UNFORGETTABLE HEROES AND UNSCRUPULOUS VILLAINS FIGHTING TO THE DEATH FOR POSSESSION OF WEALTH, WOMEN AND THE FUTURE OF THE GREAT SOUTHWEST.

JOHN COOPER BAINES—Valiant and tall, known to the Indians as the legendary warrior "The Hawk," he embraces a dangerous journey to seek fabulous riches with the same fierce courage that will drive him to fearlessly challenge a deadly enemy . . . when his only weapons are his cunning and his powerful, bare hands.

DOROTÉA BAINES—Lovely and passionate new bride of the Hawk, she becomes the sweet bait in a lethal trap set for her husband—and both their lives will depend on her sharp intelligence and indomitable spirit.

CHRISTOPHE CARRIÈRE—Behind his dark good looks lies a blackguard's heart. His ill-gotten wealth allows him a king's luxury, but with a despot's depravity he plots his twisted revenge on an innocent girl and on the Hawk.

MADELEINE de COURVENT—A proud young French woman whose sensual beauty arouses a villain's lust and whose chaste rejection of his advances dooms her to a degrading captivity—in a house of shame.

JUAN CORTIZO—Halfbreed leader of the bloodthirsty Yaqui Indians, he is driven by irrational vengeance to attack the *gringos* of Texas . . . and to stalk and kill one particular Texan—the Hawk.

D0733831

A Saga of the Southwest Series
Ask your bookseller for the books you have missed

A Saga of the Southwest
Book VII

Quest
of
the Hawk

Leigh Franklin James

 Created by the producers of
Wagons West, White Indian, and
Children of the Lion.

Chairman of the Board: Lyle Kenyon Engel

BANTAM BOOKS
TORONTO • NEW YORK • LONDON • SYDNEY • AUCKLAND

QUEST OF THE HAWK

*A Bantam Book / published by arrangement with
Book Creations, Inc.*

*Produced by Book Creations, Inc.
Chairman of the Board: Lyle Kenyon Engel.*

Bantam edition / February 1985

ISBN 0-553-24659-3

Published simultaneously in the United States and Canada

PRINTED IN THE UNITED STATES OF AMERICA

H   0 9 8 7 6 5 4 3 2 1

*To Marla and Lyle Kenyon Engel,
whose confidence in the author
has immeasurably inspired his work.*

SAGA OF THE SOUTHWEST

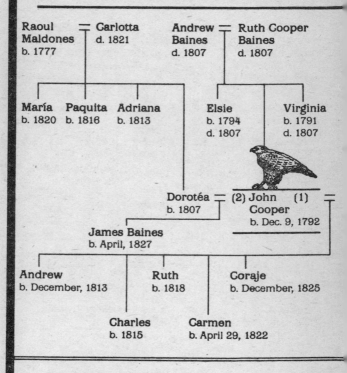

Raoul
Maldones
b. 1777
— Carlotta
d. 1821

Andrew
Baines
d. 1807
— Ruth Cooper
Baines
d. 1807

María
b. 1820
Paquita
b. 1816
Adriana
b. 1813

Elsie
b. 1794
d. 1807

Virginia
b. 1791
d. 1807

Dorotéa
b. 1807
— (2) John
Cooper
b. Dec. 9, 1792
(1) —

James Baines
b. April, 1827

Andrew
b. December, 1813

Ruth
b. 1818

Coraje
b. December, 1825

Charles
b. 1815

Carmen
b. April 29, 1822

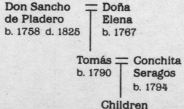

Don Sancho
de Pladero
b. 1758 d. 1825
— Doña
Elena
b. 1767

Tomás
b. 1790
— Conchita
Seragos
b. 1794

Children

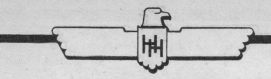

FAMILY TREE

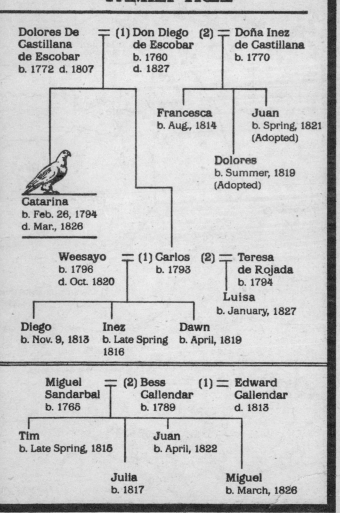

Dolores De Castillana de Escobar
b. 1772 d. 1807

— (1) Don Diego de Escobar
b. 1760
d. 1827

(2) — Doña Inez de Castillana
b. 1770

Francesca
b. Aug., 1814

Juan
b. Spring, 1821
(Adopted)

Dolores
b. Summer, 1819
(Adopted)

Catarina
b. Feb. 26, 1794
d. Mar., 1826

Weesayo
b. 1796
d. Oct. 1820

— (1) Carlos
b. 1793

(2) — Teresa de Rojada
b. 1794

Luisa
b. January, 1827

Diego
b. Nov. 9, 1813

Inez
b. Late Spring
1816

Dawn
b. April, 1819

Miguel Sandarbal
b. 1765

— (2) Bess Gallendar
b. 1789

(1) — Edward Gallendar
d. 1813

Tim
b. Late Spring, 1815

Juan
b. April, 1822

Julia
b. 1817

Miguel
b. March, 1826

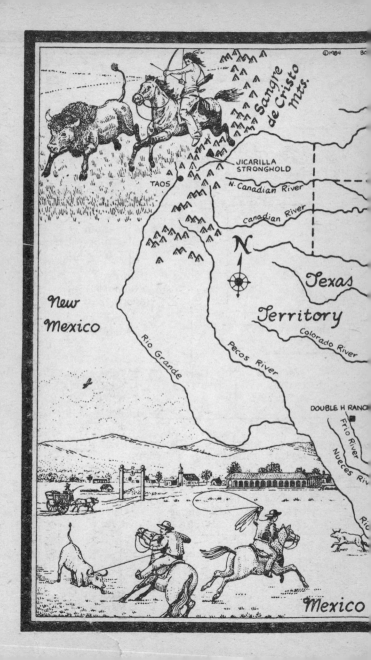

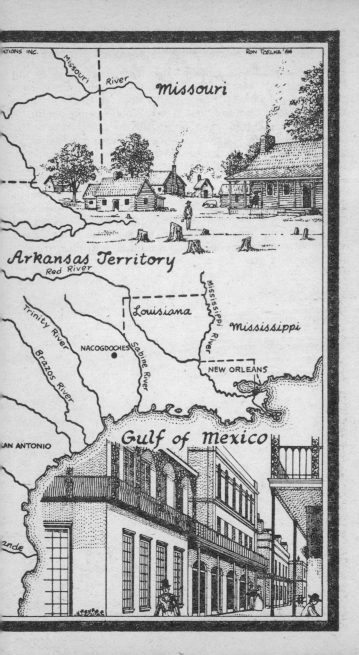

The author wishes to acknowledge his indebtedness to the Book Creations team for their infallible cooperation and suggestions that facilitated the creative process. Thanks also to Drusilla Hackl, librarian, and Tierce Whatley, lion keeper, of the Brookfield Zoo for their invaluable documentation of the jaguar, which enormously aided in authenticating a vital chapter of this novel. And thanks to W. W. Newcomb Jr., whose University of Texas-published work, *The Indians of Texas*, contains masterly data on the many tribes whom settlers confronted on our early southwestern frontier. Finally, thanks to Fay J. Bergstrom, transcriber/typist extraordinary, whose aid the past seven years has freed the author from the mechanical bondage of the typewriter and who has often contributed admirable suggestions toward the editing and improvement of his manuscripts.

One

The weather was unseasonably warm on this January day in the year 1827, when the aged patriarch of the Double H Ranch in Texas, Don Diego de Escobar, was laid to rest. All the *trabajadores* and *vaqueros* on the ranch attended the funeral, as did the household workers: the *criadas* who waited on the families living in the *hacienda*, the cooks, and all the other servants and their families. Young Padre Pastronaz, now a fully ordained priest, presided at the ceremony as the old *hidalgo* was buried near the Frio River on an upraised grassy knoll, which overlooked not only the river but also the magnificently fertile, rolling valley of the great *hacienda*.

Tall, blond-haired John Cooper Baines stood beside the weeping Doña Inez. His young wife, Dorotéa, stood on the other side of the grieving, elderly widow. Attempting to comfort his former mother-in-law as best he could, John Cooper took her hand and said, "His spirit will be with us all the time, Doña Inez. And he'll be able to see what's happening here, be able to see all the families of our *trabajadores* and all our kin grow up and find joy and face the challenges that we're going to have. You know that his health was failing ever since he was injured in that explosion in New Orleans; I think he preferred death to living as half a man. His was a glorious life, and we shall never forget his courage and his dignity. He will remain forever in our hearts. I, too, shed tears for him, as you well know, but these are tears of joy, for I shall always remember that his life here has brought new meaning to all of us."

At first she could not speak for her grief but only nodded and squeezed his hand. Then she turned to Dorotéa and huskily murmured, "*Mi corazón,* I know how happy he was to learn that you had married the man whom he most respected, the man who gave him an understanding of los Estados Unidos and the freedom and vigor it presented to all of us who came to live here from the Old World. Yes, I weep for him, but he was blessed, and I am grateful to *el Señor Dios* that I could share his life and make him happy for the time allowed us." Then she took their right hands in hers and clasped them, saying, "You are my family, you and all my other wonderful children, and we shall be steadfast and strong in the love and respect we have for one another, as well as for him who was *mi esposo*."

John Cooper now bowed his head as the young priest began speaking the words of eulogy. But the tall Texan was really thinking to himself of the problems in store for the Double H Ranch. South of the Rio Grande, the Mexican government was already becoming hostile to Texas settlers. He could foresee that, in the years ahead, the relationship between Mexico and the American Southwest would become increasingly embittered, and that the hatred and the lust for power of certain individuals might well ignite this part of the world into warfare.

Then, too, there was the recent robbery of his bank in New Orleans, from which had been taken the precious hoard of silver ingots he had originally found in a lost mine in New Mexico. Though the Double H Ranch was virtually self-sufficient, with the sale of cattle and crops paying expenses and providing income, that silver was vital for the poor and needy—the Indians and new settlers to Texas. It would be they who suffered, until John Cooper learned who had stolen the ingots and then apprehended the culprit.

He held tightly onto Doña Inez's hand and that of his beloved young wife, and when Padre Pastronaz finished his speech, he himself prayed aloud, "Dear God, grant us peace and the fulfillment of Your will. Let us make here a community of honest men and women who prepare for the future and the glory of this young country. Give us strength against our enemies and let them see that we are in the right, not by force of arms but by the pursuit of honor and worthwhile deeds. Look upon the soul of Don Diego de Escobar, who, along with my own father, was the finest man I ever knew, and grant him Your eternal rest. Amen."

Now the mourners prepared to return to their homes on the Double H Ranch, where, after supper, another service would be held for Don Diego in the ranch's newly built church. Only Doña Inez stayed behind, for she wished to remain at her husband's gravesite to be with him. A young *trabajador* waited for her, standing protectively several yards away as she knelt at Don Diego's grave and prayed silently.

She thought of all that had passed, of how Don Diego's first wife—her sister—had died on the very day he had returned from the Escorial in Madrid under the sentence of banishment from Spain. Doña Inez had long secretly loved Don Diego, and in Taos, New Mexico—where Don Diego served out his exile as intendant of the province—the then middle-aged *hidalgo* had discovered the love and loyalty Doña Inez bore for him and had made her his wife, had made her mother to his beautiful daughter, Catarina, and his handsome son, Carlos.

About that time, John Cooper Baines had entered their lives, having experienced his own form of exile. He had witnessed the brutal murder of his parents and his sisters and had traveled across the North American continent, living with the Indians and growing to manhood. He had fallen in love with and married young Catarina de Escobar, then had brought his new family to this fertile valley in western Texas, where he and Carlos and the faithful friends of the de Escobars and Baineses had built the great Double H Ranch, known also as the *Hacienda del Halcón*—so called because of John Cooper's Indian name: *el Halcón*—the Hawk. Less than a year earlier, his beloved Catarina had been murdered by a madman bent on revenge, but John Cooper overcame his grief and had recently gotten married to young Dorotéa Maldones, whom the blond Texan had met while visiting Argentina on a business trip to see her father.

By now it was nightfall. There was a full moon, and the stars twinkled about it, heralding the bright new year with its untold promise for the settlers of this frontier. Doña Inez glanced up and crossed herself and thought that perhaps the soul of her beloved Don Diego was even now on one of those very stars far in the heavens. In some ways, he had reminded her of Don Quixote, that gentle knight who tilted his lance at windmills, deeming them as giants, and yet overcame ridicule and mockery and hatred because of his own steadfast dignity and honor.

For a moment, her eyes were so clouded by tears that she could scarcely see. Then, as she took a deep breath, her eyes cleared and she could once again make out the grave of Don Diego, located on the grassy knoll above the Frio River, under a giant live-oak tree.

Esteban Morales, the assistant foreman of the ranch who had always been handy at carving wooden toys for the children of the community, had shaped a magnificent cross and inscribed on it Don Diego's name and the dates of his birth and death. It was sturdy oakwood, and it would withstand the years. But what mattered more was that his spirit lived within her and would imbue her with courage in the lonely years ahead.

At the same moment, she chided herself for such thoughts of self-pity, for they were unworthy of him, and unworthy still more of a wife who cherished him as she had done.

The soft plash of the rippling waters of the river became a kind of melody as she prayed once again. There was the twittering of night birds, and it was comforting to know that she was here with him who had been her life and whose devotion would warm her in the coldest moments of the darkest years that might yet be destined her.

And then she spoke aloud, as if they as man and wife might yet still exchange an intimate communion between them. Feeling radiant in the knowledge that he would hear her, she whispered, "*Querido,* I have already reproved myself for having mourned, for you will still live as long as I draw breath upon this earth. Until we are reunited in death and the life eternal beyond that, my Diego, I shall be still your wife, the custodian of all those happy memories and acts of love that you so splendidly and constantly accorded me. I thank you again, as I did in my prayers each day of our married life together, for the joy you gave me by doing me the honor of being my husband. *Querido,* there are not enough words and not enough prayers to tell you how beautiful you made my life after we left Madrid. I can only wish that you understood some of the happiness that you granted me, that I was able, in some small way, to give you happiness in turn.

"I shall cherish your memory until I join you, and I shall never let our daughter Francesca, nor our adopted children Dolores and Juan, nor your son Carlos and his children—no, I shall never let them forget the grandeur of soul that was yours, and how you were husband and lover to me."

She crossed herself, bowed her head, and for a long moment was silent. Then she spoke again as if he were there beside her: "And what comforts me most now is that, in your last moments, you found that even your own homeland had not cast you aside as you had once thought. You were vindicated, you were paid great honor, and those representatives of Spain who recently came to our ranch tried in their small, material way to compensate you for the anguish caused by that unjust banishment from Spain. But what is more memorable to me and will stand as an example for all my remaining days is how you adapted yourself to this strange new world of ours here, to the *gringos* and the *americanos*, as well as to the *indios*, showing kindness and consideration for all, realizing the pompous vanities of those little men who sought power, just as they did in Madrid when they sought to discredit you."

She crossed herself again and remained with her head bowed for a long moment. Suddenly there was the cooing of a wild dove not far off, perched on the branch of a fig tree. Doña Inez started, crossed herself still another time, and in an awe-struck voice murmured, "It is the voice of *la paloma*, the dove—and so it is that Catarina, sweet Catarina, my sister's child by you, Diego, is reunited with her *padre* in heaven. Both of you, sweet spirits, watch over us and over John Cooper and his Dorotéa and their child who is to be born into this new world. May God grant you both the paradise you earned upon this earth—Amen."

She rose and, without a backward look at the grave, retraced her footsteps to the *hacienda*, the young *trabajador* silently following.

Two

On the same night that Don Diego de Escobar was laid to rest, Brigadier General Antonio López de Santa Anna was at his estate in Mango de Clavo, entertaining friends belonging to his military corps. His elaborate mansion was conveniently located on the road from Jalapa to Veracruz, and Santa Anna had purchased it for twenty-five thousand *pesos*. At the moment, his wife, Inez García, and their children were off visiting Inez's cousin Madelina in San Luis Potosi. There was a legend that Santa Anna had desired Inez's prettier and younger sister but that his proposal to her wealthy parents was so awkward and fumbling that he had inadvertently become engaged to Inez. Only when he had approached the altar had he noticed the mistake, but he had shrugged and murmured to his best man, "It's all the same to me."

As was his custom, Santa Anna had ordered six of the loveliest *criadas* of the mansion to wait on his honored guests, and it was understood that at the conclusion of the banquet, each girl would be awarded to one of his favorite officers. He sat at the head of the table, resplendent in his uniform of a brigadier general, with many medals on his chest. Tall, black-haired, with brilliant dark eyes, he scanned the faces of his officers, appraising this one and that one, speculating on what he might gain through granting the man special favors.

At his left was Captain Juan Mendoza, a swarthy *mestizo* who had been fiercely loyal to him for the past fifteen years, ever since he had been orderly to the then young lieutenant at the Battle of Medina, which was one of the earliest battles between Texans and Mexicans. Santa Anna leaned toward the captain and said to him in a hushed tone, "A word with you, Juan."

Mendoza stiffened, instantly alert. "*¡Su servidor, mi general!*"

"Gently now, gently. We are all friends among friends. Do not attract the attention of the others. There are confidential matters of which I wish to speak, Juan."

"*Comprendo, mi general.*"

"*¡Bueno!* Now then, there is trouble in the government of our glorious Mexico, with various factions vying for power. You are aware of this, aren't you, Juan?"

The *mestizo* nodded agreement. "*¡Pero sí, mi general!*"

"Well, I have been sickened by all this squabbling, and that is why I came to Veracruz, where I have devoted my time for the last several years improving my personal estate at Mango de Clavo. I shall wait here until my country summons me to be its *presidente.*"

"I am sure they will soon, *mi general,*" Juan Mendoza eagerly spoke up.

Santa Anna made an impatient gesture and went on in a confidential tone, "But you must realize, Mendoza, it is my paramount wish that the people summon me, and that no one accuses me of self-seeking. I have skills; I can weld this nation into a mighty force among the other nations of the earth, but I will not seek it of my own accord. They must come to me, the people, who know my benevolence toward them."

"Just so, *mi general*."

"I am happy to find you of such an opinion, *mi capitán*. I shall see to it that you are soon promoted to *coronel*."

"A thousand thanks, *excelencia!*"

"*De nada*." Santa Anna shrugged and indolently waved his hand. "More wine, Juan?"

"*Gracias, mi general*. But let me wait on you, since you outrank me."

"If you are a faithful ally, the time may well come when you wear the epaulet of a brigadier general yourself. This is why I wish to talk to you. Perhaps you do not recall that once I had in my command a certain young lieutenant by the name of Carlos de Escobar."

"Yes, *excelencia*, I remember it well."

"Good. Then you must also recall that I had heard through my spies that this young man was the brother-in-law of that accursed *gringo* by the name of John Cooper Baines, who had, through some miracle, unearthed a great hoard of pure silver. I wished to acquire that, and not for my own ends, Juan; I swear this on the Holy Cross of our Blessed Savior! No, it was for the poor people of Mexico and for those arms that must be bought to give weapons to the valiant patriots who would otherwise fight with their bare hands."

"Of course, *mi general*," Mendoza soothingly concurred.

"I have been told that this great fortune was placed into a bank in New Orleans, and thus it passed out of my acquisition. But I heard rumors also that one of the leading banks of that city was recently plundered by an ingenious rogue who, in the process of looting it, took the silver. One of my couriers brought me a New Orleans newspaper; that is how I learned of the theft."

"It would be a great coup if you could catch the thief and regain the silver for our nation, *mi general*," Mendoza slyly proposed.

"Now you speak like a man of vision. That is precisely my intention. But we must go slowly. It is not yet known who stole the silver, and until he is found, there is no hope of getting it back. Now then, I am told that you have a good friend in New Orleans."

"That is true, *mi general*. His name is Enrique de Silva. He had a French mother and a Mexican father, and he is a well-to-do shopkeeper there."

"And I am sure he has not yet forgotten his loyalty to his native country—he was born here, was he not?"

"*¡Pero sí, mi general!*" Mendoza hastily agreed. "*Con su permiso*, I shall dispatch a letter to him at once by a special courier and ask him to learn what he can about the silver of that *gringo*."

"Do that. And if this same *gringo* John Cooper Baines makes more deposits of any substantial nature, and if these again should be silver—mark you well, Mendoza!—perhaps your friend de Silva could apprise us. He could show his own patriotism in this way—and I should be inclined even to see that he was paid for his services."

"He has excellent connections, *mi general*," Mendoza spoke up. "I am thinking that perhaps he could even find a post in the bank that was robbed."

Santa Anna uttered a startled gasp, then slapped his thigh and nodded. "By ten thousand devils, Juan, you are my best friend indeed! That would be a stroke of genius, yes, to plant one of our own spies in the very bank where the *gringo* had his fortune. Then he could report to us, and we would know the *gringo*'s every move. That money must be recovered for the nation. It will provide a loyal army, well armed, able to put down revolts, and it will restore the liberty and equality of the *peones*."

Now Santa Anna tilted the cut-glass decanter of a fine French Bordeaux and filled the goblet of his captain to the very brim. Then, filling his own, he lifted his and said, "To our eternal friendship. Each to serve the other, but both of us for the glory of our beloved Mexico!"

"*¡Salud, mi general!*" Juan Mendoza clinked his glass with that of Santa Anna and studied the face of his ruthless leader. Inwardly he could foresee great benefits from pursuing this flattering friendship. For whatever services it might demand of him, the rewards were likely to be magnificent.

As soon as he had drunk, Santa Anna rose and, clapping his hands to get the attention of his guests, announced, "You must excuse me, *mis compañeros*, for a little time. I have a personal matter of discipline to attend to, but this need not dampen the festivities. Enjoy yourselves. My *criadas* have orders to satisfy your every need, from food and wine to their own lovely embraces. I shall return in a short time. Meanwhile, I thank you for your show of loyalty. Indeed, it is a matter of loyalty that I am now going to discuss with two *soldados* who have failed in their duty. I know that you, my dear friends, my companions of the battlefield—and, I truly hope, of my glorious future at the helm of our beloved nation— could never be guilty of such lapses as these *estúpidos!*" With this, he bowed, gestured with his hands that they should go on eating and drinking and enjoying themselves, and then left the dining room.

He went down a narrow corridor and to a stairway, which he descended. There, in a subterranean passageway, his beautiful young half-breed mistress, Martina Arrigalte, awaited him. The day after his wife had left, Santa Anna had summoned Martina to spend a few days with him, and she had come some fifty miles from the little house that he had secretly purchased and put in her name.

"I can hardly wait for the hours ahead, *querida,*" he said as he took both her hands and kissed them. She purred with satisfaction as she stroked his black hair and whispered back, *"Mi amorcito."* Then, straightening, he gave her a bawdy wink and murmured, "You have told the servants how I wish to have those two stupid *soldados* prepared for me?"

"Pero sí, mi amorcito. Do I not do everything you request of me?" she asked, feigning hurt feelings.

"You do indeed, sweet Martina. You are my truest love. We must, however, be most discreet. It would never do to have my wife discover your existence. Understand, *querida,* as a power of this great state of Mexico, I must present to the nation the portrait of a family man, with a good wife and children of my body. This is expected of me; it is part of the image that every leader must put forward to his constituents. But I think you know enough of me that, when we are alone together, my love is yours and will be, so long as we are together."

"Oh, Antonio, *querido,*" she sighed, languorous with passion, "must we waste time on those two stupid ones, when I am longing for your kisses and the feel of your hands on my breasts and thighs?"

Santa Anna's face was flushed, and not alone from wine. "But, *mi corazón,*" he responded as he cupped one of her large yet superbly firm breasts, "don't you know that half of the joy of realization comes with anticipation? Think of how much more exciting it will be when finally we come together after we have witnessed this little spectacle. It may prove a somewhat arousing diversion, shall we say."

"You will have opium for me?"

"Of course. It was you who taught me how to use the pipe and how to have the sweet dreams that come from that substance made of the poppy. Come now, we have work to do before we may be alone together!" His arm around her waist, his left hand squeezing one of her lithe hips, his other hand caressing her swelling bosom, Santa Anna moved toward a door at the end of the corridor.

The room they entered was actually a dungeon, windowless and with a low ceiling. Two men, wearing only their breeches and their boots, faced each other as they sat astride sharp-ridged sawhorses. Their wrists had been bound and their hands were raised above their heads from ropes attached to the ceiling. Weights had been bound around their calves, and the torturing bite of the sharp wooden ridge into their loins was hellish, unspeakable agony. It was a torture known as the "Spanish horse," one often used by the Inquisition in Spain to ferret out not only confessions from heretics but also to reveal the secrets of what treasure they and their families had hidden that might fill the coffers of Mother Church.

Santa Anna took from the pocket of his bemedaled uniform a gold watch and fob and consulted it. "It appears that you have enjoyed two hours of riding on the Spanish horse, señores," he declaimed with an ironic smirk as he approached the trestles. Martina, clinging to him, her arm linked with his, eyed them. Her nostrils were flaring and her eyes were humid with an erotic excitement, prompted not only by the knowledge of her approaching intimacies with her beloved *libertador* but also by seeing the convulsive shudders and the rivulets of sweat that these sturdy half-naked male bodies displayed.

"You'll remember," Santa Anna pursued in the same sententious tone, "that both of you were reported to me for having slept on duty last month, when I rode to Veracruz with my troops. If we had been attacked, it might have cost me the entire regiment because of your stupidity and indolence. I have not forgotten it, but I have waited for a proper moment to punish you. Both of you are under sentence of death, as you well know, and there is no officer throughout Mexico who would deal otherwise with you. But I am merciful. I am going to say this to you: He who first begs for mercy and release from the Spanish horse will be shot at once. Console yourselves, señores, it will be a beautiful death, and not in public, not the disgrace that both of you deserve. For I shall allow the charming Señorita Martina to administer the *coup de grâce* and with my very own pistol, the one with the silver butt that was presented to me by the grateful citizens of Veracruz."

Only groans and gasps responded to his diatribe. He chuckled, turned to Martina, squeezed her buttocks, and whispered something into her ear, which made her nod and blush. Then he continued. "The other, who will have shown more courage, will be pardoned—but, in return for his life, he will execute a commission of mine. It will involve some danger, since it has to do with a fierce tribe of Indians. Still in all, it will be better than death, *¿no es verdad?*"

The man nearest him was perhaps twenty-five, stocky, with a brutish face and a short black beard. His name was Sancho Bartola, and he had been a private for three years in Santa Anna's personal corps. His companion, two years older, Rodrigo Martínez, was taller, with closely cropped hair and a short spade beard and thin sideburns. His body was wirier and more muscular, but it appeared that he was suffering even more than his younger companion, judging from his sporadic shudderings, the chattering of his teeth, and the low, dull groans that emanated from his panting mouth.

"I shall wait here until one of you has solved the matter of this disciplinary problem for me, señores," Santa Anna avowed. From his right-hand holster, he drew the pistol with the silver butt and handed it to Martina. "Whoever is first to beg for mercy, grant him what he asks. But a word of advice, *mi corazón*. Dying must not be too easy for a man who shirks his duty by sleeping like a coward when there is danger of attack to his *jefe*, to his *general*."

"*Comprendo, querido*," Martina purred as she took the gun and balanced it in her slim right hand. "You wish me to place the ball so that he will not die quickly, but in great pain; *¿no es verdad?*"

"You are veritably a treasure of intellect as well as beauty, *mi paloma*." Santa Anna chuckled. "That is exactly right. All right, then, señores. Consider your situation and let us see which of you has the greater courage to try to redeem himself in my eyes. As for the loser, we shall say it is the fortunes of war. Out of mercy, I shall not inform your kinfolk of your dereliction of duty, and I shall even see to it that a small part of your wages will be sent to your grieving family. But that is as much mercy as I shall allow. And now, do not let me disturb your concentration."

Both men, turning their livid, sweating faces toward him, seemed to implore him with their eyes. Martina licked her lips with a soft pink tongue, savoring the hellish agony the men were suffering. Bound as they were, they could scarcely shift off the fiendishly sharp ridge of the sawhorse. Both were close to breaking, and the convulsive spasms that wrenched their bodies grew more and more frequent, as did their groans and sobs.

Santa Anna planted himself with his feet spread apart, contemplating his watch as the seconds ticked on. Martina continued to grasp the pistol, her narrowed eyes fixing on the two half-naked bodies. It was Sancho Bartola who broke first, crying out, "*Piedad, mi general, por el amor de Dios*—I suffer—I did not mean to fall asleep—I had too much *cerveza*—and it was Rodrigo who made me drink it—"

"You lie, I swear it by the *Virgen Santísima!*" Rodrigo Martínez cried out hysterically, a savage spasm rippling through his thighs and along his rib cage. "*Misericordia*, I beg of you, *mi general!* What he says is a lie—I swear *por todos los santos!*"

"I am waiting, señores," Santa Anna said, smirking as he eyed them both, then went back to studying his watch. "I will say, to the credit of both of you, that you have endured the Spanish horse somewhat better than your predecessors a month ago. Unfortunately, they too slept on duty as you did, but both of them were cowards. They both asked for mercy at the same time, and I was obliged, by the anguish of their entreaties, to grant them the final, the only mercy that a military leader may grant soldiers who have failed their duty. But here, as you see, gentlemen, I give one of you the opportunity to live. There may even be great rewards and promotions, if the task is fulfilled—come now, you are keeping me from the arms of this sweet morsel, and that alone would be enough to send you to a firing squad, if I were not the merciful man I am."

His humor was lost to the two unfortunate sufferers. Their bodies were bathed in sweat, and their muscles jerked in spasms now totally beyond control. Sancho Bartola began to sob and then suddenly screamed out, "Let me die, then, my *cojones* are burning—I cannot live—kill me, kill me, *mi general!*"

"You are the first to ask for death, then? Do I understand you correctly, *soldado?*" Santa Anna said as he approached the stocky private.

"*Sí, sí, por piedad;* now, let me die now, I cannot bear this suffering any longer—"

Santa Anna nodded to Martina. She approached the trestle, calmly pressed the muzzle of the pistol against the navel of the unfortunate man, and pulled the trigger. He uttered a shriek, his body jerked violently, and then he forced his eyes to look downward at the small, bluish, powder-blackened hole from which blood began to ooze.

"*Querida,* that was an inspiration! It will take him many hours to die, and during all of that time he will remember that he failed in his duty to his *general.*" Santa Anna now approached the other trestle and, taking a fruit knife that he had brought with him from the dining room, cut the cords bound to Rodrigo Martínez's calves so that the heavy weights clattered to the floor. Then he cut the bonds that fettered his wrists. Martínez slid off the trestle with a sobbing cry and lay unconscious.

Santa Anna turned to Martina, taking the pistol from her and reholstering it. "Come, my *paloma,* my *corazón.* There is no hurry with Private Martínez, and as for poor Private Bartola, let him die in dignity and in privacy. Come, I am hungry for you!"

"And I for you, *mi general!*"

The door closed behind the two victims, while Sancho Bartola began to groan and then to shriek as the pain of his agonizing belly wound took maddening possession of him.

Three

It was on this very same January night that old Potiwaba felt that he was about to be summoned to the Great Spirit. He was nearly eighty and had been blind for the last decade. Once, long before the days of the former chief Descontarti, he had been shaman of the Jicarilla Apache in New Mexico, but he had been discredited and his powers called illusory because he had urged an alliance with a nearby band of Comanche. The tribesmen had trusted him, and they had gone forth to parley, only to be nearly decimated in the ambush that the wily Comanche had set for them.

Potiwaba and perhaps a dozen braves as well as their then chief were the only survivors. When they retreated on horseback to their mountain stronghold, the chief had turned to Potiwaba and sternly declared, "We have trusted you, and yet you have spoken with a forked tongue. What you have told us is not the will of the gods, and we do not believe any longer that the Giver of Breath has touched you with His will to make His wishes known among our people. For this day, you deserve death, but because you have been shaman, I will not break the holy law of the Apache. You shall be banished, but your punishment will be that you shall live on the boundaries of our tribal stronghold yet be shunned by every man, woman, and child. If there is one of your own children or friends who wishes to bring you food and to see to your needs, Potiwaba, he or she will live under the same banishment. Make up your mind to this, or else you may turn the head of your horse now and go wander upon the plains— perhaps your Comanche allies will give you a friendlier welcome than they gave our braves!"

Potiwaba had bowed his head and acknowledged that he had erred in interpreting the will of the Giver of Breath, and because he had once been shaman and conveyor of the words of Him who shaped all things, he did not flinch from this

14

dreadful punishment, which in its own way was worse than death.

When he had been little more than a stripling, Potiwaba had married a Ute girl, for the Jicarilla and the Ute were allies under the Spanish in those early days. (It was for this reason that the Indian tribes of the American Southwest spoke both Spanish and their own tongue.) She had given him two sons; one of them had been killed during the Comanche ambush, but the other had given him a grandson. For a time, the son and Potiwaba's grandson lived together with the aging pariah, until the loneliness and the obvious contempt with which all the villagers held Potiwaba and his descendants became too much for them to endure. And so Potiwaba's son and the grandson left the stronghold. But the boy remembered his grandfather and felt compassion for him, even as he in his turn dwelt near the Taos Plains and married a pueblo woman who had given him a daughter. Before he had even reached his thirty-fifth year, the grandson had been severely injured when a heavy beam had fallen on him during the construction of a building in Taos. On his deathbed he had said to his wife, "Before I go to join the Giver of Breath, I must make peace with my grandfather who lives high in the stronghold and yet is deemed an enemy of the tribe." Then he told her the story, and she said, "I will take our daughter, Imishba, to the stronghold to care for your grandfather, and I will instruct her in the ways of venerating an elder. You have been a good husband to me, and I respect the pity you have for him who was once shaman of the Jicarilla."

And so the mother and the little girl Imishba made the long journey up the winding trail to the mountaintop stronghold, and the girl's mother implored the then chief, Kinotatay, to allow her and the little girl to share Potiwaba's dreary life. Her prayers were granted.

Now the mother had died the previous year from a snake bite while filling a clay pot with water at one of the lower mountain streams, and only Imishba remained with her great-grandfather. She was now thirteen, at the age of puberty, but by the law of the Jicarilla and the original ordainment of banishment upon Potiwaba, she might not look to any brave to be wed, nor would she be given the ceremony of purification. Yet in her way, she adored the old man. Because he had no one else to talk to, he regaled her with stories of the ancient days, when the *conquistadores* sought to conquer all the *indios* and made allies with the Jicarilla and proclaimed them vassals to the King of Spain himself.

She knelt before him this evening, and there, high in the mountain stronghold, as a fine powdery snow fell and the wind from the northeast howled, the evil ghosts of death hovered over the rude tipi of Potiwaba. Imishba, for all her youth and despite the fact that she had not been trained in the warrior arts as a boy would have been, had learned how to trap jackrabbits and even how to make her own bow and arrows. Two days earlier, following a mountain goat along a winding trail near the summit of the great mountain of the stronghold, she had killed it and brought back the carcass, dragging it because its weight seemed almost more than her own. Her great-grandfather had taught her how to skin it and how and where to cut the best parts of the meat. Tonight she had made him a stew, and she guided the bowl into his trembling hands. He sipped at it, nodded, and smiled—a toothless smile—and mumbled, "It is good, my daughter. It warms my old bones. But the cold of death awaits me, and before dawn I shall have sung my death song."

"Do not speak so, Great-grandfather," she entreated.

"But when it is time to face the reckoning that the Giver of Breath demands of each of us, Imishba, it is wisest to face up to the truth. I ask one final boon of you, my great-granddaughter. Go to the young chief Pastanari and beg him to take pity on an old man who is about to die. Tell him that I have something of great value to say unto him, for these last three nights I have had a vision." With a feeble surge of pride, the old man tried to straighten his shoulders, and his smile deepened as he set down the bowl.

"I will go, Great-grandfather. Try to eat a little more of the stew. It will warm you. I will bring Pastanari back."

"If you were a man, Imishba, the women of the Jicarilla might stone you before you reached his wickiup, but because you are not yet a woman, I think they will have pity on you. But hurry, for my time is short and I must tell him what has come into my heart before I sing my death song." Gasping for breath, the old man leaned back upon his rude pallet, closed his sightless eyes, and began to move his lips in ritualistic incantation.

Then as he lay there, Potiwaba murmured to himself, "And now I have another vision, that the Giver of Breath will not summon me to His reckoning until I have seen the *wasichu* for whom my words are most intended. I shall resist the demons of the cold who howl outside to claim me, and I shall live until I see this man who is blood brother to our chief as he was to those two others before Pastanari. Yes, it is so, and I am comforted. I have been an outcast here among my own people for more moons than I can count now. But perhaps before I die, what I have to tell this man who is blood brother to us, though he be a white-eyes, will have gained me forgiveness in the spirit land."

Pastanari was sharing his evening meal with his wife and children when he heard the soft, high-pitched voice of the young girl Imishba outside his wickiup. Frowning, he rose and parted the flaps and emerged to confront her. "You have broken our law, Imishba," he said sternly. "Why do you come to me now, after all this time? Do you not know that you are forbidden to speak to any member of the tribe and, least of all, to me who am *jefe*?"

Imishba knelt before him and bowed her head almost to the snow-covered ground. "Forgive me, *mi jefe*. My great-grandfather is near death, and he begs to speak with you. He says that he has had a vision and that it is to be told only to the *jefe* of the Jicarilla. Please—I myself beg you, though I have no right to do so. He is so old and feeble, and I know that he will not live much longer. Take pity on him; for whatever he has done, surely he has paid the price by now."

Pastanari contemplated the crouching girl and then sighed deeply. "You have courage, Imishba, as much as any brave. Very well, then, I will come with you. Do not speak to me again, for should the villagers hear you speak, they will know that the law has been broken, and they may not be so compassionate toward you."

"I know this well, and I will hold my tongue, *mi jefe*," the young girl agreed.

Pastanari, dressed in buckskins and with a headdress to proclaim his tribal rank, walked through the village with his arms folded across his chest. Imishba followed far behind him and well to the right so that it did not appear that she would approach him. Some of the women outside at their cooking fires glanced sharply at her and muttered among themselves, and one even shook her fist at the girl, but Imishba pretended not to notice these signs of enmity. By now, indeed, she was inured to them.

Pastanari reached the tipi and, parting the flaps, moved

inside to stare down at the emaciated old white-haired man. "I am here at your summons," he said in a deep, low voice. "What have you to say to me that makes you break our law and send this child to my wickiup? The villagers might have done her great harm, and it would have been your doing, Potiwaba."

"I prayed to the Great Spirit to watch over her," the old man said. "Am I truly in the presence of the *jefe* of the Jicarilla?"

"I am Pastanari, yes. Speak, *viejo!*" I must go back to the evening meal and to my wife and children."

"You are fortunate. Wait. I do not complain; I do not pity myself; I have earned this. But now that I am about to die, I have had visions for the past several nights, so strong that I had to tell you. They concern the *wasichu* who is known to you as *el Halcón.*"

At this, Pastanari started with surprise and frowned. "How do you know the name of that one?" he asked.

The old man said in a feeble voice, "There have been times when Imishba went to get water or firewood for me, and the women around the campfires always talk in loud voices. My great-granddaughter reported to me what these women said of the *wasichu* who is the blood brother of you and of the *jefes* before you."

"Be that as it may, *viejo*, what strange secret do you hold back from me, that makes you dare break our law that was laid down long before me?" Pastanari angrily demanded.

"I know, too, of the accursed mountain where this same white-eyes found the incredible hoard of silver," Potiwaba murmured.

"And how can you know that? By what witchcraft—"

"No, no, only by the talk of loose tongues, Pastanari. But you do not know all about me. It is true that I am forsaken, that I am forbidden to mix with the villagers or to speak with them. And yet, before I became shaman of this tribe, long before you were born, I was an *esclavo* for the Spaniards who came to Nuevo México in search of gold and silver and other precious metals and stones. And I worked in a silver mine when I was not much older than poor little Imishba here."

"Is this true?" Pastanari wonderingly asked.

"As true as it is that I shall soon be summoned for my

judgment before Him who creates all things and who punishes or forgives by His will, *mi jefe*," was Potiwaba's answer.

"You speak of silver. And how does this concern the man we call *el Halcón*?"

"I thought tonight that my time had come, *mi jefe*," the old man explained, trying to raise himself on the pallet. His great-granddaughter hurried to ease his efforts and to prop him up, crouching beside him with both arms supporting his thin shoulders. "But then it came upon me when Imishba sought you out that the Great Spirit Himself had come to this tipi and told me that I must live until I can speak to the *wasichu* and tell him what I know of another mine of silver . . . the one in which I was a slave until I escaped."

"Is it possible. . . ?" Pastanari turned to the girl. "Has he ever spoken to you of this before, girl?" Imishba shook her head, and after he had pondered this a moment, the young chief of the Jicarilla declared, "I must hear you, because we have a saying that when a man stands waiting for the cold wind that lofts him from the mountain into the sky, the words he speaks are never with a forked tongue."

"I have been punished for my failure as a shaman, *mi jefe*," the old man murmured. "But by this vision that was granted to me by Him who is the Giver of Breath, it may be that I can redeem my useless life among you here, and that you will not think too harshly of me once I am dust."

"I know only of the mountain where *el Halcón* found the silver, but you speak of another, old man."

"I know it well. It is not far from Raton, near Wolf Creek Pass. It is near the mountain range that is always covered with snow, loftier than our own. How well I know it—under the whip of the *soldados* and the *padres*, I and my brothers toiled at mining the silver. I know how the white-eyes lust for this precious metal and would kill even their own mothers and fathers to obtain it. But I have kept my secret all these years, until I heard that the *wasichu*, *el Halcón*, had come to the stronghold and that he had become the blood brother of the Jicarilla because he was good and honest and he did not speak with a forked tongue. And more than this, that he shared his good fortune with *los indios* here and in the pueblo in Taos."

Pastanari's eyes brightened. "That is true. And if there is such another mountain and if there is more silver there, it can do great good. And it is true that only a man like *el*

Halcón could put it to such use." The chief now knelt down beside the old man's pallet and reached for Potiwaba's frail hand. "I will send a courier at once to *el Halcón* to tell him to come to our stronghold. But you are very ill, and the journey is a long one to his *estancia* and back to us."

"I now know that I shall live until I hear his voice, the voice of the *wasichu* who can be trusted and who is a friend of *los indios* because he has lived with them, and not only with those of your tribe, *mi jefe*."

More and more, the young chief was disconcerted by the old former shaman's uncanny knowledge of John Cooper Baines and the silver mines. Out of practical consideration, he said now, "Potiwaba, you have no covenant with the Great Spirit, and it may be that you will not live until *el Halcón* comes to visit us to learn what you have to say to him. Therefore, as your *jefe*, I charge you to say to Imishba all that you would tell *el Halcón*. And thus, if he should come here too late to hear from your own lips about this mine where once you worked as a boy, Imishba can tell him."

"I will agree to that. I trust her, for she has given up her young life to befriend me. And I thank you, *mi jefe*, for coming to hear me. Already I feel better. So much, indeed, that if you, Imishba, will hand me that bowl of stew, I shall try to eat a little more. It is very good, you know."

Pastanari nodded to Imishba and then left the tipi. He strode to one of the wickiups of the younger braves and summoned him. "Ride to the *hacienda* of *el Halcón*, Dejari, and bring him to me. Tell him that I have news of the greatest importance to him." With this, the chief told Dejari about the old shaman and what he had said about the secret mine and the treasure of silver, so that the brave could inform John Cooper.

"I shall ride off at once and bring him back as swiftly as I can, *mi jefe*," the young brave said. He saluted, and then, after bidding his wife farewell, he hurried out to the small corral behind his wickiup to choose his fastest mustang.

Four

Raoul Maldones, the widowed father of John Cooper's Argentinian wife, Dorotéa, had vastly enjoyed his stay as guest of Hortense and Fabien Mallard in New Orleans. He had been living with them for a few weeks, regaining his strength and adapting to this new land called the United States, after having been rescued by John Cooper and Dorotéa from an Argentinian prison, where he had been held by the *porteños* of Buenos Aires for alleged treasonous acts. Now, safe at last, provided with funds by his generous son-in-law, the former Argentinian ranch owner had seen his three youngest daughters, Adriana, Paquita, and María, enrolled in the Ursuline Convent School. Their *dueña*, the prim and proper señora Josefa, had come to the United States along with the rest of the Maldones family, and she now resided in a little apartment in the convent itself so that she might look after the three girls and communicate regularly with her employer.

One January evening, Raoul graciously took Señora Josefa with him to a small Creole restaurant not far from the Vieux Carré, with Hortense and Fabien Mallard as his guests. The latter were an elegant-looking, middle-aged couple, very much in love, which was obvious from the way they doted on each other and were attentive to their every need.

Raoul ordered a superlative gourmet supper from the Creole proprietor, then he leaned forward across the table and earnestly declared to Fabien, who was both his and John Cooper's factor, "Señor Mallard, I propose to leave tomorrow for the Double H Ranch. My girls are now comfortably settled in a most reliable school, where they will have spiritual guidance as well as an excellent curriculum of studies to keep them out of mischief—though this is something that Señora Josefa here assures me will never take place." He smiled and glanced at the *dueña*, who promptly blushed and began to stammer. "So I am most anxious to see my Dorotéa and my son-in-law, to whom I owe the greatest possible debt for having rescued me from a firing squad in Buenos Aires."

"Your adventures, M'sieu Maldones"—Fabien Mallard chuckled as he pulled at the end of his mustache—"would do justice to the most capable romancer of our day. I marvel that you were able to survive all the dangers and the treachery that singled you out."

"It was with the help of God, to be sure," Raoul said, crossing himself. "I shall tell you frankly, Señor Mallard, I am happy to be out of the country, for the time, at any rate. And I am fearful for my good friend, Heitor Duvaldo, who will certainly remain suspect to those accursed *porteños* for having been not only my friend but also my benefactor. It may well be that they will move against him next, for his estate is a most spacious one. Certainly those who think themselves superior to any *hacendado* of the *pampas* will be eager to acquire his estate. I have said prayers that this will not happen. But to get back to what I was saying to you—I should like very much to leave tomorrow. And since I am a newcomer to your beautiful Estados Unidos, I should like to make the journey on horseback by myself, to see more of this wonderful country."

"It would be too dangerous for you, M'sieu Maldones," the factor at once responded, while his lovely, dark-haired wife confirmed this with a sympathetic nod. "I'm sure that M'sieu Baines has given you something of the history of our young country, and particularly the situation in the territory of Texas. The land still belongs to the Mexican government, except that they have agreed to allow peaceful settlers to build homes there, through the Austin grants. But of late, a man by the name of Santa Anna, who wishes to be ruler of all Mexico, has tried to revoke the constitution, and I foresee great dangers—even a war between the Texans and Mexicans— if that course is pursued. Moreover, besides peaceful families who have come to Texas to take advantage of the land grant, there are outlaws from the so-called Neutral Ground, a kind of swampland that exists between parts of Missouri, the perimeter of our own beautiful city, and the Gulf ports of Texas. Indeed, many of these outlaws have tried to infiltrate the settlements, posing as honest men who wish nothing better than to settle on a plot of land, to farm and harvest it, and to raise a family. What they are actually doing is hiding away from the authorities in the midwestern part of our country.

And if you should run into these outlaws, you might well be killed before you ever reach the Double H Ranch. At least allow me to send two of my trusted servants with you, well armed—as you yourself will be—for I insist that you take with you a rifle, a pistol, and a good hunting knife. I should feel remiss as your host if I were to allow you to go alone, believe me, M'sieu Maldones."

"I thank you for your consideration and your candor, Señor Mallard. I shall follow your advice, then. All the same, I have said my good-byes to my girls, and I would like to leave tomorrow. You have told me that it would take about twelve days to two weeks to reach my Dorotéa and my son-in-law."

"Precisely. And yes, I will arrange for you to leave tomorrow."

They toasted to a safe trip, then finished their delicious supper in amiable companionship.

The next morning, Fabien Mallard's efficient majordomo, Antoine, saw to it that Raoul Maldones was wakened at dawn and given a nourishing breakfast to fortify him for the start of the long journey to the Double H Ranch.

In his early fifties, John Cooper's father-in-law had regained all his robust vigor, thanks to the hospitality that he had enjoyed at the Mallard house. Bearded, gray-haired, tall, with soft, friendly brown eyes that belied the stern austerity of his features, he strode out to the courtyard, where a stable boy had already brought three geldings and fitted them with saddlebags. "These men will escort you, M'sieu Maldones," Antoine politely murmured, gesturing to two young men standing near the geldings. "They are entirely trustworthy, and my master has especially chosen them for their courage and dependability. Moreover, they know the route you must take."

"I hope they will shorten the time of my journey. I cannot wait to see Dorotéa and John Cooper again!" Raoul enthusiastically avowed. "And now, Antoine, please accept this little gift and do not feel offended—it is meant in the best of taste." With this, Raoul thrust into the majordomo's jacket pocket a little sack of gold coins.

"But it is my duty to serve my master's guests, M'sieu Maldones. There is really no need—" the majordomo began to protest.

"Not a word of it! I feel part of the family here, and

much of that is to your own credit, Antoine. Well now, please convey my most appreciative thanks to your master and mistress. When I reach the ranch, I shall send back a letter by these two men that will, I sincerely hope, express my truest sentiments over the manner in which I have been welcomed here in this beautiful country. Until then, I bid you *adiós*, Señor Antoine."

"It has been an honor to serve you, M'sieu Maldones." Antoine gave him a bow from the waist and smilingly returned to the house, while Raoul approached the two men whom Fabien Mallard had chosen as his escorts. "I am Raoul Maldones," he said, "and it will be my privilege to have you journey with me, señores."

The younger of the two cordially held out his hand, and Raoul shook it. "My name is Louis Ferrand, and this is my good friend Jacques Lenoir." Twenty-six-year-old Louis was tall and wiry, a Creole, as was his companion, who was four years older, stockier, and dark-haired. Jacques Lenoir now also came forward to shake Raoul's hand, and trying to impress the Argentinian, he said, "M'sieu Maldones, you see the rifle slings attached to our mounts. These contain the finest Belgian rifles, and there is one on your horse, together with a brace of pistols in your saddlebag and plenty of ammunition in case we run into trouble. Both of us are equally armed. Oh, yes, Antoine told me to be sure to remind you that in the bottom of the saddlebag you'll find a bone-handled hunting knife. It's quite sharp, and if you know anything about knives and can throw them, you'll find the balance perfect to the hand."

"Gentlemen, I grew up on the *pampas* of Argentina, and I took pride in being able to ride and hunt with my loyal *gauchos* and not be ashamed of the way I acquitted myself. I hope that I may do equally well with both you gracious young gentlemen. And I'm eager to be off, so let us mount and you show me the way."

"It was a good idea to start at dawn, M'sieu Maldones," the tall, wiry Louis ventured, "to avoid the intense heat of early afternoon. We shall go through some swampland of which the state of Louisiana, unhappily, has an overabundance. And for the next three or four days, the difficulties that we can foresee will be those not only of the terrain but also the possibility of renegades and outlaws who make their way to the Neutral Ground and wait for the chance to slip into Texas to pose as peaceful settlers."

"I know that, Señor Ferrand, for my *yerno*—my son-in-law—told me something of the problems in the vast territory of Texas, as did your employer. But then," Raoul added cheerfully, shrugging, "if I could survive a *porteño* prison in Buenos Aires and attempts on my life by men who coveted my land as well as my daughters, I can assure you that I am not the least afraid of what we may encounter along our way."

"I think M'sieu Mallard has just come out to bid *au revoir* to you, M'sieu Maldones," Jacques now spoke up as he gestured toward the entrance to the courtyard. Fabien, who had had Antoine waken him and had taken only a small cup of black coffee for his breakfast, had hurried out to bid his guest farewell and also to entrust the latter with a small package intended for John Cooper.

"What a pleasant surprise—but truly, Señor Mallard, there was no need for you to waken from your restful slumber to see me off—" Raoul began as he hurried toward his host.

"I would never have forgiven myself if I had allowed you to ride off without a last word of good-bye. I also wish to tell you how I value your friendship and the chance over these past several years to have served you as your factor," Fabien declared as he warmly shook hands with the Argentinian. "But now, may I ask you to do me a very small favor?"

"There is no need to ask. You have already put me so greatly in your debt—"

"You must not think that way at all. But now as to this errand." Fabien took out a small jewel box and opened it. "This is the sacred Indian amulet given to me by John Cooper, which was given to him by the chief of the Charrúa in Argentina. As I expect you know, when he made his passage home with you and his Dorotéa, he had no money to pay for the journey, and so he attempted to give the captain of the vessel this amulet as security. The captain, learning I was John Cooper's factor, said there was no need for the offer of security, and when you all arrived in New Orleans, John Cooper turned the amulet over to me. He insisted that I sell it and pay for his passage and also take some money out as a retainer for my own services to his ranch. I was going to do this, but only last week, when I met a visiting jeweler who had come here from Amsterdam, and who had been recommended to me by Eugene Beaubien of our bank, did I discover that beneath the huge uncut emerald, in a sort of little secret cache, was a second emerald, not quite so large as the major one, but of great value all the same. So here is his lucky amulet back. Thanks to the discovery of the jeweler, he will still have the priceless major stone that makes his amulet of such great worth. Meanwhile, the proceeds of the second emerald more than paid for his passage and reimbursed me, leaving him with a considerable credit on my books for any supplies or equipment or the like that he may need. I have enclosed a note in the case to explain all this."

Raoul took the case and carefully thrust it into the inner pocket of his waistcoat. "It will be my pleasure to take this to him, Señor Mallard." Then again he shook hands with the factor and said, "*Vaya con Dios*, and may you and your beautiful wife know every happiness. Please, if you can spare the time from your many duties, come to visit me at the ranch."

"If I possibly can, I promise you that Hortense and I would be very happy to take advantage of your invitation. And now I can see that my two young men are anxious to be on their way, so I'd best let you begin your journey."

With a wave of his hand and a gracious smile, Fabien Mallard watched the tall, gray-haired Argentinian ride off, with the two sturdy young Creoles following him out of the courtyard.

The three riders soon reached the outskirts of New Orleans and headed toward the northwest. By late afternoon, Raoul was already on the best of terms with the escorts whom Fabien Mallard had provided, and had learned that the stocky Jacques Lenoir was actually grateful to put New Orleans behind him for a time because he had just been jilted by a mercurial Cajun girl who had promised to marry him and then, without a word of explanation, had given him to understand just two days before that her heart belonged to another man. As for Louis Ferrand (who was, in truth, the more presentable of the two men, being better groomed and dressed, as well as more articulate and outgoing), he conversely would have preferred to remain with his master. Louis was betrothed to a pretty seamstress who had promised to marry him by the end of February. At that time her apprenticeship to her elderly mistress would be at an end, and she would have a small dowry to bring to him.

The three men made camp that night about twenty-five miles away from New Orleans, not far from a patch of swampland, in an upraised clearing sheltered by a huge clump of live-oak trees. Louis made a careful inspection of the area, explaining that there was always the danger of poisonous snakes near the swampland, particularly the deadly cotton-mouth or water moccasin.

"Will we need fresh horses on this journey, do you think?" Raoul asked, having helped make a campfire and now preparing the evening meal of beans, bacon, and strong chicory-based coffee.

"M'sieu Mallard chose the very strongest horses in his stable, M'sieu Maldones," Louis explained. "I myself have ridden all three of these on long journeys, and if one gives them plenty of rest and grazing time, with just enough water so they won't become bloated, they'll be able to make the journey and back again, have no fear. If we should have some misfortune, there are small farms and ranches throughout the Texas territory and, for that matter, herds of wild horses."

"Ah, what you say there reminds me of my beloved *pampas*," Raoul said, chuckling. Then he sighed and shook his head. "My son-in-law tells me that the *vaqueros* at his *estancia* are as skillful as my *gauchos*, and I am eager to see if that is true. Naturally, since I spent so many years of my life in Argentina, I know how expert a *gaucho* is on horseback—the animal actually becomes another part of his body, as if he were a centaur from the days of mythology."

"M'sieu Mallard has told us much about your country, M'sieu Maldones," Jacques put in, eager to take some part in this conversation, "but as for myself, I've always heard that the Comanche are the best riders in all of this country, and I hope that we do not run into any of their raiding parties as we make our way to the Double H Ranch. Although it is said that they are to be found more in the northern part of Texas. I do hope so. Ah, the coffee smells good—you've a way with provender, I see, M'sieu Maldones."

"When one is a widower, even with servants, one learns how to shift for oneself," Raoul cheerfully replied as he served up the beans and bacon and poured coffee into the mugs of his two companions. "I drink a toast to the health of both of you gentlemen, and I say that I could have found no more friendly *compañeros* for this long journey."

"That's kind of you to say, M'sieu Maldones," Louis acknowledged, eyeing his stocky companion, who nodded assent. "I'll tell you this frankly: Both of us were a little afraid that we should have to look after you in the manner of nursemaids, seeing that you're so much older . . . excuse me, M'sieu Maldones, that was a clumsy thing to say—"

Raoul laughed heartily and clapped Louis and Jacques on their backs. "No offense taken, *mis compañeros*. My gray hair and my beard make me seem old, but by the Eternal, I swear that this journey has made me young again. It reminds me of when I first came to the *pampas* and I surveyed the rolling land and said to myself, 'Here is a new home away from the hidebound conventions of a royalist Spain that has lost its standing as a world power.' And that is another reason I am so glad to be with you gentlemen this evening—now I find myself in a democracy, where there is freedom to speak and to act as one desires, without fear of being called either a traitor or a heretic."

"You're right in the main, M'sieu Maldones," Louis retorted, "except that, from all M'sieu Mallard has told us, the Mexican government is beginning to get very uneasy about *les américaines* because their way of life is so different."

"Is that because of the difference in temperament or because the Mexicans are of Spanish origin, do you think?" Raoul asked.

"Perhaps both of those things, M'sieu Maldones," Jacques now eagerly contributed, "except that mainly, as I see it, it's because the Mexicans are almost to a man Catholic, which is not entirely the prevailing faith of the settlers. So many of them are Protestant, and they are energetic people who want to get things done quickly, which is not at all the Mexican way. You yourself, M'sieu Maldones, know what the words 'siesta' and 'mañana' mean."

"Only too well! And, speaking of a *siesta*, perhaps we had best turn in early so we can get a head start in the morning," the genial Argentinian suggested.

The next morning, John Cooper's father-in-law and his two companions continued on their way. They followed the principal land route to Texas, the well-beaten road from Natchitoches to San Augustine and Nacogdoches in Texas, which involved crossing the Sabine River at Gaines Ferry. They had basic supplies of food for the long journey, and Raoul welcomed the chance to add to their diet by hunting game, for the region was plentiful in wild deer, squirrels, and rabbits.

By the end of the first week, they had reached the ferry

and paid a total of six dollars to cross with their mounts. The cumbersome flatboat used as a ferry was manned by two surly, heavily bearded stevedores and a peg-legged, grizzled Missouri trader who had taken this means of earning his livelihood after a bear had clawed him so badly that his right leg had had to be amputated. He had applied the title of "Captain" to his name of Ebenezer Durrold to give himself a touch of importance, and he was extremely garrulous about the land, the people, and the Indians and ruffians that awaited travelers on the other side of the ferry. "So you gents are bound for the Frio River, are you now?" he harangued Raoul. "Say, mebbe you'd have a chaw of terbaccy you could spare the captain, mebbe?"

"I regret I smoke only cigars—but you are welcome to one of them," Raoul cordially replied as he drew a leather cigar case out of his inner waistcoat pocket and offered it to the peg-legged ferryboat owner.

"Hey now, mighty neighborly of you, mister! Believe I will jist have me a good seegar. Been a long dry spell since I tasted one, 'n that's a fact." He extracted one of the cigars and gave Raoul a sly, wheedling look, which prompted the Argentinian to add, "Help yourself to several, if you've a mind to, Captain Durrold."

"'Deed I will, 'n many thanks. You're a real gen'leman, that's a fact, too. Thank'ee!" The ferryboat owner stuffed three cigars into his vest pocket, took a fourth and bit off the end, then spat it into the river, obviously waiting for a light. Indulgently, Raoul took out his tinderbox and struck a spark, lighting a small dry twig that he held to the man's cigar until the tip glowed a bright cherry red. "Much obliged, much obliged, I'm sure."

"You are quite welcome, señor."

"'Señor,' is it? Sounds like you're Mex, mister," the ferryboat captain pursued.

"No, I'm from Argentina originally, and before that, Spain."

"Thought you wuz a furriner, no offense meant, mister."

"And none taken," Raoul replied, much amused by this garrulous, rough-hewn example of an American.

About twenty feet away, sprawled on kegs of flour that a group of five settlers had brought with them from Mississippi, two bearded, stocky men in their late thirties turned to eavesdrop on the conversation. Each of them eyed the well-groomed Argentinian, observing his shiny new leather boots that he had purchased at a New Orleans bootmaker a few days before his departure from the city. One of them, whose left cheek was badly marked by a blotch of smallpox scars, leaned forward to his companion and whispered, "Hey, Sam, that's a real fancy feller talkin' to old Cap'n Durrold, 'n he's bound to be loaded with cash. Look at them saddlebags 'n them geldin's. Bet he's got gold in 'em."

"Might well be, Jake," his crony observed in a husky whisper.

"Whyn't we follow him 'n his buddies a spell 'n see where they're headed fer? You heard that feller say he came from Argentina, wherever that is. Chances are he don't know nuttin' 'bout bushwhackin'. Now, what do you think of it, Sam boy?"

"I think yer right, Jake. Like you say, we'll follow 'em a spell 'n see what they're up to."

After they had left the ferry, Raoul Maldones and Fabien Mallard's two men had encountered no sign of either a Mexican patrol or Indians along the road they traveled. But since this was definitely Indian country, the three of them took turns standing guard at night when they camped. They had come to long stretches of canebreaks, with tall reeds rising more than the height of a man, forming huge tunnels that brushed at them and their mounts as they galloped through. Then there was a long expanse of chest-high grass and clumps of cottonwood, as well as huge pecan trees. Late that afternoon, Louis Ferrand had seen a wild deer. He quickly pulled his rifle from the saddle sheath, cocked it, fired, and brought down the animal.

That night they feasted, and Raoul drew a bottle of excellent brandy out of his saddlebag and shared it with these two men who had become his close friends. As he took a swig of his brandy, the gray-haired Argentinian reflected, "I begin to understand why my son-in-law has such a fondness for this territory of Texas, *mis amigos*. It is unconquered, like my own *pampas*. It tolerates those who seek a home on it, yet it demands much from them. Sacrifice and work and, above all, a dream—that is what I have in common with *mi yerno*." He frequently lapsed into Spanish when the words suited the exact meaning, but the two Creoles who rode with him seemed quite able to understand his meaning. He, in turn, spoke passable French, which he had learned at school in Madrid and the study of which he had pursued once he had made his home on the *pampas*.

"So far, we have made excellent time and had no difficulties, M'sieu Maldones," Jacques Lenoir remarked as he yawned and stretched. "I'm for a bit of a nap, as I'll have the last guard just before dawn, if it's all the same with you, M'sieu Maldones."

"And I shall take the first guard," Louis declared with great self-importance. "It's true that after such a feast and that fine old brandy, the temptation to sleep is very great, but I've certainly got my wits about me enough to stand guard for a few hours."

"Then I shall relieve you at midnight, *mi amigo*," the Argentinian agreed. "How do our supplies hold out?"

"We could use some cornmeal, but we have enough beans and just a little flour left. With the fresh meat from this afternoon, we'll manage three-four days, I'd judge," Louis vouchsafed. "That reminds me, I'll cut some of the venison into strips and smoke and dry them over the fire so they'll cure. And there's salt in my saddlebag, plenty of it. By the way, M'sieu Mallard says that the Indians will often trade for salt; it is something they use a great deal of. That's why he insisted I take an extra sack, and so I have." He yawned. "Perhaps just one more sip of that superb brandy, M'sieu Maldones?"

"By all means! Well then, Jacques, you and I, we shall stretch out here in our sleeping bags and rest a little until it is our turn to take the watch. I sleep lightly, so you can be certain, I shall wake at midnight."

The two men who had observed Raoul Maldones and the Creoles on the ferry had followed the trio at an ambling distance and, with nightfall, had pulled up to the southwest at about a quarter of a mile's distance from the campsite. Having tethered their horses to a gaunt, lightning-scarred cottonwood tree, they now crawled on their bellies slowly toward the faint light cast by the dying embers of the campfire.

Jake Fulton, who had nearly died from smallpox when he was fourteen, had been born in Sedalia, Missouri, the youngest of three brothers to a wealthy farmer. Jake had hated his parents because they favored his two older brothers; also, he knew himself to be so hideously scarred by the smallpox that the girls of Sedalia would have nothing to do with him. At seventeen, he had run off to Louisiana and worked as an apprentice to an overseer on a sugarcane plantation, where, despite his crude personality and ugly appearance, he was able to have his way with the female slaves. Handy with knife and gun as well as whip, he had been put in charge of many of the slaves, and he had been able to terrorize and compel the women to succumb to his carnal lusts. But five years later, he and the overseer had quarreled over a mulatto wench, and he had killed the overseer and fled the plantation with a price on his head.

Thereafter, he had gone into partnership with an unscrupulous trader who peddled guns and whiskey to the Kiowa Apache, and just the previous year he had knifed his partner, stolen his goods, and sought to deal with the Indians on his own. But when he had delivered a shipment of defective muskets, the Kiowa Apache chief had had him staked out on the plain, castrated him, and left him to die. Sam Cording, a fur trapper who had dealt with both Ayuhwa Sioux and the Kiowa Apache, found him and staunched the grievous wound, saving his life. Thereafter, the two men had joined forces: Cording was also an outlaw, having killed a man in St. Louis who had found him in bed with his wife, and the two men embarked upon a career of bushwhacking. Having observed the steady increase of settler families in Texas territory as a result of the Mexican government's grants to the Austins, they had by now killed over a dozen men and women and grown rich on the booty they took from their victims. They had already marked Raoul Maldones and his two companions as easy prey.

"Look-see there, Sam," Jake Fulton whispered as he gestured toward the shadowy outline of Louis Ferrand, who stood about a dozen yards away from the campfire, shouldering his rifle. "Stands there like a little toy soldier, don't he? Damn shame there ain't no wimmin along with 'em—"

"Shut yer trap, Jake," Sam muttered. "I know what yer hankerin' fer. All because the Kiowa cut yer pecker off, you can't git enough of watchin' me fooferaw a gal! Anyhow, there's bound to be gold in them saddlebags—them were fine geldin's, and we'll take 'em along, too. Once we sell 'em, we'll have enough cash so's I kin treat you to watch me bed down in a cathouse, mebbe in San Antone. You'd sure like that, wouldn't you, Jake?"

"You don't have to rub it in, Sam, goddamn your ornery

soul," Jake grumbled. "Let's jist tend to what we got to do right now. I'll go knife that feller standin' guard, 'n you, you'll take care of the other two in the party. Real quiet-like now, don't fergit!"

"Are you tryin' to tell me what to do, Jake? I filled more graves 'n you so far, 'n I'm likely to fill a lot more. You jist watch my style 'n do likewise, git me?"

"Shut yer trap. I'll go ahead now 'n put that feller's lights out fer him fer good," Jake growled as he drew his knife out of its sheath, gripped the handle between his teeth, and began to crawl toward Louis.

His eyes glittered as they were fixed on the young Creole. Already, he was counting the sadistic joy of feeling his knife rip through the man's heart. It was true what his partner had said: Because of his own loss of manhood, he found some compensation in watching Sam in a woman's arms. And just because of this, to kill a man who was potent and could enjoy women where he himself could not, yes, that was the sweetest pleasure of all!

The night was still, and Raoul Maldones had indeed been fatigued from the many miles they had covered that day. Yet something had made him wake well before midnight when his turn to stand guard was due, and with a grimace, he realized it was for a quite natural need. With an oath under his breath, he got to his feet, taking pains not to disturb Jacques Lenoir, who was snoring beside him in his own sleeping blanket. Raoul had his hunting knife beside him, and he gripped it now, as well as one of the loaded pistols that he had taken from his saddlebag and placed on the other side of the sleeping blanket so that he would be ready for his guard duty. It was, he told himself, a wise precaution to anticipate danger at all moments, just as he would have done himself this very night had he been sleeping out on the *pampas* with the friendly *gauchos* who had been so loyal to his *estancia*.

His vitals gnawed at him, and he grimaced again and hurried into a thicket of chinquapin, tangled, thick, and high enough to conceal him from the camp. He swiftly eased himself and then straightened, for he had just heard a sound far off to his left. Quickly belting his breeches, he grabbed his knife in one hand and his pistol in the other. Using the barrel of the pistol to push aside several of the branches of the chinquapin, he saw what was happening. A man, a shadowy figure, had suddenly risen from out of a clump of prickly cat's claw with a knife in his hand and was preparing to leap upon Louis from behind.

Raoul uttered a shout and burst out of the thicket. Startled, Louis turned, thereby saving his own life and, in the movement, leaving the figure of Jake Fulton in full view of the Argentinian. Drawing back his knife, Raoul flung it with all his strength. The outlaw's pitted face congealed, his eyes bulged, and he crumpled to his knees and then fell forward, lifeless.

"We're being attacked, *aux armes*, Jacques, *vitement!*" Louis cried out. Jacques woke with a start, just as Sam Cording, with a bellow of rage at seeing his crony killed, came rushing out of his own hiding place with pistols leveled. His first shot grazed Louis's right hip, but Raoul, without changing the pistol to his right hand, instantly pulled the trigger. The stocky outlaw staggered back, staring down at a bleeding wound in his chest. Then he dropped both pistols and fell back, rolled over, kicked twice, and lay still.

Jacques had seized his rifle now, cocked it, and crouching down, was scanning the dark clumps of trees and thickets all around him to see if there were any more bushwhackers.

Raoul now strode forward toward Louis and exclaimed, "You are hurt, *amigo!*"

"It—it's only a scratch, M'sieu Maldones—"

"I hope that is all," Raoul said in a hoarse voice and began to breathe heavily, the reaction to the danger just setting in. "If there was anyone else, the shooting probably scared them off. But we had best take no chances and get out of this clearing."

Louis had taken out a bandanna and clapped it against the slightly bleeding wound as he bent over to peer at Jake Fulton. "Was it—no, they are not *les sauvages rouges*. This one is a white man, assuredly."

Jacques came up to them now and said eagerly, "And the other is also, Louis; I checked the corpse. *Mon Dieu, je me souviens, maintenant!* Both of these men—they were on the ferry with us the other day, do you not recall, Louis?"

His Creole companion was still too dazed to respond, but Raoul put in, "Yes, now that you mention it, *mi compañero*, I recognize this one by the marks on his face—he has had the smallpox many years ago."

"They were after our horses and what we had in our saddlebags, perhaps our weapons, too," Jacques declared self-confidently, and all Louis could do was agree with an energetic nod.

"Now let us be on our way, just in case there might be others who want to ambush us," Raoul suggested. "I have had enough of sleep for the rest of the night, that is for certain."

"Then we'll saddle up and leave, but not without both of us thanking you for saving our lives, M'sieu Maldones," Louis said in an unsteady voice.

"Before we go anywhere, you will patch that wound of yours up properly, or you will not be able to ride for loss of blood," the Argentinian declared. "And you would have done the same for me. I only thank God I woke before it was my turn to stand guard."

Louis exhaled a long breath of relief. "Amen to that!"

Five

The three men came within sight of the Double H Ranch early one morning in the first week of February. One of the *vaqueros* posted to patrol the southeastern boundary rode up to the strangers and, his attitude courteous but wary, asked them their business. Learning the bearded, gray-haired man was none other than the father of his *patrón*'s new wife, the *vaquero* escorted the three men to the ranch.

Miguel Sandarbal, the white-haired *capataz* of the ranch, had just come from the bunkhouse, after having assigned the *trabajadores* their tasks for the day: putting new shelves in the larder in the kitchen, where Rosa Lorcas was presiding so admirably; reinforcing one of the smaller corrals, some of the timbers of which had been broken by the energetic kicking by a few of the wild mustangs the *vaqueros* had been training. He caught sight of the three men being escorted by one of the ranch's *vaqueros*, and he dashed to the *hacienda*, calling out, "John Cooper, I think it is your *suegro*! Come quickly! I am certain it is he!"

Dorotéa, who had just finished dressing, heard Miguel's call and came hurrying out of the bedchamber, donning her *mantilla*. Here on the ranch, she had already quickly adapted herself to the easygoing, casual life of the outdoors that her vigorous husband so loved, and so she rarely put on the formal *mantilla*, which devout Spanish matrons were expected to wear. But the news that she would again see her father safe upon this good, fertile land made her remember that, as his eldest daughter, there were certain proprieties to be observed. With a coquettish smile, she realized that the wearing of the *mantilla* signified that she had indeed happily accepted her status as a wife and soon-to-be mother.

John Cooper, in his customary buckskin garb, met his wife in the hallway of the grand *hacienda*. He chuckled and made her a low, sweeping bow. "Doña Dorotéa, allow me the honor of escorting you to meet your father," he teased.

"I should expect nothing less from my well-domesticated *esposo*," she twitted him, but took away the sting of that formal remark by giving him a quite unmatronly hug and a very passionate kiss on the mouth. Then, assuming a sedate mask of expectation, she linked arms with him and went out of the *hacienda* to meet her father.

Raoul Maldones flung himself out of the saddle and came running toward her. "*Mi* Dorotéa! *Mi yerno!*" he joyously exclaimed. And then, catching sight of her *mantilla*, he burst into uproarious laughter and slapped his thigh. "My sweet one, *mi corazón*, that is a charming way to greet your father, and to tell him that the marriage is a happy one."

"In more ways than one, dear *padre*," Dorotéa said, putting her arms around him and warmly kissing him. "You know that I shall have my husband's child in the spring, and the blessed joy of it will be that you will be here to hold either your grandson or your granddaughter in your arms."

There were tears in Raoul's eyes as he stepped back and then hugged John Cooper, who looked somewhat embarrassed at this overly enthusiastic display of paternal affection. Miguel could not help smiling, hugely pleased at the reunion.

"You had a safe journey?" John Cooper stepped back and demanded, his cheeks still flushed from the embarrassment of the bear-hug embrace of his father-in-law.

"Quite safe, and very scenic," Raoul said. "I have learned a great deal about your country already in the two weeks it has taken us to arrive here. Later I will tell you about our journey, and a nasty little encounter with some renegades that my friends here and I had to dispose of."

By now, Louis and Jacques had dismounted, and Miguel gestured to the *vaquero* who was with them to take their horses to the stable. Then the *capataz* greeted the newcomers, saying, "Señores, welcome to the Double H Ranch! I'll see to quarters for you directly, and I am sure you're hungry and thirsty. Meanwhile, we'll take good care of your horses, never fear. It is a long journey you've made all the way from New Orleans."

"This, undoubtedly, must be your famous *capataz, no es verdad*, John Cooper?" Raoul said, turning to shake hands with Miguel. John Cooper chuckled and responded, "Yes, the legendary *capataz*, I should say. And if I know Miguel, he's a little envious that he wasn't along with you on the trip."

"You're reading my mind, *Halcón!*" Miguel answered. "But all the same, let me go into the kitchen and tell Rosa to prepare a feast! This is an occasion worthy of celebration!" he excitedly declared. "Excuse me, señora, señores!" And with this, he hurried to the *hacienda*.

"I am happy to say, dear Dorotéa, that María, Paquita, and Adriana are doing very well at the school in New Orleans. They send you their love, as does Señora Josefa. Oh, yes, John Cooper, I have something for you from Señor Mallard. It is the amulet."

"The amulet?" the tall Texan echoed, mystified. "But I told Fabien to sell it and to pay my passage back to New Orleans, as well as to reimburse him for the expenses he had on my behalf."

Raoul reached into his pocket and pulled out the jewel case. "Here you are. There is a note with this. I think it will explain everything."

John Cooper opened the case, took out the letter, and quickly read it. He shook his head with admiration. "It's very good indeed to have the amulet restored to me, for as you know, it was good luck for all of us in Argentina. What lucky men we are to have such a factor as Fabien Mallard. And now, *mi suegro*, let me see to a room for you in our *hacienda*. You must rest and get ready for the *fiesta* we shall have to celebrate your safe homecoming!"

*   *   *

The feast was a great success, and Rosa Lorcas received many plaudits for her culinary skill. The elderly Tía Margarita, the former cook, was retired now, married to the old prospector, Jeremy Gaige, and living with him in a fine new cottage on the ranch. Rosa had replaced her and was ideally happy, married to Antonio, one of the *vaqueros*. She knew that her gentle husband was a tower of strength and that he had a great, promising future on the Double H Ranch, maybe even becoming assistant *capataz* here himself someday.

But perhaps the most exuberant guest at the celebration was none other than the *gaucho*, Felipe Mintras, who had worked for Raoul Maldones in Argentina and had come to the United States with John Cooper Baines after the Texan's first visit to South America. Seated at the huge table with his wife, Luz, and his two young boys, he ecstatically welcomed his former *patrón* and proposed a toast to the reunion with the man to whom he had pledged lifelong loyalty on the Argentine *pampas*.

"*Mis compañeros, mis amigos y amigas,*" the *gaucho* exclaimed, "I know that you here in the Estados Unidos are often given to boasting. Now that I have been here for several months living with you and making friends with you, I rise to say that we *gauchos* of the *pampas* knew what boasting was long before *americanos* thought of it. I say this: No man anywhere else in the world ever had a finer *patrón* than the señor Raoul Maldones, and I do not miss my *pampas* now that he is here, for together we shall work and show all of you how it is that we care for the *ganado* and make the *estancia* safe for all who live upon it."

There were cheers at this, and Raoul himself rose to acknowledge the toast. "*Señores, señoras, amigos, amigas,* I, too, may be eloquent in my praise of a *gaucho* who, with his men, came to me on the *pampas* of Argentina. That is the greatest tribute a man can be paid, señores and señoras, believe me—to be accepted by a *gaucho*. And now that he has changed countries as I have, and he still professes to be loyal to me and to be my friend, then I say that this long journey was well worth all the hardship. I give you, *mis compañeros,* Felipe Mintras, *gaucho* extraordinary and *gran vanquero!*"

Again there were cheers, and then John Cooper rose to add his own toast as Dorotéa squeezed his hand and gave him a loving look. He said, "This proves exactly what we on the

Double H Ranch propose to create here: a community where even the humblest *trabajador* need never feel that he is less than the *patrón*; for his own contribution, in the spirit of teamwork, strengthens all of us. Most of you know that this land of Texas, where we have our great ranch, still belongs to the government of Mexico, and it is by sufferance of their government that we exist here. I think that there will be increasing hostilities until one day, as is my fondest hope, this land becomes a state of the great new country of which I am proud to be a citizen. And so I pledge to all of you that now that my *suegro* is here beside me, I shall put him to work along with Miguel Sandarbal and Esteban Morales and my brother-in-law, Carlos de Escobar, so that we may constantly strengthen our defenses against any foreseeable troubles. In addition, we intend in the not-too-distant future to have an exchange in manpower between the brave Texans living in the settlement on the Brazos River and our own fine *vaqueros* and Texans, who have pledged themselves to work for Jim Bowie and his Texas Rangers. If we work to such an end, we cannot be conquered, and one day, I hope before my own time runs its full measure, all of us will be proud to say that we are citizens of the State of Texas of the United States of America!"

The next morning at breakfast, John Cooper again thanked Raoul Maldones for bringing him back the amulet. "I can see that it might be valuable one day, if you and I should ever have to go back to Argentina—and I do hope that you will be able to regain your estate, *mi suegro*," he told the Argentinian.

"I shall not hold my breath until that day, John Cooper," his father-in-law replied. "The *porteños* are in power now, and they will not give it up so readily. There would have to be a kind of *junta* among all the landholders of the *pampas* region, and even so, it would mean recruiting an army, which the *porteños* already have. No, it would lead to bloodshed and no one would win, and the *gauchos* would be poorer than ever. As for myself, I am quite content to be here with you and Dorotéa and the child that will bless your union."

"What I should like very much, *mi suegro*," John Cooper went on in a sober tone, "is for you to gradually undertake the stewardship of our ranch here. It's true that Miguel is our *capataz* and Esteban Morales his very good assistant. But Miguel, though he would never admit it and would challenge me to a duel if he heard me say this, is getting old. You know, he accompanied my father-in-law, Don Diego, from the Old World to the New. Now he should start having the time to spend with his family. As his children grow, he will be more and more concerned with their well-being and, perhaps, the arduous affairs of this ranch will demand more and more with the years. Esteban is a good man, but he has no ambition to replace Miguel, I know that already. Still in all, I could ask for no more loyal *trabajador*. But you, *mi suegro*, with what you know about cattle and horses, you can help instruct our *vaqueros*, for you had conditions on the *pampas* like those we have here."

"Indeed, and I look forward to the challenge, John Cooper. I am ready to begin learning about the ranch at once." Raoul rose from the table, patted his belly, and chuckled, "But what I am afraid of most, now that I am here with you, John Cooper, is that I shall put on a good deal of weight. That sweet cook of yours, Rosa, is a treasure. I have already eaten more for breakfast than is my custom."

"The exercise this morning will work off whatever extra weight you may have put on from your breakfast, and you ate no more heartily than I did, if the truth be known." John Cooper laughed as he rose and accompanied his father-in-law out to the bunkhouse.

Esteban and Miguel were standing chatting, as the white-haired *capataz* prepared to give the orders for the day. Both men broke off their conversation and turned eagerly to John Cooper and Raoul. "*¡Buenos días, Señor Maldones, bienvenida!*" Miguel exclaimed.

"*Gracias, mi compañero*," Raoul replied with a smile, using the term than indicated they were equals, not *patrón* and *trabajador*.

Miguel turned to John Cooper and shook his head with a chuckle. "I swear by all the saints, *Halcón*, that this father-in-law of yours is a man after my own heart. I say to you, the luckiest thing you did for yourself was to go to Argentina because you brought back a wonderful wife and a *suegro* like Señor Maldones."

"Señores"—the mature Argentinian laughed with pleasure—"if this continues, we shall spend all the day praising one another, and no work at all will be done. And that was not my intention at all when I came here."

"I am with you in spirit and deed, then," Miguel assured

him. "Esteban, be a good fellow and round up the *trabajadores*. By now, they should be finished with their breakfast."

Esteban went at once into the bunkhouse to summon the *trabajadores*, who came out cheerfully and of their own accord greeted the Argentinian. His exploits in saving the lives of his two companions on the trail from New Orleans, about which he had told John Cooper and Miguel the previous evening, had already reached them, thanks to the two young Creoles who were temporarily residing in the bunkhouse. Thus, the *trabajadores* regarded Raoul Maldones as one of themselves.

John Cooper himself took over the introductions, by asserting that his father-in-law had left Argentina to live in Texas when his own estate had been confiscated by a hostile government faction. "You may look upon Señor Maldones just as you would yourselves. Because he was a *hacendado* and shared my own ideas, as well as those of your late *patrón*, Don Diego de Escobar, and your loyal *capataz*, Miguel Sandarbal, he believes all men should be treated as equals."

Raoul shook hands with his son-in-law. Then he called out to the *trabajadores*, "And now, I think your *capataz* has work for you to do, so do not let me interrupt your duties, or I will be guilty of causing you to fall under his displeasure, which must not happen."

There was laughter and a few sporadic cheers at these words, while Felipe Mintras, who was in the foreground with the *trabajadores*, turned to them, lofted his *sombrero* above his head, and shouted, "*¡Viva Señor Maldones, viva!*"

"It is certainly a warm welcome, *mi yerno*," Raoul murmured to John Cooper. "I wish to be worthy of it, and I welcome the chance to be put to work."

"I thought that this morning we'd round up some of the stray cattle on the edges of the ranch and brand them, *mi suegro*," John Cooper proposed. "You remember that when I brought you some of our Texas longhorns, you exclaimed over the size of their horns. Well, now you'll see thousands of them—all belonging to us. However, every so often a considerable number of strays come onto our ranges, and once they come on our land, it's best to brand them, so that we can make use of every cow or yearling or bull as part of our herd. As for stunted stock, we can drive those away."

"You have a good market for your cattle?" the Argentinian asked.

"Yes, and it will get increasingly better. New Orleans uses all the cattle we can send, and there are other towns, like San Antonio and even Corpus Christi, where fresh meat and hides are in great demand. Of course, they are plentiful and the price isn't too good, but since the cattle have really cost us almost nothing—except for the prize bulls I bought for interbreeding—we still do very well. And, of course, with the many workers on our ranch, fresh meat is a staple part of our daily diet. Besides, there is a growing new American settlement on the Brazos River, and occasionally we send them a hundred head or so."

Miguel approached him now and said, "I couldn't help overhearing some of that, *Halcón*. I agree: The weather is so unseasonably pleasant, we may as well get to some of the rounding up and branding of the strays. And I'd like to break in two young *vaqueros* who came to us while you were still in Argentina."

"A good idea. Well now, we'll saddle up and join you out on the western side of the ranch, Miguel," John Cooper replied. Then, turning to his father-in-law, he said, "You'll want to have a good look at our horses. You've already seen in Argentina some of the fine palominos I brought you, but perhaps until you're used to our range and the feel of our saddles, you might make do with a docile gelding. Believe me, I don't say this to disparage your horsemanship, for I remember how magnificently you ride."

Raoul grinned. "Well, I have put in a good two weeks in the saddle coming from New Orleans, and I think I am used to anything you could give me. But I admit that this morning I feel at my ease, and not like showing off my horsemanship to all your fine *vaqueros*."

More and more, John Cooper found himself on the warmest terms with his father-in-law, who did not stand on ceremony, and who, despite having been wealthy and an aristocrat, in no way conveyed any attitude of superiority. Now he could understand very well why the *gauchos* of the *pampas* had been so fiercely loyal to such a man. "Then I'll give you a gelding. There's a bay in the stable with spirit enough, and certainly as good as the horse that brought you to me, *mi suegro*," he declared.

Meanwhile, Miguel gestured to two young Mexicans to

saddle up and follow them, and they eagerly nodded, wanting to make friends of the *capataz* by their diligence and to be accepted by the other *vaqueros*. They were in their midtwenties, cousins who had come from Nuevo Laredo after having heard that the *capataz* of the Double H Ranch was a man who gave employment to those who wished to work hard and did not care if they came from the poorest villages. Ruiz Malendo was a year older than his cousin José, short and stocky, quite soft-spoken and self-effacing, where José, slim and two inches taller, was voluble and excitable. The two had formed a perfect contrast in their first weeks at the Double H Ranch, and Miguel soon saw that they were eager to please and would accept any task given them to justify his having employed them.

Raoul mounted the bay gelding, tested the saddle cinches, approved of the reins and the saddle itself, and affably nodded to his son-in-law. "A fine mount, *mi hijo*. And now let us see this vast property of yours. There seems to be plenty of good grazing land."

"There is, not only near the river but also farther west, as you'll soon see. We brought some sheep from Taos, when Don Diego de Escobar and his family came to live in Texas. There have been no problems with the sheep, so long as the *vaqueros* keep them off to themselves on grazing land that does not intrude upon what is available for the cattle. There is still a good market for wool, not only in New Orleans but also in Taos and Santa Fe. It's true that the trip back to New Mexico is long and not without some dangers, but whenever I've a mind to be off outdoors by myself, a drive like that is ideal for me."

The sky was cloudless, and a gentle wind blew from the southwest across the river as the two men rode easily, side by side. "We've really been very lucky this winter, from what Miguel tells me," John Cooper observed. "Weather like this brings out the game, and I know that Yankee will want to go hunting with me very soon, now that I'm back."

"Oh, yes, your wolf-dog. You have told me about your valiant Irish wolfhound Lije, who accompanied you across the country to Nuevo México and then gave up his life for yours. And then his offspring Lobo, the sire of Yankee."

John Cooper was lost in thought for a time, remembering that incredible journey he had made as a young man, when for weeks on end Lije was the only creature he could talk to or be with. He remembered how he had come to rely on his dog and how he had learned from the dog's instincts when to be warned against dangers. Then he was brought back to the present as he looked out at the vast ranges of the ranch, and he said to his father-in-law, "Well, what do you think of our land, *mi suegro?*"

Raoul rose from his saddle and stared around him, then chuckled. "It is an empire, beautiful, majestic. There is certainly more grass here than on our *pampas*. Wonderful grazing land. I see now why you left Nuevo México."

"If we had stayed there, *mi suegro*, we should still run afoul of the Mexican authorities, as we did the Spanish. And the tariffs are still far too high to encourage open trade. That was our real concern when we were there before the independence of Mexico. And, of course, I'm still concerned about the poverty of the Pueblo Indians. But that's another matter. Now I think I see some of the strays that recently came across our borders. We've work ahead of us."

About half a mile ahead, John Cooper and his father-in-law could see a small herd of longhorns, moving about in desultory fashion. John Cooper beckoned to Miguel. "Let's try Ruiz and José out in branding a few of those, Miguel," he said.

"*Si, Halcón,*" the *capataz* replied. "I didn't think so many of them had clustered in that spot. When we go back, I'll have about six *vaqueros* out in the morning, if this pleasant weather holds, to finish the job. But I'd like to see how José and Ruiz work. They came from farms, so they should certainly know something about horses and cattle."

John Cooper declared, "Let's ride on at an even pace; I don't want to frighten the herd. They're skittish, and there are a lot of calves. Some look like runts and should be culled, but that can be done tomorrow, when the older *vaqueros* who know cattle better can get out here."

"My thought exactly, *Halcón,*" Miguel agreed. He drew on the reins and turned his mustang back to the two young *vaqueros*, giving them instructions. They nodded and rode ahead, Miguel following them, while Raoul and his son-in-law brought up the rear at a leisurely pace.

As they neared the milling herd, John Cooper frowned. Most of these new cattle had come onto his range in search of good grazing land. But new animals, not yet branded and accounted for, nor merged with the main herd so that they would acquire the placidity of the others, were likely to be unpredictably skittish.

"I wish," he muttered almost to himself, "Miguel had brought a few more *vaqueros* along. Those two young fellows will hardly be up to a chore like this. Still in all, it will be good experience for them . . . what the devil—"

He suddenly reined in his horse and uttered an angry oath. Some fifty yards ahead of him, a covey of mallard ducks had taken flight from a patch of swampland not far from a winding branch of the Frio River and flew directly over the heads of the young *vaqueros*. José Malendo, without thinking, seeing only the prospect of game for the evening meal, had impulsively unsheathed his rifle, cocked it, and fired, even before Miguel could halt him. One of the ducks plummeted to the ground a few feet away from the young *vaquero's* horse, but the sound of the shot had suddenly made the herd stiffen, prick up their ears, and then turn tail and come charging in the direction of the men.

"The young fool, he's caused a stampede!" John Cooper shouted. "Ride off there to the left, *mi suegro*! I'll try to head them away! They're gathering speed! Hurry!" Spurring his mount, John Cooper rode directly for the oncoming herd, yelling and seeking to distract the beasts. But they were frightened at the sound of a gunshot, which was so new and terrifying to them, and they would not be halted.

Raoul had reined his gelding off to the left to go toward the riverbank, but it suddenly stumbled in a gopher hole and fell. The Argentinian jumped off the animal before he could be crushed, but now the gelding had regained its footing and raced off, frightened by the pounding hooves of the menacing longhorns.

Ruiz Malendo did his best to turn the herd, but the animals were already past him, and Miguel, swearing ferocious oaths of what he would do to the unthinking José, saw Raoul's plight. Quickly turning in Raoul's direction, kicking his heels pitilessly against the mustang's belly, Miguel urged it on. As he came toward the Argentinian, he shouted, "Reach out your hands; I'll catch you and haul you away from them. Don't miss, *por el amor de Dios!*"

John Cooper turned his horse this way and that, expertly avoiding the frightened animals that surged past him, but the herd could not be stopped. The long, sharp horns of the bulls in the foremost row of the stampeding cattle seemed to head now right for Raoul. Miguel, with a final effort, urged the mustang forward a few feet ahead of them and, leaning from the saddle, seized Raoul's hands in his and hauled him up, flinging him across the body of his mustang—and in front of him. "Hold tight, with all your strength! I'll outrun them!"

John Cooper, racing alongside, still shouting, had turned some of the cows to one side and thus minimized the danger. Miguel continued to kick his mustang's belly and to urge it on, shouting orders, until at last it raced ahead and turned swiftly to the right and back toward the stream. The rest of the herd went by, and a cloud of dust rose to mark their passage. At last the frightened animals came to rest in a little gully surrounded by high boulders.

Raoul was pale, the blood having drained from his face, but he clung tenaciously with both arms around the horse's neck. When Miguel drew the mustang to a halt, the Argentinian slid down to the ground and stood unsteadily. Then, staring up at the white-haired *capataz*, he panted, "God is very good. You have saved my life. It is a bond between us. And it is a sign that my future life is truly here, Miguel, *mi amigo, mi compañero.*"

"That young idiot, to fire at game when he is rounding up untried cattle!" Miguel savagely declared. "I'll flay him alive; I'll rub salt in the wounds—"

"No, no," Raoul murmured as he slowly regained control of himself. "He just did not think; he is young. He is a good man; do not destroy his faith in himself. Oh, yes, point out to him what might have happened—and I am sure he knows it already. But give him work to do right now. Have him and the other man round up some of the cattle and start branding them. Put him to work so he will forget what might have happened. It did not, thanks to you, my good friend, *mi compañero.*"

In order to hide his emotion, Miguel abruptly wheeled his mustang around and galloped off toward the two frightened cousins. Already, Ruiz was telling José what a fool he had been, and the impulsive, slim *vaquero* hung his head and made the sign of the cross, as Miguel rode up to him.

"I—I am discharged, *¿no es verdad?* I know now—" he began in a faltering voice.

"The fact is, you imbecile, you know nothing! What are you sitting on your horse for? Get to work! What are the branding irons for? You, Ruiz, start the fire; and you, you idiot, let's see if you know enough to lasso a cow and brand it!"

José looked up, and there was a look of intense gratitude on his face. *"Gracias, mi capataz. Gracias por mi vida,"* he said softly. Then, untying his lasso from its coil, he galloped off toward a stray cow, docile now after the mad charge.

Six

For the next several days, Raoul Maldones, refusing to be shaken by the almost tragic accident that had befallen him, continued learning about the expansive Double H Ranch as he rode with the *vaqueros*, Miguel Sandarbal, and John Cooper. By now, Miguel had chosen some of the older men to brand the cattle, and they had headed at once for the western range. By the end of the second afternoon, every new cow, calf, and bull had been roped and branded, then allowed to graze, with the unsuitable animals turned away and culled out of the herd. John Cooper instructed Miguel to have one of the *vaqueros* drive some twenty of these scrawny animals back across the Frio River and direct them to a particularly verdant grazing patch where they might fatten and, perhaps by fall, return to be counted as part of the Double H herd.

One evening at supper, Raoul expressed some of his views on what he had seen and made some recommendations, which both Miguel and John Cooper enthusiastically agreed to put into operation. One of these was a running tally of all animals branded with the ranch's mark and entered into a ledger book, which would enable the *capataz* to know exactly how many head of cattle would be ready for market when there were orders to be filled in San Antonio or at the settlement or in New Orleans. Another suggestion was that the best of the herd be given supplements to their rations of tall, verdant grass, including maize and some barley, in order to fatten them and make their flesh particularly succulent for cooking.

During this time also, Raoul was introduced to Ramón Santoriaga, in charge of the defense of the Double H Ranch. The two men became fast friends at once, and the former Mexican soldier listened with interest to the Argentinian's stories of how he had attempted to defend his own *estancia* against attacks from both hostile Indians and *porteño* soldiers.

Thus, after only a short time, Raoul Maldones had made his presence felt, and he had won the friendship of all the *vaqueros* and *trabajadores* by his open, friendly demeanor and his utter lack of arrogance.

Meanwhile, Carlos de Escobar, John Cooper's brother-in-law, was absorbed with the raising of his children by his first wife, Weesayo—the lovely daughter of the Jicarilla Indian chief Descontarti—who had died several years earlier. Carlos's eldest, Diego, was of particular concern to him, and he shared his thoughts one afternoon with his wife, Teresa, and his stepmother, Doña Inez.

"Do you know, *mi madre*," he said as they sat out on the *patio* of the *hacienda* in the warm February sunshine, "I'm thinking about my son, Diego, and your daughter, Francesca, and what's going to happen to them."

"I, too, am greatly concerned about Francesca, dear Carlos," Doña Inez nodded. "Francesca is precocious and she is already a little beauty as she nears thirteen. And I can see that she likes your son very much. You know, of course, that such a relationship would be against all church law because of the blood ties. Though she is the same age as he, she is his aunt by blood."

"That's understood. Both my son and your daughter, dear Doña Inez, are of an age when we must nurture them very carefully and see to it that their good instincts are encouraged so that one day they will find the right *esposa* and *esposo*. If they are kept together here in proximity, as they grow older, they may forget their relationship and then it would be tragic. My son has no one else of his own age to love, just as your daughter, *mi madre*, is almost inevitably attracted to Diego. They began as children hating each other, and yet hate is the first step toward love, as we all know."

"Frankly, it worries me, dear Carlos," Doña Inez said as she bit her lips and glanced at Teresa, who was holding the sleeping Luisa—her and Carlos's newborn—on her lap.

Teresa nodded and, in a sympathetic tone, put in, "When one is nearly in one's teens, sometimes there are overpowering attractions toward the heart rather than toward the mind. One can make mistakes very easily. Carlos and I have already spoken of this, Doña Inez, and we both think that Diego and Francesca should be sent away from here to good schools, where their own lives can be developed and they can be able to decide what their futures will be. You and I have already discussed for Francesca the Ursuline Convent School in New Orleans, where Señor Maldones has left his three younger daughters."

"Yes," Doña Inez agreed. "New Orleans is a cosmopolitan city, and I think Francesca should learn languages, some of the genteel arts of being a lady, and perhaps take an interest in music and the theater, which is quite active in that port city."

Carlos slowly tried to express himself in exactly the proper terms. "You know from my own experience, I've never cared much for books and schooling. And when I came here from Spain as a youngster, all I wanted to do was hunt and shoot and ride my horse. But now that I'm a father, I begin to see that this is no life for a son of mine because it has no chance for improvement. I think that Diego should look forward to something more than being just the heir to my share of this ranch. True, it will keep him comfortably provided for, so far as *dinero* is concerned, but ranching to me was never a way of life. And I know enough about my own son to realize that it would bore him to death if all he could expect would be revenue from taking over my share of the ranch when the time comes. No, I think that Diego would be the first to tell you that he'd like to fill his mind with something useful, something that will allow him to develop his own abilities and make his own choice of what sort of career he wants to pursue."

Doña Inez leaned forward, an earnest question in her lovely eyes. "And what do you think that would be, Carlos?"

"I should not be unhappy if my son turned to the profession of law," Carlos declared. "Then he could interpret the formal rules by which men govern themselves and see to it that there is justice. Here on the frontier, we have had to take matters into our own hands, by the *pistola* or the rifle. When this country is great enough, and that is not too far off, it will no longer be the way. Only savages live by force. No, I should like my son to learn what ways there are to control communities by laws of order and discipline and peaceful conduct."

"Why, that is a perfectly marvelous idea, Carlos!" Doña Inez smilingly declared. Teresa meanwhile took her husband's hand in one of hers and gave him a warm, loving smile.

Carlos gave his wife's hand a squeeze and leaned back with a sigh of satisfaction. "I think we have accomplished a great deal, my dear ones. And I think that I'll have a little talk with Diego this very evening."

Thus it was that that evening, Carlos, after enjoying brandy and a cigar with Raoul Maldones and John Cooper, went to Diego's room and gently knocked on the door. Diego lay on his bed, still fully clothed, his hands locked behind his head, and he was dreaming, though not yet asleep. He was dreaming of Francesca's lovely face and how, more and more each day, he was becoming drawn to her. How curious it was that only a few years earlier—and he had almost forgotten it—he had really hated her for calling him such awful names as boor and stupid and too *macho*. Now he did not want to be that way at all, and it was important to him to shine in Francesca's eyes. How lovely she had become all of a sudden—he hadn't noticed before. . . .

"Come in!" he called, interrupted in his reverie by Carlos's knock.

"Forgive me, *mi hijo*. I hope I didn't disturb you?"

"Why, no, *mi padre*."

"I haven't been alone with you as much as I would have liked, and so I'd like this opportunity, if you'll permit, to sit down and, man to man, talk things over with you."

Diego grinned, for the expression "man to man" delighted him. "But of course, *mi padre*." He swung his long legs down to the floor, stood up, and beckoned his father to a chair. Then, seating himself on the edge of the bed, he folded his arms across his chest and tried to look important and grown-up. Intuitively, he sensed that this was a matter of the utmost concern, and he wished to show his father that he was capable of being treated no longer like a boy, but rather as a man.

"Thank you, *mi hijo*. Well now, I've been doing some thinking about you. We must think very seriously about what will happen in the future. You see, Diego, there is a limit to what you can achieve simply as my heir. Yes, to take over the ranch, to develop its resources, to make money so that the

trabajadores as well as our families may live comfortably—
that's all very well. But that may not be enough, Diego. If
you want the truth, I'd like very much for you to think about
the prospect of becoming a lawyer."

"An *abogado, mi padre?*" Diego wonderingly echoed.

Carlos nodded, shifting his chair and trying to phrase his
words so that his son would understand precisely what was in
his mind. "Exactly, *mi hijo*. You see, Diego, this is still wild
country, but law and order will come to it. I'm sure that one
day this Texas of ours will become part of the Estados Unidos.
Now, you've already met Jim Bowie and his group of Texas
Rangers, who propose to patrol this entire vast land and
protect it against bushwhackers, thieves, murderers, and
outlaws."

"Yes, *mi padre*."

"But in order to protect such a vast country, we must
have not only men who can use a rifle and a knife the way Jim
Bowie does, but men who can use their brains to bring about
laws in the legislature in order to protect the poor and the
oppressed who have no one to fight for them. It is a worthy
cause, *mi hijo*, and it gives one a good feeling to fight for a
cause and to make oneself skillful so that one can outwit those
who try to profit out of greed and dishonor and evil. Your *tío*,
John Cooper, has fought all his life against injustice—but you
see that even he, wise and courageous though he is, had little
schooling and does not know the written law. I am like him,
and that is why both of us must look to someone like you,
young and strong and intelligent, to become a leader of the
people here in Texas."

Diego lowered his eyes, greatly flattered at his father's
confidence in him. And then he thought to himself, a smile
crossing his lips, that if he were to go to school to be a
lawyer, lovely young Francesca would be highly impressed
with him.

Carlos had apprehended this instinctive reaction and
quickly went on, "It would please me greatly, and Teresa and
sweet Doña Inez as well, if you would agree to go to New
Orleans and become an apprentice to a good lawyer."

"Well, I think I should like that, *mi padre*."

"As for Francesca," Carlos continued carefully, knowing
what his son was thinking, "she will go to school with the
Ursuline nuns, along with Señor Maldones's other three
daughters. Now I have watched, as has Doña Inez, how you

and Francesca have progressed from hatred to what I should say would be the first feelings of love—isn't that true?"

Diego could not help blushing and lowering his eyes as he meekly nodded.

"Well now, I know you're very fond of each other. That's good. But you mustn't forget that you can never expect to marry her. The church would never sanction such a thing, and the two of you would be miserable if it were ever attempted. Look, the simple facts are that I am your father and Weesayo was your mother, but Don Diego, peace to his great soul, was my father and also the father of Francesca. It would be a mortal sin if you and Francesca were to think of any permanency in your relationship."

"I—I understand."

"Good!" Carlos leaned forward now, his face gentle, choosing his words with the greatest care, so as not to be harsh. "Seriously, I want you very much to continue your friendship with her, by all means. But when you're in New Orleans studying to be a good lawyer, as I know you will be if you put your mind to it, try to look about and see if there aren't other young women who have much to offer you in warmth and kindness. Do you understand me?"

"Yes—*mi padre*, I—I understand. I thank you for taking me into your confidence this way. I know what I shall do now. I want to please you, and Doña Inez—and—and Teresa—my new mother."

Carlos rose and went to embrace Diego and held him closely. "Yes, your new mother. She is a wonderful woman, and I love her very much, as I love you."

"And I love you, *mi padre*. I will try to be all that you wish of me."

"God Himself could ask no more of you, my dear son. This evening, *mi* Diego, you have truly become a man, and I'm going to be very proud of you, I know I am!"

For the next ten days, John Cooper spent a good deal of time at the *hacienda* with his beloved Dorotéa. Knowing that she was with child and that it would be born about April, he felt presentiments from out of the past. He remembered how his son Andrew had been kidnapped when he was an infant by Don Sancho de Pladero's traitorous *capataz*, Ramirez, in league with the bandit Santomaro. About ten years after that, when Francisco López had directed an attack

of renegade Comanche and deserters and outlaws against the
Double H Ranch, Catarina had given birth to Coraje, his
youngest child. He did not want Dorotéa to be exposed to
the dangers that Catarina had endured during her marriage
to him.

He had had supper and had chatted with Dorotéa for
over an hour in their bedchamber, kissing and caressing her,
professing his love for her and telling her how happy he was
that her father was living with them now. Then he told her
that he would come back later to be with her, but that he
wished to go to the *hacienda*'s little chapel to pray, to thank
God for the happiness given to him by having so wonderful a
wife and *suegro*.

She kissed him longingly and whispered, "I'm in love
with you more than ever now, with each new day, dear John
Cooper! I have thanked the Holy Virgin many a time for
having brought you to Argentina to find me!"

He could not speak, his emotions welling up within him
at this exquisite avowal, and he contented himself with kissing her lingeringly. "I shall be back, my heart, my joy, my
sweetheart," he whispered. "And I will pray that our child is
strong and well and will have the happiest life *el Señor Dios*
can afford one born between a man and a woman who love
each other as we do."

He left the bedroom now and went to the chapel, closed
the door behind him, and sank down on his knees. Reverently,
he crossed himself, and then he prayed, "Dear Lord God,
look down with favor upon my sweet Dorotéa and the child
she bears in her womb. Grant her and the child long life and
happiness, and accept my vow of lifelong gratitude for the
great kindnesses with which You have showered me throughout my life."

He bowed his head again and was silent for a long
moment. Then again he prayed aloud, "Lord God, I have
saved my *suegro* from the prison in Buenos Aires. I have also
avenged the death of Catarina, that foul and vicious and
needless murder. In doing these things, I know that I have
taken Thy will into my own hands, and wrongfully. I do not
ask for forgiveness, save that if I am to be punished for it, it
be visited upon me, and not sweet Dorotéa and the child who
is to come. I know deep within me, even as I pray to You
Who hears the humblest prayers from the lowliest of men,
that I shall not be spared more violence. It comes now in the

dangers between our countries of the United States and
Mexico; I know this well. And then the bank robber who
stole the silver that You let me find—this thief is unknown to
me, and yet he is also my enemy. Well, whatever else You
decide for me, I pray You to let me recover that treasure, not
for my own selfish use but for the poor and the needy and for
those here who give such loyalty and hard work to our
community."

He crossed himself, and his eyes were wet with tears as
he turned from the chapel and went back to join Dorotéa.

His Excellency, the marqués Santiago de Viñada, had
remained at the Double H Ranch as a guest, having come
from Spain a few months earlier to award Don Diego de
Escobar the Order of St. James of Compostella. He had also
brought the down payment of a pension that the king of Spain
had ordained to be given to the former *hidalgo*, whom a
junta had cleared of the charge of treasonable utterance decreed against him twenty years earlier. Before his death,
Doña Inez had suggested to Don Diego that he send the first
payment of twenty thousand silver *pesos* to Fabien Mallard,
to help the New Orleans factor recover from the grievous loss
he had sustained after the robbery of the bank in which his
and John Cooper's savings and the silver ingots were deposited.

The marqués, a tall, haughty-looking man in his early
sixties, who wore the brilliant, bright-blue costume of an
hidalgo of the Spanish court, with lace ruffles at his neck
and cuffs at his wrists, had been accompanied by two attachés,
Arturo Mendez and Pasqual Dorada, and his valet, Francisco
Pernari, as well as by his temperamental personal cook,
Corbacco. Understandably, not having learned in Spain that
Don Diego de Escobar had accompanied his son-in-law, John
Cooper, to the Double H Ranch in Texas, the marqués had
first come to Taos and had been greeted by Don Diego's old
friend, the widow Doña Elena de Pladero. She had accompanied him along with Carlos de Escobar back to the ranch, and
she, too, remained a guest at the *hacienda*. Already it was
evident that she and the mature *hidalgo* were becoming fast
friends.

Several days after Miguel Sandarbal had saved the life of
Raoul Maldones, the marqués de Viñada had made the decision to remain for a little while longer in this thriving new
country. He had arranged for his attachés to return to Spain

in the next few days with the news that the king's mission had been carried out in every detail, and also the news that Don Diego de Escobar had died, but not until he had expressed his humble gratitude for the generous gesture of his monarch.

This evening at dinner the marqués absently twirled the ends of his waxed mustache of which he was inordinately proud. A thoughtful frown on his aristocratic face, he diffidently declared, "Doña Elena, I am certain that you will wish to return to Taos to see your son and daughter-in-law. My thought is that since my attachés are going to leave shortly for New Orleans, there to board a vessel that will take them back to Barcelona, I should like very much to see such a famous American city. It was, you know, Spanish in origin, although the French also claimed it as their very own. Now it belongs to the Americans. Perhaps you would do me the great pleasure of accompanying me. Then I would see you safely back to Taos and consider my own future plans. Very frankly, Doña Elena, the strength and vigor of this new country interest me a good deal, and I should like to see quite a bit more of it. Particularly the famous port of New York, of which I have heard so much and which I am told may one day surpass the great port of New Orleans."

Doña Elena blushed and lowered her eyes. "It is most gracious of you, *excelencia*. How thoughtful you are! I, too, would very much like to visit New Orleans. I am sure I can do some shopping there for my dear son, Tomás, and also sweet Conchita. And some presents for their little ones. How happy I am that I was able to see dear Don Diego and know that his last hours were made happy by the wonderful news you brought him all the way from Spain, marqués!"

The *hidalgo* inclined his head with an exquisitely courtly gesture. "It was my duty, Doña Elena." Then he sighed and shook his head. "I must confess—and I trust that this conversation will not go beyond the walls of this room"—here, he turned to John Cooper, Carlos, Doña Inez, and the other family members, who all nodded their assurance of that promise—"that although I am a royalist as was my father before me, I begin to have grave doubts about the vitality of our monarchy. It is evident that Spain has lost virtually all of its colonies in this new world. México is, of course, gone, and also Nuevo México, which I just visited and where I had the joy of meeting Doña Elena here." At this, she blushed again and made little coughing noises with her napkin to her mouth.

"And so it seems," the marqués continued, "that while this young country grows almost daily in strength, Spain slips farther into the shadows of the past. Ah well, I should not complain too much. I have a beautiful villa on the outskirts of Madrid, my loyalty has never been questioned, and I am by birth and by heart a Spaniard. Except that now I have become a realist, as well as a royalist, shall we say."

"I applaud your candor, marqués," Carlos smilingly declared. Turning to John Cooper, he added, "But isn't it possible, John Cooper, that if the marqués sees enough of this country of ours, he can go back to Spain and try to teach that doctrine of realism?"

"I do not think so, though with all my heart I wish it were possible," John Cooper answered after a moment's reflection. "Don't forget, the Spanish have traditions that have lasted for centuries. These are hard to break, and Spain has never forgotten that it was a great world power in the days of Queen Elizabeth and the vaunted Armada. It has never been able to be as realistic as the marqués now says he is."

"Well, I for one am glad that there is no member of the *junta* here to overhear our discussion, señores," the marqués said, chuckling as he lifted his glass of Malaga wine. "At any rate, may I toast all of you and tell you how greatly I have enjoyed my visit here. I suppose ultimately I must return to Spain, for my property and my life are there, however much I should be tempted. And besides, I am a little too old to change continents."

"But you are not old at all, marqués!" Doña Elena inadvertently blurted out, and then, as all eyes turned to her, she blushed even more violently and took refuge by reaching for her wineglass to acknowledge the toast of the handsome *hidalgo* who sat across from her. He considered her warmly and then, pouring a little more Malaga into his glass, lifted it to her and said gently, "I drink to your very good health, señora. And I thank you for the friendship that you have accorded me to make me welcome in this country that I have come to love."

Immediately after dinner, Doña Inez asked to speak to Carlos and John Cooper in the little study that had once been her husband's. "You know," the elderly woman said, "we have discussed sending Francesca off to the convent school in New Orleans with the señor Maldones's other daughters. The nuns there have already said they would be delighted to enroll her; perhaps it would be an ideal time to send my sweet girl to school now, with Doña Elena and the marqués acting as chaperones."

Carlos and John Cooper enthusiastically supported this plan, and so, just before bedtime, Doña Inez went to Francesca, sat beside her, her arm around her, and said, "My darling, how would you like to leave tomorrow for New Orleans, to go to the convent school and be friends with Paquita, Adriana, and María?"

Francesca's eyes shone with delight. "You mean, go with the marqués and Doña Elena?"

"Yes, it could not come at a better time. There are plenty of escorts, and the marqués has his carriage. And it would be a very pleasant time for you chatting with them both. You know, Francesca," Doña Inez added with a little wink, "I should not be surprised if Doña Elena and the marqués decided to get married one of these days."

"That would be so romantic, *mi madre!*"

"Yes, indeed, it would, my darling. And speaking of romance, Francesca, you know, I have thought a good deal that if you stayed here on this ranch, inevitably there would be all too few young men whom you could come to love. You know how my Catarina was pampered because she had so little contact with others, and she lived unto herself, until John Cooper came to us in Taos. Well, I have a feeling that in New Orleans you will have a chance to meet the man who one day will win your heart. And although it is far too early for you to think of marriage, my darling, you are so grown-up already and you have such good common sense and sensitivity as a girl, that I know you can rely on your heart and your mind when he does come to you. You will have much more chance to meet him there."

"I know you're right, *mi madre.* I also know what you're thinking about Diego. I love him—because he's my friend, because he showed me how a boy can be friendly and helpful and reliable. But I could never marry him."

"I love you so very much, my darling. Your dear father was as proud of you as I am now, and his spirit will watch over you wherever you go, as will my prayers, sweet Francesca!" Doña Inez took Francesca in her arms, tears brimming her eyes as they communed in tender understanding.

And after she left Francesca's bedchamber, Doña Inez

went to the chapel, where she said a prayer for her daughter's happiness.

So the next afternoon, the two attachés, the valet, the marqués and Doña Elena de Pladero, Francesca, and Fabien Mallard's two Creole aides started out for New Orleans, with the cook, Corbacco, bemoaning his fate at having to ride horseback all that long distance. John Cooper sent four of his ablest *vaqueros* with them, well-armed and driving a supply wagon so that the party would not lack for provender and defense in the event of any hostility shown them. The uniform and medals of the *hidalgo* would, John Cooper was certain, act as a guaranteed safe conduct, even if Mexican patrols should come upon them.

Carlos and John Cooper, their wives, and Doña Inez bade farewell to the marqués, Doña Elena, and Francesca, while young Diego came up to Francesca and blurted out his best wishes for a safe journey and hoped that she would do very well in school. "Do please write me, Francesca."

"But you told me you'll be there in New Orleans studying to be a lawyer before much longer, dear Diego," she teasingly replied. "In that case, you'll be able to see me now and again. I am so excited. It's going to be wonderful being able to see fine stores and clothes and things—"

Diego's face fell. "Just like a girl!" he murmured, for, to tell the truth, he was not entirely over his infatuation with Francesca, and now he was suddenly aware that she was about to be lost to him for all time.

"Just like a boy, you mean!" Francesca sniffed. Then, giving him a hasty peck on the cheek, she climbed into the carriage beside the marqués and Doña Elena.

Carlos put his arm around Diego's shoulders. "I'm very proud of you, my son. You're going to make a good lawyer. And one of these days, you'll be writing me ecstatically that you've found the most beautiful woman in the world and want my permission to marry her. Better than that, you'll bring her here—or else your uncle and I will go there and look her over and make certain that she lives up to your expectations," Carlos told him.

Diego made a long face and sighed. "I suppose so. Well, I hope it won't be too much longer before I can get there."

"We plan a cattle drive to New Orleans in the next few months, Diego," John Cooper spoke up. "You'll have a chance to ride with us, and it will be good entertainment before you lock yourself up in a world of books."

They all stood there as the carriage and the wagon started off for New Orleans, with the radiant Doña Elena waving out the window. Doña Inez sniffled and dabbed at her eyes with a handkerchief, trying to remind herself that this parting with her beloved daughter and her friend from Taos was not a time of sadness but one of joy. Nevertheless, both Carlos and John Cooper comforted her by putting their arms around her and leading her into the *hacienda*, where, with their wives, they sat down with glasses of brandy and toasted Doña Elena's future with the marqués de Viñada, wherever that might take her.

Seven

Dejari, the twenty-five-year-old Jicarilla Apache brave, was not daunted by the long journey on which his *jefe* had sent him, though it was over five hundred miles. For him, it was a challenge to prove how swiftly he could reach *el Halcón*. And since the Jicarilla were at peace with the Mescalero, their ancient enemies, as well as with the Ute and Comanche, there was little danger of being waylaid over the long trail that led into the fertile valley of the Frio River. His only concern, indeed, was about itinerant Mexican patrols, whose hatred for all Indians, and particularly any of the Apache tribes, was only too well known. Thus, Dejari had with him not only his bow and quiver of arrows but also a fine new Belgian rifle that Pastanari had given him, a pouch of ball and gunpowder, and an extra flintlock. Indeed, *el Halcón* had given the tribe many such fine weapons, along with ammunition and other supplies.

To be sure, Dejari hoped to use the rifle only to procure game, for he had taken sparse provisions with him, knowing that he could live off the land. But even if there was no time to hunt, there would still be some berries even in winter, and nuts and roots at the very worst, and he had maize and some strips of dried jerky in a saddlebag made of deerskin. The mustang would graze on wild grasses and drink from streams.

As he rode, Dejari saw a small herd of buffalo and sadly sighed at the sight. In the early days, his grandfather had told him, the Jicarilla had come out of the mountains to hunt the buffalo on the plains, but then the buffalo had moved to the south and other Indian tribes had pursued them. And the Spanish had tyrannized the Jicarilla, forcing them away from the nomadic life that they had known from the very beginning of their existence and driving them into the mountains. The legend was that Monster Slayer, the war god, had created a country for the Jicarilla in northeastern New Mexico and southeastern Colorado and had decreed that they live in it always, or they would perish by his prophecy.

Nonetheless, Dejari, with the bravado of youth, decreed that he would prove his daring by bringing down one of the shaggy beasts with his bow rather than with the rifle. Besides, buffalo meat would be a welcome addition to his sparse diet on his arduous journey. And so, looking up to the sky and beseeching the Giver of Breath to look with favor upon his foray (and also secretly praying that Pastanari would never learn how he had delayed in fulfilling his urgent mission), Dejari fitted an arrow to his bow and, guiding the mustang with his knees, approached the small herd. They scattered at once, but Dejari had notched his arrow and directed it toward a young cow. It struck home, and the cow crumpled to her knees and then rolled over with a few convulsive kicks. With a triumphant shout, the Jicarilla brave galloped up to his fallen quarry, leaped from the mustang, and drawing his hunting knife, prepared to begin the job of butchering the animal. He would put strips of the best meat into a pouch with salt, together with the dried jerky, for it was the best way to cure it; the rest of the carcass he would leave for the vultures and other predators. But tonight, at least, he would gorge himself and then make up for it tomorrow by spending more time in the saddle as he headed southeastward. Also, before he was through, he would slash off one of the ears as a trophy to prove his daring.

Suddenly, Dejari uttered a cry of horror. From the herd, a young bull had disengaged itself and now came at him, horns lowered, snorting ferociously. Evidently, the dead cow had been the mate of this bull who was intent upon avenging her death.

There was no time to reach either his bow and arrows or the rifle in its sheath, and so Dejari crouched, his bloody hunting knife in his hand, warily watching the oncoming bull. Terrified, his mustang reared, pawing the air. The bull, distracted, gored it. There was a shriek of agony from the wounded mustang as it toppled, and Dejari was aghast: Now he was horseless, with most of his journey still before him and speed of the utmost essence by the decree of his *jefe*.

Out of maddened desperation, with little time to think of the consequences, Dejari flung himself forward and leaped onto the back of the bull, which was worrying the dying horse it had gored. His left hand clutching the thick shaggy mane, Dejari plunged his hunting knife repeatedly toward the buffalo's heart. Madly, the wounded animal tried to shake its unwanted rider from its back, twisting its terrible bloodstained horns, its eyes bloodshot and rolling. But a final thrust, with all his strength, found the bull's heart, and Dejari was just in time to leap from the dying monster before it fell heavily onto its side and lay still.

His horse still screamed in pain, and Dejari, tears in his eyes, bent to the mustang and swiftly dispatched it by cutting its throat. Then, removing his saddlebags of food and ammunition, taking the bow and arrow quiver and the rifle, he began disconsolately to trudge in the direction in which he had been riding, forgetting all about the buffalo he was intending to butcher. He cursed himself for a fool, and he prayed to the Great Spirit to let him rectify this blunder that would disgrace him forever and perhaps have him driven from the tribe as a wanderer marked for death by anyone who found him. The stern law of the Apache was inexorable, and to fail a chief in such a mission brought with it the most drastic penalty, Dejari well knew.

He adjusted the quiver of arrows to his back, shouldered the musket, held the heavy saddlebags over the other shoulder, and walked on. The air was crisp and cold, but he was unaware of anything except the immensity of his mistake. There were some five hundred miles to be traversed, and on foot—he did not even want to think of how long it would take him. And assuredly that old shaman who awaited *el Halcón* would pass to the Great Spirit long before he, Dejari, could bring back *el Halcón* to the stronghold.

He had walked at least two hours, still alternately praying and damning his own brash stupidity, when suddenly he saw a dozen wild mustangs feeding on herbs that grew in a thicket near a little dried-up creek. He caught his breath and feverishly began to think how to catch one of them. But he had no lasso, and of course to shoot down one of these wild creatures would do him no good, either. They were upwind and not aware of him as he crept toward them, holding his breath and saying more prayers than he had known he could ever express. He pledged to be the most courageous warrior of all the Jicarilla if only the Great Spirit would grant him this one chance to redeem himself in the eyes of his *jefe*.

And then, as if the Great Spirit had taken pity on him and sent a silent message, Dejari knew what he must do. If he could come close enough to one of the mustangs to loop his bow over the animal's neck, he might be able to hold the skittish animal and mount it. Once astride, he could conquer it, he could break it, for he had done this before in the stronghold while the other braves watched and while the woman who was promised to him had shown by her smile that she found him valiant and good to look upon.

Quietly, he discarded everything except the bow and the quiver of arrows over his shoulder. Crouching low, praying that the wind would not change or any of the mustangs suddenly glance about, he crept forward. Then suddenly he sprang, and fortune was with him, for he managed to loop the cord of the bow around the neck of a black mustang. The rest of the herd snorted and whinnied and raced off, and his own momentarily captured prey kicked wildly and lunged forward to break the unexpected restraint. But in the same moment, Dejari had leaped astride the mustang and now, holding the end of the bow in his left hand and digging the fingers of his right hand into the thick mane of the animal, shouted at it, saying in Apache, "Ride, devil. I am your master; ride. You will not shake me; you will take me where I must go; it is the will of the Great Spirit! Do your worst, devil, I have you now!"

The mustang bolted, suddenly stopped short, then began to kick and buck. But Dejari, swearing under his breath and at the same time almost tearfully praying that he would not be thrown off, held on grimly with the tenacity of despair. This was his only chance. His ribs ached from the jolting shock of the mustang's ferocious plunges and bucks and kickings, but he held firm, and now he pulled the bow toward him, cutting off the animal's windpipe, until at last the mustang weakened and, snorting, tossed its head several times, then bowed it in defeat.

Now Dejari was gentle, soothing it, praising it with the softest of terms while his right hand stroked the animal's shuddering neck. At last he knew that he had found a mount to take him to *el Halcón*. But he dared not dismount to retrieve his rifle and provisions; to do so would mean that the mustang would take to its heels—no, he must pay the penalty for his earlier folly, and he must survive now with just the hunting knife in his belt and his bow and arrows. It was enough that the Great Spirit had sent him this *caballo* out of the sky itself, as it appeared, and the rest was up to him.

When he was certain that the mustang would follow his commands, he removed the bow at last, let it drape around his own neck, and with both hands plunged into the mustang's mane, urged it toward the southeast.

By nightfall, his body drenched in sweat and aching in every limb, Dejari realized that he must at last halt the black mustang. For the past few hours, it had shown itself to be thoroughly docile, obedient to his slightest direction of fingers or knees. Yet he must rest and find some kind of provender for both his new mount and himself, and he would have to risk releasing the mustang while he did so.

These last few miles, he had leaned forward and soothingly talked to the mustang, as if it could understand the Jicarilla tongue. "You are not a devil, but an angel sent by the Giver of Breath to save me. What you do for me, black one, is truly for *el Halcón*, and he would respect you as I do, for he trains horses. I will find you something to eat and to drink, black one. You have a great heart; have compassion on me also, for I do not mean to take you from your herd. It was the will of Him Who gives life to all of us, believe this. I am your friend. When I reach the ranch of *el Halcón*, I will have the *trabajadores* give you all the oats you can eat, yes, and sugar, too, which I know you have never tasted. Be gentle now, for I must dismount, and I must find something for our evening meal. How well you have ridden, black one, greathearted one!"

The black mustang shook its head and whinnied, turning back, its eyes no longer rolling and bloodshot with anger but seeming to understand what the young brave was saying to it.

Greatly heartened, Dejari at last halted the wiry wild horse and cautiously dismounted. He held the end of his bow in his left hand, ready if need be to use it again as the improvised lasso around the mustang's neck. But to his great joy, the horse stood quietly, shivering a little, and regarding him with its great brown eyes.

Crouching, Dejari listened to the low call of a small screech owl not far from a thick clump of mesquite. As he strained his ears, he could hear the flow of water, and that was a good thing; they were both parched with thirst. First they would drink, and then he would see to food. He stood facing the mustang and made a gentle sweep with his left arm. "Come to me, black one, come; there is water. Do you not hear it? Come, we shall both drink together, as *compañeros!*"

His heart was pounding violently, for he feared that at any moment, knowing its freedom, the mustang would at last bolt off into the darkness and leave him there helpless. But again, to his astonishment, the mustang followed him, dipping its head now and again as if to acknowledge that it would obey its new master.

They came to a little creek, and the water was fresh. Dejari flung himself down on the ground, leaned over, and drank avidly. He could hear the soft clop of the mustang's hooves as it followed him, and then he heard the horse drink. He straightened slowly and quietly, so as not to startle the animal. "That was good, wasn't it, black one? Now to find us some food. You cannot eat the mesquite; it would poison you, swell your belly, and give you pain. But there must be some kind of tasty grass not far from the mesquite. I will find it for you, do not fear."

The black mustang stood quietly, seeming to stare after the young Jicarilla brave as he made his way past the mesquite thicket. He came upon a clump of thick dried buffalo grass and tore it with both hands from the ground. He came slowly back and, speaking gently to the mustang, placed the grass on the ground before it. Then he moved away. After a moment's hesitation, the horse dipped its head and began to chew. Dejari permitted himself a small smile of triumph, but the danger was not yet over. He must find food for himself, and then some kind of reins to guide the mustang.

He heard a scrabbling in the brush just beyond him and, drawing his knife, stealthily crept toward the source of the sound. It was a small jackrabbit, and with a lucky leap and thrust, he killed it. This would do for food, and he would make a fire by rubbing dry twigs together over more of that thick grass, to cook the rabbit. And there was water enough in the little creek. Yes, the Great Spirit had shown him a sign of favor. He would reach *el Halcón*. Almost in the same moment, while he was thinking this, he came upon a huge yucca plant and beside it a small cypress tree with thick vines. Yes, here was what he needed to make the reins and a *reata*.

An hour later, having fed the mustang plentifully, he cooked his rabbit, and the horse nuzzled his back as he did so. That was a very good sign.

After he had finished his meal, Dejari squatted down and began to string the lengths of vine he had cut from the tree until he had formed a suitable lasso and a bridle with reins. Now that they had rested enough, it was time to travel onward to make up for the lost time. He came quietly toward the mustang, advancing with his left hand held out and speaking in the same kind of soothing voice that had first gentled it.

The mustang made no skittish movement as he vaulted astride it and then expertly adjusted the bridle and reins, keeping the *reata* in his right hand. His belly filled and his throat no longer dry, he beamed with satisfaction. Surely he would reach his goal because the Great Spirit had forgiven him his dreadful blunder. Kicking his heels against the mustang's belly, he urged it on at a gallop. In the starry night, Dejari rode at topmost speed, saying his prayers to the Giver of Breath that this time he would not fail in his quest.

It was on the morning of the thirteenth day since his departure from the Jicarilla stronghold that Dejari saw in the distance the church and the *hacienda* and the bunkhouse of the Double H Ranch. He rode in under the huge gate that formed the boundary of the ranch, with its insignia of the head of the hawk at the top and the legend "*Hacienda del Halcón*" on one side and "Double H Ranch" on the other. The twin *H*'s—which were the sign of the ranch's brand—were inscribed in the very middle beneath the hawk's head.

Dejari rode up to the largest of the corrals and dismounted; Miguel Sandarbal, who was chatting with a group of the older *vaqueros*, at once hurried up to him. "*¿Qué pasa, amigo?*" he asked. Then, glancing at the mustang, he said admiringly,

"That's a fine horse, and you've ridden it a good way, from the sight of it."

"*Si, mi compañero,*" Dejari responded, "I have been sent by the *jefe* of our tribe to find *el Halcón.*"

"I'll bring him out to you directly. Ho there, Jaime, take this man's horse and give it a good stall and see that it's watered and fed. It's a wild mustang, I'll be bound."

"*Es verdad,*" Dejari admitted. "My own horse was gored by a buffalo bull, and I was very lucky to find this one in a small herd and to capture it."

"A trick like that would earn you a job here as a *vaquero, mi amigo,*" Miguel affably averred. "Now wait a moment, and I'll bring *el Halcón* out."

Miguel had long ago learned to tell from the costume and markings of an Indian to what tribe he belonged, and he had at once recognized Dejari as a member of the friendly Jicarilla, to whom John Cooper was blood brother, as was Carlos. A few moments later, he had summoned the tall Texan, who hurried up to the young brave and exclaimed, "Welcome to the Double H Ranch, *amigo*! Miguel tells me you've come from Pastanari."

"*Si, Halcón.* We have in our stronghold a very old man who was once our shaman. He lives at the very edge of our camp, and by our law he is not permitted to speak to any of the tribe. Once, I am told, he urged an alliance with the Comanche, and he was betrayed and many Jicarilla died. He who was then *jefe* said that from that day forth he would be punished by living with us and yet never being one of us."

"A terrible sentence, but I know the Apache law. And what has this to do with me, *amigo*?" John Cooper asked.

"The great-granddaughter of this old shaman sought out Pastanari and brought him to the tipi of the old man. And there he told Pastanari of a vision he had had of a mountain where there was silver, and he said that he knew of you and wished to tell you of it before he went to join his ancestors in the sky."

John Cooper shot a wondering look at Miguel and then echoed, "A mountain of silver? But perhaps because of his great age, his mind is wandering, and he remembers only that sacred mountain from which I took the silver ingots years ago."

The brave shook his head. "No, *Halcón,* he knows of that one, it is true, but what he spoke of to Pastanari was still another mountain near Raton, where he was a slave to the Spaniards long moons ago when he was only a boy."

"What is your name, *mi amigo*?"

"It is Dejari, *Halcón*."

"Well then, Dejari," John Cooper went on, "go with my *capataz*. You've had a long and hard journey, and I will go back with you after you have had time to rest."

"It is my prayer that the old shaman will be given time by the Giver of Breath until you reach him, for he is very weak," Dejari declared.

"In that case, the sooner we leave, the better. I must go tell *mi esposa*, Dorotéa, and the others and make my preparations."

John Cooper went back into the *hacienda* and directly to the large sitting room, where Dorotéa and Doña Inez were busily chatting and knitting clothing for Dorotéa's newborn, due in April. Greeting Don Diego's widow and bestowing a kiss on her cheek, John Cooper then asked his wife to accompany him to their bedchamber. She gave Doña Inez a quizzical look but immediately put down her knitting and followed her husband down the long hall to their room.

"*Querida*," John Cooper said, taking her hands, "I must leave at once for the Jicarilla stronghold. A brave has just ridden here with news that is of the greatest importance. It concerns a hidden mountain in which there is another cache of silver. If this story is true, if there is truly another mountain, then I can replace the silver that was stolen, and the money will benefit the *indios* of the mountains and the pueblo, as well as the poor and needy of Taos. Also, it will help me do many things to make this ranch even stronger against attack, as well as to help new settlers begin their fruitful lives here."

Dorotéa wound her soft arms around his neck and looked deeply into his eyes. "I hope you will be back before our child is born, *mi corazón*."

Again John Cooper felt a twinge of conscience, remembering how Catarina had once been vexed with him for not being on hand during her delivery of their child. And yet, this was such vital news that even the occasion of a birth might not halt the undertaking of it.

"I will leave this very afternoon, my sweetheart," he said. "It will take about two weeks going and two weeks back, and then such time as is needed to determine the location of the new mine. But I'm certain I'll be back in time to be with you, Dorotéa. And each night when I make camp, I will say prayers to *el Señor Dios* for you and the little one who will bring such great joy to our lives together."

"Be careful; do return to me safely, *mi corazón*," Dorotéa earnestly whispered as she held him tightly to her bosom.

Eight

——◆————————————————————————◆——

Dressed in buckskin, with the Spanish dagger in its sheath around his neck and his strong, sharp Bowie knife in a belt sheath, John Cooper added only "Long Girl"—the Pennsylvania long rifle he had inherited from his father—to the arms he would take with him on the long journey to the stronghold. Saddling one of his young palominos and attaching saddlebags with ample provisions for several days, John Cooper led the horse out of the stable, having given Dejari a palomino also. The young brave was overwhelmed by the generosity of *el Halcón*, but he did not forget the mustang he had tamed and made his friend. The animal was led behind them by a rope, and it followed obediently.

John Cooper turned and whistled, and with a happy bark, the sturdy wolf-dog, Yankee, raced up to his master. The wolf-dog looked up, tongue lolling out of his mouth, showing his great joy at being allowed the privilege of accompanying his master.

He was sturdier than his sire, Lobo, and his jaws were even more formidable. Yet John Cooper and Carlos, and Miguel at times as well, had skillfully trained this mixture of the savage wolf and the Irish wolfhound, a strain that had begun with John Cooper's first dog, valiant Lije, some twenty years before.

In John Cooper's opinion, Yankee was as valuable as a man in the event that he was subjected to attack, for the animal's cunning and strength were powerful weapons, often more capable than rifle or pistol or knife at close range. And the ferocity of the wolf-dog, when loosed upon an enemy, was certain to strike terror, a valuable advantage in battle.

John Cooper and Dejari rode side by side, and the first rays of the setting sun touched their horses and cast shadows. In the past, especially during the formative years of his young manhood when he had made his way from Shawneetown across the plains, John Cooper Baines had known moments of intense premonition, as if that which was about to happen had been long ago foreordained. At first, he had not been able to explain these feelings, except that they grew out of an instinct for self-preservation. Undoubtedly Lije's presence had also alerted him many times to dangers that he might have only vaguely felt. But after having lived with Indian tribes and having learned many of their customs, particularly those of the Jicarilla whose blood brother he was, John Cooper had begun to believe that these feelings were mystical in origin, and more and more he put aside the pragmatic, realistic core of his nature to prepare himself in a spiritual way for what these premonitions augured. And on this journey back to the stronghold where he had lived so many years ago after his perilous flight from the Dakota Sioux, he felt an impatient eagerness to know what was in store for him when he arrived.

Along with his eagerness for what lay ahead, the tall Texan welcomed this rare opportunity to be on horseback and to make camp, to forage for food and live off the still-wild land. He saw the majestic stretch of the land beyond him, the hills and the canyons and the mesas, the mountains far in the distance, the incredibly flawless blue of the sky intensified by the floating fleece of clouds like a thousand sheep gently marching across the heavens. He smelled the grass and the wildflowers and the herbs, and he heard the sounds of their horses' hooves.

He glanced at the stalwart young brave who regarded him with open admiration. They had spoken hardly a dozen words between them since they had begun their journey, and yet each seemed to know the other's ways. Was this not in itself proof that the Great Spirit had made all men and blown into them, divergent though they were in skin and race, in religion and color, the same divine breath that let them perceive all those great things upon this earth? And perhaps because of these very feelings that had been inculcated within him by the Indians for so many years, he felt an angry sadness at the thought that there were so many white men who regarded every Indian as a bloodthirsty savage and a usurper of peace.

The palominos were tireless, and on the fourth evening, as they made camp, Dejari permitted himself the luxury of higher praise than an Apache is wont to give. "Halcón, the more I ride this palomino of yours, the more impressed I am. He has courage and strength—as much as the fine mustang I tamed. He is wise, too, and he can sense danger. My father once told me that the spirit of a warrior is sometimes brought back in the shape of an animal, and thus it is that we are taught to respect the four-legged creatures of the land."

"It is a good thought, Dejari. There are times, perhaps because of this, that we are more willing to trust a horse or a hunting dog than one of our own kind. The animal acts by instinct, where a man acts all too often from forethought and cunning."

"That is true. Well, we must not make camp for too long, Halcón," Dejari said to him. "There is within me the fear that the old man may not be alive when we reach the stronghold. And I have not forgotten how very nearly I did not come to bring you the message."

"But you did, and you see it was ordained. That is why I have the feeling now that we shall find him alive, that he will live until he tells me the secret that he has kept for so long," John Cooper answered.

On the eleventh day of their journey, on the day before they would reach the stronghold, John Cooper and the Jicarilla brave rose at dawn, made a frugal, hasty breakfast, and then mounted their horses and rode onward. "With luck, we might make the stronghold by tonight," the tall Texan remarked to his companion. He glanced up at the sky, and he frowned, for thunderclouds were forming. "But if there's a storm, we'd best settle for arriving there tomorrow."

Yankee was tireless, loping ahead of the two riders, his tongue lolling out of his mouth, his eyes gleaming with pleasure. The long trek had been a happy adventure for him, and he had eaten well, for he had contributed several times in bringing provender for the evening's meal. Each time, John Cooper had praised him, rubbed his knuckles over the wolf-dog's head, and given him a tidbit. Then, when the food was cooked, he had seen to it that Yankee received a share. Dejari had overcome his initial caution of the sturdy wolf-dog and by now was not afraid to rub his own knuckles over

Yankee's head and to elicit the contented sound, not unlike that of a dog or a cat when it is petted by a beloved master.

The storm began a little after noon and compelled the two riders to take refuge in a cave along a slope of low, rocky hills. The rain drenched the trail, and the thunder and lightning lasted for nearly an hour. Finally, the sky brightened, and the sun again emerged.

As they continued on, they passed a low mesa and then entered a rocky canyon, out of which they came onto an uneven plain abundant with live-oak trees and thickets of mesquite, bushes of yucca, and tangled chinquapin.

To their left, there was a row of hills, diminutive as compared with the towering mountain range well beyond them, where the Jicarilla stronghold lay. Now the air was so clear that those mountains seemed only half an hour's ride away, but that was most deceptive: It was at least a forty-mile journey.

Dejari glanced over to his left and commented, "This is good hunting country, *Halcón*. It was not far from here that I found the herd of buffalo. Sometimes our braves come down here to hunt the *jabalí* and the wild deer and antelope. And there are many rabbits and squirrels, which are good to eat the way our squaws cook them."

"Yes, and if we weren't in such a hurry, I wouldn't mind sending Yankee out on another hunt. He'd love it!" John Cooper suddenly stiffened in his saddle. "Wait a minute—I heard someone cry out over there, way up at the top of the hills!"

"I heard it, too, *Halcón*. Let us go see what it is!"

They spurred their palominos up the gradually ascending slope toward the topmost hill and came upon a stretch of level ground abundant with thick foliage and many tall trees. Again the cry came to them, a cry of desperate pain. It was off in a clump of trees, and John Cooper quickly dismounted. His palomino snorted and tossed its head, and Dejari, as he dismounted, muttered, "I have the scent of bear in my nostrils!"

John Cooper swiftly turned to the saddle sheath and drew out "Long Girl," already primed and loaded. Then, beckoning to Yankee, who had followed the two riders up the slope, he and Dejari advanced toward the forest.

All at once they saw a black bear, three feet at shoulder height and five feet in length, snarling at the base of a live-oak tree. Perhaps fifteen feet above, a young brave clung to a heavy branch, armed only with his hunting knife. At a glance, John Cooper could see that the Indian's bow and quiver of arrows lay on the ground where they had been abandoned. And there was another sight, even more ominous: a pool of blood and the drops that fell from the badly mauled left leg of the brave in the tree.

"*¡Mata, mata!*" John Cooper called to Yankee, gesturing to him.

Yankee understood. With a low growl, his ears flattened against his skull, the wolf-dog warily circled toward the bear. Just as the angry animal extended its front paws and, standing upright, began to ascend the tree toward its victim, Yankee darted forward and nipped at the bear's leg, then stepped back, growling.

Angered, the bear turned, its bloodshot eyes seeking out its attacker. Then, looking upward at the Indian, the bear again began to climb.

"Do you see the arrow shaft in the bear's side? He has wounded it," Dejari whispered to John Cooper. "It is not a wound that kills, but it has made the bear savage. And the brave has only a knife."

"But I have 'Long Girl'," was John Cooper's answer as he squinted along the sights. Then again he called to Yankee, "*¡Mata, mata, amigo!*"

Once again, Yankee launched himself at the black bear, nipping its leg. This time, the infuriated wounded bear dropped to all fours and made a vicious swipe with its right paw toward the wolf-dog who, his fur bristling, eyes narrowed, watched his enemy's every movement.

John Cooper took careful aim and, just as the bear shuffled forward, fixing its baleful gaze on Yankee, he fired. There was a roar. The bear seemed to jerk convulsively, made as if to rise on its hind paws, and then fell heavily onto its side, kicked several times, and lay still.

Dejari, to whom John Cooper had given a Belgian rifle when they had left the *hacienda*, had already cocked and aimed it, and now he pulled the trigger, sending a shot into the bear's side. There was no movement.

"Yes, we killed him, Dejari." John Cooper lowered his rifle with the butt on the ground. Cupping his right hand to his mouth, he called out in Apache, "It's safe to come down now!"

"The Great Spirit be praised!" the Indian called in a

hoarse voice. "I have only my knife—and I had wounded him—I had forgotten that the black bear can climb a tree. I had to leave my bow and arrows on the ground when I ran for the tree." He slowly and painfully descended, grimacing with the effort as he carefully made his way down. Finally, he let himself down to the ground and stood with his back against the tree trunk, his eyes closed, his face damp with sweat.

The bear's claws had gouged his leg badly, from the uppermost thigh to the knee, and there was a welter of blood from the wound. John Cooper immediately took charge. "In my saddlebag, there's an extra blanket. Take your knife, Dejari, and cut it into strips; I'll make a tourniquet. I'll also have to make a fire." To the wounded brave he said, "The bear's claws may poison the wound; I must cauterize it for you."

"I know you, H–Halcón." The brave gasped, wan with his pain. "I am Masikaya."

"Yes, I know you, too," John Cooper exclaimed as he helped make the Jicarilla brave comfortable, then began collecting dry wood for the fire. "Your father was the brother of Nadikotay, mother of the *jefe*, Pastanari."

"That is so. I had thought to hunt for the *jabalí* or the wild deer, but this bear came out of a cave and chased me, until I faced it with an arrow. In my haste, the arrow did not speed true and only wounded the beast. I thank the Great Spirit that you came in time. I could not have killed it with a knife, weak as I was from my wound. You have been sent by the Giver of Breath that I may return to the stronghold of my people."

Dejari brought strips of the blanket, which he had cut with his own hunting knife, and he also brought John Cooper's tinderbox. Swiftly, taking the strips of blanket, the Texan bound them around the brave's thigh and knotted them as tightly as he could. Then John Cooper squatted down, lit a little piece of moss with his tinderbox, then with that lit the twigs. He put the blade of his hunting knife into the flame, turning it to and fro until it was glowing with heat. "Now I must burn the wound, Masikaya," he warned.

"I am ready." The brave folded his arms across his chest and tilted up his head. The muscles of his jaws stood out as he steeled himself for the agonizing ordeal of cauterizing the wound.

There was the hiss of hot steel on raw flesh, but only a

faint groan escaped the Indian as John Cooper, as quickly and mercifully as he could, saw to it that the long bloody furrows left by the bear's claws were cauterized.

"Where is your horse?" John Cooper asked as he finished his work.

Masikaya shook his head. "He ran off. The smell of the bear and the sight of it, as well, frightened him. It is the first time he has ever seen a bear."

"Well, there's no help for it. Anyway, you're too weak to ride alone, even if I were to let you ride the tame mustang we brought with us. No, you'll have to ride on my horse, and I'll ride behind you to steady you. But first, you'll rest and eat a little something and drink some water, to give you strength to reach the stronghold."

"My life is yours, *Halcón*. I will do whatever you think best. One day, may the Great Spirit grant that I can repay this gift of life, perhaps by killing one of your enemies."

"You mustn't think of a thing like that now. Here now, lie down and rest." John Cooper gestured, and Dejari brought one of the sleeping blankets from his palomino, folded it, and made a pillow of it for the wounded brave who was, at thirty, five years older than the young chief of the Jicarilla.

This done, John Cooper prepared a quick meal of beef jerky and some corn. With the little flour he had remaining, he also made some biscuits over the fire. Masikaya ate gratefully and drank half a canteen of water. Then, exhaustion claiming him, he slept.

The sky was clear now, and there was no hint that there had ever been a storm. John Cooper murmured to Dejari, "It was very lucky the storm ended when it did. If it hadn't, we might never have found Masikaya in time to save him from the bear."

"I have cut off the ears of the bear, and also some of the claws," Dejari said, his voice filled with awe. "I shall take them back to the stronghold to show that you are still the great *Halcón*, and that no hunter can do greater deeds than you with the long stick that speaks with thunder and lightning."

Before the sun set, Masikaya agreed that he was strong enough to return to the mountain camp of the Jicarilla, and both John Cooper and Dejari helped him mount the former's palomino. The tall Texan then mounted behind the wounded Indian, putting his arms around the latter's middle and taking the reins. "We shall go slowly, so that your leg will not hurt too badly."

The next morning, as Dejari, John Cooper, and the wounded brave neared the mountain of the stronghold, Dejari turned to the tall Texan and asked, "Do you see the smoke signals? The scout on the lowest ledge of *la montaña* has seen us and tells of our coming to the *jefe!*"

John Cooper nodded. Then he solicitously asked his wounded companion, "How does your leg feel this morning, Masikaya?"

"It is very stiff, but thanks to you, much of the pain is gone. And the heated knife drew out the poison, of this I am certain. You have within yourself, *Halcón,* the gifts of a true shaman."

With Yankee in the lead, they reached the summit where the camp was sited. Pastanari himself emerged from his wickiup at the very head of the clearing and uttered a cry of joy to see the three men riding toward him. John Cooper dismounted and helped the wounded brave down, while Dejari hastened to Pastanari and explained what had happened. Then he produced the pouch that contained the gory trophies of the ears and claws of the black bear.

Pastanari took the pouch and murmured, "Once again, we of the Jicarilla see how you have strengthened the bond between us, *Halcón.* The son of my mother's brother is my good friend and advises me at the council. I thank you for his life."

"I was lucky to be there to help him, Pastanari. And now, I have come to the stronghold to learn of the old man and the mountain of silver of which he told you. Does he still live?"

"Yes. I will take you to him." Pastanari turned to two younger braves who had hurried up to greet Dejari and John Cooper and bade them take the two palominos and the mustang and place them in the corral at the edge of the village. Meanwhile, Masikaya had begun to hobble back to his own wickiup to greet his wife and children; Dejari, after Pastanari had touched him on the shoulder and thanked him for having brought back *el Halcón* so speedily, went to his own dwelling place.

Pastanari and John Cooper walked to the end of the village and approached the isolated, unadorned tipi of Potiwaba. His young great-granddaughter emerged and at once crossed her wrists over her bosom and bowed her head in acknowledgment of the *jefe*. "How is he, girl?" Pastanari asked.

Imishba nodded, then volunteered in a low voice, "Each day I thought would be his last, *mi jefe*, but each morning, when I wakened, he was there to tell me that he could not die until he had seen the *wasichu* to whom he must speak. Go in. I know he awaits you. Even this morning, as I brought him a little broth, he said that the *wasichu* was not far from the stronghold and that it perhaps would be today that he would come."

She drew aside the flap of the tipi, and Pastanari and John Cooper entered, with the wolf-dog ordered to wait outside with the girl.

The emaciated old man lay on his pallet, but now, hearing them, he tried to raise himself on his elbows. Then he sank back, gasping for breath with the effort.

"Do not try to rise, *viejo*," John Cooper soothingly murmured. "I am the one you sent for, and I am called *el Halcón*."

"I saw in my dream last night that you came to my tipi, and that we spoke. I have heard much of you, *wasichu*. You who are blood brother to the Jicarilla, a man whom all trust because he is a friend and an ally to *los indios*. And that is why, knowing of you and recently having had this vision from the Great Spirit, I have decided after all these years to tell my secret. For I know how the yellow and silver metals turn the heart and the mind of a man and make him ready to kill his friend, even his brother, for it. But you are not a man like that, and I know, too, what you have done with the silver you took from that other mountain not far from our stronghold. *Los indios del pueblo* speak your name with honor, and you are known for what you have done."

John Cooper seated himself in cross-legged fashion, and Pastanari emulated him. "You say that there is another mountain in which there is a treasure of silver, Potiwaba?"

The frail old man nodded. "It is so. Should I not know it well, having worked there for three years when I was a boy? The Spaniards came to our village, and they chose the strong ones; I was then strong, and they led me bound like a wild animal to a horse, and two *soldados* flanked me as I was taken to that mountain, there to be an *esclavo*." He paused now to gain breath and strength and then feebly raised his voice. "Imishba, come to me, help me sit up. I must show the *wasichu* and my *jefe* that I do not lie."

The girl swiftly entered, came to her great-grandfather, and gently helped him sit up on the pallet, crouching beside him and supporting his back and shoulders with her slim arms.

"Take off my jacket, Imishba," the old man ordered.

She obeyed, and then Potiwaba said, "Look at my back. The marks of the whips of the Spaniards and their *padres* bit deeply into my flesh, and the scars have been all the days of my life written upon me."

It was true. John Cooper winced at the sight of that emaciated, dull, coppery-toned flesh angrily gouged by crisscrossing welts, some so deep they assuredly had drawn blood when they had been inflicted.

"You speak the truth, Potiwaba," Pastanari murmured, himself greatly moved.

Potiwaba continued earnestly, "I escaped; that is why I am here to tell you this story. It was a stormy night, and the soldiers had not bound my wrists and legs too tightly. I managed to work free of my bonds, and I crawled to the mouth of the cave. There I saw that the storm had driven away the *soldados*. I crawled out of it, and I hurried along the slope until I came to another cave; there I waited until the storm abated. When I looked out again, two of the *soldados* had come back. They had the long guns that speak with fire and thunder to guard the poor slaves inside. They did not see me, and so it was that I made my way down the mountain and then to the south. I came upon a village of my fellow Apache, and for a time I lived with them, until I came to you in your mountain stronghold. I became your shaman, and you know the rest."

Almost exhausted, Potiwaba now gestured to his great-granddaughter that he wished to lie back on the pallet, and for a long moment he lay there with his eyes closed.

John Cooper exchanged a wondering look with Pastanari and was about to speak when the old man, in a feeble voice, resumed. "It is time for me to leave for the great land in the sky and to visit all of my friends. I have had another vision from the Great Spirit that the silver you once found was taken from the place where you had it safely kept, far to the south and east of here. I know also, for the Great Spirit has told me, that it will be returned to you."

"Incredible!" John Cooper murmured, and crossed himself in awe.

"The cave that I now speak of is a second cave of silver that monks mined with the help of their *esclavos indios*. And I know where the hiding place is. Now that I am about to die, I do not wish the secret to be lost. I am a Jicarilla, though I have been banished, and perhaps by this telling of the secret that will benefit my people, I may be pardoned so that my spirit will go into the sky and be received by the Great Spirit in a kindly way. For I wish the Jicarilla to benefit from this treasure, as well as you, *Halcón*. I know that you will build a mighty ranch and help the emerging *wasichus* of the north, the *americanos*. Your future lies with them, *Halcón*, not with any of the Mexicans."

For a moment again he was silent, and Imishba looked worriedly at him, then appealingly up at John Cooper, who was lost in reverie by what he had heard. A hush had come upon the tipi, and only the strained breathing of the old man could be heard. Then there seemed a flicker of animation within him, and he again spoke. "I have seen many visions as I have lain here alone with only Imishba to tend me. I see a great war coming, and in it the Mexicans will try to take away the territory from you. You and your people must be prepared for this. Beware, too, of the Mexican general who wants your silver."

"Santa Anna!" John Cooper inadvertently blurted out. Then, glancing again at Pastanari, he shook his head in awed admiration.

"Watch out for yourself and for your people, and watch over my people, too, *Halcón*. If ever you and your people on your *hacienda* should be in need of help, I know that the war chief of the Jicarilla will join you in driving your enemies off. I see many great things happening in the future for your ranch and your family. Yes—but there will be many misfortunes along the way, and you must be prepared, you and your children and your friends, to overcome them."

Pastanari murmured to John Cooper, "He is near his death, I know this. And that is why he speaks with a tongue of prophesy. So it was with my father, whose name I cannot speak."

Imishba's eyes were wet with tears as she again glanced at Pastanari and John Cooper. She bent over her great-grandfather, touched his cheek with her soft hand, and mur-

mured a few inaudible words, which professed her concern
and her love for him.

Once again he spoke. "Listen well, for my time is upon
me, *Halcón*," Potiwaba murmured in a feeble voice. "It is a
mountain by itself, and it is near Raton. At the base of it, you
will see three great oak trees, into which the Spaniards
burned the sign of the cross. And then, on a higher level,
along a winding trail, there is a great rock shaped like a
buffalo, yes, even to the head of it and the horns."

"I hear you, and I mark it well, Potiwaba," John Cooper
said in Apache.

"Good! Remember these signs. After all these years, the
trees may not be there, but the rock surely will be. Not even
the *soldados* could budge it, for at first they wished to block
one of the large caves with it, but they failed. Now, after you
have found this rock, you ascend by a narrow trail that goes
steeply up to very nearly the top of the mountain. And there
is a huge cave, on a ledge high above a clearing. In that cave,
you should find the silver; I do not think it will have been
taken by anyone else. Use it well, *Halcón*. And if the Great
Spirit pardons me and receives me into the heavens, then I
will know it is because I have kept the secret for one like
you."

Now, with a sudden final flare of animation, he sought to
sit up, while Imishba cried out in distress, "No, no, please,
mi bisabuelo!"

He seemed to stiffen, then his eyes glazed even as they
stared into nothingness. And in that moment, he died.

Imishba began to sob softly, and Pastanari watched her
for a moment, then said aloud, "I as *jefe* revoke the law that
banished Potiwaba. We shall bury him in the Apache way, for
what he has said now has the voice of great truth, from the
Great Spirit Himself, and thus it is that he has redeemed
himself, and the punishment is lifted." Imishba continued to
sob softly, bending over her great-grandfather, touching his
wrinkled face and his lips.

"We shall leave her to her grief, *Halcón*," Pastanari
murmured. "I will have our shaman prepare the burial ceremony at dawn tomorrow."

John Cooper spoke almost as if to himself alone. "To
have lived with that secret so long! And to have chosen me
alone to make use of it—I do not know if I am worthy."

"You are worthy, *Halcón*," Pastanari stoutly declared.

"Do not forget that you saved my life when I was only a boy of ten summers, when I stole my father's horse and rode down the mountain. I would have been killed if you had not halted the horse and brought me back safely to my father. I will tell you now that he told me a few days later that the Great Spirit had led you to our stronghold and ordained that you be of great aid to the Apache. And that was true. You have been a loyal friend, a blood brother of great honor. Yes, *Halcón*, Potiwaba did well to keep the secret for one like you. And when the burial has taken place, you and I and six of my strongest braves will ride to find the new treasure."

Nine

On the morning of the next day, Chief Pastanari and the gray-haired Marsimaya, shaman of the Jicarilla Apache, emerged from their wickiups and moved to the center of the clearing within which ceremonial dances and rituals were held in the mountain stronghold. Two elders of the tribe, frail and white-haired, sat upon the ground, their legs crossed, and beat upon gourd drums with the flats of their hands to summon the villagers.

John Cooper came to stand behind Pastanari and the shaman, arms folded across his chest, as Marsimaya now intoned a blessing to the Great Spirit: "O Giver of Breath, here before Thee and under Thine own sky, we make petition for the spirit of Potiwaba. Until this moment, he has been like one cast out, and yet condemned to live among us without speech from any villager, dishonored and reckoned as among the dead—but as one whose spirit has not been summoned unto Thee. Now, for what he has done to redeem himself and to aid the people who pray unto Thee, we call out his name for the last time, and we restore to him the rights of a warrior and a shaman of the Jicarilla. Hear these drums which announce it, O Giver of Breath!"

Once again, the two old men beat upon the drums until

the very mountain seemed to reverberate with the echo. All the villagers, even the children and the old women, had clustered into the clearing and stood gravely silent.

"And also, we petition unto Thee to hearken unto the prayers of Imishba, who equally from this moment forth is no longer outcast and is the only living relative of him whose spirit we commend into the sky with his ancestors. It was she who helped prepare him for the burial. And when the funeral is done, the purification rites for a maiden will take place, honoring Thy eternal laws, O Giver of Breath!"

Pastanari's mother, Nadikotay, had, at Marsimaya's order, gone to the forlorn tipi in which the old man and his great-granddaughter had eked out their isolated days in the stronghold. She had brought with her the white buckskin jacket, skirt, and moccasins that a maiden just emerging from puberty would wear in the ceremony of purification. She made Imishba dress herself and then briefly instructed the girl in what she was to do in the preparation of old Potiwaba's body for burial. And the girl's thin, hollow-eyed face brightened now, when she understood that the terrible shadow that had blighted the old man's life and condemned her into the same merciless darkness had at last been lifted.

Pastanari made a sign to one of the young boys, who quickly ran toward a small corral to the far left of the clearing and brought out a brown mustang. It was saddled, and the cabalistic markings of the Jicarilla tribe appeared in colored beads on the buckskin cinches. Two mature braves now lifted the body of old Potiwaba and placed it astride the horse, binding it into place with rawhide thongs. Then Marsimaya took the reins and began a slow processional down from the stronghold toward a lower ledge of the mountain, as the villagers followed.

He came at last to a large level area from which jutted a small hill, and at his sign, several of the braves began to dig a hole in the hill. As the villagers made way for her, Imishba, in her white buckskins, carried Potiwaba's pitifully few possessions: a blanket, a small totem that he had had when he had once been shaman of the Jicarilla, and his hunting knife, its bone handle dyed in the tribal colors. When the excavation was deep and tall enough, Marsimaya turned to intone an incantation to the Great Spirit, and the braves led the horse into the opening, the white-haired frail corpse seated stiffly in the saddle, his head bowed as if in prayer.

Then Marsimaya took the blanket and the totem from the hands of Imishba, murmured an incantation over them, and carried them into the cave. Next, he took the knife from the girl's hand and swiftly and expertly killed the mustang. Then the braves and the young boys began to shovel back the dirt to cover up the cave. Thus old Potiwaba would have a horse to ride when he was summoned forth by the Great Spirit, He Who is Giver of Breath to all mankind.

It was a solemn and moving ceremony, and John Cooper watched with an awed reverence, for the primitive meaning of it was as true as any religion he had ever known. Man who came from earth was given back to it, that man might again be reborn—was this not in a sense the same teaching his own father and mother had given him all those years ago in Shawneetown? He was also reassured by the knowledge that this slight young girl, who had spent years with her great-grandfather in as brutal an isolation as the latter himself had known, was now to be redeemed and to be proclaimed marriageable.

Now Marsimaya whispered to Imishba. At once she straightened, and her head held high and her eyes filled with tears, she walked slowly back toward the clearing and the village of the stronghold, leading all the others who had come to honor the old man who had lived so many years as a pariah. And she murmured her own prayer of thanksgiving to the Great Spirit for the bounty of restoration to life.

Shortly after the funeral, Pastanari, who had invited John Cooper into his wickiup for the noontime meal, declared, "*Halcón*, the journey to the mountain will take at least two days and two nights. I shall go to make the preparations."

John Cooper rose and stretched, his eyes alert and eager for this new adventure. "I shall be ready when you are, *mi jefe.*"

An hour later, the preparations were made. Six braves had been chosen to accompany them, and in the saddlebags of the horses were strong thongs made of cured rawhide that could be used to bind around the silver bars and lower them, should the mine of which Potiwaba spoke actually contain the treasure after all these years.

Pastanari mounted his strong roan stallion, while John Cooper sat astride the palomino that had carried him so obediently on the long journey from the Double H Ranch to the stronghold. Of the six braves whom Pastanari had chosen,

Dejari was youngest; and when John Cooper smilingly nodded to the young brave, he drew the palomino John Cooper
had given him up alongside the tall Texan's horse and
murmured, "I asked our *jefe* to choose me because I wished
to prove myself again. And also, as only you and I know,
Halcón, to make up for the mistake that very nearly made
me fail in my vow to our *jefe*."

"I think you have done more than that, Dejari. I am
happy to have you with us."

"As you can see, I have chosen to ride this fine palomino
you gave me," Dejari exclaimed proudly. "Indeed, I even
think he is superior in swiftness and courage to the mustang I
tamed."

And so they rode out of the stronghold down the winding trail of the mountain and northward toward the mountain
that old Potiwaba had described.

By nightfall of the second day, John Cooper, Pastanari,
and the six accompanying Jicarilla braves reached the base of
the mountain. Time had not changed its physical appearance
from the old man's description, and the landmarks that he
had detailed to John Cooper were identifiable beyond the
least doubt: the three great oak trees and, above them, a
great rock shaped like a buffalo. There was snow on the peak
of the mountain, and a northwest wind howled about it, with
swirling gusts of snow.

"We must try it in the morning because the wind now
would make it dangerous to climb," John Cooper told the
young Jicarilla chief.

"Let us make camp here at the side of the mountain,
where the wind will not reach us," Pastanari decided.

They had brought with them sheets of thick bark, drawn
in a travois by one of the horses. Once they had determined
on their campsite for the night, the braves set to work forming tipis, lifting the bark up and holding it while other braves
set up at a triangular angle two sharpened sticks bound
together by thongs. The bark was pushed onto the unyielding
wood to take its shape and was stuck to the wood by means of
a thick glue made from the juices of herbs and the *cacto*.
These shelters were then placed along the side of the mountain away from the wind and would form temporary sleeping
quarters until the dawn, by which time it was hoped the
sudden wintry storm would pass.

John Cooper shared one of the hastily constructed tipis

with the Jicarilla chief, who produced a calumet and tobacco, struck tinder, and made a fire to light the pipe that he passed to his blood brother. They smoked for a time in silence, listening to the swirling wind beyond them. Then they retired for the night.

Yankee had slept outside the tipi that John Cooper and Pastanari shared, and he was first to waken, uttering a low growl and nuzzling at the door flap to waken his beloved master. The latter and Pastanari, as well as the six braves who had accompanied them, came out of their tipis and made a swift breakfast of dried corn and jerky, washed down with water from their canteens, and then discussed what they might find when they ascended the rugged mountain.

"If there is as much silver as was found long ago in that hidden cave in *La Montaña de las Pumas*," John Cooper declared, "I shall ride into Taos to give Padre Madura a share for the church, for the poor of the village, and especially for the *indios* of the pueblo. For the time being, it might be well to keep the rest of the silver in the mountain, to be used eventually for your people and my ranch, as well as deserving settlers, such as are in the Austin settlement and on my own *estancia*."

"I agree, *Halcón*," Pastanari said. "And I can arrange to have six well-armed braves guard this place. Now that we have discovered it, others might see signs of our presence and also come this way. I do not wish to take that chance. I will post the braves, and I will exchange them every fourteen suns, so that the task does not become too wearying for the young men."

"Good! If there is a silver treasure here, Pastanari, it will one day buy the guns and ammunition against that day, which I feel is not too far off, when we *americanos*—and that means you and your people, as well, Pastanari!—must do battle against the Mexicans. And with some of the treasure that I shall take with me today, I shall buy arms and ammunition for my own ranch, as well as for your stronghold."

"It is well to be prepared for evildoing," Pastanari admitted, "though you know that the Jicarilla have been at peace since the treaty with the Mescalero was signed."

"Do you think that the Ute would come near this mountain, Pastanari?" John Cooper asked.

The *jefe* of the Jicarilla shook his head. "They have gone farther to the north into what is called Colorado, beyond the

Sierra Blanca Mountains, for the hunting is good there, and there are still many buffalo. And also, since they had reason to hate Spaniards, they retreated farther to the north to be away from the *soldados* and from the *padres* who came ahead of the *soldados* to preach peace, when what they really wished was the yellow and the silver metals that the *wasichu* covets even more than some braves covet a comely squaw. No, there will be no trouble with the Ute. We have been at peace with them for long years, *Halcón*. Should any hunting party come near this mountain, we shall place a totem showing that the Jicarilla have marked it as their sanctuary, and the Ute will respect that totem. If not, they will face our guards."

"Excellent! Then let us begin our work. I shall need the long strips of rawhide thongs that have been made into ropes." He looked upward at the towering mountain and frowned, making mental calculations. "The ropes must be very long, for I think it will be at least fifty or sixty feet from the ledge of the cave that the old man described to the lower summit where a horse might be brought."

"Let us first have one of my men take a horse up to that point, *Halcón*. Then you and I will follow."

"And Yankee, too." John Cooper chuckled as the wolf-dog rubbed up against him and uttered a low whine. Yankee wagged his tail, impatient to be ordered to hunt or at least to accompany his master.

The horses, which had been hobbled during the night with soft doeskin thongs, had remained sheltered out of the wind by the southeast side of the mountain. Dejari volunteered to follow the trail to see how far his horse would take him, and he declared that he would call down and signal to his *jefe* and John Cooper when he had reached the lower summit. Mounting his palomino, he rode to the north about a hundred yards and called that he found a narrow pathway but that it was wide enough for the horse and himself and that he would attempt it.

Yankee stood barking after him, turning repeatedly to gaze at John Cooper, awaiting his signal to accompany the Jicarilla brave. But John Cooper merely chuckled and smiled, rubbed his knuckles over the wolf-dog's head, and then murmured, "No, Yankee, not yet. Wait a bit."

Pastanari stood, his hands to his temples, straining his eyes to watch the palomino climb, losing it in the trees and the shrubbery. There was a light coating of snow on the lower slope of this mountain that thickened as it rose, for here the winters were longer and far colder than in Taos or the Frio River Valley of the Double H Ranch. It would be treacherous footing for a horse, and there would be dangers for the brave who rode it, skillful horseman though he was.

Nearly half an hour later, Dejari hailed them, standing on the edge of a wide ledge, waving his hand and then cupping his hands to his mouth to magnify his shout. "I see the smaller ledge above; no horse can reach it. One must climb by hand and foot, *mi jefe!*"

"You and I will make the climb," Pastanari said to John Cooper. "We shall follow the trail that Dejari has found for us. Then we shall climb to the ledge and see if the silver is still there."

Leaving the other braves at the site of the camp to await further instructions, John Cooper and Pastanari mounted their horses and rode off to follow the narrow trail. They had in their saddlebags several lengths of the sturdy rawhide thongs, made into ropes fifty feet long and now neatly coiled to minimize their size.

Yankee, barking joyously, followed behind the heels of the horses, taking care not to come too close lest they grow skittish. His eyes sparkled with the joy of adventure, anticipating the game that his master would order him to kill and fetch.

They reached Dejari at last, and his palomino tossed its head and whinnied, recognizing John Cooper's own mount. Pastanari, dismounting, stood beside the young brave and stared upward, then frowned. "It is a more difficult climb than I had anticipated." Turning back to Dejari, he demanded, "You have looked around the side of the mountain? Does this upper ledge circle it?"

"*Sí, mi jefe,* but nowhere is there any easier way to reach the ledge above us," was the answer.

"Then there is no help for it; we must climb here." Pastanari shrugged and eyed John Cooper, who nodded agreement.

"I'll carry the rope around my middle, and you do likewise with yours, Pastanari," the Texan told the *jefe*. Then he said to Dejari, "If we find the treasure, we will tie these ropes around several ingots and lower them down to you."

"Shall I have the other braves bring up extra saddlebags or the travois?" Dejari inquired.

"No," Pastanari answered. "We have both decided that if there is truly much treasure here, we shall leave it under guard. What we can get down by these ropes, we shall put into the saddlebags of *el Halcón*, who will take a portion to the good *padre* in Taos, so that he may help our brothers, *los indios del pueblo*."

John Cooper nodded to Pastanari and then moved to the face of the cliff. There were outcroppings of rock here and there, and as he worked himself slowly and cautiously upward, he very carefully tested the rocks with his moccasined toes to make certain that they would hold his weight. Pastanari watched him and then imitated his method, starting at the base of the steep cliff and gripping the projecting jagged edges of rock and boulder with his hands, as he carefully lifted first one leg and then the other, slowly ascending.

Yankee, left behind with Dejari, barked furiously and then growled in his anger at not being able to accompany his master. Several times he loped first to his left and then to his right, as if seeking some narrow pathway that would help him reach the summit to greet his master and the young Jicarilla chief, but at last he realized that there was no other access save this climb, which he could not make. Baffled, angry, he let out a fierce growl, his hair bristling, and then sat down on his haunches and watched with unblinking yellow eyes the figure of his master moving inch by inch up the cliff toward the jutting ledge.

It was cold here, but at least the wind was not an enemy this morning, as it would have been the night before. John Cooper paused several times to get his breath and to summon his stamina, while Pastanari moved below him some ten feet, not looking down but looking up at the buckskin-clad figure of his blood brother. John Cooper had come halfway up the cliff, and now he moved slightly to his right, seeing a patch of rock untouched by snow or ice. Once again, he reached with one hand toward a jutting, jagged fragment of boulder, and it held securely as he tugged at it with all his might. Fortified thus, he continued to ascend now with more confidence. His muscles ached, but the challenge exhilarated him. All the same, he could not help wondering how the Spaniards had managed to get the slaves up to the mine and to bring down the mined treasure after it had been melted and formed into ingots. For indeed, this access was far more difficult than he had experienced at *La Montaña de las Pumas*, where he had found the first silver mine.

Now he had very nearly reached the ledge, and he drew himself up, glancing down at Pastanari to encourage the young *jefe* to follow him. As he clambered onto the ledge and lay on his belly, he swiftly removed the coil of rope from around his waist and uncoiled part of it. It was an intuitive gesture, and it chanced to save Pastanari's life, for in that same moment, with a terrified cry, the Jicarilla chief lost his footing and clung frantically with both hands to two narrow, jagged pieces of rock that jutted out from the cliff.

"Catch hold of the rope—I'll pull you up, Pastanari!" John Cooper called as he shifted on his belly and angled the rope down toward Pastanari. With a supreme effort, retaining his balance with his left hand, Pastanari reached up for the rope and seized it just as his left hand slipped off the snowy piece of rock. For a terrifying moment, he dangled from the rope with just one hand, shuddering and kicking, until he got hold with his other hand. Then John Cooper pulled on the rope with all his strength and began slowly to draw Pastanari up toward the ledge.

At last, Pastanari rolled onto the ledge beside him, breathing hard and his face flushed with exertion. His eyes sought John Cooper's tautened face, and wanly he held out a hand to touch the tall Texan's shoulder.

"Truly are we blood brothers. Once again I owe you my life, *Halcón*," Pastanari said.

"Let us rest and get our breath before we look for the cave, Pastanari," John Cooper said in a casual tone, not only to move swiftly away from any talk of indebtedness but also because inwardly he had been shaken by the near death of the young Jicarilla chief. He closed his eyes for a moment and drew in deep breaths of the pure mountain air.

Below, he could hear the renewed barking of Yankee, furiously thwarted in his desire to be reunited with his master, deprived of this new adventure. The Texan could smile now, however, for the tension had eased.

Now John Cooper rose and cautiously moved along the narrow ledge toward the east. He found that it was almost a complete circle, but at the northeast point, on the other side, there was a pile of huge stones. With pickaxes or some other such implements, the ledge had been covered over with rubble to prevent anyone from reaching it from the lower summit, where Dejari and the horses were. Had it been the Spaniards themselves who had done this, in order to close off the access they must have used when they first came here? Or perhaps it had been hostile Indians, who had killed off the Spanish invaders and then hoped to prevent anyone else from getting to the mine.

Most mystifying of all, unlike *La Montaña de las Pumas*, there was not a sign of any skeleton in armor or the rotted cloth of an attendant priest to tell the story of what had happened to end the usefulness of this ancient mine.

He came back to tell Pastanari what he had discovered, and the chief shook his head and mused aloud, "Perhaps a tribe of Ute came up this mountain and found the *soldados* at their work, then threw them from the top of the mountain to their deaths."

"Yes, perhaps indeed, but then we should have found their bones on the lower summit," John Cooper responded, frowning with perplexity. "Perhaps the interior of the cave we seek will tell us what happened."

"Yes, and I think I discovered what we are looking for. Over there, to my left, there is a huge slab of stone that may seal the mouth of the cave, though the old man did not speak of this stone before he died," Pastanari wonderingly exclaimed.

John Cooper followed the young chief along the ledge to the left, and the two men stood before a heavy stone slab. There were markings on it, as if cut with some kind of crude chisel, and Pastanari brushed away the faint glaze of snow with his hand and then uttered a cry of amazement. "It is in the Ute sign language, *Halcón*. Yes! This is indeed the treasure cave of which the old man spoke—come, look at these signs!"

John Cooper stared wonderingly at the face of the heavy stone slab that sealed the mouth of the cave on the narrow ledge. The markings had been cut with extraordinary depth, and thus they were still clear after all these years. Pastanari turned to him. "You will remember the wampum belt given to you by the Ayuhwa," he said, "how you were told that it would be understood by other tribes, even those who spoke different tongues, because the signs were known to all?"

"Yes, I remember it well. It said that I was a hunter and a friend."

"Just so," Pastanari nodded excitedly. "I do not speak

the Ute tongue, but these signs I can read, for many of them
are like our own that we put upon the totems and dye on the
bark of our wickiups. See here—" He pointed with his right
index finger to one of the hieroglyphics. "This is the sign for
the Spanish oppressor, the peaked metal helmet that the
soldados wore. And this"—his finger traced another sign—
"this shows the war party of the Ute. Wait—it tells the tale,
and now I see why we found no skeletons. The Ute came
upon the *soldados* and the *padres*, killed them, and took
their bodies away and buried them without a sign, that their
spirits might never reach the sky. And because the *esclavos*
were of my people, the Jicarilla, with whom the Ute were
then at war, they dispatched these also and carried away their
bodies and buried them as ignobly. Then, so that no one
might regain the treasure of the mine that the Ute had no
need or wish for, they sealed the cave with this slab, then
they pried away the rocks on the other side of the ledge to
block the easier passage—this is why we had to climb by
hand and foot, *Halcón*."

"Then the old man who told us this story must have
escaped just before the attack on the mine," John Cooper
declared.

"That is how I read the signs and relate them to what I
heard him say to us, *Halcón*," Pastanari agreed.

"Well, now that we have found the cave, we must try to
remove that heavy stone slab," John Cooper said. "Do you
think the two of us can budge it, Pastanari?"

"We shall try, *Halcón*." The Jicarilla chief took a deep
breath, flexed his muscles, and, standing to the right of the
heavy stone slab, placed both hands on its edge and pushed
with all his might. "It is very heavy, and I cannot move it by
myself. I hope the two of us can move it, otherwise we must
ask some of the braves to climb this dangerous little cliff and
help us."

"Probably it's stuck because of all the years it's been
here," John Cooper averred. "Well, let's see what the two of
us can do, Pastanari." He crouched a little below the young
chief, placed his hands on the stone, and shoved with all his
might, while Pastanari emulated him. "That time I felt it give
just a little," John Cooper said, panting. "Let's save our
energy and try from time to time."

They waited a few moments, each drawing in gulps of
the cool mountain air. Then again they put their shoulders to

the slab and, leaning forward with both hands pressed hard against the edge, gave a vigorous shove. "It moved, yes, this time I felt it move!" Pastanari exclaimed.

The seal between earth and stone had been broken, and now it was easier. Once again, after taking several deep breaths, Pastanari and John Cooper exerted all their strength in the attempt to move the stone, until at last there was an opening large enough for a man to get through.

"We shall need to make torches, *mi hermano*," John Cooper advised. "I'll break off some of the branches of this scrub tree growing above the top of the cave, and we can use my tinderbox to light them so that we can see inside."

After John Cooper broke off some of the dead branches, they moved just inside the mouth of the cave. The Texan squatted, took his tinderbox out of his buckskin jacket, and struck the flint against the thatch of moss he always carried inside the box. He blew on the moss until the tiny flicks of fire began to spread, then he held out one of the branches until its end kindled and began to burn. From this, he lit another torch for Pastanari, then he extinguished the thatch, put the box back into his pocket, and moved forward into the cave.

At once he saw a huge table, and it reminded him of the other cave that he had found fourteen years earlier. As with that other cave, there were benches around the table, and undoubtedly here the Indians had worked under the surveillance of the monks and the soldiers. Unlike the first cave, the mummified bodies of the Indian slaves were not there to cast their terrifying aura and recall to him the cruelty with which the Spaniards had treated their Indian captives, left them there to die of thirst and starvation. But on this table, just as in that other cave so long ago, he saw bars of pure silver, ingots nearly two feet long, three inches thick, and as many inches wide.

He turned to Pastanari. "The old man's story is true. And what you read upon the stone slab explains why we have found no *esclavos indios*."

"Yes, and I am glad that I lifted the ban against him that his spirit might be summoned to the Giver of Breath," the young chief answered.

"Padre Madura will be able to take this silver to his friend, who will make costly trinkets of it to be sold in the shops of Taos and Santa Fe and at the fairs in Santa Fe and

Chihuahua. And the money that is earned will aid the Indians of the pueblo. Meanwhile, I will take some of the ingots with me to Texas and then on to New Orleans, where I can buy supplies and weapons for my ranch, as well as for your own people, Pastanari. But first let's see what else is in the cave. We must look about for better torches, for these branches will not burn too much longer, and they cast very little light."

"Look there, *Halcón!*" Pastanari suddenly exclaimed, pointing to the floor at his left. "A silver candlestick and a tallow candle. That will give much better light. Undoubtedly some of the slaves were taught to make the silver into useful objects. The Jicarilla have always been craftsmen, yes, even in those early days. Let us light the candle; it will give good light!"

John Cooper hurried over to his blood brother, picked up the silver candlestick, and set it on the table. Then, using his torch, he soon kindled the wick. "The tallow must have been made from buffalo fat," he commented. "I remember how candles like these were made in the village of the Ayuhwa. There, it's a very good light. Now we can see everything."

Lifting the candlestick, he moved to the end of the large room and through a lower, narrow archway in the wall. There he observed, to his left, the opening of the mine shaft. And to his right, there was the shadowy outline of another opening, which he surmised to be a storage room, not unlike that which he had found in the cave in *La Montaña de las Pumas.* Pastanari followed close behind him, and when they entered this room, the young *jefe* gasped at the sight. Here there were stacks of silver ingots placed against one side of the wall, and to the right, on two crude tables, religious artifacts, crosses, rosaries, and, just as in that first cave, a massive cross with the figure of the Christ crucified upon it, worked into a huge stand made itself of the same pure silver. Indeed, Pastanari had been right: There had been many craftsmen among the Jicarilla, and their reward had been the lash, meager food and drink, and, finally, death at the hands of their age-old enemies, the Ute. Yet that, he reflected, must indeed have seemed a boon after their enforced servitude by the Spaniards.

There were chains as well, and medallions and brooches, all made of the same refined metal, and there was also a silver box on the very edge of one of these tables. When he opened it, John Cooper was startled to see a superb silver necklace into which large turquoises had been expertly set.

"I shall keep this as a present to my Dorotéa, to thank her for the child she will give me," he murmured as he started to lift the necklace out of the silver box; then, thinking better of it, he closed the box and slipped it into his jacket pocket. "One of the rosaries I shall give to Doña Inez, and one to Carlos for his Teresa. The crucifix on the chain I shall give to our own Padre Pastronaz at the ranch. Let us see if we can find some sort of leather pouch or bag in which we can let down these objects, rather than trying to rope them and lower them."

Then suddenly, as he glanced over to his right, John Cooper added, "Wait, there seems to be another room beyond this one. Do you not observe that narrower opening in the wall?"

"I see it. Can it be still another room with treasure?" Pastanari marveled.

Pastanari took the candlestick and moved through the archway, which was just wide enough to allow him to slip inside. Then he uttered a cry. "There is a body here, the body of a Jicarilla. And it is not a skeleton, but preserved by the sealed cave and the lack of air."

John Cooper moved to the archway, edged inside, and shuddered at the sight of the long-dead Indian slave. Pastanari, sensing what his blood brother felt, urged, "Come, my brother, Dejari will wonder what has happened to us. We shall lower the silver bars we found in the workroom to him, and then I will help you look for something in which to put the crosses and the other objects."

They returned to the main cave, and John Cooper inhaled deeply. Quickly, he and Pastanari brought seven of the ingots outside on the ledge and tied the ends of their ropes around the silver, Pastanari binding three and John Cooper four. Then, lying on their bellies and moving toward the very rim of the ledge, they slowly lowered the long ropes while Pastanari called out, "Dejari, can you reach what we are lowering to you?"

The young brave called back, "I see it, *mi jefe;* yes, I can reach it. There now, I will untie the rope so that you can pull it back up. And this one, also."

"Good! Wait—do we not have a large pouch in one of

the saddlebags in which we brought tobacco from the stronghold?" Pastanari called.

"Sí, mi jefe. It is in one of my saddlebags."

"¡Bueno! Put the tobacco into something else, then attach the rope to the pouch so that it will hold and I will draw it back up," Pastanari called down.

A short time later, this was done, and Pastanari lifted the pouch onto the ledge. "I'll fill it with some of the relics, Pastanari," John Cooper declared, "and then we'd best see to getting back down. We're going to have to go down the way we came up, I'm afraid. One good thing about it, it won't be easy for anyone to climb up here and get the treasure."

"Still, I will have my men guard this mountain," Pastanari promised. "We must take no chances of discovery."

But the presence of that one mummified body troubled John Cooper, and he said to Pastanari, "I wish that we might bury the body of that unfortunate indio, for he is too grim a guardian of this cave, now that your braves are here."

"You are right, Halcón. But I will not call the shaman Marsimaya to this desolate place. As jefe of the Jicarilla, just as I revoked the ban on the old man, so I am empowered to perform the burial rites on this ancient tribesman. I saw a pickax near the mine shaft, and I will bury the body outside on the ledge and consecrate it by a prayer to the Great Spirit. Thus, the poor man will be brought out from darkness into light, and when the sun of the Giver of Breath shines down upon his grave, his spirit will ascend."

And so, after tying the pouch securely at the end of the improvised rope, John Cooper lowered it down to Dejari, who called up that he had received it safely and would store it in the saddlebags of John Cooper's horse. After that, Pastanari used the pickax he had found to break the ground of the ledge until he had hollowed out an adequate grave. Then he and the tall Texan went back into the cave to bring out the mummified body of the poor slave who had sought to escape the carnage wrought by the vengeful Ute. As they carried it into the open, the cool air did its work, and the body began to crumble in their grasp. John Cooper gasped and closed his eyes.

They covered the grave, and then Pastanari stood, his arms uplifted to the sky, and intoned a prayer to the Giver of Breath to receive the spirit of the unjustly slain warrior, a tribesman of the Jicarilla, who sought redemption and release from the obscure limbo of the cave of servitude. When it was done, he began to lower himself down the steep wall of the cliff, the way he had come, this time with the rope tied around his middle and John Cooper holding the other end. The wiry chief tenaciously clung to the rocks and sought with his moccasined feet the rocks below to aid his descent, until at last he reached the lower summit. John Cooper followed him without benefit of the rope, and he descended to the clearing without mishap. The two men stood facing each other, as Pastanari gravely put his right hand upon John Cooper's left shoulder and said, "We are closer than before, *Halcón*. My life is always yours, and it will make me a better chief to know this."

And John Cooper, his right hand clasping Pastanari's shoulder, replied, "For the rest of my days, I swear to you, *jefe* of the Jicarilla, that our lives shall be intertwined, that each shall share the other's dreams and hopes, and that each shall stand as ally against the enemies of the other."

Pastanari turned to Dejari. "When I reach the stronghold, I will send food and containers of water to you and your companions, Dejari. And, fourteen suns hence, other braves will come to take your place so that you may return to your families. We shall guard this mountain, and as we do, though we do not speak his name ever again, we shall remember the old man who redeemed the error of the past by his own self-sacrifice and the cherishing of a secret that will strengthen our people against our foes."

With this, he, John Cooper, and Dejari filled the saddlebags of their horses with the silver ingots, each of which weighed about twenty-five pounds and was wrapped in a piece of deerhide to prevent its jangling against another bar. They returned to the main camp where the rest of the Jicarilla waited, and there John Cooper transferred most of the bars into the saddlebags of one of the Jicarilla mounts, which he would now use as a packhorse for his return journey. John Cooper was careful to load up the ingots while the horse was standing on a rocky ledge, so that no stranger coming upon the scene would see the deeply embedded hoofprints and thus surmise that some kind of treasure had been loaded up. As for the ride into Taos and then back to the Double H Ranch, it would appear from the tracks of the packhorse that it was merely a horse and its rider.

Now John Cooper and Pastanari left the camp and rode

away, Yankee following happily. Two days and nights later, the young Jicarilla *jefe* and the Texan parted, as the former took the winding trail up the mountain to the stronghold while John Cooper headed his horses southward toward Taos and Padre Madura. They would communicate again once John Cooper had disposed of the silver and purchased many fine guns and knives for the people of his blood brother.

"My son, it warms my heart to see you again," Padre Madura said, extending both his hands and clasping John Cooper's in a warm grip of friendship. "It has been a very long time since we last visited."

They were in the rectory, and at Padre Madura's invitation, John Cooper breakfasted with the courageous priest. The latter's housekeeper, who had come from the pueblo village after his old housekeeper had died, smilingly served them the simple meal. John Cooper turned to her and said, "Tell me, Dalcaria, what is the news from your village? Does the *alcalde*, Cienguarda, show greater compassion to the *indios* of the pueblo?"

The handsome Indian woman nodded. "Yes, señor. Our good priest, Padre Madura, has put the fear of *el Señor Dios* into his heart. And then also, he knows how Carlos de Escobar became an avenging angel against the *hacendados* who committed evil deeds and used the *indios* as *esclavos*."

"Carlos did your village a great service," John Cooper admitted, remembering how his brother-in-law had visited Taos the year before and had threatened to go to the governor if the mayor did not put a stop to the intolerance and bigotry he displayed not only with the Indians of the pueblo but also with the Americans who came to trade at the fairs. "I am glad that the *alcalde* has learned his lesson. Thank you, Dalcaria. The food is very good."

"It is prepared with love, because it is for a man all of us respect and love," she murmured as she left the dining room of the rectory to return to the kitchen.

"Now, my son, I am eager to hear your news," the priest said to his guest.

John Cooper related to Padre Madura all that had happened in the past months: his voyage to Argentina to save the life of his young bride's father, their return to the United States and the discovery that the silver had been stolen from the New Orleans bank, and finally the death of Don Diego de

Escobar. "And there is more," John Cooper said. "I come to you today because what I have brought you is God's compensation for what was lost."

"Now you leave me in the dark, John Cooper," the gray-haired priest responded.

"I went to the stronghold of the Jicarilla because a courier had ridden to Texas to urge me to go with all speed," John Cooper continued. "I was told that there was an old man who was once shaman of the Jicarilla, who had a message of the greatest importance. The message was that he had, as a boy, labored as an *esclavo* in a secret mine in a mountain near Raton, where there was another treasure, which he had kept secret all these years."

"The ways of *el Señor Dios* are inscrutable. And did you find the silver?"

"Indeed I did, and I believe it to be richer than the original mine. Pastanari's braves will guard it until such time as all the treasure can be taken and put into a safe place where, I hope, it cannot again be stolen. I bring you today three silver bars to be given to Fra Peramonte. He can melt them down and fashion them into jewelry items to sell at the trading fairs. And there are many relics, crucifixes, rosaries— some of these I have brought you, also. Distribute what monies can be derived from the silver bars to your own poor and to the needy in the pueblo."

"This is wonderful news, indeed. Although Mayor Cienguarda has not raised the taxes, the villagers in the pueblo still have fallen upon bad times. There are now fewer *hacendados* here in Taos than there were when you first came to Nuevo México, *mi hijo*," the priest explained. "So there are not enough to contract with *los indios* to do work for them, and thus there is little money to help these poor people provide for their families. In my church, when there are donations that are extremely liberal—and it is not too often, these days—I see to it that a goodly portion is given to the pueblo, for they are most in need of all. This will be a welcome gift, and God will bless you for it, *mi hijo*."

"There will be much more of it, *mi padre*. And now I must ride back to my Dorotéa, for I promised her that I would be on hand for the birth of our child."

"I will pray that you reach your home safely, and that the child conceived between you and your new wife will be strong and healthy and as dedicated to the Christian ways as you have always been, my son." Padre Salvador Madura made the sign of the cross, and John Cooper bowed his head.

The priest rose from the table, as did John Cooper, and then he turned to the tall Texan and said with a smile, "I wish you could stay longer in Taos, *mi hijo*."

"This town brings back many memories," John Cooper said. "Most of them are very happy. Now come; we will go out to my horses and get the silver bars I promised, as well as the religious objects. God is truly looking after His people of this great land."

Ten

On the same March day that John Cooper left Taos to return to the Double H Ranch, three men sat in the lavishly furnished council chamber of the stately *cabildo*, or government building, in the City of Buenos Aires. One of them was Gregorio Pordoña, a man in his late forties, with a thick, drooping mustache, a corpulent body, and cruel and calculating eyes—the very portrait of avarice and cunning. His two companions were the men who had accompanied him on the same ship that John Cooper Baines had boarded for his first visit to Argentina and his meeting with Raoul Maldones. These men were Luis Toriano, a foppish, slim man not quite fifty; and Geraldo Viseyama, a pompous man in his early forties, with a trim black beard and enormous sideburns, who wore a ruffled silk shirt and a gaudy cravat, not unlike the Creole dandies of New Orleans.

Gregorio Pordoña, the Minister of the Interior, had taken up the cause of Porfirio Ramos, who had attacked John Cooper in ambush during the latter's second visit to Argentina, when he had come to rescue his father-in-law from prison. Ramos had ultimately been killed by the *bola* of Felipe Mintras, who had acted as leader of the *gauchos* loyal to Raoul Maldones, Ramos's intended victim.

"Señores," Pordoña began with an unctuous smile, "there

is great news from Uruguay. A courier has just come to my office, which is why I have summoned you for this meeting. He brings news of a great battle at Ituzaingo. Yes, señores, a combined Argentine and Uruguayan force under the direction of Carlos María de Alvear has decisively defeated our Brazilian enemies. You know that our beloved Argentina and those accursed Brazilians have both claimed Uruguay. I am certain that now there will be a peace. And in the treaty, I am sure we Argentinians shall annex Uruguay because of our victory in the war, and our power thus will be greatly increased. When that happens, the *hacendados* of the *pampas*, those detestable upstarts who defy our fine government, will be entirely under our control."

He paused to observe the effect of his words on his companions, then exclaimed, "The occasion calls for a toast with the best wine, señores!" With this, and a florid gesture of his plump right hand—on the third finger of which there appeared a gold ring with an enormous ruby—Gregorio Pordoña rose. Lifting a cut-glass decanter, he poured a vintage Bordeaux into the three silver goblets that were placed before him and his two companions, then lifted his own goblet. "¡Salud, amigos! To the damnation of all *hacendados*, and to the victory of our glorious *unitarios*. Buenos Aires will be, henceforth, the chief power of all Argentina. Those who attempt to dispute this fact will meet the fate that the traitor Raoul Maldones should have met before a firing squad."

"Which he avoided through the contrivance of that demon *gringo*, who escaped our *soldados*," Luis Toriano growled as he set his goblet down on the magnificently handwrought, beautifully scrolled council table.

"It really does not matter, señores," Pordoña continued as he seated himself and belched, then sipped more wine. "Maldones is gone from Argentina forever; he is no longer a problem to us. As to his land, I am told that the sons of Heitor Duvaldo, who maintains an *estancia* near Lobos, live there with the *gauchos* faithful to that fugitive traitor. What confronts us now is the obstinacy of Señor Duvaldo. He was, as all of us know, a very good friend of Maldones. And I am not so sure that he was innocent of the death of our beloved comrade, the *caudillo* Porfirio Ramos—peace to his memory, señores." Here he crossed himself, and all three men bowed their heads for a moment in respectful silence. "Now, as you know, I have assumed his role as leader of the *porteño*

movement because I was most in his confidence and I share
his views on the extermination of the *hacendados* who will
not subscribe to our unitarian rule. If progress, culture,
education, and wealth are to come to Buenos Aires, all this
must be brought about by a strong central government located here where our port is and where we engage in com-
merce with the rest of the world. These advantages cannot be
disseminated among the scurrilous dogs who are called
gauchos, and the traitors they see fit to follow on the
pampas!"

"I share your views, *mi jefe,*" Toriano glibly responded,
lifting his silver goblet to toast the fat *porteño* official.

"Now then, it is true that there was no proof that Heitor
Duvaldo had anything to do with the death of Porfirio Ramos,
but we do not have to stand by idly wondering about it, doing
nothing whatsoever. I propose that we send an emissary to
him at once to offer him a price for his property, which he
will be told will be used for the benefit of the fatherland.
Once he has quitted the land—and he would be wise to do
so—it will be an easy matter to take over the Maldones
property as well. Do you concur with me, *señores?*"

"¡Pero sí, Gregorio!" Toriano eagerly nodded, and Geraldo Viseyama lifted his goblet to toast Pordoña and to signify
his own assent in the matter.

On the *estancia* of Heitor Duvaldo, some three miles
northwest of Lobos, the *hacendado*'s teenage sons, Benito
and Enrique, were being welcomed by their father upon
their return from the Maldones ranch. The bearded, now
completely gray-haired Heitor had been a longtime friend to
Raoul Maldones, who was several years his junior. Heitor had
promised to have his sons watch over his friend's *estancia*
and to protect it with the help of his own loyal *trabajadores*
and *gauchos,* as well as those who had become attached to
John Cooper's father-in-law. These included Oudobras, who
had been *capataz* to Dorotéa's father.

After John Cooper and Dorotéa had rescued Raoul from
prison and brought him back to the United States, Oudobras
returned to his master's *estancia* and there rallied the
gauchos. They swore to help him watch over the Maldones
estate until such time as its rightful owner could return to
Argentina to claim it.

Heitor's sons were nearing manhood, and their genial

father had determined that they should assume important responsibilities despite their youth so that they might be better equipped to confront the enmity of the *porteños*, which was certain to increase against all *hacendados* of the *pampas*. To that end, he had been glad to have them look after the Maldones *estancia* and to familiarize themselves with the property and think about how they themselves might manage it, if it were theirs. And thus, for the past few months, they had lived on the Maldones property with the *gauchos* and Oudobras, who instructed them in every detail concerning the assets of the rich *estancia*.

On this gala evening at the end of the month of February, Heitor sat at the table with Benito and Enrique and half a dozen guests: other *hacendados* like himself, and their wives. Now he rose to salute his sons, holding in his hand a letter that one of the *gauchos* had brought to him that very afternoon from his old friend Raoul Maldones. *"Mis hijos,"* he smilingly declared, "I have great news. My old friend Raoul has arrived safely in los Estados Unidos, and he has gone to the *estancia* of his *yerno*. He remembers you both, Benito and Enrique, and wishes you well. He thanks you for your vow to help watch over the land that was once his home and on which he met the *yanqui* who is now his *yerno* and as valiant a friend as any man could ever hope to have. My sons, I respect you as men for already you have shown your loyalty, not only to me, but to my dearest friend. No father could ask more of his sons, and in the presence of these my guests who, like Raoul Maldones and myself, are *hacendados* who love the *pampas* and will never yield to the tyranny of the *porteños*, I express my paternal pride and my deep gratitude."

Benito Duvaldo, at fifteen, was slim and wiry, and he looked older than his age. Beardless, with a frank, earnest face, aquiline nose, and high-set cheekbones, he was perhaps more the student than his brother, who was two years his senior. Indeed, one of his own secrets, for which he would have died at the stake rather than to have revealed it either to Enrique or to his father, was that he was secretly in love with Raoul Maldones's thirteen-year-old daughter, Adriana, and in his possession had several poems written in her honor that he had never dared to give her. To be sure, he well understood that she was in the United States and was very nearly betrothed to that *gringo*'s son, the señor Andrew. And he respected Andrew, who had visited Argentina with his father, because Andrew had shown great skill and courage.

Enrique Duvaldo, seventeen, was stockier, more outgoing, and constantly smiling. He was an expert horseman, adept with weapons, and like his father and, indeed, like Raoul Maldones himself, had no feelings of superiority because he possessed money and land. The *gauchos* as well as the *trabajadores* openly admired him, and he was on the best of terms with them, knew their names and those of their families, and had also made a powerful ally in Oudobras, who placed loyalty above all else.

Heitor's mood changed now as he addressed his guests. "We are beset with tyranny and treachery on all sides, *mis amigos*," he declared. "We must weld together an even stronger bond against our enemies. Although Porfirio Ramos is dead, his associates in the government of Buenos Aires will increase their war against us. Have no doubt of this, *mis amigos*. If we unite, we can overcome them. Now that the war with Brazil is over, the *porteños* will concentrate on us and redouble their efforts to drive us from the land that we have earned by our settlements and our travail. We need not seek this war, but it is being forced upon us. We may take heart from the lesson that los Estados Unidos has taught us, that to yield to tyranny is to become a slave, and that only by a concerted and united effort can we hope to defeat those who would enslave us and strip us of our possessions. Their motives are high-sounding, but their real aim is as old as evil itself: the theft of what they covet and which they have not earned, and the destruction of those who dare stand against them."

His guests applauded, and a dignified-looking *hacendado* in his early sixties, Santiago de Arcana, rose to lift his goblet in a toast. "*Mis amigos*," he said, "the words of our good friend Señor Duvaldo fill our hearts with pride and with a patriotic fervor. With him as our friend, and with sons like his, I have no fear of the future, and I, too, cast down a challenge to the accursed *porteños!*"

Three days after the meeting of the *porteño* officials at the *cabildo* in Buenos Aires, a courier rode into the courtyard of Heitor Duvaldo's *hacienda*. The man dismounted and abruptly ordered one of the *trabajadores* to stable his horse, to give it a good measure of grain, and to rub it down, especially taking pains not to let it drink too much water.

Such a discourteous order from a stranger made the *trabajador* gawk uncomprehendingly at the courier, an importunate, insolent-faced man in his late thirties. Scowling and tilting up his pointed Vandyke beard at a belligerent angle, he barked, "*Perro*, do you not understand me? I am Emilio Vargas, envoy from *su excelencia* Gregorio Pordoña, and I seek your master. Now do as I have ordered. I'll give you a thrashing if after I have delivered my message I find that my horse hasn't been properly cared for, ¿*comprendes?*"

Hearing the loud-voiced diatribe, Heitor came out of his *hacienda* onto the porch. "What is the trouble, señor? I am Heitor Duvaldo, *hacendado* of this *estancia*."

"¡*Bueno!* Then it is you I seek, Señor Duvaldo. I have a message from the Minister of the Interior, His Excellency Gregorio Pordoña."

"In that event, señor, enter my *hacienda*, and I shall have some refreshment prepared for you. You have ridden all the way from Buenos Aires, I assume?"

"Of a certainty!" Vargas glowered, then shrugged with almost a pitying smile. "I should think, Señor Duvaldo, that a glance at my horse would tell you that I have ridden a long way. And that should convince you that the matter is of an extreme urgency to His Excellency."

Always genial and courteous, Heitor opened the door and gestured to the courier to enter, inclining his head in a sign of respect. But inwardly, he was greatly concerned; an urgent message from one of the leaders of the *porteño* government was hardly an announcement to brighten this sultry afternoon.

His majordomo, Tomaso Troganos, who recently had been ailing from a touch of what was called lung fever, now entered the salon and inquisitively eyed his master.

"Tomaso, be good enough to bring refreshments for my guest." He turned to Emilio Vargas. "Since it is midafternoon and I am aware that you have made a hard and swift journey, would you care for something substantial, a *carne asada*, perhaps?"

"Of course," was the insolent retort of the courier as he leaned back on the stuffed sofa toward which his gracious host had directed him. He crossed one booted leg over the other, indifferent to the mud he was leaving on the carpet, and looked around the salon with a sneer, his upper lip curling with visibly insulting contempt.

Once again, Heitor was rankled by the man's boorishly overbearing behavior, but discretion was the better part of valor when it came to dealing with the *porteños*, as he well knew. Therefore, forcing a polite smile to his face, he turned to the majordomo and said, "Please be good enough to have Carmen prepare a *carne asada* for my guest. And have her make some fresh tortillas, as well—they will be useful in dipping into the gravy. My *cocinera*, Señor Vargas, has a way with sauces that will please you greatly."

"So long as it is brought to me quickly, it is all the same. Now then, if we can be alone, I have a message for you. My *patrón*, Señor Pordoña, wishes me to convey to you his offer to purchase your land. I was told that in the register book in the Bureau of the Interior, your acreage is listed at a hundred and ten hectares. That is a very large *estancia*. However, His Excellency is anxious to acquire it. He bids me offer you seventy-five *pesos* for each hectare."

Heitor stared incredulously at his guest. "But, Señor Vargas," he at last protested, "such a price is certainly out of the question. Surely Señor Pordoña must know the value of land on the *pampas*, and particularly land as productive as my *estancia*. It is within reach of a town that furnishes supplies, there are good water sites, and I have loyal *trabajadores*. Also, my cattle thrive, and I have a section set off for the growth of grains and another for fruits and vegetables. Any *hacendado* who manages an estate as large as mine would tell you that such assets command a far higher price than your *patrón* offers."

"I am not interested in your views on the price of land, Señor Duvaldo," Vargas said, sneering. "I am simply the envoy chosen—and it is a great honor, I assure you—by the Minister of the Interior to transmit his legitimate offer to you. He bade me tell you that because Argentina has just won the war against the Brazilians, the government of the *porteños* is now in complete power in the province. Cooperation with the *unitarios* is to the advantage of every loyal Argentinian —and I trust that you so count yourself, Señor Duvaldo."

At this moment, Benito and Enrique entered the salon, then stopped short, seeing that their father was conversing with a stranger. But the former beckoned to them. "That is quite all right, *mis hijos*. This gentleman is Señor Emilio Vargas, from Buenos Aires, sent by the Minister of the Interior with an offer to buy my *estancia*."

"But I am sure you don't want to sell it, *mi padre*," the outgoing Enrique said, chuckling. He glanced over at the courier, who sent him a malevolent look and plucked at his beard, his narrowed eyes considering the young man who dared make light of an announcement from the powerful *porteños*.

"I agree with you, Enrique. And there is your answer, Señor Vargas. Be good enough to tell your master that I have no intention of selling my *estancia*. Even if I had, it would never be at so ridiculously low a price. Why, my neighbor and friend Felipe Tortinqua, who has only half the acreage I do, would gladly purchase my land from me at at least triple the price your *patrón* offers."

"And that is your final answer, Señor Duvaldo?"

"Yes, I am afraid it is. Understand, Señor Vargas, I mean no offense to His Excellency. And I do not think my loyalty to Argentina needs be questioned."

"Of that I am not so certain, nor is my *patrón*," the courier said with a sneer, just as a *criada* brought in a tray laden with the *carne asada*, a plate of *tortillas*, and a cup of strong coffee. She set it down on the tabouret beside the sofa, then, curtsying, hurried out of the salon.

Emilio Vargas turned to the tray and could not help licking his lips at the heaped plate of meat and sauce and refried beans. He took a mouthful with a fork, smacked his lips, and nodded. "You told the truth when you said you had a fine *cocinera*, Señor Duvaldo! This is very good. By the bye, do you have any wine you can serve me?"

Enrique and Benito exchanged a startled glance between themselves at such outlandish discourtesy, but their father pretended not to have noticed. "But of course, forgive me; I am remiss as a host." He clapped his hands, and the majordomo returned to the salon. "Tomaso, be good enough to bring a bottle of the French claret that I prize so highly. Open it, let it breathe a bit, and fill to the brim one of my silver goblets, which I use only for honored guests."

"At once, *señor patrón*." The majordomo bowed.

"You may bring me a goblet also, Pedro. I shall toast Argentina," Heitor said with a gentle smile.

At this nuance of elegant sarcasm, Vargas lifted his attention from the plate of *carne asada* and, holding a half-eaten *tortilla* in one hand and his fork in the other, his mouth still filled, blurted out, "His Excellency has often said that loyalty does not come by the expression of words, Señor Duvaldo. It comes by acts. That is why he urged me to use all my powers of persuasion to induce you to sell your *estancia*. That would be the swiftest, truest proof of your loyalty to our great country that you could offer."

"Perhaps that is true," Heitor mused, again with a sarcastic little smile, "but in the event that I sold all my hectares to your *patrón*, where should I live? I should have to become an exile, and then how indeed could I prove my loyalty to Argentina? No, surely you must see for yourself, Señor Vargas, that His Excellency asks the impossible."

The majordomo returned with the bottle of wine, which he placed on the sideboard after filling two goblets. He handed these to his employer and his guest.

The *porteño* emissary mopped up the sauce from his plate with a last bite of *tortilla*, then greedily gulped down the wine in his goblet. Belching, he looked around with an arrogant frown, lifting the goblet to indicate that he wanted it refilled. Glancing at his sons with a covert little smile, Heitor himself rose from his chair, went to the sideboard, and solicitously filled Vargas's goblet to the brim. "My pleasure, Señor Vargas," he blandly murmured as he resumed his chair.

The latter took a long swallow of the wine, set the goblet down, belched again, and then, scowling at his host, rejoined, "I detect in your conversation, Señor Duvaldo, a disrespect for my *patrón* and, indeed, for our unitarian government. I am to warn you that such conduct is frowned upon by the Minister of the Interior and his associates. Indeed, they believe that it is akin to treason."

"Sir," the gray-haired *hacendado* retorted in as steely a voice as he could muster, "no one before has ever questioned my patriotism. I believe in Argentina, in its people, in the rich land that gives us food, in the dignity of labor. I have no stomach for politics, but it seems to me that a sound government is one that believes in its people and does whatever it can to aid them, rather than to usurp their land and take away their right to free speech and the pursuit of their own lives."

"That, very definitely, is treason, and I fear I shall have to report what you have just said to me to the minister, Señor Duvaldo," Vargas said, sneering. "I take it, then, that you will not reconsider, that you refuse the offer that His Excellency has been kind enough to tender?"

"You and he may both take it exactly that way, Señor Vargas. Now do you wish more refreshment?" was Heitor's ironic answer.

Emilio Vargas belched again as he rose and flung down his napkin on the floor. "You *hacendados* of the *pampas* are all alike! You are stiff-necked, obstinate, and blind to reality. Those who stand in our way will be dealt with, you may be certain. And it is well-known that you befriended the condemned traitor Raoul Maldones, who, luckily for him, escaped the firing squad."

"Do you threaten me with a firing squad also, Señor Vargas?" Heitor asked calmly.

Vargas snorted, drew himself up, and with an insolent look, responded, "It may well come to that, if you persist in your treasonable outlook on our government. But you leave me no alternative. I shall return to Buenos Aires and tell the minister that you will not sell your land to him."

"If the land were to be sold, it would be sold to a government, not to an individual. You see, Señor Vargas, you have unwittingly betrayed the real motives of your illustrious master. History is filled with the biographies of men who worshiped power above all else, and who counted life's successes by the acquisition of wealth, whether it was in gold or silver or in land."

"You will not need to wait for history to deal with you, I'm afraid, Señor Duvaldo," the emissary retorted as he turned toward the door of the salon. "There are immediate ways of dealing with dangerous rebels."

"You will do me the honor of leaving my *hacienda*, Señor Vargas, now that you have had your refreshment. And you may tell His Excellency that if he and his colleagues continue to judge every *hacendado* who believes in freedom as a dangerous traitor, then I fear he may defeat himself by fomenting a veritable rebellion—yes, Señor Vargas, a rebellion formed by the coalition of men like myself and, yes again, my friend Raoul Maldones, who stand united against tyranny and greed and corruption. It is true that you may acquire a good deal of land by your bluster and your threats, but you will never enslave the *gauchos*. A piece of advice: Beware of them, for they are free men, and they go as the wind goes, as they please, and no one can dictate to them. That they have befriended Raoul Maldones and myself is a rare honor, and it tells me more about my patriotism than your specious moralizing about your absolute power of government."

"You have not heard the last of this, be certain of that, Señor Duvaldo!" Vargas snapped as he stalked out of the salon without a glance behind him.

"It was all I could do to keep from making him apologize to you for his insolence, *mi padre*," Benito angrily spoke up.

"I, too, felt the same way," his older brother added with an energetic nod of assent, and for once he was not smiling.

"Gently, my sons. Your loyalty touches me, but we should gain nothing by a physical encounter with that lackey, for that is all he is. What we must do is to be on our guard now, for I am certain that Gregorio Pordoña will plan retaliatory measures against this *estancia* . . . and, as well, against my neighbors who feel as I do."

Shortly after his return from the *estancia* of Heitor Duvaldo, Emilio Vargas hurried to the council chamber, knocked peremptorily, and was at once admitted by Gregorio Pordoña himself.

"I have been waiting for you, Emilio," the fat *porteño* official exclaimed. "Well now, what was the outcome of your meeting with Señor Duvaldo?"

"He has refused your offer, Señor Minister! And he made a long speech about defying our government, saying that there were other *hacendados* like himself who would fight for freedom."

"So," Pordoña purred as he went back to his desk and gestured to his courier to seat himself. He opened a teakwood box, took out a long Havana cigar, lit it, and indicated that Vargas should help himself. Puffing at the cigar, he scowled as he meditated for a moment, and then, watching the wreaths of smoke ascend to the ceiling, declared, "Measures must be taken against this traitor. He is more dangerous than that accursed *hacendado* Maldones because he remains a landowner, and no doubt he has allied the *gauchos* who protected Maldones."

"That is true, Your Excellency! He said as much to me. He said that the *gauchos*, too, would rise in revolt against the *unitarios*."

"A treasonable remark, sufficient to send him before a firing squad. But I have a much better idea. I do not wish to make a martyr of him, but if he should die, shall we say accidentally, through the savage elements of nature—his traitorous friends would possibly understand that *el Señor Dios* was punishing him for his treason."

"A superb idea, Señor Minister!" Vargas exclaimed.

"As it happens, after the escape of Raoul Maldones from his execution, I immediately took certain precautions, anticipating that Duvaldo would be a difficult man to deal with. There is now on his *estancia* a new worker, a man named Manuel Forlana, who was hired by the majordomo. He has great skill with horses, as well he should, for he trained them on my own little farm outside Buenos Aires. A week after Maldones escaped, I sent him on to Lobos, and I gave him a story to tell Duvaldo's majordomo. It was a very romantic one, Vargas. Poor Manuel was the victim of a thwarted love affair; the widowed mother of the *novia* with whom he was enamored made false accusations against him, saying that he had besmirched her daughter's honor, and that she wished him imprisoned and publicly flogged. So he fled to the country, to the *pampas*, where he could be free to lead his own life until such time as he might come back for his beloved."

"Most ingenious, Señor Minister!" Vargas beamed and nodded.

"I thought it rather good." The fat minister smirked. "At any rate, he has been a *trabajador* on the Duvaldo *estancia* for a few months now. And he reports to me by leaving letters in the hollow of an old *ombú* tree some three miles to the west of the *hacienda*. I have another courier as faithful as yourself, Vargas, who rides there and brings back these letters to me."

"I begin to follow Your Excellency." Vargas puffed at his cigar, then leisurely leaned forward in his chair, his face eager, regarding the minister with almost servile veneration.

"I chose well when I made you my courier, Vargas. You exhibit a loyal intelligence that will make you go far in my administration."

"I will do everything I can to justify your faith in me, Señor Minister!"

"I am sure you will. And your devotion will have its own rewards, have no fear of that. But now, back to business. Manuel Forlana's last letter, which arrived only three days ago, informs me that it is the *hacendado*'s daily custom to go riding on his finest stallion for about three or four hours after dawn. Invariably, he takes a path to the west, and of course beyond the secret tree that acts as our mailbox."

Vargas arched his eyebrows, waiting for a further explanation.

"Now let us suppose that one fine morning while he is out riding, an accident befalls him. A tragic accident, of course, in which his life is terminated. There would be no connection between myself and that accident, and his friends would indeed look upon his death as an act of *el Señor Dios*, would they not?"

"Of course they would, Your Excellency!"

"Once he is dead, it will be an easy matter to seize his lands and declare that they are forfeit to the government because of his treason. And such swift action immediately after his death will certainly tell his traitorous neighbors and friends that they may expect a similar Divine reprisal followed by, shall we say, a legal one. Are you with me, Vargas?"

"I think it is a brilliant stratagem, Señor Minister, and I am proud to be in your employ," was Vargas's answer.

"I thank you for your sentiment. Go see Coronel Matisa, who occupies an office at the other end of this wing of the *cabildo*. He is Assistant Minister of War, and he will have a sum of money to be paid into your hands, Vargas . . . your wages for carrying out this errand of mine so admirably. I am glad that you provoked Duvaldo's hostility, for you caused him to burst out with his own true feelings about us, and now we know what a villainous traitor he really is."

"Your Excellency is much too generous. I am happy to serve in the cause of the *unitarios*, and I do not look for *dinero*—"

"Yes, yes, your loyalty is never to be questioned," Pordoña interrupted with a brusque wave of his hand. "Go collect your wages, and keep yourself in readiness for the next time I summon you."

Seeing that he was dismissed, Vargas gave the Minister of the Interior an obsequious bow and then, leaving the council chamber, his face radiant with such high praise from his *patrón*, went in search of the colonel.

About an hour later, one of the clerks in the *cabildo* entered Pordoña's office in the company of a wizened, stoop-shouldered man in his early fifties, whom he introduced as Tiburcio Llamas. "Here is the *hombre* you asked to see, Señor Minister," the clerk said.

"Good," Pordoña replied, without looking at his underling. "Now go away and let me talk to this man."

The clerk departed, and at once Pordoña put on all his oily charm for the little man standing in front of him.

"Be at your ease, Señor Llamas," the *porteño* purred with an ingratiating smile. "On the sideboard, you will find a decanter of excellent Canary wine. Be so good as to help yourself."

"*Gracias, excelencia.*" Tiburcio Llamas genially nodded, then poured himself a generous glass of the wine and sat in the chair that the minister indicated to him. "To your health, *excelencia.*"

"Add to that the damnation and extermination of all enemies of our valiant unitarian government, Señor Llamas, and I will drink with you," Pordoña pompously intoned as he rose, filled his own goblet with the red wine, and returned to his desk. "Now tell me about yourself. I already know that you are a renowned animal trainer, in charge of the *corrida de toros*. I have seen one or two of the contests, and they are quite good, although you might do with wilder bulls, I think. Of course, one must go to Madrid for the great *corridas.*"

At this, the little man's face froze in an expression of annoyance, and in a piping, high-pitched voice, he querulously retorted, "Señor Minister, my men scour the provinces for the wildest bulls. I have heard that there are better ones in the *america del norte*, but thus far no vessel has imported them. Perhaps, since you are in charge of the government of Buenos Aires, you could use your influence—"

"Never mind that," Pordoña said impatiently, waving his goblet to dismiss the topic. "With what other animals have you had experience? I mean those that would be dangerous for the average man to face, and especially unexpectedly."

"Well, señor, I have worked with many kinds of *culebra*, with the *jabalí*, and several times with the wild dogs of the *pampas.*"

"I see. It is true that those are dangerous creatures, but I am thinking of something even more dangerous, and I will tell you the reason once I learn from you the full range of your experience, Señor Llamas."

"Ah, perhaps this will interest you, *excelencia.*" The little man's face brightened. "Slightly more than two years ago, a friend of mine who was traveling in Brazil found a jaguar cub, had it caged, and brought it back to Buenos

Aires. He made me a present of it, although he thought that it would be much too dangerous to train. But since he made a wager that I could not do it, I was honor bound to take up the challenge—and I succeeded."

Pordoña leaned forward in his chair, his eyes narrowing with interest. "And how well have you succeeded? Let me see, now—after two years, the animal should be full-grown."

"You are right, Señor Minister. It weighs nearly three hundred pounds, and it is a very ferocious beast. But I have trained it to hunt and to kill at command. It takes patience, and of course the secret is that the animal must trust the trainer. And though the reverse is true, that the trainer must trust the animal, still in all he must use a certain amount of wisdom and know when things may go wrong."

"I cannot afford to have anything go wrong with what I have in mind, Señor Llamas. Of course, when you say 'hunt and kill,' you refer to wild game, do you not?"

The little man drew himself up, affronted. "*Excelencia*, I would be sent to prison and perhaps shot if I let Diablo hunt and kill a man."

"But do you think you could train it to do just that?"

Now a look of wary alarm replaced the hurt look on the trainer's face. "Perhaps—but you must understand—"

"I would pay you a thousand silver *pesos*, Señor Llamas, and apart from that you would have the gratitude of the entire *porteño* government. You see, I have in mind a traitor, an enemy of our great city, who must be taught a lesson that will impress his equally traitorous neighbors and friends."

"A thousand *pesos*, Señor Minister?" the animal trainer almost reverently echoed. "But it's not easy. You must understand, first of all, that while you can train a *perro de busca*, a hunting dog, by command, you cannot do this with any member of the cat family, to which the jaguar belongs. Cats are extremely independent and self-willed. It is true that when they're hungry, they are amenable to reason—but there again, one cannot hope for total success each time."

"But could you do it?"

"I think so. But I should need several things from you, *excelencia*."

"Name them."

"First, I must know whether this man has a beard."

The *porteño* official scowled. "And why is that, Señor Llamas?"

"One way to train a cat like a jaguar to kill is for the trainer to represent the game or, in this instance, the human quarry that is to be hunted and attacked. You see, *excelencia*, you reward a cat with food. But also, you teach him to hate by not only looking like this man, whoever he may be, but also by associating that look with the man's smell and also with pain. I have a cattle prod with which I sometimes punish Diablo when he does not obey me. He has learned to respect it. To be sure, he is in his cage all the time now, as he has become too ferocious for me to take out on a leash and expect to be able to return without a scratch from those terrible claws." The animal trainer permitted himself an ironic little laugh.

"Naturally. What do you mean by the man's smell?"

"I should require some clothing belonging to this individual, Señor Minister. Brought to me as quickly as possible so that the scent may be fresh enough to be identified by the animal. In fact, it would be an excellent idea to have several parcels of such clothing over the period of time it will take me to train Diablo."

"And how long do you think it will take, Señor Llamas?"

"Several months—"

"Impossible!" Pordoña rose from his chair and paced the room for a moment. Then, whirling and confronting the animal trainer, he said in a conspiratorial whisper, "I cannot give you much more than a month."

"That is really not enough time, although of course I shall try—"

"I will make it two thousand *pesos*, and you will have it out of my own personal funds. My word should be good enough for you."

"Oh, but, *excelencia*, it certainly is!" the little man fawningly responded. "I know how important you are in Buenos Aires. The whole city knows of the Minister of the Interior."

"Very well, then. A month. I have a courier who is in communication with the *estancia* where this enemy of the people resides. I shall send him off this very night to procure what clothing he can. Now then, you asked if the man has a beard. He does, and it is short and pointed and gray."

"That is easy. You see that I have a beard now, Señor

Minister, and I can easily trim it. As to the gray, I am already graying. That's the easiest part of all. May I ask the name of the man?"

"No. For all of us concerned, it is better that you know only that I wish you to train your Diablo and to have him ready within a month. When that is done, you will come here again and tell me that the beast is ready. Then I shall have specific orders for you."

"Very well, Señor Minister."

"Good. Now here, I will give you fifty *pesos* on account. It shows you that I am in earnest, and you have my word for the rest. Once the traitor dies by the claws of Diablo, you shall have the full two thousand, so let this be an additional incentive for you to do your best, Señor Llamas."

"Your Excellency is most generous. I shall begin as soon as your courier arrives with the clothing." He began to leave the office, then turned to look at Pordoña with a conspiratorial little smile. "You know, Señor Minister, when Diablo finishes with the man, it will not be a pretty sight. I think this traitor you mention is going to be taught a very nasty lesson."

"Good," Pordoña replied, sitting back in his chair and allowing himself a smile. "That is very good indeed."

Eleven

Manuel Forlana had waited until he was certain that everyone in the household was asleep for afternoon *siesta*. Then he saddled his horse and rode to the *ombú* tree with its huge hollow that he used as a depository for the letters sent on to Gregorio Pordoña in Buenos Aires. In the past few weeks, he had also deposited in the tree sacks containing several of Heitor Duvaldo's *camisas* and *calzoncillos*. A courier had been dispatched from Buenos Aires every third or fourth day to bring back what was found in the hollow of the *ombú* tree, and only two days earlier, Manuel had found a little pouch containing fifty silver *pesos* and a note expressing Gregorio Pordoña's appreciation for his valorous services to the nation.

It had been easy to obtain the job of *trabajador* from Heitor's majordomo, for Manuel Forlana was expert with horses, his father once having lived on the *pampas* for a decade as a *gaucho* before wearying of the monotonous life and coming to Buenos Aires to become a shopkeeper. His father had taught him all that he knew about horses and cattle, and Manuel had worked for a year on Pordoña's own farm. And since Manuel was in his midtwenties, personable and soft-spoken, with warm brown eyes and an appealingly earnest face, the ailing majordomo had readily engaged him to work at the corral. More than this, his personable manner and good looks had swiftly attracted one of the *criadas* on the *estancia*, eighteen-year-old Carmen Norgaldo, and he had already promised to wed her one day in a church in Buenos Aires—it would not be too far off, he had glibly assured her.

He had told Carmen that he was desirous of becoming a gentleman, and that, like his father, who had gone to his eternal rest just six months before, he hoped to be a shopkeeper. His father had set aside money and a small inventory of merchandise as his last legacy to his only son, he had told the ingenuous young woman, and so, to prepare himself for a change of status in their new lives together, he wished to dress as befitted a *porteño*. Carmen, who was virtually an orphan, with only an old aunt in her seventies to care what happened to her (and she in a little village some thirty miles from the Duvaldo *estancia*), had doted upon his every word. He had paid her rapturous homage, for he was as fluent with words as he was expert in breaking in and training horses and driving cattle.

So he had wheedled Carmen, telling her that the *señor patrón* had so much underlinen that he would never miss a few *camisas* and *calzoncillos*, and that he wished to keep some of them. Then he would know the kind of garb he would wear when the happy day came that he and Carmen could be husband and wife and joint proprietors of a charming little shop on the calle de Arbolas in Buenos Aires.

This afternoon, as he rode toward the *ombú* tree —ostensibly to round up a mare that had bolted at the sight of a snake and run off before a *trabajador* could seize her reins and halt her—he carried more of the *patrón*'s garments that had been worn against his skin. The *patrón*, after his lengthy horseback ride in the morning, invariably bathed and changed his clothes, and some of these Carmen brought to her young suitor.

It pleased Forlana that the *patrón* did not vary from his thus far predictable schedule of his solitary early morning horseback ride. That would make it even easier for the señor minister to accomplish what was to be done—though he had not been told in detail what would occur. Moreover, it was not his concern. He was shrewd enough to realize that the less he knew about Gregorio Pordoña's plans concerning Heitor Duvaldo, the less turbulent his own future life was likely to be.

He reached the *ombú* tree, looked carefully around to make certain that no one was following him or could see what he was doing, lifted out several handfuls of grass and briars that were used to camouflage the hollow, and dropped the sack into the bottom, then replaced the vegetation.

He could not help wondering why the señor minister was so insistent upon obtaining the *patrón's* garments in this manner. One of the *trabajadores* had told him that a courier had come some weeks before with an offer from the *porteños* to buy the *estancia* of the *patrón* and that the latter had brusquely refused. This provided Forlana with a glimmer of understanding: Something, no doubt, was being planned to punish the *patrón* for defying the señor minister. But that was all he needed or cared to know. He permitted himself only the inner observation that he was happy that he was not in the señor Duvaldo's boots, for the señor minister was known to have a savage temper when crossed.

He would come again to the hollow in a few days and perhaps find further instructions. Now it was time to find the runaway mare, whose location he had already guessed, and then he would have a little *siesta* and then visit with the delicious Carmen. It was torment not to be able to take her into the thickets far beyond the *hacienda* and show her that he was by no means impervious to her charms, but she was religious and would not engage in any intimacies with him without the sacrament of marriage. Well, he could also console himself with the thought that once he had accomplished the task on which the señor minister had sent him he would marry Carmen and have her as often as he wanted. And by then, to be sure, if he should tire of the *muchacha*, there would be many others in Buenos Aires, finer ladies, and he, Manuel Forlana, appreciated by those in power, might well be able to pick and choose.

"Tiburcio, *querido*, a man on horseback just delivered this for you, and he says you are to use it at once," Madalena Llamas exclaimed as she hurried into the kitchen where her husband was busy devouring a bowl of *chiles rellenos*, dipping a *tortilla* into the spicy broth. She was a plump woman in her early forties, who doted on her husband. Indeed, it had been her dowry that had set him up as an entrepreneur who trained bulls for the occasional *corrida* that was held just outside Buenos Aires and sometimes, if the fce was large enough, in the provinces.

Tiburcio Llamas sprang up from the table, his eyes glittering when he saw the sack of Heitor Duvaldo's clothing. "*¡Gracias, mi corazón!*" he exclaimed. "I'll take that, and I shall get to work at once."

"With that dreadful cat of yours downstairs, I assume?" she murmured with a grimace of distaste.

He drew himself up to his full height and rebuked her in a harsh tone. "*Mujer*, what I do is for the good of my fatherland. It is an order from the Minister of the Interior himself. You will know better than to question it. I should say that our future depends upon my success."

"But please be careful, dear Tiburcio! Diablo—his very name makes me shudder each time I hear it, and I cannot bear to go downstairs and see him in the cage. Whenever those horrid yellow eyes of his fix on me, he snarls and bares his dreadful teeth!"

"Then, wife of my bosom," he sarcastically retorted, "I'd advise you to be a good wife to me, if you do not wish me ever to turn this cat upon you."

"How can you say such a thing, *mi corazón!*" she said reproachfully. Then, with a philosophical shrug, she left the room, only to pause on the threshold and murmur in a wheedling voice, "I assume you will be hungry again after you have done your work. Well, when you are finished, I shall have prepared your favorite meal—*pollo con arroz.*"

"Now you are being a good wife. Go then, occupy yourself, for I have work to do." The little man took the sack that the courier had brought and went out by the other door and down the steps at the end of the passageway to the cellar. As he unlocked the door, he heard the angry snarl of the caged jaguar and chuckled to himself. It had been hard work indeed, but the fee agreed upon would more than pay for it. And beyond that, there was the inestimable service to the *porteños* that would assuredly make his fortune. He had trimmed his beard to the size of the man whom the minister had described; and with the clothing sent on by the courier at regular intervals during the previous few weeks, he had begun training the jaguar to associate the scent with the pain he inflicted until, when the moment came, Diablo would be certain to kill. There were, to be sure, difficulties, for one never knew if at the exact moment of unleashing the jaguar the quarry would be well in range, particularly as regarded the jaguar's catching the scent of the hated enemy. But then, he had done all that any man could, for it was not easy to train a wild beast, even though it had been under his care these past two years.

He opened the cellar door and locked it behind him. The jaguar gave an angry roar, for it was hungry. At the outset, Llamas had trained it by rewarding it with food, but for some weeks he had calculatedly shortened the beast's rations, to put it into a more ferocious mood.

Now he approached the cage and stared at the almost full-grown animal. It was about six feet long with a tail nearly two feet in length and black spots forming a pattern against the reddish-tan background. Its yellow eyes considered him as he stepped before the heavy wooden cage and then, seeing the short-trimmed, graying beard, the animal hurled itself against the door of the cage.

"*¡Bueno*, Diablo!" He chuckled. Going to a chest near the cage, he opened it and drew out a pair of black velvet gloves and a cattle prod. Donning the gloves, he turned to the sack that the courier had brought, opened it, and carefully took out the *camisa* enclosed. Then, holding this almost daintily by left thumb and forefinger, he took hold of the cattle prod in his right hand and squatted down to face the jaguar. It lashed its tail in a growing fury, and it gave a horrible roar as again it hurled itself at the door of the cage.

Carefully wrapping the *camisa* around the top of the prod and making a knot, Llamas moved quickly, almost like a cat himself, to the right side of the cage and thrust the prod against the jaguar's side. Again it uttered an angry roar, twisted, turned, and tried to cuff at the prod with its great paw. Llamas could see the claws bared, and he shivered at the thought of how lethal a swipe from those claws would be. The trainer believed that, within a few more days, the jaguar's killing instinct would be sharpened to its zenith. Then, all that would be necessary would be to await word for the time to take the caged animal and to place it so that it would intercept the traitorous rider.

Once again, he thrust the prod against the jaguar's side. There was a furious snarl as the great cat twisted and struck at the prod. Its fangs were bared, and its eyes blazed with fury and hate. "That's the way, Diablo, that's the way! He is your enemy!" Llamas hissed,

For more than an hour, he continued the tormenting of the jaguar, moving all around the cage, prodding here and there, and always managing to let the beast be aware of the scent of the garment wrapped around the prod. Finally, when he was satisfied that the jaguar's fury was unrestrained and that there could be no mistaking the association between the pain and the scent conveyed by the *camisa*, Llamas tossed the prod into the back of the chest and went to a large clay bowl. Earlier that morning he had placed into the bowl half a dozen strips of fresh meat, and now he rewarded Diablo by tossing the jaguar the food. Then, his left hand concealing his beard, he resumed the tone of voice with which the jaguar had, until this training had begun, always associated him and quelled the angry rage of the predator cat.

"Diablo, you are assuredly a weapon more terrifying and deadly, by far, than any rifle or *pistola* or *cuchillo*," he said with approval. "Do not be impatient; your time is at hand. I am sure of it. *Adiós* until *mañana*, Diablo!"

The jaguar lay in the cage, its glowering yellow eyes considering him. But it was calm now and showed no sign of the fury to which the prod and the clothing had driven it. It was true, Llamas suddenly thought with a wry grimace, that once the animal had done its work, it might be very hard to catch it, especially if the cat were loose in the jungle. But at the moment, that was not his concern. So long as Diablo accomplished the task for which he had been training the beast, that sufficed. Surely the Minister of the Interior, learning how reliable he could be on so enormously difficult a task, would find other uses for his services. The future was very bright indeed.

He ran his hands down his sides, and his nostrils dilated.

He could smell the aromas of the food his wife was preparing for him. Good, plump Madalena. He would eat a delicious meal, and then, his stomach satisfied, maybe he would take his wife into their bedroom and lose himself for a while in her ample flesh. She was a passionate, eager lover, and she was capable of satisfying all his appetites in a way no young *criada* ever could.

The last Saturday in the month of March was, as the Argentinian summer had been almost all along, unseasonably warm. Indeed, it was one reason why Heitor Duvaldo wakened at about dawn, and then, to shake off his lethargy from the heavy sleep into which he had fallen, dressed and went out to the stable. A solitary ride at daybreak was an ideal time to be alone with one's thoughts. And his were with his old friend Raoul Maldones, from whom he had received a new letter only a week before . . . the day, alas, when his majordomo, poor Tomaso, had died from a lengthy bout of fever that not even the town *médico* had been able to cure.

His sons, Enrique and Benito, had returned to the Maldones *estancia* early the previous week, and they would be coming back this morning. In a way, it was a pity they were not here now so that he could ride with them. He had much to tell them. The letter from his old friend was full of optimism, and already he could sense Raoul's love for his new homeland. There was much to be said about a democracy where all men were given the opportunity to lead their own lives, without constraint or repressions. No longer was that true of his beloved Argentina. Now, even the *pampas* were threatened by the ruthless inroads of *unitarios,* the *porteños* who, after learning of the decisive results of the great battle against the Brazilians, would have no check to their headlong rush for total power. It was certain to affect him, just as it had done Raoul, though up to now, praise the Lord, there had been no repercussions from the unfortunate meeting with Gregorio Pordoña's emissary several weeks earlier.

Knowing his master's habits, Pablo, the fifteen-year-old stable boy, had already saddled the beautiful black stallion that had been named Triunfante because Heitor swore that there was indeed always a look of triumph in his mount's eyes, satisfaction at always meeting the demands of his rider.

"Buenos días, señor patrón," Pablo warmly greeted his master "I've saddled your horse, and the cinch straps are

tight. Yesterday, when you came back, the one on the left was a little worn, so I replaced it."

"You are a thoughtful young man; *gracias*, Pablo. By the way, if memory serves me right, won't you be celebrating your *cumpleaños* next week?"

The tall, slender youth, with an unruly mop of black hair, blushed like a girl, overwhelmed that his *patrón* should remember the birthday of a humble stable boy. Then, not forgetting his manners, he stammered, "*Sí, señor patrón*, I shall be sixteen then."

"That is what I thought. And very soon you will be a fine man . . . you have proved it already, Pablo. I shall have a little present for you next week, and some silver *pesos*. Now then," Heitor added, holding the reins of Triunfante in his left hand and patting the stable boy on the shoulder with the other, "go to the *cocinera* and tell the cook to give you a very good breakfast. You have pleased me very much this morning." With this, Heitor mounted his stallion and rode out of the courtyard.

Suddenly, he heard a voice hail him: "*¡Patrón, patrón, momentito, por favor!*" Turning, he saw a thickly mustached, genial-featured *trabajador* mounted on a brown gelding behind him. Curious at the interruption, he wheeled the head of his stallion around to meet him. "Oh, it is you, Joaquín. What is the matter?"

Joaquín Ortega, carrying his rifle, drew up abreast of his *patrón* and stammered, somewhat embarrassed, "Please do not take offense, *patrón*, but I know that you often ride out toward the place that they call *La Selva de los Espectros*, the jungle of ghosts, and it is not always safe. Sometimes there is a wild boar, or a deadly snake—please allow me to ride with you, *patrón*."

Heitor smiled. He had recently hired the *trabajador*, whose parents had been killed by a roving band of Indians, and no doubt the young man, unaware that his *patrón* rode out daily without anyone accompanying him, was offering himself as an escort out of gratitude for what Heitor had done for him. It touched the older man deeply, and so, continuing to smile gently, he nodded. "I should be pleased to have you as my riding companion, Joaquín. It is a beautiful day, is it not?"

"*Pero sí, mi patrón*, and—*gracias*."

"*De nada, hombre*. Well then, let us go. I need my

morning exercise, if I am to do justice to the breakfast our fine *cocinera* will have ready for us when we return—and you will eat at my table with me, Joaquín."

"You are too kind, *patrón*. And I will ride behind you, because I am only a *trabajador*."

"You will ride alongside of me. In the eyes of *el Señor Dios*, we are of the same stature, *hombre*, though when we reach the jungle, the trail is so narrow that there is room for only one horse."

"As you wish, *patrón. Gracias* again." Joaquín touched his right index finger to his forehead, and then he and his master went on their way.

Manuel Forlana had left his bed well before dawn, for three days earlier he had found in the hollow of the *ombú* a note from Gregorio Pordoña. The minister indicated that the *hacendado* would be dealt with on the morning of this day and that he, Manuel, should make certain that Duvaldo took his usual morning canter through the wooded and jungle stretch northwest of his *estancia*, as was his custom. There he would be met by some men in hiding, whom Forlana was to ride out to warn of their approaching quarry.

Peeking around a shed, he observed the distinguished-looking ranch owner about to mount his black stallion and grinned to himself. It was working out very well. Not seeing the *trabajador* join up with the *patrón*, Forlana hurried to a small penned-in corral on the other side of the *hacienda*, where some of the stock horses were kept. He chose the best-looking of the lot, did not bother to saddle it, for he was an expert bareback rider, and headed his mount at a gallop so that he would be well in advance of Heitor Duvaldo and not be seen by him.

He rode as if the devil were behind him for about three miles, and then he saw the huge *ombú* tree where the minister said he would meet the men in hiding. Here, the trail was narrow, and thick foliage and trees surrounded it on both sides. He reined in his horse, which pranced and neighed, foam slavering its muzzle, for he had driven it pitilessly. Then, putting his right hand to his mouth, he gave the call of the wood dove. After a moment he shivered, for he thought he heard a low growl ahead of him and to the right, well inside the abundant bushes and grass that made this stretch seem like a miniature jungle, such as one would find in the sultry regions of Brazil. Immediately there came the answering call of the wood dove, and a moment later, a stocky, black-bearded man emerged. "You're Forlana, *hombre?*" the stranger demanded.

"*Sí, amigo.*"

"We are ready. The *hacendado* comes this way for certain?"

"I've seen to it. After he mounted his horse, I went off to get another one on the other side of the *hacienda.* Then I galloped ahead so that he would not suspect that I know where he is going."

"*¡Bueno!* You'd best not stay here, *hombre.* The *patrón* says that you are to go on to Buenos Aires and report to him. With the death of the *hacendado*, your work at his *estancia* will be done."

"But I thought—" Forlana began, remembering the pretty *criada* Carmen, whom he wanted to marry.

"You are to obey His Excellency, *hombre,*" the stocky man growled. "It wouldn't be wise for you to be found at the *estancia* after your *patrón* is taken care of, *¿comprendes?* His friends will be certain to investigate, and you might tell all you know out of fear—"

"Now that's not true!" Forlana angrily drew himself up. "I am loyal—have I not served His Excellency well?"

There was another low growl from beyond, and the stocky henchman of the *porteños* smiled grimly. "Take care Diablo does not include you in his morning meal, *hombre.* Now get back on your horse and ride away from here, *pronto!*" As for food, you can beg, borrow, or steal it until you get to Buenos Aires; it's of no consequence."

"Well then, I suppose I'd better—all right." Hesitantly, still thinking of Carmen and wishing that he could get word to her somehow to join him in the city, Forlana turned his horse and headed toward Buenos Aires.

Now the stocky man who had accosted Manuel Forlana went back into the thicket and joined Tiburcio Llamas and his other assistant, an older, gray-haired but powerfully muscled man in his early fifties. The animal trainer now exclaimed, "So he's on his way! Quickly, we'll climb the *ombú* tree, and I'll hold the cord tied to the top of the door of Diablo's cage."

"Will it work, Señor Tiburcio?" the stocky man respectfully inquired.

"*¡Caramba!* You insult me, Juan! I have worked for a

good month with Diablo, and he knows the scent. He is starved, and he is angry. He will catch the scent of the *hacendado*, will see his pointed, gray beard, and he will go for him. There is no man alive who can survive the attack of a full-grown jaguar thus trained! Are you sure that our wagon is well hidden from the trail?"

"Of course, Señor Tiburcio," the stocky man replied. "And I tell you this, my insides are still not in place from all the jolting we had in the wagon making the journey from Buenos Aires with those spavined mares."

"Stop grumbling. We shall be well paid for this. Now quickly, climb the tree, both of you!"

The two men obeyed, Llamas also swiftly climbing to an upper branch of the huge *ombú*. In his right hand, he held a strong cord that he uncoiled gradually from his arm as he ascended. Diablo growled, hurling himself against the cage. "Patience, Diablo, patience, you will soon have your freedom!" Tiburcio called down.

Heitor was now within fifty yards of the *ombú*, with Joaquín Ortega riding about five lengths behind him because by now the trail had narrowed. The *trabajador* was uneasy, though why he could not tell. Instinctively, he cocked his rifle, which he had already primed and loaded before leaving the *estancia*. With his other hand, he made the sign of the cross, for *La Selva de los Espectros* had a reputation that even the *gauchos* spoke of with not a little awe and fear around their campfires. According to legend, the king of an Indian tribe had been led there by a man who professed to be his dearest friend but who wished to replace him as king. And in this junglelike terrain, the Indian king had been hacked to death with knives and spears. Since that day, his ghost was said to haunt *La Selva de los Espectros*, and those who did not respect the ghost of one who had been king long before the white man had come to these lands met with bad luck—if not death by violence, then perhaps the loss of their fortune or their *novia*.

The trail was indeed narrow, as the *patrón* had said, and so Joaquín was obliged to hold in his impatient horse, who wished to catch up with the stallion. By then, Heitor had come abreast of the huge *ombú*.

High above, his left arm wound around the sturdy uppermost branch, Llamas pulled with all his strength at the cord with his right hand. The door of the cage rose in its grooves, and the jaguar sprang out onto the trail with a roar. Its gleaming yellow eyes fixed on the rider turned in profile to it, and it saw the pointed, short beard streaked with gray hair. With a snarl, it launched itself in the air, its terrible claws extended, eager to rip and rend its prey.

Joaquín saw the great cat leap and uttered a warning cry of horror. *"¡Patrón, patrón,* take care, *el gato demonio!"* But it was already too late. The beast had sunk its claws into Heitor's upper thighs, and the shock, together with the momentum of the jaguar's leap, had propelled the *hacendado* off his saddle to the ground.

Sobbing in his agony, Joaquín lifted his rifle and pulled the trigger. The jaguar uttered a hideous yowl. It stiffened, lifted its head from the unconscious, bleeding body over which it crouched, and then with a rattling cough rolled over onto its side and lay still, the fierce yellow eyes slowly glazing in death.

Hidden in the tree, Llamas swore under his breath, but he did not utter a sound. He only prayed that his two colleagues would have brains enough to imitate his silence so that they did not give themselves away.

Joaquín fell on his knees before his master, sobbing, "I was afraid that something like this might happen—oh, *mi patrón, mi patrón,* how horrible—if only I had shot more swiftly—I could have prevented this attack—you who have given me new life—*Dios,* why must a good man like this be struck down, without purpose or plan?"

Joaquín vigorously ripped his *camisa* to make strips of bandage. The blood poured from both the *hacendado's* thighs, and the marks of the jaguar's brutal fangs could be seen just above the left hip bone. Holding his breath, praying for strength and dexterity, he managed to wrap several of the improvised bandages around the deepest wounds left by the savage claws, then wound other strips tightly in order to act as tourniquets.

Now, very gently, he lifted Heitor's body in his arms, slapped his own horse on the rump, and bade it return home, which it at once began to do, for he had trained it well. Then, approaching his master's stallion, which snorted and reared, terrified by the sight of the dead jaguar, he soothingly murmured, "Triunfante, brave Triunfante, you did not run when the devil cat struck at your master—do not run now, be kind to a poor *trabajador*—I must take your master back and perhaps a *médico* can save his life. Please, Triunfante, allow me to sit upon your back—unworthy as I am, I have your master with me; let us go back to the *estancia, por favor,* Triunfante!"

The black stallion turned and regarded him, then bobbed its head as if understanding. It stood docilely as Joaquín carefully put Heitor's limp body over his shoulder, then tentatively placed his left foot into the stirrups. Supporting the body of his unconscious master the whole time, Joaquín exerted all his wiry strength, gripped the saddle pommel with his right hand, and swung himself up. Then, grasping the reins and getting a tight hold with his right hand, he put his left arm around the legs of the *hacendado* who was carefully draped over his shoulder. "Now home, Triunfante, with all your speed, in the name of our most beloved Lord God!" he called, his voice choking with sobs.

After he had galloped for nearly half an hour, cradling Heitor's limp body as best he could, Joaquín at last rode into the courtyard of his master's house. He began to shout, "¡*Ayúdame, hombres!* The *señor patrón* is badly hurt—come help me, *por el amor de Dios!*"

The young stable boy Pablo was first to hear Joaquín's agonized cry and came running out of the stable. Quickly, Joaquín told him what had happened and implored, sobbing, "Ride for *el médico!* Take this horse, it is the fastest; go to Lobos and call *el médico* Arribante and bring him back quickly! Even with the tourniquet I made, the *patrón* bleeds badly, as you see. Here, I will lower him down to you. Be very careful—oh, thank you, *Dios,* for letting me return in time—if only I can save the *patrón's* life! A man like this should not die this way, it is not worthy!"

By this time, other *trabajadores* had hurried out of the bunkhouse, as well as some of the servants from the *hacienda,* while the young stable boy, swiftly mounting the black stallion, rode off in the direction of Lobos in search of the doctor. There were cries of concern and horror at the sight of Heitor's limp, bleeding body, which Joaquín now stood holding in both arms, tears flowing down his cheeks. Gently, they took Heitor from him and moved slowly toward the *hacienda,* thence to his bedchamber where one of the workers drew the sheets so that he might lie at his ease. Another began to tug off his boots as gently as possible, while Joaquín himself carefully removed the blood-soaked bandages and tourniquets, then unbuttoned and removed the remains of his master's sweat-and-bloodstained breeches.

Joaquín now turned to the others. "It was a devil cat, a jaguar, *mis amigos!*" he exclaimed. "I do not know why, but something made me want to ride with the *señor patrón* this morning and to take my rifle. I killed it, and *el Señor Dios* guided my aim with the single shot I had in that horrible moment—but it was too late to save the *patrón.* Some of you, give me those cloths to use as bandages and tourniquets so that the blood will not pour forth too much—he has already lost so much; *¡que lástima!*"

Two of the workers at once hastened to obey, while two others gently lifted the unconscious man's legs so that the new bandages and tourniquets might be applied. Benito and Enrique, who had just returned from the Maldones ranch, had been told what had happened to their father, and they hurried into the bedchamber, their features taut and incredulous. Shouldering their way among the workers who had gathered around the huge bed, they stood looking down at their father; Benito, the younger, burst into sobs. Enrique looked around, his eyes wild, his face haggard. "How did it happen? Where did he get such terrible wounds?"

"It was a jaguar, Señor Enrique," Joaquín spoke up. "I rode with him this morning. I took my rifle. I do not know why it was, but the saints must have warned me—and yet, not in time—I will always be ashamed that I could not have killed that devil cat before it leaped at my master!"

"A jaguar near Lobos? I have never heard of such a thing before," Enrique said. "But I do not doubt you, and I am grateful to you for bringing my father back." Enrique regained control of himself with a visible effort. "Has someone sent for the doctor?"

"*Pero sí,* young master," Joaquín again spoke up. "I sent the young stable boy Pablo on your father's stallion to ride to Lobos."

Heitor's eyelids wanly fluttered, and slowly he came back to consciousness. When he opened his eyes, he saw the faces of his two sons bending down close to him, Benito's streaked with tears, Enrique's grim, with tightly compressed lips and jaws. "My sons—I am glad you are here," Heitor faintly murmured, a slight smile creasing his trembling lips. Then he closed his eyes again, fighting for strength and breath.

"Lie still, *mi padre.*" Enrique solicitously touched his father's shoulder. "A doctor has been sent for; you will be fine. Rest, please rest."

Within the hour, Pablo returned to the *estancia* with the doctor, who rushed into the *hacienda* and examined the wounded man.

"The gashes of those claws are very deep," the doctor pronounced as he straightened. "He has lost so much blood that his pulse and his heartbeat are very weak."

"Will he live, *señor médico?*" Enrique anxiously demanded.

"It is in the hands of *el Señor Dios*, my boy," the old doctor admitted with a weary sigh. "I cannot tell you any more. Whoever put those tourniquets on kept him alive, that is certain. He must rest, and all we can do is pray and hope."

Again, Heitor's eyelids fluttered and finally opened, and he stared with almost a pathetic earnestness to see his sons again. Then, perceiving them, he made a weak beckoning gesture with his left forefinger.

Enrique bent down to him. "Yes, my father? What can I do to make you feel better?"

"You must not think of me now, but of both of yourselves. I think it was the *porteños* who brought this about—I cannot prove it, but it is my feeling, after I had sent off the emissary of the Minister of the Interior—you will remember how he threatened me."

"Yes, my father! And I wish I had killed him then!" Benito fiercely burst out.

"You must not harbor such thoughts now, my son." Heitor's voice nearly trailed away, and he lay back for a moment, eyes closed, fighting for his last reserves of ebbing strength. Presently he murmured, "Here in my bedchamber, on that wall opposite me, near the floorboards, you will find a secret compartment. There is a small round circle, like the indentation of a knob. If you press it, the section of the wall will open, for I had a carpenter make it when this house was built. And in there is a bag of gold."

"Do not talk as if you were dying, *mi padre*," Enrique groaned.

"Listen, my son, every man must die. That is the debt we owe *el Señor Dios* for having put us into this world. But you, you and Benito, will replace me. You are to take the gold—and you will go to the Estados Unidos in search of that *gringo* who visited here, the one who married Dorotéa Maldones, do you understand me?"

"Sí, *mi padre*." Enrique nodded, blinded by his tears. Benito also nodded, too choked up to say anything.

"He is in a country that is called Texas, *mis hijos*." Heitor's voice began to be fainter still, and his words very nearly indistinct. Enrique had to bend down with his ear nearly to his father's mouth to understand them. "You must find the Señor Baines and my friend Raoul, do you hear?"

"I swear it on the cross of *Jesucristo, mi padre*." Enrique sobbed as he made the sign of the cross.

"*Bueno*. You will be safe then, in a land where there is freedom. And when the time comes, when my friends overthrow the *porteños*, there will be time enough to return. I wish—I wish I could have been with you more, Enrique, Benito. You are—oh, *Dios*, into Thine hands I commend my spirit—look after *mis hijos*, I pray to Thee—" He tried to raise himself on the pillow, his eyes starting from their sockets, wide and glazed with a feverish glow. Then he fell back, and the doctor quickly put his hand to the *hacendado*'s heart. He sadly shook his head.

Those who had been at the bedside murmured words of commiseration; some of them wept openly, others swore profanely at the injustice of such a death. All of them had revered Heitor Duvaldo as a kind, generous master, who treated them as if they were his equals.

Enrique moved toward his brother and said, "Benito, now we must see to the burial of our father. And then we must ask the *trabajadores* and the *gauchos* of the *pampas* to help protect this place so that one day, when the *porteños* have lost their power, we can return and live here again, perhaps—and build a chapel to our father's memory."

"I would like to do that very much, Enrique," his brother murmured.

Enrique turned to Joaquín Ortega, who had bowed his head and was weeping silently. The sturdy young man put his hand on the *trabajador*'s shoulder and said, "From this moment on, I make you majordomo of the *estancia*. Tomaso died, and you will take his place. You have earned it."

"I am only a humble man, señores, I can scarcely read and write—it is too important a task—" Joaquín began, in a tone of near alarm as he stepped back and shook his head.

"I know that my father would have wished this. You will

learn to read and write, but what you have in your head is loyalty and common sense. No, you will make a very good majordomo. And when we leave for Texas—though we cannot do it now, there is too much else to be done on this estate and also at the Maldones *estancia*—then you will be in charge here, and I will ask you to protect our father's *estancia* and to send us letters telling us what is being done to the land for which my father gave up his life. Perhaps one day we shall avenge him—if God so wills."

Joaquín's voice was hoarse as again he fought for self-control. "I swear to you, *señores*, as before all the other *trabajadores* in this room and the *señor médico*, too," he said, "that I shall devote my life to guarding this *estancia* and that of the señor Maldones also. And I swear also that I will send news to you, if the *porteños* try to move against your father's property."

"I could ask no more than that from anyone. May God bless you, Joaquín!" Enrique Duvaldo extended his hand, and the *trabajador* warmly shook it.

Manuel Forlana reached Buenos Aires three days later, having paused at little farmhouses to beg for food and drink and provender for his weary mount, grandiosely promising that his benefactors would be hugely rewarded because he was on a most important mission for the government of the *unitarios*. Once he had tethered his horse to a hitching post outside the *cabildo*, he made his way to the office of Gregorio Pordoña. A uniformed soldier wearing corporal's stripes and shouldering a rifle barred his path. "Tell His Excellency that I am Manuel Forlana, and I come with news he is eager to have," the false *trabajador* insisted, puffing out his chest.

Ten minutes later, by which time the spy was almost beside himself with angry impatience, the corporal reappeared and, opening the door, gestured and said, "Go in; he is waiting for you."

"And about time, too!" Manuel insolently drawled as he strode into the foyer of the luxurious office and thence into the private office of the fat *porteño* official.

"Your Excellency, I have fulfilled my mission. The señor Duvaldo rode out, and I met your man who was waiting at the *ombú* tree. He told me to ride on and that the *patrón* would be taken care of," he at once averred.

"That is very good news indeed."

"Then I have pleased Your Excellency?"

"You have delivered an enemy up for execution, yes. But to be sure, you were a traitor in so doing, a traitor to the *hacendado* who trusted you."

Forlana did not like the turn the conversation was taking. "But, Your Excellency," he protested, taking a step forward and holding out one hand in a propitiatory gesture, "that was the task to which you assigned me. And besides, why should I be called traitorous to a man you yourself condemned as a traitor to our government?"

"It is a matter of degrees, Forlana," Pordoña said slowly, choosing his words with care while he lit a cigar. The man who stood before him looked greedily at the box and obviously hoped that he would be invited to take one, but the Minister of the Interior made no such offer. Instead, he went on, "The difference between you and the man who accomplished the execution is that you know the name of the victim. That could be dangerous for you."

"But he is a condemned traitor; you yourself practically said as much, Your Excellency!" Forlana's brow was furrowed with anxiety.

"For your own safety, you will be lodged in a cell—oh, do not worry, it will not be for long. There have been some inquiries regarding the *hacendado*, you see, and I do not wish anyone to recognize you."

"Oh, yes— yes, I see that now—forgive me, Your Excellency." Forlana almost babbled with a sigh of relief, for he was sweating as a result of the impersonal tone and biting words with which his illustrious *patrón* had welcomed him. "I will do whatever Your Excellency tells me."

"I am glad to find you of a sensible disposition, Forlana. Ah, here you are, Capitán Mendez!" Pordoña smiled and rose from his desk. Forlana turned his head, and he saw a bemedaled, tall man in the uniform of a captain of the Argentinian army, flanked by two subalterns. "Will you convey this man to a cell, as we have agreed on?" the minister said.

"At once, *excelencia!*" The captain smartly saluted, then gestured to the two subalterns, who took their places on each side of the still-mystified traitorous *trabajador*.

The two men marched Manuel Forlana out of the office and down a corridor and into another wing that led to the city jail. It was the jail in which Raoul Maldones had been imprisoned awaiting execution.

But Captain Mendez remained behind to await the further orders of the Minister of the Interior. Pordoña puffed a time at his cigar, then gestured to the captain. "Help yourself, *mi capitán.*"

"*Gracias.* I have not often had the pleasure of enjoying so superb a cigar, *excelencia.*"

"Take several to smoke later. *Bueno.* Now, as to that traitor. You will send for a priest to shrive him. You will gag him and blindfold him and then take him out to the courtyard. A firing squad will do the rest."

"I understand perfectly, *excelencia.* It will be done within the hour."

"*Bueno.* Bring me word when he is dead. As for the body, a traitor does not need Christian burial. He betrayed his master; he might well have betrayed us all. Throw him into the river and let the piranha dispose of his carcass."

Twelve

On his way back to the Double H Ranch, a sudden sandstorm had delayed John Cooper Baines for nearly two days, and he and his animals had had to take shelter on the leeward side of a giant, isolated hill. His concern was not for the possibility of running short of supplies, for he was always able to live off the land, but for the fear that he might arrive too late to be with Dorotéa when she gave birth to their child.

And so he was enormously relieved when, on the third day of April of this year of 1827, he rode through the gate of the Double H Ranch, Yankee in the lead, the packhorse following John Cooper's palomino.

The *vaquero* Antonio Lorcas was there to greet John Cooper as he dismounted in the courtyard. He had seen the tall Texan come through the gate and had also roused all the *trabajadores* and Miguel to welcome back *el Halcón.* John Cooper gripped Antonio's hand and anxiously demanded, "How is my wife, Dorotéa, *amigo?*"

"She is near her time, *Halcón*."

"Thank God I'm not too late!" He turned to the horses and patted their necks, then turned back to Antonio. "These animals were courageous and strong. Have them rubbed down and given an extra ration of grain and some carrots and sugar as a reward. Meanwhile, have some of the men bring the saddlebags to the *hacienda*. They are heavy, and their contents are valuable, so choose your best men. Many thanks, *amigo*." And then, to Miguel, who had come up, grinning from ear to ear and holding out his hand in welcome, "You old scoundrel, have you been behaving yourself while I've been away?"

Miguel assumed a hurt look of utter dejection. "*Mi compañero*, how can you say such a thing to a man with white hair on his head? Of course I have behaved myself—all is well. And with you, *Halcón*?"

"Miguel, God has been very good." And with this John Cooper told his *capataz* all about the second silver mine and the new-found riches.

"But that is wonderful, *Halcón!*" Miguel delightedly exclaimed. "It will make up for what was stolen in New Orleans—what I wouldn't give to get my hands on that clever thief!"

"One day, I'm sure, Fabien Mallard will learn who the thief was, and then there will be time to regain the silver. I only hope that can be done before this man, whoever he is, uses all that money for evil, instead of for good, as I intended to."

John Cooper now hurried into the *hacienda* and there met Doña Inez, who was walking down the hallway, having come from Dorotéa's bedchamber. She uttered a cry of joy and hurried to him. "John Cooper, I am so glad you have come back! Within a day or two, I am sure, Dorotéa will have your child."

"I, too, am grateful that I'll be here to be with her this first time. And you, Doña Inez, how goes it with you?"

"Wonderfully, dear John Cooper. Last week I had a letter from Francesca. She loves her school, and she is very much drawn to Paquita and Adriana and María. She is making new friends there, and she is most excited about it. But do not let me stand here chattering away. Dorotéa has been asking for you."

"I'll go to her at once, Doña Inez." He kissed the handsome woman on the cheek and then knocked gently on the door of the bedchamber. Dorotéa bid him enter. She was propped up by two pillows, and her face brightened with joy as she held out her arms to him. "I was praying you'd be back in time, my sweet John Cooper, *mi querido, mi corazón!*" she exclaimed.

"I thank God, too, my dearest." He cupped her cheeks in his hands and kissed her gently. "And I've come back with wonderful news, Dorotéa. The silver stolen from us in New Orleans has been replaced by a miracle—at the stronghold, an old man told me the secret of another cave to the north, which was filled with silver. I brought back four bars of it, and when I ride to New Orleans again, I'll put them in the vault. But I also found something for you, my sweetheart." From the pocket of his buckskin jacket, he now brought out the silver box containing the magnificent turquoise necklace. He took the necklace out, and as she gasped in wonder, he clasped it around her slim throat. "It becomes you, Dorotéa. And God Himself provided it as a sign that you and I are blessed, and blessed the more by the child we shall have."

Dorotéa studied the beautiful turquoises of the necklace, gently touching them with her fingers. Then she looked up at her husband, her eyes brimming with tears.

"I've got gifts for Doña Inez and Teresa as well," John Cooper said, taking Dorotéa's hand. "I found some silver rosaries in the mine, which I will present to the ladies at dinner tonight. I also have a beautiful crucifix on a chain, which I will give to Padre Pastronaz. Now you rest, my dearest one. I will visit the children and the rest of the family and be back with you shortly."

Two days later, Dorotéa's labor pains began, and she was attended by Bess Sandarbal and Concepción Morales, the good-natured wife of the assistant *capataz*, who had often served as midwife to many of the families on the Double H Ranch. Dorotéa's old nurse, Estancia, was also present, sitting by her bed and murmuring comforting words to her beloved young charge. Meanwhile, John Cooper paced up and down in the courtyard of the *hacienda*, as any father from time immemorial might have done while waiting for the birth of a child. And he prayed ardently for a son, for he had vowed that he would name the child after his first father-in-law, the late Don Diego de Escobar.

Doña Inez herself hurried out a little after midnight with

the joyous news. "You have a son, dear John Cooper! And Dorotéa and the child are well and strong—her time was very easy."

"God be praised! A son, as I prayed for—and it shall be named after your husband, Doña Inez. He will be called James, the English name for Diego. Now, may I see my wife?"

"For just a little time, *querido*. Of course, she is exhausted, and she should rest."

"Just for a moment, then. *Gracias*, Doña Inez."

"I shall go to the chapel to pray for long life to all of you," Don Diego's handsome widow declared.

Hesitantly, the tall Texan knocked at the bedroom door, and it was Bess Sandarbal who admitted him, a finger to her lips, whispering, "Not too long, John Cooper; she's done fine, but she's trying to drift off to sleep."

"I shan't keep her awake, I promise. Thank you, Bess, and you, too, Concepción."

He smiled warmly at old Estancia, who was sitting by the bed, watching over Dorotéa, her eyes filled with tears of joy. Then he knelt down and took his wife's hand. She blinked her eyes and slowly looked at him, and then an exquisite smile came to her face.

"I've given you a son, *mi corazón*," she whispered. "And he shall be named James Baines, after your father-in-law, just as we discussed."

Greatly moved, John Cooper leaned over and kissed her on the forehead. "Now you must sleep, my darling, so you'll be strong again. And thank you, thank you, Dorotéa, for being my love."

She gave a little sigh and went to sleep as he watched, and then he turned and reverently tiptoed out of the room, quietly closing the door behind him.

On this beautiful April afternoon, the church at the Double H Ranch was filled with the *vaqueros*, *trabajadores*, and their families, who wished to attend the baptism of the newly born son of John Cooper and Dorotéa Baines. Dorotéa, radiant in a white muslin dress and slippers, tenderly carried the child in his blanket, with John Cooper beside her facing the young priest. Behind them stood the godparents, Carlos de Escobar as godfather and Doña Inez as godmother.

Padre Pastronaz, wearing the silver crucifix John Cooper

had given him, turned to the congregation after having genuflected before the altar and, in a loud, clear voice, declared, "Beloved of our dear Lord, gathered here to pay homage to Thee and to thank Thee for Thy works upon this bounteous earth, today is truly a time for rejoicing. By this act of baptism, we prepare to bring another soul toward Him Who is the Maker of us all. It is a time for the reaffirmation of the faith of each one of you here, man, woman, and child, and an augury for the future of this lifetime, for which we pray that peace and prosperity and the fulfillment of hope and love be granted to us."

After a low chorus of "Amen" from the congregation, Padre Pastronaz turned to John Cooper and Dorotéa. "What name do you give your child?"

John Cooper looked at his beautiful young wife and nodded, and she returned his smile and said, "It is that of James, *mi padre*."

The young priest now asked, "What do you ask of God's church for James Baines?"

"Baptism, *mi padre*," Dorotéa answered.

The priest waited a moment and then said, "You have asked to have your child baptized. In doing so, you are accepting the responsibility of training him in the practice of the faith. It will be your duty, thus, to bring him up to keep God's Commandments by loving God and our neighbors. Do you clearly understand what you are undertaking?" He glanced at each of them, and John Cooper and Dorotéa said in unison, "We do, *mi padre*."

Now, making a sign to Carlos and Doña Inez to step forward, he turned to them and asked, "Are you ready to help the parents of this child in their duty as Christian parents?"

"We are," Carlos and Doña Inez chorused.

Then the priest lifted his hand and made the sign of the cross and said, "James Baines, this Christian community welcomes you with great joy. In its name I claim you for Christ our Savior by the sign of His cross, which I now trace on your forehead." With this, he made the sign of the cross on the baby's forehead, then turned to the pulpit and read from the Gospel according to the Apostle Matthew. Doña Inez and Carlos, who knew the words by heart, repeated them aloud, as did Dorotéa, while John Cooper bowed his head and said a prayer, as he glanced at the baby in his young wife's arms.

A hush fell upon the congregation as Padre Pastronaz took from the altar a little vial of sanctified oil and came forward. At the priest's sign, Dorotéa held out the child, and Padre Pastronaz declared, "We anoint you with the oil of salvation in the name of Christ, our Savior. May He strengthen you with His power, Who lives and reigns forever and ever." And as all said "Amen," the priest anointed the child on the breast with the oil.

Now he moved toward the font, and after addressing the congregation once more and then asking the child's parents and godparents to reaffirm their belief in God and in Jesus Christ, he baptized the child, saying, "I baptize you James Baines in the name of the Father." Pouring water upon the child's breast, he said, "And of the Son." And then for the second time he poured water upon the baby's breast and said, "And of the Holy Spirit." Finally he poured water for the third time.

There was a long pause as he knelt to pray. Finally, the priest rose and stood before the altar, addressing the whole assembly: "In the name of this child, let us pray together in the words our own Lord has given us."

From the lips of the congregation, there came the Lord's Prayer. John Cooper glanced up at the altar once and was greatly moved to see the priest, his head bowed in prayer, lovingly touching the beautiful silver crucifix around his neck.

Now Padre Pastronaz blessed the mother, who held the child in her arms, then the father, then the godparents, and finally the entire assembly. And then he knelt before the altar, bowed his head, and prayed.

John Cooper put his arm around Dorotéa's waist and proudly led her out of the church. There were tears in his eyes, for he felt the true mysticism of the ceremony and the beauty of it. Men of good works and of good will would stand to confound the evil ones, he knew. That was what his mother had once told him, and now that memory was revived by this ceremony of eternal faith.

The day after the baptism, the young New Orleans doctor named André Malmorain took leave of the friends he had made at the Double H Ranch as he began his return journey to New Orleans. He had stayed on many weeks after the death of his patient, Don Diego de Escobar, at the request of Sister Eufemia, who had discovered that a number of the workers' children had come down with the whooping cough. The doctor had been able to cure all of his young patients and had made several recommendations to Sister Eufemia for the provision of medical supplies that, indeed, he volunteered to have shipped back to the ranch as soon as he reached New Orleans. By now, the resident doctor of the ranch, Pablo Aguirrez, had returned with his family from a visit to Mexico City, and he thoroughly approved of everything Dr. Malmorain had done in his absence.

"You are taking the Jicarilla brave, Lortaldo, with you, aren't you, Dr. Malmorain?" Carlos de Escobar asked as André packed his belongings. It had been Carlos who had brought the young brave to the *hacienda*, promising to provide him with the opportunity to learn the ways of white man's medicine.

The doctor replied, "Yes, he's a fine, intelligent young man, and I see that he has a healing gift already and a desire to learn all he can. He will go back with me as my apprentice. He will spend some time in the hospital, for occasionally I provide a clinic for those who cannot afford medical treatment. And it's quite possible that after his apprenticeship is up, he could return to his people and use his knowledge to help them."

"That's excellent!" Carlos exclaimed. "And Epanone? They are such a loving couple, it will be hard for her to remain here while he is away in New Orleans."

"But I have already talked with them both, M'sieu de Escobar," the genial young physician answered. "Epanone is even now attending Sister Eufemia's school, for she wishes to acquire greater knowledge in reading and writing so that she can be a better wife to a husband who intends to be a doctor. In addition, she has volunteered to help with the little ones. It will keep her busy and cheerful. Perhaps when M'sieu Baines goes again to New Orleans on a cattle drive, she might be able to accompany him and visit her husband at least once or twice during the year ahead."

"You have found an ideal solution to a problem that greatly concerned me," Carlos averred. "I will send two *vaqueros* with you, with plenty of provisions for the journey and also arms enough in the event that you and Lortaldo should be in need of a guard. I would advise you to watch out for Mexican patrols—my *vaqueros* know by now the areas in which these patrols are most usually found and will avoid them." His face sobered, and he held out his hand. "I wish to thank you again for the loving care you gave to my father, Dr. Malmorain. You made his last days easier, and what I am most grateful for is that you were able to preserve his life long enough for him to know the vindication that came from his native country. I am in your debt. Do send letters back to us to let us know how Lortaldo progresses with his studies."

"Of a certainty. I am happy to have made your friendship, M'sieu de Escobar. And as I said, I'll see to it that a wagonload of medical supplies useful for your needs here will go back with your *vaqueros*."

"If you will see Fabien Mallard, our factor in New Orleans, he will pay you at once for whatever you send us."

"I shall communicate with him directly when I reach New Orleans, M'sieu de Escobar. Again, my sincere thanks for the hospitality you've extended to me. And may I say also that your fee was far too generous—"

"I do not wish to hear you say a thing like that because I do not measure life in terms of *pesos*." Carlos's friendly smile softened the abrupt words. "Well now, may your journey be pleasant with nothing to mar its enjoyment."

Thirteen

Christophe Carrière had proceeded cautiously since his return to New Orleans the last week of the previous December. He had rightly reasoned that the display of too much sudden wealth would draw unwanted attention to his presence in the city and might lead banking officials, who were notoriously inclined to gossip and to brag about their clients, to think that perhaps this wealth might have come from the daring robbery of the Banque de la Nouvelle Orléans. Apart from the purchase of the elegant house on the rue de Carondelet, he had sensibly kept from mingling too often with the elite of New Orleans society. It was true that he enjoyed the theater and an occasional operatic concert, but to be seen often at such entertainment might expose him to needless risks.

So he was content to live quietly with Amy Daroudier, whom he had met on a ship out of Le Havre and whom he had persuaded to become his mistress. She returned with him to New Orleans after he had completed his affairs in depositing substantial amounts of the stolen money in Paris, Amsterdam, and London banks, as well as selling the jewels stolen from the vault to an unscrupulous Parisian jeweler for half their value so that he might have usable funds without touching any of his bank capital.

The illegitimate daughter of a count and the count's seamstress mistress, Amy Daroudier was as fiercely opportunistic as her lover. Not acknowledged by her father, who had given her impoverished mother hardly any money for the child's support, Amy had grown up in a squalid Parisian house to find herself snubbed and insulted by her schoolmates because she had no father. And she had resolved to lift herself out of the obscurity and squalor of poverty by whatever means were presented to her. Having briefly been the mistress of a wealthy English businessman she met in Paris, she adopted the name of Amy, the anglicized form of Aimée.

Thus far, she had not regretted her bargain with Carrière. She knew him to be wealthy, even though he had carefully hidden from her the secret of his wealth, simply telling her that he had made speculative land investments and bought up properties condemned because of delinquent taxes. So long as he provided her with the finest food and wine, elegant clothes and jewels—and even more so, because he was still young and handsome and virile enough to satisfy her exceptionally passionate nature—she was quite content to remain with him. She sensed at times, even in his moments of reticence, that he was capable of outlandish deeds that would bring him even greater wealth and, for her in turn, even more gratifying material rewards in exchange for her erotic submission to his often sadistically tinged whims.

Of his previous life, he had told her only that he had a score to settle with a certain young lady named Madeleine de Courvent, whose father had insultingly refused to consider his suitorship for her hand in marriage. When he told her these things, his eyes glittered and his jaw worked convulsively, and Amy thought him a man possessed. But she had readily agreed to help him get his revenge. It would be, in a sense, her own revenge against the pampered, high-born young women in Paris who had never had to want for a meal, a fine new dress, or a jeweled bauble, while she had had to sell her body to the highest bidder like any *putaine*.

Carrière had allowed Amy to hire the servants, so that there was a majordomo, Joseph Lacombe, a distinguished-looking, tall, gray-haired man who had been bankrupt and who with almost pitiful gratitude had accepted employment in this menial and domestic role, because at least it would give him a further taste of the luxury he himself had once been able to afford. There was also an excellent Belgian cook, Maurice Arnaut, a man in his midforties, plump and jovial, which spoke well for his enjoyment of gourmet foods and a temperament that presented no problems to the Carrière household. In addition, Amy had engaged a personal maid, a twenty-eight-year-old former *midinette* named Élise Barlier, whose face was pitted with smallpox and, perhaps even because of her earlier misfortunes, worked with a diligence and perseverance rare in domestics. Finally, Amy had hired a coachman, Georges Meunier, for Carrière had purchased both an enclosed carriage for bad weather and a calash. Georges Meunier was expert with horses, having grown up on a Missouri farm; he now resided in the living quarters of the small carriage house at the back of the courtyard of Carrière's fine house.

During the first week of February, Carrière had sent a note to his newly appointed factor, Étienne Remontrier, a Creole like himself. Remontrier was a man of forty-five, heavyset, with thick jowls; shrewd, narrowly set gray eyes that held a constant look of suspicion; and a luxuriously thick, dark brown beard flecked with gray. He had sideburns to match. He dressed like a dandy, with audaciously bold cravats and ruffled silk shirts and gaudily buttoned waistcoats made to his order by the most expensive tailor in New Orleans. Carrière admired this, for it issued a challenge to the entire world, as if to say, "I am who I am, and to hell with you, *messieurs*! Are you not envious of my elegance and grooming?"

The note Carrière sent had invited his factor to supper with him. Because he wished Amy to realize the total scope of his power and his unflinching determination to gain his revenge on Madeleine de Couvrent, Carrière asked her to attend, also, as *maîtresse en titre*.

In a beautiful blue brocaded gown, a necklace of tiny but perfect pearls around her slim throat, the tall, black-haired Amy Daroudier presided at the head of the table. Étienne Remontrier could not take his eyes from her during the lavish supper, which the Belgian cook had taken special pains to prepare.

Carrière let the conversation drift from topic to topic, without once coming to the chief point of information, until after the dessert, when coffee and brandy and cigars were served by the majordomo. Then he said to his mistress, "*Chérie*, if the smell of strong tobacco offends you, you may withdraw. Otherwise, you will certainly be welcome, if you choose to stay."

"I should like to very much. And I love good, strong tobacco, *m'amour*," she huskily murmured, giving him a lascivious glance.

He smiled, dabbed at his sensual lips with a fine lace-trimmed napkin, and then pushed the cigar box over to his factor, who lit a cigar and leaned back, luxuriating over its bouquet. "M'sieu Carrière, you know how to live," he at last declared. "I don't think I've had a finer supper anywhere in New Orleans. That's the highest praise I can pay your cook."

"Arnaut will be enchanted to hear you say so, M'sieu Remontrier," Amy put in with a dazzling smile, her green eyes luminous as she considered the two men. Her quick mind was alert for all the nuances of the discussion that she was sure would be of particular interest to herself.

Carrière drew on his cigar and sent a cloud of smoke up toward the ceiling. "Now then, M'sieu Remontrier, you'll recall that when I engaged you not quite two months ago, you mentioned to me that M'sieu Joseph de Courvent owed the city tax collector something like eight thousand dollars, and that his note to the bank would fall due within two weeks."

"I remember it very well. And knowing how you felt about the matter, I did not wish to come to you until I had news that would really please you, M'sieu Carrière," the factor declared. He poured himself some of the brandy, took a sip, smacked his lips, took a larger sip, then reluctantly set the goblet down and drew on his cigar. Finally he put that down and then went on, "After that daring robbery last year at the Banque de la Nouvelle Orléans, in which M'sieu de Courvent kept his savings, he found himself in dire financial straits. He was not able to meet that note, and so the property was declared forfeit. Just yesterday, M'sieu Carrière, as per your instructions, I went to the tax collector's office, paid up the delinquent taxes, and received title to the house of M'sieu Joseph de Courvent."

"Excellent! You've done well, Remontrier!" Carrière exclaimed, his eyes narrowing and a cruel little smile curving his mouth. "And what else?"

"You told me that you wished to see M'sieu de Courvent out on the street. Well, he has not yet reached that degree of poverty, but he and his daughter have been obliged to take a very inexpensive apartment in a rather unsavory section of our city."

"Even better! And what else have you learned about his financial affairs?" Carrière pursued as he leaned forward toward his factor, his eyes intent on the latter's thickly jowled face.

Remontrier, who was perspiring from his overindulgence in food and wine, drew out a silk handkerchief and mopped his face. He took another sip of brandy before continuing, "Some of his investments were in shipping, M'sieu Carrière. Unfortunately, two vessels in which he had a large financial interest were sent to the bottom of the ocean by buccaneers, and the cargo was lost without hope of redemption. As to the cash he had on hand, he has been tempted into playing *baccarat*, *chemin-de-fer*, and *vingt-et-un*. One of my friends attends the most luxurious gambling salon in all New Orleans and told me last week that he observed M'sieu de Courvent at the roulette wheel and that when the night was finished, the gentleman had lost at least two thousand dollars. He rose from the table and walked out of the salon as if he were in a trance. And the despair in his face, my friend told me, could have been done justice only by the finest of portrait painters."

"Better and better!" Carrière grinned. "If he plunges into gambling, it must be that he knows how shaky his financial situation is. And because of that spoiled daughter of his, he naturally seeks to recoup."

"Exactly, M'sieu Carrière," the factor agreed. He reached a hand toward the decanter, then drew back, perhaps out of fear that Carrière would consider him too greedy.

"Go ahead, help yourself, *mon ami*," Carrière graciously urged. "You've already earned the two-thousand-dollar bonus I promised you for buying de Courvent's house for me."

"I took the liberty of putting it in my own name, M'sieu Carrière," the factor said with an unctuous smile, "because title can be transferred whenever you wish it. There's no need to call any suspicious attention to you. If, for example, M'sieu de Courvent were to find out from information in the records at the courthouse that it was you who purchased the house, he would know who his enemy really is."

"I told you I like your intelligence, Remontrier, and you show even greater signs tonight." Carrière sat back in his chair and smiled indulgently at his factor.

"It is really none of my affair, M'sieu Carrière," the factor tentatively began, "but I'm curious to know why you hate this man so much. Oh, yes, I understand that he refused to let you marry his daughter—"

Remontrier suddenly stopped speaking. There was something about the way Carrière's eyes glittered and the way he gripped the end of the table that made the factor think he was talking to a madman. But at last the other man relaxed, and his handsome face resumed its normal expression.

"I will tell you something I did not mean to tell you, Remontrier, because now I think I can trust you," Carrière began slowly, gaining control of his emotions. "My father was once one of Napoleon's most admired seamen. When Lord Nelson's English fleet attacked the French and destroyed almost all of Napoleon's ships, my father fled and outdistanced all of his pursuers. He made his way to Cuba, signed on an additional crew that would be loyal to him, and became a pirate."

"*Mon Dieu!*" Étienne Remontrier gasped, and promptly helped himself to more brandy.

"He had married a lovely young woman from an aristocratic French family, my mother. When she discovered that my father had become a pirate, she took her own life. I was then five. My father made his base in Florida, where he brought me and an attractive wench he had found in Havana and married so that I might have a mother in my early years. Later, he purchased a fine little house here in New Orleans itself, as well as a plantation upriver. But five years after that, he was captured by the crew of an American frigate, brought ashore at Charleston, and was hanged in the public square."

"*C'est incroyable!*" the factor said, setting down his goblet and staring at Christophe Carrière with openmouthed astonishment.

"So here I was at nineteen, once the news had reached New Orleans, treated little better than a leper. It was foreordained that no matter what I did, I would go through the rest of my life known only as the son of an executed pirate. I could have become one of the most wealthy men in New Orleans, but it would not have mattered to a man like Joseph de Courvent. No, *mon ami*," he said with a little laugh, his eyes once again glittering, "I swear he would rather have married that virginal daughter of his to a drooling old fool smitten with the French pox because at least that man's antecedents were impeccable, than have her wed to me. You see, my friend, by bankrupting Joseph de Courvent and by forcing Madeleine de Courvent to come to me on her knees, I get back at these pretentious snobs who can judge a man's life by what happened to his father. I can assure you that, had my father not been so unlucky as to have been captured, but had become a great buccaneer like Henry Morgan or Sir Francis Drake, why, these fine citizens of New Orleans would today sing his praises and look upon me as the most eligible of bachelors. Now you understand. And I need not say that what I have told you is not to be bruited around the city. It will be our secret together, M'sieu Remontrier." Once again he leaned back in his chair and contemplated the factor, who was convinced he was working for a madman.

"To be sure—I wouldn't violate your confidence," Étienne Remontrier began, attempting to pacify him. "You've made me a pretty penny already, and besides, I rather like the idea of turning the tables on the snobs. *Le bon Dieu* knows that I myself have met enough of them. Yes, the thing to do is to have money enough so that you needn't bother about their jibes and petty little judgments."

"I have all that money and a good deal more. Well then, let us shake hands to our mutually profitable association and to the day M'sieu de Courvent and his daughter are out on the street. You shall be well rewarded for that day, so make it come as quickly as you can, *mon ami*." Carrière rose from the table and held out his hand, which his factor firmly gripped. Amy Daroudier watched them and smiled to herself, thinking what a fool that de Courvent girl was to have turned her back on someone like Christophe Carrière.

Joseph de Courvent uttered a soft groan and looked down at the floor in an attitude of total dejection as he sat before the desk of the genial Eugene Beaubien, president of La Banque de la Nouvelle Orléans.

"Courage, *mon ami*," Beaubien soothingly placated. "I know that you've had staggering reverses, what with the unfortunate robbery of our bank and the loss of your ships. Alas, you were not the only one who lost nearly everything—if only I could find out the identity of that clever scoundrel, I'd see that he was dangling from a lamppost in the Vieux Carré! And indeed, I'd help pull the rope myself—but only after I'd forced him to reveal the hiding place of all the monies and jewels and other articles of value that he cleared out of our vault."

"So you've found nothing to date on that score?" De Courvent slowly looked up, his eyes pleading, a patina of sweat on his flabby jowls. In his fifties, nearly bald, with a small, ascetic mouth and the prominent beak of a hawklike nose, he looked as if he had had little sleep in the last several weeks—and that indeed was true. His clothes unkempt, his beard in need of trimming, his eyes bloodshot, he no longer looked the part of one of the most affluent and distinguished citizens of New Orleans.

Beaubien shook his head and said, "M'sieu Mallard, factor for my esteemed client in Texas, M'sieu John Cooper Baines, has been scouring the city for news of any unusual shows of good fortune ever since the robbery. Thus far, he's found nothing. No, M'sieu de Courvent, I cannot offer you any hope, at least not in the immediate future, of regaining what was stolen from you. And unfortunately, there is no existing law in these young United States that provides indemnity for those whose funds are stolen by acts of violence or cunning theft. But so much for that. I wish I could help you, but the fact is that I have barely enough for my own family, let alone offering you a loan."

"No, that's all right. I still—I still have some ready cash at my disposal," de Courvent said in a dull tone as he rose from his chair. "The worst blow of all was to lose my fine house that my father left me and to have my daughter cast out of her birthplace and have to make do in a squalid little apartment. Well, I didn't mean to burden you with my problems, M'sieu Beaubien. Tonight I shall go to La Maison d'Espoir and pray that my luck will turn."

"I wish you all the luck in the world, M'sieu de Courvent."

But the bank president's wishes for Joseph de Courvent's

good fortune were never realized. That night the unfortunate older gentleman lost all his remaining money at the gambling salon and was so distraught he fainted as he left the establishment. A driver of a calash saw him and kindly took him home—to the little apartment on DuBoisset Square, where de Courvent's daughter, Madeleine, saw that her father was put to bed.

The next morning, matters turned for the worse—if such was possible. Étienne Remontrier had done his work well and had bribed the de Courvents' landlord to evict the father and daughter. Charging Joseph de Courvent with irresponsibility and penury, the landlord called in the bailiff, who gave Madeleine and her father one hour to vacate the premises.

After the bailiff left, Joseph promptly shoved the bolt home and, trembling uncontrollably, turned to his daughter. It was only with the greatest effort that he forced himself to speak audibly. "Come into the study, my dear," he murmured. "I have something to give you. Please hurry—there isn't much time."

Wonderingly, the young woman followed her father. She wore a simple blue frock, and now at the age of twenty-one, she was in the full bloom of her virginal beauty. The mournful poignance of her large eyes, the pure oval of her face with her slightly high-set cheekbones, the firm yet sweet mouth that bespoke a latent sensuousness . . . these things stamped her as an eminently desirable beauty and explained Christophe Carrière's almost obsessive passion for her.

Father and daughter entered a small room that he had converted into his study. In one corner was a large, ornate satinwood secretary, and Joseph opened it, then put his forefinger to a circular indentation in a wooden panel at the left, causing a secret drawer to spring out. He put his hand into it and drew out a leather pouch. "It has a few gold pieces, my dear. It's all I have to bequeath to you, I'm afraid. I can't give you any advice, except to go to my friends and see if they can place you in some situation."

"Please, dear Papa, it sounds so f–final. But we'll be together—"

"Madeleine," he interrupted, pressing the pouch into her faltering hands, "you were bred to be a lady, but alas, now that you must earn your own living, you may have to descend to the role of governess or tutoress to some wealthy family. I can think of two families who may yet have some sentiment for you, the de Mourniers and the Lachises, for they at least have always befriended us." He uttered a heavy sigh. "I approached some I thought were my true friends, asking them to help me out of this dreadful situation—and I found that they were simply fair-weather friends. I hope I am not disappointed by the de Mourniers or the Lachises."

"I—I'll remember—but where shall we go now? This money you've given me—I'll use it to find another apartment—"

"It's most important that you think of yourself now, more than ever, and of your livelihood, *ma chérie*," was Joseph de Courvent's only response. "And now, if you'll excuse me for a moment, I must make myself more presentable. I tell you what—go out to the stairwell and tell that importunate bailiff that we will be out presently."

Distraught by her father's strange attitude, Madeleine hesitated. Then, as he kissed her on the cheek and gave her a very gentle shove toward the door, she at last left him.

Joseph made the sign of the cross against his clammy forehead and then pressed another circular hollow in a panel on the other side of the secretary. Once again, a drawer opened, and he reached for its contents: a pearl-handled pistol. He looked up at the ceiling and murmured a silent prayer, then put the pistol to his forehead and pulled the trigger.

Madeleine was in the act of opening the apartment door when she heard the shot. With a terrible premonition, she uttered a shriek as she hurried back into the little study room. She found her father lying on his back in front of the secretary, the pistol still gripped in his right hand, a small, bluish hole in the center of his forehead.

"Oh, no! Papa, why did you do this? I would have helped—I wouldn't have been a burden to you—oh, dear God, I'm lost now—I'm all alone. Oh, Papa, Papa, you didn't need to die. It doesn't matter that we've lost all the money; I've such faith in you. I know you would have gotten it all back—you were so good and wise. Oh, what am I to do now?" She wrung her hands, bursting into hysterical sobs.

The bailiff, a fat, bearded man carrying the official eviction notice, was puzzled by this outburst, and he stomped into the room. He was about to order the couple out at once when he saw Joseph de Courvent's body. "Holy Mother of God!" he muttered, crossing himself. "He couldn't face being out on the street without a red cent—well, I don't think your landlord counted on anything like this. Now I'll have to get the civil guards to remove the body—devil take it to be in a profession like mine, because I can't help feeling that if I hadn't brought this eviction notice, he'd still be alive this minute. It's a shame what a decent man has to do to earn an honest living these days!" Then, in a tone he sought to make kindly, he cleared his throat and said to the kneeling, distraught young woman, who scarcely heard him, "I'm awfully sorry, young lady—twasn't my doing, I'll have you know that. I'm sorry. Take your time about getting out of here. I'll have the civil guards come for him directly. Well, I guess that's about it." And then, as she continued to sob and to cup her father's dead face in her hands, the bailiff winced, shook his head, and hurried back down the stairs to tell the landlord of the tragic event.

Outside, three tough, insolent-looking street urchins between the ages of ten and thirteen watched the bailiff and the landlord come out onto the street. The oldest one of them, with dirty face and tattered clothes, crept closer so that he could eavesdrop on the conversation. "It's a clear case of suicide, Mr. Jacquinot," the bailiff was saying to the landlord. "He had the pistol in his right hand, so there's no question of the young lady doing him in. I'm afraid you'll have to be a bit patient—I'll have the civil guards take the body away at once."

"The reputation of my house—it will be difficult for me to find another tenant if the scandal of this gets out!" the landlord wailed.

The bailiff gave him a contemptuous look and then shrugged. "That's your affair, Mr. Jacquinot. Me, I just did my duty. And I don't mind telling you I didn't relish what happened for my having done it, either. Look to your own conscience. And leave everything as it is. I'll have to make a report to the civil guard, but as I said, they'll be here directly."

The dirty urchin crept back to his two cronies and muttered, "I'll go back to the boss, now, 'n I betcha he'll pay us good fer what I jist found out!"

"What's that, Tom?" the youngest boy piped up.

"The old man did hisself in jist now. The civil guard's comin' fer his body. Wait a bit—the boss said we wuz to find out what happened to his girl—you better stay on here, Jeremy, 'n you too, Benny, 'n see what she does. I'll tell the boss you'll be watchin'."

"Sure, Tom. Only mind you don't spend the cash he gives you fer wut we done so far," the youngest urchin warned.

"Fat chance, with you 'n Benny here always keepin' tabs on me," the oldest boy retorted. "Well, I'm off, now." And with this, he began to run down the street on his way back to Étienne Remontrier.

Her eyes swollen from weeping, Madeleine de Courvent went out into the street an hour after the civil guard had removed her father's body. She had given one of the men a gold piece from the little purse that Joseph de Courvent had handed to her before taking his own life, and she pleaded with the man to see to it that her father received a Christian burial. Feeling sorry for the plight of the young woman, he solemnly assured her that he would.

Not having the heart to see her beloved father laid to rest in some pauper's cemetery, Madeleine went on her way. Carrying her reticule and an old, worn leather case in which she had hastily packed a few dresses and changes of undergarments, she began to walk toward the center of the city. Perhaps there would be a rooming house where the money her father had given her would keep her for a few weeks until she could find some way of earning her livelihood.

Two of the street urchins who had watched the bailiff and his men come to the house had remained, at the older boy's order, to keep surveillance over her and to learn where she went. They ambled at a good distance behind her, so that she could hardly suspect that she was being followed. At last she came to the rue de Jaboulet and saw a hand-lettered sign in a shuttered window offering a room for rent. With a sigh, she climbed onto the little porch just off the fenced-in yard and, setting down the case, put her hand to the knocker and rapped it three loud times.

A blousy woman, who came to the door wiping her hands on a dirty dishtowel, confronted her. "I—I'm here about the room," Madeleine stammered.

"All right, now. It's two dollars a week, 'n you gits breakfast, if you ain't too fussy. All I serve my boarders is coffee 'n biscuits most of the time—"

"That—that will be quite satisfactory," the young woman wearily responded.

"My now, ain't you a lady, though; I kin tell jist by the

way you talk. All right, then, come in—cash in advance now, mind!"

Madeleine opened the purse and took out another gold piece, which she pressed into the woman's grimy hand. The latter eyed it, bit it, and grinned, revealing several missing and several decayed teeth. "Well now, you kin stay here for a month on this, missy, 'n I'll see if I can't also scrounge up somepin' fer yer supper every so often—but don't you go talkin' about it when yer at the breakfast table with my other boarders. I got two, 'n one's an old lady who's deaf, 'n the other's an old man who's the worst busybody I ever done seen in all my born days. Come in, come in, I'll show you where the room is. On the second floor, the last one at the back on the right."

"I—I can find it, thank you so much," Madeleine said sighing. She ascended the stairs, while the woman waited below, still wiping her hands and calling directions. Then, grinning, she took out the gold piece, bit it again and pocketed it, then marched back to her kitchen with a thoroughly satisfied air.

The following day about noon, after a virtually sleepless night, Madeleine chose her best frock and walked a good two miles to the house of the de Mourniers. It was on St. Louis Avenue, a stately old house behind a high metal gate and with a balcony set with wrought iron in the form of the *fleur-de-lis*. She hesitated a moment, then took a deep breath, opened and closed the gate behind her with a soft clang, then ascended to the porch and rapped on the door. After a few moments, an elderly woman servant opened to her knock and quizzically peered at her. "Yes, missy?"

"I—my name is Madeleine de Courvent, and I should like very much to see Madame de Mournier, if I may."

"I'm real sorry, missy; they sailed off to France last week, and I don't know when they'll be back. I'm the housekeeper, you see. A pity you missed them—they friends of yours?"

"I—yes—yes, and of my poor father. Well, th-thank you."

"I tell you what, missy, I'll write them you came here to see them. Maybe when they get back they'll come looking for you—do they know where you live?"

"No—not now—I—when they come back, I—I'll come see them again. Thank you very much."

"Quite welcome, I'm sure. Sorry I can't be of any more help, missy."

"It—it's not your fault. Thank you again." Madeleine went out, closing the gate behind her, and stood for a long moment, a feeling of desolation sweeping over her. It would be all too easy to give way to tears, and she had already shed enough for her father. Perhaps the Lachises—they were only a few blocks away, as she remembered. She brightened and turned in that direction.

Five minutes later, she knocked on the door of the Lachise house, and a black butler in livery opened the door to her and then unctuously bobbed his head and wished her a good afternoon.

"Would you please tell Madame Lachise that Madeleine de Courvent would like to see her for a moment, if I'm not disturbing her?" Madeleine anxiously asked.

"Y'all jist come right in now, missy, and y'all sit yoself down and make yoself comfortable. Ah'll go tell madame directly."

"Thank you very much." Madeleine was able to force a grateful smile. Perhaps this was a sign of a light in the darkness of her desolation. She seated herself in the fashionably furnished salon and, touching her hair with her slim fingers, tried to make herself as presentable as she could. She had not used any rice powder, and she should have brushed and combed her hair until it was glossier, she knew. But after the past week or two, such primping had been the least of her concerns.

A few moments later, Madame Genevieve Lachise entered the room, a woman in her early fifties, elegantly gowned, her fingers bejeweled and a pearl necklace around her plump throat. Her husband was a factor with offices at the wharf, and he represented a number of mercantile firms in France whose cargos were regularly shipped into New Orleans. On several occasions, Madeleine and her father had attended a special supper or a gala ball given at the Lachise home for visiting members of the French nobility.

"My dear girl, how nice of you to call!" Genevieve Lachise held out her hands, and Madeleine gripped them and nodded with a smile. "Now, as you see, I'm all in a dither because some important clients have just arrived from Paris and Louis is taking me to a restaurant with them this evening. He may have a new account, you see, and we must make a very good impression. What can I do for you, dear Madeleine?"

"You—you haven't heard, then?"

"Why no, what should I have heard?"

"That—that my father is dead."

"*Mon Dieu!* What dreadful news! You poor darling! You have my deepest condolences."

"I—I came to ask a great favor of you, Madame Lachise."

"Oh?" The plump dowager arched her eyebrows and regarded Madeleine with a wary look. "And what is it, *ma chérie?*"

"Madame Lachise, you—you have two sons, as I remember—"

"Yes, my dear, so I have."

"And they have little children, do they not?"

"That's true. But I fail to see—"

"Please—I—my father died, as I said, and he was almost penniless. He gave me a little money, and it's all I have in the world. Madame Lachise, I must earn my way. I thought that perhaps you might recommend me to your sons, as a nurse or governess for their children."

"Oh, my poor girl! Really, Madeleine, you don't know what you're asking!"

"But—"

"Please, my dear. Why, they would be as offended as my husband and I would be to offer you such a domestic or menial position—you, so elegant a young lady. You see, my dear, the fact is that both of them have already engaged nurses. Besides, the position wouldn't suit you. The wages are really very low, if I say so myself. They would hardly keep you in the fine clothes a well-reared young woman like yourself should wear. My advice to you is to seek something worthy of your station—and then, too, you are at an age, as I recall, for marriage. That would solve all your problems, my dear Madeleine."

"It would, if I had any suitors. But my father's financial losses—"

Madame Lachise's face congealed, and she nodded, putting a plump forefinger to her lips. "Oh, yes, now I recall. Louis was saying something to me about that only the other day. My, my, my, such a shame, such a tragedy. I wish there were something we could do."

Madeleine understood only too well. The Lachises were

not really such close friends to her father as that unfortunate man had believed. And the insincerity of the woman's voice was like the lash of a whip to the sensitive, sheltered young woman. She rose abruptly. "I've taken too much of your time. Please excuse me," she said coldly.

"Jasper will show you to the door, my dear. I would do so, but I really must finish my preparations for this evening, you understand. I wish you *bonne chance, ma chérie*. And do please come tell me how you've made out. I should really like to know."

But Madeleine had turned her back to the dowager and was going to the door by herself. Opening it without a word, she went out into the street.

During the two following days, Madeleine tried to find a domestic post, her landlady having mentioned that there was a woman on Eglantine Street who occasionally sent young women out as governesses and maids. The proprietress turned out to be a brothel owner who had come from Natchez after her competitors had forced her out of business. When she learned Madeleine's background, she sniffed and shook her head, "Forget it, dearie, a high-toned fancy lady wouldn't do for these swells, but I can put you in a place where you'll make lots more money and maybe get yourself a fancy gentle-man to look after you permanent-like." When she intimated how this could be brought about, Madeleine uttered a horri-fied cry and, her face scarlet, hastily left the madam's small office.

The next day, having placed a small advertisement in the newspaper, she received a letter urging her to come for an interview. She spent a dollar out of her dwindling handful of gold coins to take a calash to the address, for it was on the eastern side of the city in an isolated, luxurious old house. Out of forethought, she had the driver wait for her, and it was well that she did: The house was occupied by an old satyr and his domineering housekeeper, a woman in her midforties, coarsely handsome and viciously perverse. To her horror, Madeleine learned that if she accepted the post, she would be expected to cater to the carnal whims of both her em-ployer and the housekeeper. She fled back to the calash and had herself driven to the boardinghouse.

Once in her room, she gave vent to a hysterical fit of crying, for never had things seemed so black. There was enough money for perhaps three more weeks, if she were frugal, but her experiences in seeking work had already proved so shattering to her morale that for a moment she even thought of leaving New Orleans and seeking her livelihood elsewhere. Yet common sense told her that such an attempt might prove as fruitless as what she had already experienced.

The urchins Étienne Remontrier had hired to keep an eye on Madeleine had done their work well and had reported Madeleine's whereabouts to the factor, who in turn passed the information on to Christophe Carrière. But Carrière and Amy Daroudier had no need of this news as they had already read Madeleine's advertisement seeking work. Now the son of the executed pirate determined that he would pounce upon his long-awaited prey. Accordingly, Carrière told Amy, "You'll go to Madeleine de Courvent's boardinghouse this evening and tell her that you saw the advertisement. Tell her that you're ready to offer her steady employment, and that she will be tutoring a very clever boy."

"How deliciously cruel you are, *m'amour*." Amy giggled as she wound her satiny arms around his neck and intimately pressed her body against his. "And you promise you will let me help make her your slave? It will pay me back for my own unhappy times."

"I'm counting on you to enslave her, *mignonne*," he said chuckling, his hands fondling her hips and breasts. "You will make my revenge the sweeter by enjoying your own. But take care; she must suspect nothing. Bring her back to me, and this very night you shall begin training her in her new life as a slave who must expiate her family's insolence to me—so he would rather have seen himself in hell than accept me as his son-in-law, would he? Ah, in a sense, *ma belle* Amy, I hope that there is life after death so that the estimable Joseph de Courvent will be aware of how Madeleine herself, his precious virginal daughter, will be in hell because of his erroneous judgment of me!"

"Missy, there's a smart-lookin' carriage outside, 'n a mighty fancy lady come callin' fer you!" the landlady excitedly exclaimed. She had come upstairs to knock on Madeleine's door about two hours after the young woman had eaten a meager supper at the landlady's table.

"Someone in a carriage to see me?" she gasped. "Who could it possibly be? Who would know—?"

Before she could finish, the landlady interrupted, "Sez

she saw your notice in the paper lookin' fer work, 'n she's come to talk to you about it!"

"*Dieu soit béni, milles fois merci, Seigneur!*" Madeleine said, crossing herself. Her eyes bright now, she hastily put her fingers to her glossy dark brown hair and did her best to push a stray lock back into place. Then she hurried out of the room and down the stairs.

In the unkempt little living room that served as salon to this squalid boardinghouse, a tall young woman stood, black-haired, green-eyed, wearing an elegantly brocaded frock and wide-brimmed hat. She held a parasol between her daintily gloved hands, and a necklace of beautifully matched pearls encircled her slim neck.

"I am M'amselle Daroudier. You are M'amselle de Courvent, I take it?" Amy asked with an engaging smile.

"Yes, that's my name. And you—you saw my notice in the *Times-Picayune?*"

"That is exactly what brought me here, m'amselle. I have a situation to offer you. That is, if you are free and are at the moment not contemplating any other offer?"

"Oh, no! I mean—" Madeleine did not wish to seem overly eager, but the prospect of steady employment in a decent home (which the elegant costume of this tall young woman hinted at) made her blurt out her real feelings. "That is, I'm very much interested in finding a post where I can be of service."

"I can promise you that. And the wages are quite good."

Madeleine smiled, a smile of genuine relief and gratitude. Perhaps at last her ordeal would end, and though nothing could bring back the father she so greatly mourned, she could at least become self-reliant and raise herself in her own self-esteem.

"My employer has authorized me to engage a personable young woman of good education and breeding to tutor a charming boy. I presume that you have been well schooled?"

"Oh, yes, m'amselle," Madeleine hastened to assure the other woman. "My father sent me to the best seminary in New Orleans."

"And of course you speak French fluently. That is an advantage. Your pupil is most fluent in that language," Amy blandly responded. "The wages will be ten dollars a week. The house is most comfortable, and you will have a room, yes, and a bath as well, all to yourself. We are located on the rue de Carondelet."

Madeleine recognized this as a highly fashionable neighborhood, and she eagerly nodded. "Oh, yes, that's most generous, and I'd like very much to try for the post."

"Nothing will be easier, m'amselle. You have only to accompany me. My carriage is outside. It will take you to the employer, who, of course, will have the last word as to whether or not you qualify for the post."

"I shall certainly do my best to impress him," Madeleine ingenuously replied. Turning to the landlady, who, eager for gossip, had come to the threshold of the living room, she explained, "I'm going with Mademoiselle Daroudier, and I may be a little late if the interview takes some time. But I have my key."

"Go along with you, dearie, 'n I wish you luck."

"Th—thank you." Turning back to the tall, exotic brunette, Madeleine exclaimed, "I can go with you now."

Amy opened the door of the boardinghouse and let Madeleine precede her onto the street. At the sight of the elegant carriage, Madeleine was certain that this time destiny was altering its harsh treatment of her, and when the liveried coachman clambered down to open the door for her, she was quite sure of it. Amy entered and sat beside her, the coachman returned to his post, whipped up the two sprightly black geldings, and drove off.

Madeleine turned to her benefactress. "Tell—tell me about the boy I shall have to tutor, M'amselle Daroudier."

"He's most precocious," was Amy's sly answer. "And, I might add, somewhat demanding. But of course you'll be able to cope because I can see you're quite intelligent, M'amselle de Courvent. Besides, he's used to tutoresses, as he has had quite a number until recently. I assure you that he appreciates the opposite sex and has impeccable manners. And you're so very lovely, I'm sure you will make an immediate, yet lasting, impression on him."

At this, Madeleine could not help blushing, and the flattery was so unlike what she had been used to during the past several weeks that she quite overlooked the fact that Amy Daroudier had very cleverly refrained from telling her the exact age of her future pupil.

Madeleine leaned back against the stuffed seat of the carriage and closed her eyes with a weary little sigh. It was like coming out of a blinding storm into a peaceful haven, and perhaps, distracting herself by trying to teach her new pupil all she could, it would help her forget her father's terrible death and all the ugly things that had been said about both of them. Perhaps one day she might even hope to find a man of honor and status who would understand that she was not besmirched by the ugly taint of poverty but could offer him the love of a virgin who would be his tender wife and solicitous mother to their children.

Her reverie was broken as the carriage came to a halt and Amy leaned toward her, murmuring, "We have arrived, M'amselle de Courvent."

The coachman descended from his seat, opened the door, and helped Madeleine out onto the narrow sidewalk. It was made of cobblestones, unlike the perilously muddy sidewalks and streets of much of downtown New Orleans. Other houses in this elegant neighborhood had banquette sidewalks, utilizing driftwood from some of the ships that had grounded on the shoals of the port.

Amy opened the door on the other side and got out, then dismissed the coachman. "*Merci*, Georges. We shall not require you further."

Madeleine overheard this and frowned questioningly, wondering how she would be taken back to her boardinghouse after the interview. But Amy Daroudier gave her no time to pursue her train of thought as she linked arms with the young woman and airily averred, "Come along now, my employer is eager to meet you, and so is your pupil."

Unsuspectingly, Madeleine let herself be drawn toward the door, which Amy herself opened, for it had not been bolted from the inside. Madeleine found herself in a magnificently furnished foyer, in front of which was a winding stairway with a gleaming mahogany handrail. To her right was the narrow archway that led into the main salon.

"This way, *s'il vous plaît, m'amselle*." Amy had already taken hold of Madeleine's arm again and was leading her through the archway into the salon.

"*Bon soir*, Madeleine," Christophe Carrière drawled. He stood in front of the fireplace, in a black velvet dressing robe, under which he wore only his drawers. He also wore a pair of supple leather slippers. He was smoking a cheroot, and he took it out of his mouth to make her a low bow.

Madeleine stood, as petrified as if she had been suddenly turned to stone. Her eyes grew wide and her mouth gaped, but no sound emerged. She stared at the suave, tall Creole and then, taking a step backward, blinked her eyes rapidly, as if to dispel what must surely be a hideous hallucination.

Behind her, Amy burst into mocking laughter. "As I said, *ma chérie*, your employer and your pupil—did I forget to mention that they are one and the same? Do forgive me; I was so eager to make certain you were engaged for this most important post!"

Fourteen

Madeleine tottered, a hand to her mouth, as she stared at what appeared to be a terrifying apparition out of the past, one that she had dismissed and completely forgotten. But it was not a dream: He stood there as tall and poised as a ballet dancer or fencing master, and she now remembered the trim beard, the distinguished patch of gray at the center of his jet black hair just above his forehead, and the bushy eyebrows. As he raised his right hand, she saw a gold ring into which was set an enormous black onyx, and that ring she also recognized as something he had worn when she first met him and he had attempted to court her.

"I am touched, M'amselle de Courvent," he began, and again he made her a low bow, "to find you so affected by our reunion. Yes, it has been quite some time. Four years, to be exact, since I approached your father and asked, most honestly, for your hand in marriage. And I'm sure you'll recall his reply, that he would sooner burn in hell than have a son-in-law like me."

"You—oh, *mon Dieu—c'est incroyable!*" Madeleine gasped, her voice faint, for she felt herself reeling. Amy, standing behind her and to her left, uttered a triumphant little laugh and said, "This *pigeonne* of yours, *mon cher* Christophe, does not seem too intelligent."

Carrière held up an admonishing hand to his mistress. "Wait a bit, *ma belle*. Your turn will come in due time. Let me relish this reunion." He turned to Madeleine. "You recall also, M'amselle de Courvent, how you rebuffed me despite my ardent and sincere protestations of love for you."

"My father had forbidden me to see you—I loved my father; I obeyed him! And you, I did not love you. How could I marry you, knowing what my father told me about you?" Madeleine burst out. "But now he's dead, and no one can hurt him anymore, least of all you!"

"That's true. Oh, yes, I know of it. He died by his own hand. I should have believed that a man of great honor and especially a good Catholic, *ma chérie*, would never have taken his own life."

"How dare you speak in that way! Yes, I see you for what you are. I thought you overbearing and a fortune hunter—" Madeleine indignantly began.

Carrière tilted back his head and burst into laughter. "That is the greatest jest of all, dear M'amselle de Courvent! Let me tell you: I possess more money than most of the citizens of New Orleans, and I should not be surprised to find out that I might even be the richest in this city that has rejected me because of what happened to my father. And that is why your father, dear M'amselle de Courvent, forbade you to see me and denied us the joy of union—because my father was hanged—isn't that it?"

"Yes!" Madeleine exclaimed with a flash of spirit, "And you deserve the same because you had me brought here under false pretenses! I will inform the civil guard—"

"I'm afraid, my misguided m'amselle," he interrupted with still another bow, "that you will not be able to reach the civil guard tonight. Nor, for that matter, for some little time. My coachman will return to your boardinghouse, to collect your things and to inform your landlady you are now in my employ. Actually, you are really my prisoner. You owe me a debt, you and your father. And since he has seen fit to escape me by taking his own life, I am very much afraid, my dear M'amselle de Courvent, that you will have to stand as surrogate for him. Thus you see, *chérie*, you will have two debts to repay."

Then he brusquely commanded, "Amy, now you may take charge of her. Down to the cellar, which will be her new abode until she accepts her role as tutoress." And both of them burst into laughter as the black-haired woman suddenly seized Madeleine by her wrist and bent it behind her back until, with a cry of pain, the younger woman bent over and tried to ease the cruel hold on her. Amy then swiftly tied a cord around both of Madeleine's wrists, and once they were bound behind her back, Amy triumphantly plunged the fingers of her left hand into Madeleine's thick dark brown hair and twisted viciously until her victim's head fell back and another cry of pain was torn from her lips. "Now, my pretty one, we shall go down the stairs to the cellar." Amy purred. "I shall be in charge of you, and I do hope that you will resist me. It will give me the excuse to give you a good whipping, you aristocratic bitch!"

"*Brava*, Amy, *brava!*" Carrière applauded as he followed his mistress and the struggling young woman out of the salon.

Near the kitchen, there was a small door, and Carrière now unlocked it with a key that he alone possessed, not even allowing any of the servants to have access to the cellar. Having lighted a lantern that rested on a little taboret beside the door, he led the way down the stairway. "Careful, M'amselle de Courvent, I don't wish you to trip and fall and injure yourself," he sarcastically called back. "Amy, be careful with her. No harm must befall our new tutoress on her first evening's employment!"

"You monster, you've no right to keep me here against my will—I demand that you let me go. I shall complain to the civil guard—" Madeleine now regained her spirit and tried to struggle. But Amy, her fingers still twisted in Madeleine's long hair and her right hand gripping the young woman's bound wrists, gave her hair a sadistic tug and hissed, "Down the steps with you!"

With a cry of pain, Madeleine was compelled to descend the steps, while Carrière set the lantern down on a table beside a huge upholstered armchair and watched his mistress force the writhing, protesting victim to the level of the cellar floor.

When Amy released her grip on Madeleine's hair, the latter was able to see, with an incredulous gasp, that this cellar had been converted into what seemed like a chamber of horrors, with its ominous-looking apparatus. Indeed, as soon as he had purchased the house, Carrière had employed workmen to prepare the cellar in anticipation of his ven-

geance on Madeleine de Courvent. Not far from the upholstered chair, there stood a huge bed, over which the low
ceiling had been mirrored. Opposite the bed at the other wall
stood a mirror set in a lustrous mahogany frame; in front of it
was an old-fashioned pillory, such as had been used in the
New England colonies to punish the intemperate and the
immoral. It had a raised platform, and the cross piece provided grooves in which to pinion the victim's wrists and neck.

To the right of the pillory was a low, flat bench on which
lay a leather-handled whip with five long thongs. Beyond the
bench, opposite the bed, was a windowless cell with bars on
the door. The cell contained only a little footstool and a large
chamber pot.

All of this Madeleine viewed in a long, consternated
glance, and her heart began to pound wildly as both Amy and
Carrière silently and gloatingly relished their prisoner's
discomfiture. Presently, the suave Creole drawled, "This will
be your new home, *ma belle*. In some ways, you may find it
even more comfortable than your present quarters. That, to
be sure, will depend on your own conduct while you are,
shall we say, employed in your new situation. However, I
don't expect you, in your first few hours of new employment,
to be thoroughly adaptable to what is required of you, *ma
chérie*," he sarcastically continued. "So you will spend the
night in the cell, and you will be able to watch what takes
place in this very delightful private apartment. All right,
Amy, put her into the cell!"

"Gladly, *m'amour*," the tall, black-haired beauty purred.
"*Allons, vite, sale vierge!*" she said as she forced Madeleine to
stumble forward and pushed her in front of the cell. Carrière
had already gone ahead of her and unlocked the narrow iron
door. Madeleine's wrists were left bound behind her back,
and she was unceremoniously shoved into the cell, upon
which her vindictive captor turned the key in the lock and
then stepped back to contemplate her. Amy, standing beside
him, an arm around his waist, shamelessly used her other
hand to stroke his loins, while Madeleine turned scarlet with
mortification and shame at this obscene display of the brunette's
triumph over her.

"For the present," Carrière continued, his voice hoarsen-
ing as Amy's sly caresses began to exact their full erotic
effect, "my belief is that you need a lesson in how to please a
man, *ma chérie*. Accordingly, Amy has very graciously con-

sented to edify you on that score. I trust that you will watch and learn."

"You—you despicable, contemptible monster! You can't keep me here against my will—you can't—"

"I know that your grief for your dear lamented father presently prevents you from seeing things clearly, dearest Madeleine," he interjected as he began to cup his mistress's breasts. "But I think that in time you will be brought around to a more sensible and practical viewpoint. At least, for your own sake, I trust you will. And now, Amy grows importunate, I fear, and you must excuse us both. *Viens au lit, ma belle mignonne!*"

So saying, he took Amy by the hand and led her to the huge bed. Then, with a mocking little bow toward the horrified Madeleine, who recoiled up against the rear wall of her narrow cell, he doffed his velvet robe, drew down his drawers, and stepped out of them, his manhood standing out stiff and erect. Amy also swiftly disrobed until she was naked, save for her stockings, held up high on her sleek thighs with purple rosette garters. The couple then got on the bed, and like a cat, Amy rolled over onto her back and held out her arms to receive her lover.

Madeleine turned her back and closed her eyes, shuddering with mortification. Carrière, lowering himself onto his naked mistress, turned his head to observe and uttered a sardonic laugh. "Though you close your eyes, my dear Madeleine, you will still hear us. Perhaps even from this you will learn what I shall require of you." Then, clasping Amy in his arms, he entered her as she uttered a cry of ecstasy and, entwining her long legs around his back, dug her fingernails into his shoulder blades.

Madeleine uttered a groan of horror and despair as the amorous sounds reached her, the gasps and sighs of Amy Daroudier, the groans and muttered obscenities of the pirate's son, while, above, the mirrored ceiling reflected their feverish carnal gymnastics.

And when it was done, as Carrière rolled over on his back and Amy's head lay cradled on his heaving hairy chest, the Creole languidly turned to stare at the silently weeping young woman, her back to him, her wrists still knotted by the tight cord that cut into her tender skin. He gloatingly declared, "Take a practical outlook on your situation, *ma belle* Madeleine. You are almost penniless. I promise you that no one will engage you in this city because of the disgrace your father brought upon you."

"Oh, *mon Dieu, sauve-moi, je t'en prie!*" the young woman hysterically cried out.

Once again, Carrière laughed, and in the low-ceilinged cellar, the laughter came back in sinister hollow reverberations to the victim's ears. "Your prayers will not be heeded, I fear. Alas, my aristocratic virgin, you, whom I would have made my fiancée and then my wife in the most honorable manner, had best face the facts. Your only hope is to accede to my desires, because you will be my prisoner and without power to reach anyone outside this house who could help you. Submit yourself, and things may be easier for you. I do not wish your death or even to destroy or permanently harm you, be assured of that."

"I would rather die!" Madeleine panted, leaning her forehead against the cold stone wall of her cell, her eyes still tightly closed and her back to her mocking persecutor.

"Suit yourself. When the pangs of hunger and thirst begin to assail you, sweet Madeleine, I think you will sing a different tune. And now, since you have nothing further to say to me at the moment, allow me the pleasure of amusing myself with a woman who at least is honest enough to know how to try to please a man—a lesson from which you would inestimably profit, once you put your mind to it, *ma chérie!*"

Amy had extended a soft hand and begun to fondle him, and now, rekindled, Carrière mounted her with a hoarse oath of lustful joy. Again Madeleine groaned and shuddered as the sounds of their lovemaking reached her.

After having made love for the second time, Carrière and his mistress left the huge bed in the cellar. Heedless of their nakedness (the servants had been given a week off), they went out of the room that was to be Madeleine's dungeon, leaving her with her wrists still bound behind her back, without food or water, not caring that the only way she could sleep would be to lie on the cold stone floor.

Madeleine cried herself to sleep, and when she awakened a little after dawn the next morning, her body ached from the cramped quarters and the hard floor. With a groan, she rolled over and got to her knees, then managed at last to stand, though waveringly.

Now a further humiliation grew imminent. The chamber

pot, mortifying enough to have to use under such circumstances, represented a further sadistic ordeal, since she could not use her hands. For a time, she sought to drive the growing discomfort out of her mind, but at last it was intolerable. Finally, again bursting into tears, she managed to drag up her frock and petticoat, unbutton her drawers and wriggle out of them, then ignominiously squat the way an impoverished slavey who lived in a hovel would be obliged to do.

She had scarcely rearranged her skirts when Amy Daroudier, clad only in her negligee and slippers, entered the cellar and, arms akimbo, laughed heartily at the young woman's distress. "*Tiens*, how bedraggled you look this morning, *chérie*!" she exclaimed. "I regret that we can't furnish you with your own maid, but, you see, *petite*, the servants have been given leave. In this way, there will be no other distractions for you, and you'll be free to concentrate on the education of your pupil." She paused and emitted another peal of mocking laughter, and Madeleine turned her back.

"*Morbleu*, you still think yourself superior to me, do you! I know precisely how to cure that impertinence of yours. You shall taste the whip!"

With these words, she unlocked the door of the cell and rudely seized Madeleine by the hair and dragged her out toward the pillory. Weakened by the stiffness of her limbs, Madeleine could scarcely protect herself, the more so since her wrists were still bound. She attempted to kick, but Amy nimbly moved to one side and punished her for such maneuvers by vicious yanks at her tousled dark-brown hair until at last her captive cried out for mercy.

Swiftly, Amy unlocked the headpiece of the pillory and lifted the top part up, holding it with one hand while, with her left hand still plunged in Madeleine's hair, she compelled the unfortunate young woman to move forward and bow her head until her neck was set into the center groove. Then she shoved down the headpiece and locked it.

Now, standing back a moment to gloat over her triumph, revelling in the notion that her lover would reward her well for breaking in this aristocratic beauty, Amy now viciously tore at Madeleine's frock until it fell in tatters to the floor. Then she did the same with the chemise and the petticoats until Madeleine stood on tiptoe, her head bowed by the

pillory yoke, her wrists chafed from straining at the cord that
had been tightly wound and solidly knotted against her wrists.

The sight of her naked skin provoked a new sadistic
tirade from Christophe Carrière's sensual mistress. "It's plain
that you've never been whipped in all your life, *chérie*. Such
soft white skin, and I'm sure it's the first time you've ever
exhibited it to strangers! Hmm, your figure is really quite
good, I'll give you that. I can see why *mon amant* wants to
take you to bed—and he will, Madeleine, be certain of that!"

Shuddering, half-fainting, the pillory yoke cruelly com-
pressing her slender neck, Madeleine nonetheless was able to
cry out indignantly, "No, never, I would sooner die—I'd kill
myself before I'd let that monster touch me, do you hear?"

"Oh, yes, you're very brave and proud, but this is only
the start. You've had a little discomfort, but only the slightest
taste of it. Now you will experience pain, and you will tell
yourself that I, Amy Daroudier, born a bastard—yes, even
though my father was of the nobility—will have the pleasure
of thrashing your aristocratic *derrière* until you act more
humbly toward me!" She stepped forward and glided her
palm lingeringly over Madeleine's buttocks. At this defaming
touch, the young woman in the pillory uttered a cry of rage
and shame and tried again to kick her tormentor.

"You wish to dance, little one? I'll accommodate you,
but it will be I who calls the tune!" the brunette sibilantly
exclaimed as she strode to the bench and picked up the
five-thonged whip. Returning to the pillory, she placed herself at the victim's left and let the thongs dangle onto the
floor. Then she drew back her arm and, her eyes narrowed
and gleaming with sadistic joy, lunged forward. The leather
bands curled with a noisy crack over Madeleine's hips and
buttocks, and the burning sting wrested an involuntary cry
from the helpless young woman, as well as a convulsive
twisting of her pinioned body.

Again and again Amy lashed her, and each time Madeleine cried out. "Now you've had a taste of what's in store for
you, and perhaps from now on you'll keep a civil tongue in
that haughty head of yours when you speak to me!" Amy
taunted. Satisfied, panting and shuddering with lustful pleasure,
she flung the whip to the floor. Madeleine sagged in the
pillory, her thighs and buttocks striped from the flogging.

"Now I'm going to put you back in your little cell,
petite," Amy announced. "Reflect on the good lesson I've

given you—and tell yourself that it will be worse the next time. You will address me with humble respect, *comprends-tu?* And you will never again try to kick out at me. You are little better than a slave, *chère* Madeleine, and I am your trainer. A disobedient slave is always whipped, remember that well!"

So saying, she unlocked the top piece of the pillory, again twisting her fingers in Madeleine's hair, and fairly dragged the sobbing young woman back to the cell into which she rudely pushed her, then locked the door.

Now there was a long period of silence for the prisoner, for Carrière and his mistress did not return until late the next evening. Through these long, terrible hours, Madeleine alternately wept and prayed, trying almost pitifully to find some position on the cold stone floor that would enable her to sleep. But sleep had been virtually impossible. Her body ached, her hair was disheveled, her eyes red and swollen from all her weeping. The pangs of hunger and thirst had made her weak and almost feverish. She thought with a wretched despair that no one would be concerned about her not being seen in society or on the streets or in the shops. No, there was no one who could help her. No one except *le bon Dieu.* And it would take a miracle for Him to remove her from the clutches of this monster and his vicious paramour.

When Amy and Carrière entered the cellar on the third evening of her captivity, they carried a tray with them on which there were plates of food whose tempting aroma reached her nostrils and made her awkwardly scramble to her knees and press her face against the bars, if only to gain a glimpse of the savory viands. And there was also a pitcher filled with water and there was wine in cut-glass goblets of the most exquisite patterning, reminding her of those halcyon days when her father's table was one of the most beautifully set in all New Orleans and when attentive servants brought her just such food and wine and saw to her every comfort.

They completely ignored her as if she were not there, and sat at a table, discussing the food. "You are becoming as good a cook as Arnaut," Christophe complimented his mistress. "I have thought of a way in which you can have a career all your own while still being *m'amie.*"

"Oh? And what is that, *mon cher?*" Amy paused with a forkful of jambalaya halfway to her mouth.

"Why, I'd open a little restaurant for you because you are certainly a *cordon bleu, pigeonne*," her lover complimented her. "This sauce is really superb. It takes skill to know exactly what herbs and spices to add so that the final dish becomes a culinary *tour de force*."

"You flatter me, *m'amour*. And how did you like my *blanc mange*?"

"Exquisite!" He paused to put right index and median fingers to his lips and convey a kiss to her, showing her that he awarded her the highest accolade of praise within his power. "But now, I wonder if the Burgundy we've chosen this evening is not a little too overpowering for the jambalaya?"

At this point, poor Madeleine could not suppress a faint groan of total anguish. Amy crinkled her nose at her lover and, by rolling her eyes, indicated that she found their captive's reaction hilariously diverting.

"No," he solemnly pronounced after a moment, having taken a sip of the wine, "it's true that it has a strong bouquet, and it lingers. Yet you must remember that the jambalaya sauce is in itself strong enough to overcome even that. No, indeed, to my palate the wine prepares it for the jambalaya."

"I'm happy to hear you think so. I wish always to please you."

With this, she leaned forward to him, put her arm around his neck, and pressed her mouth to his in a passionate and noisy kiss, which he purposely prolonged.

Again Madeleine could not help groaning.

"Did you hear something just then, *pigeonne*?" he drawled.

"Very faintly. But there are no rats in this cellar. Perhaps it was a little mouse, too shy to come out and beg for food," Amy purred.

"Oh, *mon Dieu*, in pity," Madeleine hoarsely cried out, "give me something to drink and eat—surely you won't starve me to death this way? Have pity on me; it's been nearly three days now since I've had food and water—it's not human. Surely I couldn't have hurt you as much as that, M'sieu Carrière. I beg of you—"

"That time, I distinctly heard something, didn't you, *mon amant*?" Amy gleefully exclaimed. She leaned over to whisper to Carrière, who nodded and turned his chair so that he might contemplate the naked victim, kneeling, trembling, pressed against the bars of her cell, her swollen eyes dilated and fixed almost hypnotically on the water pitcher and the plates of food beyond her.

Amy rose and approached the cell. "Are you really hungry and thirsty, my poor darling?" she cooed with false solicitude. "Would you like some water, some jambalaya, and some good red Burgundy?"

Madeleine licked her lips in a reflex that went beyond her own will and pride, so weakened was she now by her ordeal.

"Well then, one must pay for everything in this life, I'm sure you know. If you wish to eat and drink, you have only to say that you'll give yourself to my lover. Well, now, Madeleine, what is it to be? Or shall we go back to our bedroom and entertain ourselves while you remain here and dream about bowls of gumbo and plates of roast chicken and *tournedos* of the finest beef and—"

"Stop it, stop it, you devil!" Madeleine burst into hysterical sobs. "I can't bear this any longer—please have pity on me—I beg of you as one human being to another. You're a woman; how can you act like this to me, who has always been chaste and innocent?"

"Why, my poor darling, it's very easy," Amy laughed pitilessly. "As I said, my father was a nobleman, a count of France. I might have stood higher in society than you ever could, you whining little goody-goody! But you don't hear me sniveling or carrying on about my virtue, do you? And you see how much better it is for me. There's a lesson for you, dear Madeleine. And that's why I despise your sort, who wring their hands and shed floods of tears and think that men will give in to their every wish. My lover is not like them—so you may as well make up your mind to it. All right, now, we've wasted time enough with you. Do you want food and drink, or shall we leave you?"

Madeleine slowly bowed her head and closed her eyes. A violent shudder shook her naked body, and at last, in a tremulous, faint murmur, she answered, *"Oui, je me soumets."*

Carrière wiped his mouth with the linen napkin, rose from the table, and made a gesture toward his mistress. "Bring her out and put her on the bed," he said matter-of-factly. "I shall test her newly found submission. If indeed she proves docile, we shall permit her to eat our leavings and to have some water, even whatever wine is left in both goblets.

I think that is being reasonably generous under the circumstances, don't you, *mignonne*?"

"It's really more than she deserves, *m'amour*," Amy responded with a vicious smirk at the crouching, shivering, naked victim, who began to sob softly, her head pressed against the bars. Amy unlocked the door of the cell and said coldly, "To the bed, and let's see if the lesson has taught you anything. If not, be very sure I shall take the lash to you again."

Madeleine staggered to her feet and, her wrists still bound behind her back, made her way to the huge bed. Her eyes were blinded with tears as she eased herself down onto it and lay passively, closing her eyes now, as she saw Carrière cast off his robe and then his drawers and come toward her, an evil grin on his flushed face.

"Open your eyes and look at a man for a change," Amy scornfully commanded, taking a threatening step toward the bed.

Madeleine forced herself to open her eyes as her captor mounted her and, his fingers digging into her shoulders, silenced her frantic cry of loathing with his mouth.

She writhed, moaning as he ruthlessly probed her, and in his vindictive triumph, her ordeal this time was mercifully short, for after a few moments he uttered a bellow of lust and lay shuddering atop her, satiated.

At last he raised himself from her, flung himself off the bed, and contemptuously declared, "You certainly earned no more than what we've left for you on the table, you pampered slut! But mark my words, Madeleine de Courvent, you'll show more alacrity and submissiveness before I'm done with you, or you won't eat or drink at all."

Trembling uncontrollably, she now looked up at her captors and pleaded, "Some water—please, some water!" Laughing, Amy took the pitcher from the table and, with an encouraging nod from Carrière, slowly poured the contents over Madeleine's head, causing her to gag as she tried to swallow as much of the precious liquid as she could. Amy stood gloating, enjoying the spectacle, then she commanded, "Now get to the table and eat. No, I shan't untie your wrists. Eat with your mouth and teeth, the way the poor do who can't afford the finest silverware as you and your father did. Do it, I say, or I swear I'll put you back on the pillory and thrash you to the blood!"

"You'd best heed Amy's warning, my dearest one," Carrière ironically told her. "Amy has my full authorization to discipline you as harshly and as often as she sees fit. So you'd best try to make a friend of her by obeying her swiftly, as you would your new master. Eat—you claim to be so hungry, and you've earned a slight recompense, though I must say that you gave me far less pleasure than I've anticipated all these years."

Bruised and bleeding, her face and hair wet from the dousing, Madeleine crouched on the chair before the plates that her cruel captor and his mistress had left. Her hunger overcame her shame and revulsion, and she bowed her head and began to eat, gulping down mouthfuls and almost choking in her ravenous hunger.

"How disgusting, *mon cher*," Amy purred. "And this is supposed to be a young lady of good breeding, from one of the finest families in New Orleans? She eats like a pig, and I'd expect better manners from a scullery maid in her household."

"True enough. Don't forget your wine, Madeleine. Drink a toast to your departed maidenhead. Amy will teach you that once that obstacle no longer exists, a female can become readily trained in the ways of pleasing a man who is as insatiable and demanding as you'll find me to be."

Madeleine's cheeks were flaming as she listened to these insults, but her only thought was to assuage the overwhelming hunger to which her lengthy incarceration had forced her. Tears ran down her face; she believed that she had reached the very lowest point of existence, that no further ordeal could surpass in degradation that which she had endured these days and nights in the cellar of the house on the rue de Carondelet.

She attempted to drink some wine at Amy's insistent order, but there was only about an inch or two in each goblet, and she could hardly put her mouth down into it. When she feebly tried, she knocked over one of the goblets, only to be met by Amy's vituperative, "Lap it up with your tongue; don't waste good Burgundy, you stupid bitch!"

Finally, she was ordered back to her cell and locked in for the night, and at last Carrière and Amy went out of the cellar and locked the door behind them. Madeleine rolled over onto her side and wept bitterly, praying aloud for salvation from this demonic ordeal to which there seemed to be no end.

Fifteen

Madeleine's situation improved somewhat after her initial incarceration and degradation. Amy visited her and allowed her to bathe in a wooden tub filled with warm water. She was given a cot to sleep in, her bonds were untied, and though Amy watched over her sternly, snapping out orders, she at least did not use the whip or the pillory. Madeleine was given a clean chemise to wear and food to eat and water to drink, and only after she looked presentable and was reasonably well fed did Christophe Carrière make his appearance.

He continued to demand that she submit to him on the huge bed, and she did so, not daring, even by a grimace, to show her distaste, lest Amy take up the whip again and punish her. Then, after her captor was through with her, Madeleine was sent back to her cell and locked up for the rest of the night.

Now, on the seventh night, as he lay satiated after enjoying her submissiveness, Carrière bade Amy bring him a cigar. Puffing it and sending huge smoke wreaths up to the ceiling, he boasted, "I have a secret to tell you, my dearest Madeleine, since we've become so intimate. I may say that tonight I take great joy in revealing to you that it was I who bankrupted your father."

Madeleine, lying beside him helplessly, stiffened and regarded him with an incredulous look.

"Oh, yes, it's quite true. Don't you recall that a certain person robbed La Banque de la Nouvelle Orléans last fall? In that robbery, your father's capital was part of the robber's loot. It was I, my charming Madeleine, who conceived the master plan for that daring robbery, which still, to this day, has not been solved—nor will it ever be."

"It was you—" she gasped, still not believing her ears.

"Oh, yes, it was I. I could even tell you what I took from

your father's strongbox in the vault of that bank. Certain bills of lading on cargos that your father had shipped, together with a great deal of cash and a fortune in jewels. Of course, it was an extremely rich haul—what with the contents of the other boxes and the bars of pure silver—and your father's contribution was only a small part—though for him, I daresay, it represented most of his solid capital."

"It was you! Oh, *mon Dieu*—and because of you, my father took his life—and—and—"

"And you find yourself here in bed with me, a man whom your father would rather have seen in hell than see you marry, is that it, *mon chérie*?" he finished for her. "Yes, it's quite true. And why did I do all this and why did I go to such lengths to plan so daring a robbery? I'll admit it was a challenge, but the real challenge was to pay you and your father back for your insults to my dead father, a better man than ever was your father—"

"You monster—you liar!" she began, but he slapped her viciously across the mouth, almost drawing blood.

She shrank to the other side of the bed, propped up on her elbows, regarding him with horror and loathing. He tilted back his head and laughed satanically. "I see you're properly shocked. But you see, my dear, the information will do you no good whatsoever. First of all, I'll compel you to marry me. There is no court of law in this country that permits a wife to testify against her husband. Moreover, it would simply be your word against mine. Everyone would think, if you brought any sort of charge against me, that you were simply being vindictive and spiteful because your father died. So you see, your protests will avail you nothing."

"You are a devil! I would to God my father had killed you—hired thugs from the levee to put an end to your horrid life! And to think that he died because of you—" Madeleine gasped.

"Take care, you've very nearly earned a good, sound thrashing. But because I'm indulgent, and because after all I owe a present to my bride-to-be, I shall spare you the whipping this night. But let me again hear such insults, Madeleine, once we are married, and I promise you that you'll be whipped three times a day, if need be, until you've learned to lower your eyes and your voice and, in a word, to be a total slave, an instrument to my will and pleasure—that, in essence, will be your future life. It can be pleasant, all things considered, if you take heed of my warning. Otherwise, you will never leave this cellar. And now, your anger and revulsion have excited me again—it's your fault, you know. Amy, stand by, and if she resists me, whip her!"

He now flung himself upon the unfortunate woman, and his wiry strength easily mastered her piteous attempts at evasion. Once again, Madeleine de Courvent knew the demeaning humiliation of being used at his sexual convenience, in which there was only hate and self-aggrandizement.

Amy had persuaded her lover that it would be most advisable to keep Madeleine isolated away in the cellar for several weeks before compelling the unhappy captive to marry him. "If as your wife-to-be, *m'amour*," she said, "you grant her access to the house itself, the servants, who have returned from their holiday, will see her. Even though you've told them that she's become sadly deranged as a result of her father's bankruptcy and tragic death, they might conceivably feel some sympathy for her. And if she were to have a moment unguarded with them and beg them to aid her, it's just possible that one of them might be tempted by his conscience to let her leave the house."

"You're right, of course. Well, I'm in no hurry. Indeed, the prospect of maintaining her as my slave in a dungeon excites me even more than the prospect of having her as my wife. Also, by the time I do marry her, if I am to grant credence to your suggestion, *ma chérie*, she will be so totally disciplined and degraded that she'll have no spirit left, and she'll certainly not think of trying to escape."

Thus, for the next several weeks, Madeleine endured incarceration in her cellar cell, with Amy as her sadistically joyous trainer. All track of time was lost by now, and it was early April when Carrière at last entered the cellar, carrying a white gown, white veil, white slippers, a white chemise, and white silk hose with blue rosette garters to hold them up. He led her out of the cell, and then he ordered, "Now then, *pigeonne*, today is your wedding day. You'll do me the favor of putting on this bridal finery, and very shortly we shall become man and wife."

"I—I don't want to marry you. For God's sake, haven't you done enough to me? Aren't you satisfied yet with your vengeance?" she said in a husky, trembling voice.

"No, I'm not at all satisfied. Don't forget, I want to take

every precaution against the possibility of your ever going to the authorities. As my wife, you won't be heeded if you do manage it, which I'll see that you don't. Now," he continued, his tone incisive and his face tautening with cruelty, "be quick about it, Madeleine. If you should dream of refusing, I shall have Amy give you a flogging three times a day until you finally agree. And I shall move you to another part of this cellar that does not have even the conveniences of the one you now occupy, and where I know there are rats."

"Oh, no! *Dieu me sauve!* I—I will do what you wish," Madeleine blurted, then slowly began to get dressed in the wedding costume, her husband-to-be watching with an evil little smile.

Meanwhile, a plump, smiling, bald-headed man in dress coat and black trousers was being ushered by Amy down the narrow stairway to the cellar. His name was Wilfred Gummage, and he was a minister who had come to New Orleans from Pittsburgh after his congregation had learned that he was pocketing church monies and threatened to have him defrocked. Christophe Carrière's factor, Étienne Remontrier, had recommended Gummage as just the man to perform the unusual marriage ceremony, and so for a substantial fee, Carrière had engaged the corrupt minister and had had Amy bring him to the house on the rue de Carondelet.

The plump little man showed surprise as he took in his surroundings. "Do you mean that the wedding is to take place in the cellar, my dear Miss Daroudier?" he asked.

"Why, yes, M'sieu Gummage," Amy nonchalantly retorted. "The young lady is suffering from a peculiar malady. Her father took his own life, you see, being penniless, and the shock proved upsetting. A doctor whom we consulted thought it best that she be isolated from the servants, you understand, until she has regained her composure. She is subject to fits of melancholia."

Seeing that he frowned, she pursued in a blithe, engaging tone, "M'sieu Carrière, my employer, wishes me to tell you that for your services you will receive a bonus of five hundred dollars."

Wilfred Gummage's frown was replaced by a beaming, fatuous smile. "Why, that is most generous! I sympathize with the young lady, and I hope that your employer, marrying her as he now will under my auspices, will be able to return her to every harmonious joy of a long and fruitful wedded life."

"That, too, is my wish," Amy retorted with a little smile. "Here we are, Reverend Gummage. I see you've brought your Bible."

"Why, I could hardly perform the marriage ceremony without it, Miss Daroudier," he said sarcastically.

"So long as the marriage is legal—" she intimated, halting a moment and giving him a searching look.

"I've already told you that, with this license, notarized as I've done it, and with my ordainment as a minister authorized to perform just such a service as I'm about to now, you need have no fear. The marriage will be recognized throughout these United States, and nothing can be done to challenge its legality."

"You relieve my peace of mind, M'sieu Gummage. And I'm sure that my employer will be equally grateful. Now, we shall go in. I'll be a witness, of course, as is required by law, I believe."

"Quite right."

Amy smiled again and ushered Wilfred Gummage into the cellar ahead of her. Madeleine stood, clad in her white gown and veil and white slippers, her eyes downcast, beside the tall, suave, handsome pirate's son, who had put on black trousers and a matching waistcoat, with a bright red cravat. He looked exceptionally debonair, and he had already ordered Madeleine to link her arm with his so that they might appear to the minister as a truly devoted couple. To this order, needless to say, he had added the warning that, should she in any way try to halt the ceremony or make any kind of outward protest, she would spend a week in the rat-infested part of the cellar, be flogged, and kept on bread and water.

Gummage cleared his throat and approached the couple. "My felicitations to you both on this happy day of your union. If you will join hands, now. Oh, yes, I forgot to ask Miss Daroudier—is there a ring?"

"I have one," Carrière smilingly avowed as he took out of the pocket of his waistcoat a gold ring with a sapphire stone and then turned to his downcast captive. "Let me have your left hand, my darling."

Listlessly, Madeleine extended her hand, and Carrière slipped the ring on the requisite finger; then he grasped her hand with his right and stood facing the obseqious minister.

The ceremony proceeded apace, for Madeleine offered no objections. Thoroughly cowed, thinking only of survival, she responded to the questions that Gummage put to her as the ceremony unfolded, until at last he declared, "I now pronounce you man and wife by the laws of the State of Louisiana. You may kiss the bride, Mr. Carrière."

"My darling! My bride!" Carrière exclaimed in a convincingly ardent tone as he enfolded Madeleine in his arms and kissed her lingeringly on the mouth. His hands slipped down to her hips, and he pinched her there cruelly.

But Madeleine submitted, and Gummage exhaled a long sigh. "It delights me to be a part of this union," he said, "for I feel that I have joined you two lovers, and I foresee the happiest and longest of lives ahead for you both. It has been my privilege to serve you, Mr. Carrière."

Carrière broke off the embrace and turned to the portly, pious-featured minister. "A fine service, Reverend Gummage. And here is the fee I promised you, with a little bonus for the inconvenience of making you leave your office and come to my dwelling." He handed the man an envelope filled with crisp banknotes. Wilfred Gummage beamed again, blurting out his effusive thanks as he tucked the envelope safely into his own waistcoat pocket. Then Amy quickly intervened, saying, "I will have you driven back to your office, M'sieu Gummage. Thank you so much."

"I was happy to do you this service, Mr. Carrière. And to you, my dear," he addressed Madeleine, who remained still with eyes downcast, passive and listless. "I know that you'll be very happy. May I wish you both the happiest of lives together."

"Your servant, sir," Carrière said, bowing to him. Then he took Madeleine's hand and said, "My dear, don't you want to thank the good Reverend Gummage? I thought it was a lovely ceremony. And now you're truly, legally mine, my darling, and I shall always care for you."

Forcing back a sob, Madeleine at last raised her head and, staring through tear-blurred eyes at the grinning minister, managed a thank you.

As Amy led the minister up the stairs and out to the street, Carrière gloatingly contemplated his young wife. "Now, Madeleine, you'll find that if you obey and put aside your airs of coquetry and insolence, your life will be infinitely more pleasant. I may even permit you to occupy my luxurious

house, if you give me your word that you will not try to
escape."

"I—I can't. I know you have trapped me, so cleverly, so
very cleverly—as you did my poor father. All I pray is that I
may die soon and escape you. I hate and despise you—"

"Excellent! I would rather have some show of spirit than
a passive body in my bed," he jeered at her. "We shall
consummate our marriage tonight. And in bed you will show
how properly grateful you are for my having rescued you
from a debtor's prison, or perhaps even the disgrace of being
an indentured bondservant. At least you have escaped that
indignity, for you are now Madame Christophe Carrière."

Carrière remembered Amy's warning that immediate restoration of their captive to the normal living in a house,
rather than incarceration in the cellar, might induce Madeleine to attempt to escape—or, at the least, to create unpleas-
ant scenes that the servants could not help witnessing. Thus
he kept Madeleine in the dungeon that had been her quarters since Amy had tricked her into coming to the house on
the rue de Carondelet.

For nearly a fortnight, this regimen was continued, with
the husband periodically visiting his wife in her prison. Then,
at the end of the twelfth night, having just made love to her
in the big four-poster bed, Carrière pronounced himself satisfied that Madeleine had been converted to the total docility
of a slave. She had, surprisingly, actually been aroused by his
ardent and skillful lovemaking, partly the result of her own
carnal wakening, but also the result of her knowledge that
she could perhaps do a lot more for herself by not only
submitting but even feigning her enjoyment of the sex act.
For Madeleine de Courvent, now Madeleine Carrière, realized that by showing complete submission, she could perhaps
effect her own escape.

"I think we may safely trust my dutiful wife to take her
rightful place in the house, Amy," Carrière said to his mistress,
who, as usual, enjoyed being a spectator when her lover
bedded Madeleine. "She's aware now who is her master."

"Perhaps you are right, *m'amour*," the brunette said
after a moment's thought. "All the same, I shall still watch
her very carefully. I'm not sure I trust her quite so fully as
you do—but that is because I'm a woman and you're a man."

"I trust no one, not even you," he responded with a

cynical laugh. "But so long as we both watch her, I doubt that she can do us any harm." Then, turning back to Madeleine, he smilingly announced, "Starting tomorrow morning, Madame Carrière, you will take breakfast with us, and you will meet the servants. I will warn you in advance, however, that they are incorruptible and that they certainly would not help you escape. I have already prepared them with a little story that is most convincing. Now then, my dear, I'll allow you to sleep in this bed while Amy and I go to sport ourselves. We'll call for you in the morning."

"Merci, mon mari," Madeleine murmured, lowering her eyes.

His triumphant laugh echoed as he and Amy left the cellar, locking her in for this last night in what had been her dungeon.

The next morning, as promised, Carrière and Amy went down to the cellar and escorted Madeleine up the narrow stairway and into the huge master bedroom that the pirate's son occupied. Amy then went to the kitchen to order breakfast for three and presently came back with a tray, serving her lover, then Madeleine, and finally herself.

"You see, my beloved wife," Carrière sarcastically remarked as he sipped his coffee, "we have here an admirable *ménage à trois*. To be sure, when you continue to show greater prowess in the amatory arts, I may be inclined to reward you by excluding Amy from this connubial setting. But meanwhile, until I am certain that your decision to be a very obedient and obliging little wife is not some kind of ruse, she will continue to be your disciplinarian."

"If—if I'm truly your wife, Ch-Christophe," Madeleine faintly responded, "I should feel much happier if—if when we—made—made—"

"Made love?" he prompted, turning to Amy with a sardonic wink and smile.

"Yes—yes—that—that we be alone together. It is more—more seemly—it is certainly more proper between husband and wife."

"Why, so it is, but that thinking is part of your prudish heritage, which doubtless you gained both at the convent school and from your father. I do not wish a prudish wife. I prefer a woman who is wanton, and yet clever enough as well as intelligent enough to be able to assume the pose of modesty when such a pose adds spice to the dish."

"I—I will try to please you, *mon mari*," she faltered.

"And so you do, especially when you're humble like this. Who would have dreamed"—here, he turned to Amy for corroboration—"that the chaste, insolent virgin, Madeleine de Courvent, now comes to the point of wishing to please me? Decidedly, if you continue in this vein and studiously devote yourself to doing exactly that—pleasing me—then I shall not regret the encumbrance of a wife. Let me serve you more coffee, dear Madeleine."

She thanked him in a low voice and made a pretense of sipping the coffee that she did not want. Her mind was focused only on her desperate resolve: to lull him into believing that she was totally conquered, totally incapable of revolt, totally his slave and dependent upon his every whim for her existence. Because then, she prayed, he might be less vigilant, and Amy, too, in keeping her a prisoner in this beautiful house.

At noon, Amy again brought in a tray from the kitchen, and the three of them took the midday meal together. Madeleine was offered a fine white wine, which she savored, and the Belgian cook had shown his skill in preparing a chicken dish of which she had always been very fond, even as a little girl.

"Tonight, *m'amie*, as a reward for being so well-behaved, you shall dine in the salon. And you shall meet the servants. I think it's high time they were introduced to you—but again, let me warn you that not one of them would believe any fabrication you might concoct as to your being held a prisoner here against your will."

"I—I would not lower myself asking a servant for help," Madeleine said in a low, trembling voice.

"Now that is wisdom, too. I applaud you, my dear wife. And now we shall leave you until it is time for supper."

Amy returned just before the evening meal with a dress that Carrière had had his middle-aged majordomo, Joseph Lacombe, purchase at one of the leading dress shops of the city the day before, Amy having given Joseph Madeleine's measurements. It was a yellow silk frock, which set off her dark brown hair and matching eyes in a most appealing way, giving her an even more youthful look. Its *décolletage* was daring enough to show the cleft of her superb bosom.

They ate dinner, with Madeleine seated at the other end of the table from her husband, and Amy directly to her right.

One by one the servants were brought out to be introduced to their employer's new wife, and Madeleine dutifully and shyly acknowledged each of them.

Afterward, as Amy was accompanying her back to Carrière's bedchamber, the latter turned and said, "Tonight, I shall grant my wife her request of being alone with me. We are still on our honeymoon, *tu sais bien*, Amy."

"As you like, *m'amour*." Disappointment flashed for an instant on Amy's sensual face. This was the first time she had been left out of the activities that gave her and her lover such pleasure, and for a moment she was afraid of losing her own sense of power and control. But she pushed these thoughts from her mind and said, "All you need do is pull the bell rope if you wish me, and I shall be ready if Madeleine misbehaves."

"I know that," he replied absently, his eyes fixed on Madeleine. "We shall see if my wife means all that she says."

Amy shrugged and went next door to her room, closing the door behind her. Carrière, meanwhile, led Madeleine into his bedchamber, then took her hand and brought it to his lips, bowing his head over it as if he were courting her. "Madame my wife," he said in an unctuous tone. "Will you do me the honor of sharing my bed tonight?"

"Yes, my husband," Madeleine whispered.

She was trembling, but with a supreme effort she managed to show no aversion as his hands roamed her supple young body. She was growing more and more certain that her hold over Carrière was increasing, that his obsession for her was actually weakening him and putting him in his captive's power. And so, when he said in a voice grown husky with mounting lust, "Now then, to show how truly you wish to please me, I want you to undress, as slowly as you can, to excite me," she obeyed. When she was naked, Carrière seized her in his arms and flung her down on the huge bed. Grinding her teeth together, she dug her fingernails into his back, scoring his flesh as he thrust and probed her with all his wiry strength. By force of will alone, she compelled herself to respond to him.

When he was done, Carrière rolled onto his back and sighed, then contemplated her in the darkness. "*Mordieu*, I no longer recognize the haughty creature who could not bear the sight of me," he muttered. "Perhaps this was what you were destined for after all, dear Madeleine, to meet a man who would know how to strip away all the veneer of your snobbery and hypocrisy and make a woman of you. For your body is that of a woman, and your responses equally so. And now, come lie in my arms and sleep."

She did not fall asleep at once, but when she heard his steady breathing and knew that he was asleep at last, she began to think with all her might as to how she could escape another such night that made her flesh crawl.

The next morning, true to his plan for the total subjugation of his beautiful young wife, Carrière commanded Madeleine to dress herself in only chemise, slippers, and dressing gown. "We shall breakfast in the dining room, my sweet wife," he sarcastically declared. "Thus the servants will see how happily united we are, that you cannot even bear to think of leaving off your bedclothing for proper dress, so anxious are you to return me to your ardent arms."

Her face flushed under the overt insult, but she meekly murmured, "I will do as you wish, *mon mari*."

His smile was gloating. "That's the wisest course of all, dearest one. Now let me watch you adorn yourself, as befits a bride still on her honeymoon who, if she had her truest wish, would prefer to spend all day long, and night as well, in bed with her attentive husband—myself, to be sure."

And so again Madeleine was obliged to stand naked before the tall Carrière, whose eyes scanned her from crown to toe, as if he were appraising either a slave on the auction block on Chartres Street or purchasing a pedigreed heifer at the fair held just outside the city. She put on the chemise that Amy had brought before and a red silk dressing gown, and she thrust her feet into dainty fur-trimmed slippers. "Excellent! And now, take my arm and let me escort you to breakfast, my dear wife," he exclaimed.

The Belgian cook himself served breakfast to the trio. Amy sat at Madeleine's right and amused herself throughout the repast by taunting the unfortunate woman with ribald comments. "That costume really becomes you, *chérie*," she drawled. "This morning you really look like a high-class *poule à grand prix*. Christophe tells me that you've turned out to be quite passionate in bed. But, of course, you've a long way to go before you can really please a man to the utmost."

This last remark she made with a glance at Carrière, to see if he still responded to her as before. She was rewarded with his customary, lascivious little smile, but she was not aware how intently he was looking at Madeleine.

In the afternoon, Carrière took his young wife—still dressed in her chemise and robe—on a tour of his magnificent house, proudly showing off all the wonderful furnishings he had purchased with his ill-gotten gains. He was so taken with his success and power—and with her—that, as Madeleine had hoped, he was indeed letting down his guard more and more. As if sensing this, his eyes suddenly fixed on her and he said, "Though I am allowing you to share the comforts of this great house, do not for a moment think you can escape. I will be watching your every move, and if I am unavailable, Amy will be with you. You do not want to incur Amy's wrath and feel her whip again, now do you?"

She shook her head rapidly, her expression one of meekness and submissiveness.

"And do not think that any of the servants will help you. You see, I've told them that you've not been quite well after your father's suicide, that you've become a very nervous young woman and may say and do foolish things at times. They are totally loyal to me, and they would not lift a finger to aid you. Thus you see, Madeleine, if you continue to try your best to be an obedient wife in all things to me, your life will be relatively pleasant and carefree. Remember, however, that my so-called humanitarian actions toward an innocent girl in dire straits can only be stretched so far—" With this, he laughed sardonically.

They went up to the bedroom, where once again Carrière had his way with the beautiful young captive whom he had made his wife.

Afterward, he slept, and as Madeleine lay there, she tried to form cogent thoughts and plans. Somehow, in some way, she must escape from this house and tell what she knew. *Oh*, Dieu, *let it come about that way*, she prayed to herself. Then she, too, fell asleep at last.

A few hours later, she was wakened by the opening of the bedchamber door. Amy entered, pushing a little four-wheeled cart holding trays of food and wine. After placing the cart near the large bed, Amy returned to the door and locked it.

"Tonight we shall have a party, Madeleine," announced Carrière sleepily, also awake now and stretching languorously, unembarrassed about his nudity. "I wish Amy to teach you certain little games that keep a man's interest and passion prolonged—though I must say you are already becoming a most ardent and satisfying lover. But first, we shall eat and drink. Then, when we are comfortably relaxed, we shall begin our little *ménàge à trois!*"

Arnaut had baked a ham with cloves and sweet yams, snap beans with bits of pecan, and almonds cooked in butter and added to the vegetable dish. And Carrière had instructed Amy earlier to bring out two bottles of a twenty-five-year-old Burgundy that he proclaimed a particularly excellent vintage year "in honor of my sweet little wife's progress in the art of love!"

Madeleine ate ravenously and drank two glasses of wine, but made them last throughout the supper. Conversely, both Carrière and Amy emptied one of the bottles between themselves, and then the Creole drank two glasses of the bottle from which Madeleine had been served. He bade Amy go to the kitchen to bring back the dessert, a *bombe surprise.* "And don't forget the decanter of brandy, *m'amie,*" he added to his command.

Amy, looking forward to the pleasures the evening promised, happy and relieved to be playing an active role with her lover once again, giggled foolishly. She bent to give him a kiss, her robe opening to show that she was naked save for hose, garters, and slippers. She whispered something into his ear, and he tilted back his head and laughed as his fingers fumblingly stroked her belly and breasts. Then, giving her a resounding smack on the bottom, he ordered, "Be off, bring back the dessert and the brandy. And of course the coffee. Tell Arnaut it must be very strong. Oh, yes, while you're about it, *pigeonne,* ask him to give you another bottle of that same wine. It goes down well. It has a smooth and mellow taste to it."

Madeleine's heart began to beat faster. He had already drunk much more than she had ever seen any man drink before, and suddenly, like a flash of light, she vaguely comprehended that here might be the way to escape the living hell to which she was obviously being consigned.

Amy returned in about fifteen minutes, carrying a tray with the dessert, a silver coffeepot, the decanter of brandy, and the uncorked bottle of Burgundy. These she set down on the sideboard, staggering somewhat and giggling at her own ineptness as she sliced the dessert into three portions, then served her lover and Madeleine—who were still sitting on the bed—and finally herself. In a slurred voice, Carrière reminded her that he wished his coffee with the dessert, and she again bent over him and let him fondle her, whispering endearments, before she went back to the sideboard, poured out the coffee, and brought the three cups to the bed on a little tray, which she set down on a nearby taboret.

"It's so warm in here!" Amy complained, staggering again as she cast off her robe, then turned to regard Madeleine with an owlish expression. "Now my lover has *deux filles bien nues* waiting for him, *n'est-ce pas*, Madeleine *chérie*?" she said with another tipsy giggle.

"Serve me brandy, Amy; there's time enough to tutor my dear wife. We've all night ahead of us," Carrière grumbled as he gulped down the last of his coffee and shoved away the dessert plate and the cup onto the nearby taboret.

"Whatever *mon amant* desires he shall have," Amy agreed as she moved over to the sideboard and, uncorking the heavy decanter, poured a generous portion of brandy into an Italian hand-blown snifter goblet. She brought this to him, standing beside him and pressing her body against him. His left arm encircled her waist, his fingers edging toward her loins as he reached around, while with his other hand he brought the brandy goblet to his lips and took a long sip. "Magnificent! It sets fire in the blood, but then the two of you will help extinguish that fire, isn't that so, *pigeonne*?"

"May I have some brandy, too, *m'amour*?" Amy asked.

"Of course. Give Madeleine some, also. I wish her to shed the last vestiges of her hypocritical purity tonight." His voice became thicker now, and he paused to gulp down more of the brandy.

With an exasperated sigh, Amy ambled over to the decanter again, and this time she stumbled, righted herself, and managed to fill another snifter almost to the brim. Madeleine's eyes widened as the brunette turned to her and proffered the goblet. She was about to refuse it, when she decided to remain docile and await developments. Accordingly, she took only a small sip, while pretending to hold the snifter for a long time to her mouth, and passed it back to Amy. The brunette scowled at her, then put the goblet to her lips and gulped down at least a third of it before setting the goblet down on the taboret near the bed. "*C'est fameux, ce cognac!*" she announced.

By now, Carrière had emptied his brandy goblet and himself rose to refill it, stumbling toward the sideboard with an annoyed and inaudible oath and almost losing his balance. At the sideboard, he stood swaying, finally uncorking the decanter and gripping it as solidly as he could with his right hand to tilt it toward his empty goblet. Then, with hardly a pause, he put it to his lips and gulped down another generous amount, smacking his lips and holding the half-empty snifter in his hand.

Amy eyed him, then contemplated Madeleine, who shrank back in the bed but forced a smile to her lips. She could see that Carrière's head was beginning to nod and that he had very nearly dropped the beautiful hand-blown goblet in which only an inch or two of the brandy remained. She herself timidly took a sip of coffee to clear her own head, and she watched them both, while trying to look meek and totally passive, believing this to be her only chance.

Amy then tilted the brandy snifter to her lips. She did not set it down until it was almost empty. "How good it is! You and I, *mignonne*"—her voice was even more slurred now than that of her lover—"will have much drollery in bed tonight, *n'est-ce pas?*" With this, she put out one slim hand and cupped Madeleine's naked breasts, then leaned forward to kiss the young woman. Madeleine suffered this also, closing her eyes, unable to repress a shiver of disgust that Amy mistook for passion. "Ah, you tremble, you palpitate, you and I will be lovers, while dear Christophe watches and teaches us both. I will make you a true *putaine*, never fear! And when he tires of you—oh, yes, he will, be sure of that!—we shall send you to one of the best houses on Rampart Street. There you will be able to earn a very good living, *mignonne*. And every man will be a stranger, so that you may receive him warmly with all the ardor you have been taught—how hot it is in here—*mordieu*, it's so very hot!"

Carrière had finished his brandy and now turned back to the open bottle of wine and poured himself a snifterful, ignoring the empty wineglass. His hand trembled noticeably, and some of the red liquid splashed onto the thick carpeting of the floor, but he did not notice this. He staggered back to the bed, carrying the snifter and the wine bottle, and when he put the bottle on the taboret, he tilted it and it fell to the floor, gurgling out its contents. He laughed thickly, lifted the snifter to his lips, and downed the wine at a gulp.

A few moments later, he closed his eyes, dropped the

snifter, and sank back along the foot of the bed, his feet dangling toward the floor. He began to snore.

Amy blinked her eyes, regarding first Madeleine and then her unconscious lover. "Christophe—*que fais-tu donc?*" she shrilly demanded, bending over her lover and prodding him with a forefinger. She had completely forgotten Madeleine, whose eyes turned toward the floor and saw the empty wine bottle that had been overturned by Carrière. Stealthily, Madeleine swung her legs out of bed, crouched, and picked up the bottle, while Amy went on urging her lover to waken. Drawing a deep breath, Madeleine lifted the bottle and then brought it down with all her strength on the back of Amy's head. There was a choking gasp, and the brunette crumpled, falling atop Carrière, arms outstretched, motionless.

Trembling violently in reaction, Madeleine glanced frantically around the ornately furnished bedchamber. Now she could escape—but not naked, not out into the street like this, or she might be apprehended and judged insane before she could even have a chance to tell her story. She quickly donned her discarded chemise and slippers, then ran to a closet door and flung it open. She saw Carrière's robes, and she hastily rummaged among the hangers until she found one with belt and buttons. She put this on, and it covered her completely, down to her ankles.

Then, still warily watching the two prostrate figures, she hurriedly went through the closet again and took out two of the cloth belts from Carrière's robes and came back to the bed. Swiftly, she tied the first one around and around Amy's ankles and made several knots, panting and shivering in her feverish haste to escape from this house of evil. Then, going around to the other side of the bed, she took the other belt and fixed it as tightly as she could around Amy's wrists. Finally, from Amy's own discarded robe, she tore wide strips and bound them around the brunette's mouth, knotting them at the back of Amy's neck.

She was going to do the same with Carrière, when he stirred and his snoring broke off. But then his head turned to one side and he lay inert as before. Her heart had nearly stopped beating. Now her only concern was to leave as soon as possible, without being seen by any of the servants.

She drew the bolt of the bedchamber door and peered out. There was no one in the hallway. Very carefully, closing the door softly behind her, she made her way toward the

front door of the house. Here there were two bolts, and these
she drew back. She put her hand to the knob and turned it,
and the cool yet humid air of the night wafted to her. *"Merci,
mon Dieu, merci pour ma vie!"* she said. And then, closing
the door as quietly as she could, she began to run down the
street and toward the central section of the city.

Sixteen

Christophe Carrière stirred and moaned, blinking his
eyelids and breathing heavily. He winced, for his head was
pounding as if a thousand hammers were being beaten on an
anvil at the recesses of his brain. Yes, he'd had too much to
drink; he could feel it now. *Dieu*, how his head ached!

He lifted his head and saw Amy lying atop his body; saw,
too, the strips of cloth bound around her mouth and the belt
of his dressing robe binding her wrists.

"Diable!" he bellowed, almost sobering at once with the
sudden shocking realization of what must have happened.
With both hands, he impatiently shoved her body off his to
tumble onto the floor beyond the bed. Then he got to his
feet, swaying, still unsteady from the wine and brandy he had
imbibed.

The bed was empty. And there was no sign of Madeleine.

"What in the devil has happened here!" he said in a
savage, hoarse voice, and then turned to contemplate his
mistress. Amy now stirred, turning slightly, and her widened
eyes fixed on his rage-contorted face as he towered over her.

"Ah, you've come back to life! And perhaps you can tell
me what has gone on here!" he growled as he stooped and,
with the strength of his lean fingers, tore away the strips of
cloth that had gagged her. "Where is Madeleine? What did
you allow to happen, you stupid *putaine?*"

"I—I don't know—you had had too much liquor—you
were drunk, *m'amour*—and all of a sudden something struck
my head. I don't know anything more until just now—"

"It was Madeleine! Oh, that cunning bitch! All this time pretending to be thoroughly enslaved, to be afraid of both of us, and all the while she was plotting something like this!" He was storming. "But it was your fault! All right, perhaps I drank too much—but you should never have turned your back on her. What did she hit you with, I wonder? I see now—this empty wine bottle—my best Burgundy! You've really botched it now, Amy!"

"But perhaps she hasn't been able to leave here—perhaps the servants saw—please untie me—"

"Lie still there; I'll settle with you later. I'm going to look through the house—maybe Joseph saw her—if he did, he would be certain to stop her—"

Beside himself, Carrière belted his robe and ran out of the bedchamber, calling, "Joseph, Joseph, *venez ici! J'ai besoin de vous!*"

A few moments later, the middle-aged majordomo, his face puffy with sleep, hurried into the foyer, frightened by the furious urgency in his master's voice.

"Where is my wife, Joseph?"

"But, M'sieu Carrière, I don't know—I thought she was with you—"

"You were supposed to watch—"

"I did, M'sieu Carrière, and I heard nothing. I know the doors were locked; and besides, M'amselle Amy was with her and with you—"

"Then she's escaped—while you were sleeping. But it's not really your fault. Look, Joseph, I must leave now. I shan't tell you where I'm going so you can't tell anyone else. You and the other servants have been well paid. You can look out for yourselves."

"But, M'sieu Carrière, I—I don't understand—" the majordomo faltered.

"Never mind. Go back to sleep—what's done is done, and the hell with it."

Joseph shrugged and went back to his room. Carrière hastened to the bedroom, locked the door behind him, and then methodically dressed. Amy, meanwhile, had sat up and was grimacing with pain from the blow to the back of her head.

"Well, she's gone, thanks to you, *ma petite,*" Carrière said sardonically. "That means I shall have to leave New Orleans. For certain, she'll be able to reach the civil guard or someone she knows to tell her story. Even if they don't believe her, they're certain to investigate. And it will lead to prying into facts I'd just as soon not have come to the surface, if you don't mind."

He contemplated his mistress, standing with his hands on his hips, looking down at her with an icy smile on his compressed lips, his eyes cold and narrowed.

Amy began to be afraid. "Please—please untie me—she tied the knots so tight." Seeing that Carrière was making no move to help her, she tried another tack. "I can help. I'll go out—I'll have Georges drive me in the carriage, and we'll go looking for her—"

"You stupid fool, how long ago do you think it was that she hit you with that bottle? Half an hour—an hour? At least that—and by now, she's reached someone and told them everything. Oh no, Amy, thanks to you, I must abandon this house and New Orleans. Happily, I have my stake in this world well hidden—several stakes, indeed, and not only in the European banks. So I shall say *adieu* to you, *m'amie*. I regret it, for you served me well until this fatal mistake—but I can take no further chances."

"What do you mean, *mon amant*—no—why do you look at me like that—oh no, *mon Dieu, sauve-moi, aide-moi, je—*" But his hands had closed around her throat, and though she struggled, trying to break that murderous hold, her eyes bulged and her nostrils dilated wildly as she fought for breath. And then at last her eyes dimmed, and he held only a lifeless body.

He let her go, and her head thudded back on the carpet as she lay in that final hideous agony, her face twisted.

He turned and strode out of the bedchamber, hastily rummaged in his study for some money as well as two guns and ammunition, and then hurried to the stable at the back of the house. He saddled a black mare, affixed two sturdy saddlebags to the heavy saddle, then mounted the horse and rode off toward the southwest.

Swearing under his breath, Carrière felt the gusts of wind buffet him as he rode. The cool air and the approaching storm, together with his sudden realization that he might well be in mortal danger, had served to sober him sufficiently now to think of the difficulties in unearthing the buried silver ingots. There had been about sixty of them, each weighing roughly twenty-five pounds. He had needed two men before to help him hide the ingots, and of course he had killed the men and buried them in one of the huge holes they had dug for the disposition of the stolen silver. His horse, sturdy though it was, could at best carry only about three hundred pounds of weight, including his own—and he had no desire to leave any of the silver bars behind. But how the devil was he to transport some fifteen hundred pounds of pure silver to the ship that would take him across the Atlantic and to a hiding place where he would never be found?

He would have to employ some men, perhaps get them to take a small raft and pole the raft upstream to the abandoned plantation and there help him dig up the silver. When he went back to New Orleans, he would have to carry the silver bars in strong canvas sacks; then he would have to pole the raft downriver to the levee and have some of the roustabouts help him lug the heavy sacks onto the ship he chose. But he would be able to pay the captain of the vessel an extravagant sum to look the other way and ask no stupid questions about the contents. Yes, it could be done. Men were venal, and silver and gold were the way to overcome the scruples of even the best of them, he was certain.

He halted the horse, which snorted and reared and pawed the air with its front hooves, its eyes wildly rolling. There was a clap of thunder off to the east, and the wind seemed to freshen and grow colder. As he recalled, there was a tavern, just beyond the northern side of the levee, where men who hoped for a berth on a ship or a post as roustabout or stevedore on the docks often gathered to talk over their hopes and misfortunes. He could engage some of those men. And as for weapons, thank the *bon Dieu* he had had the presence of mind before rushing out of the house to arm himself with the brace of pistols and the pouch of gunpowder and ball. Also, he had taken along some banknotes as well as a little leather sack of gold pieces, so that he might pay his passage; it would not be wise to tempt the captain of a frigate with a silver bar, for the latter might infer that the sacks taken aboard probably contained more of the same, and then it would be easy, one night while crossing the Atlantic, to have the roustabouts or the stevedores overpower him and throw him overboard.

He grinned as a flash of lightning darted its jagged course across the dull dark sky. He had not lost his wits, even though he had been sodden with drink. He could still outsmart the virtuous and the upright, and perhaps this was the heritage his father had left him: how to live by his wits and to cope with sudden, supposedly overwhelming adversities. It was exhilarating, and then once in Paris or London, he would truly lead the life of a gentleman, which was his rightful due, and which would have been his father's except for the meddlesome and sanctimonious piety of those who had captured him. Indeed, Carrière had often wondered why his father had not been able to buy his way out of prison and escape that final hangman's noose. But then, to be forewarned is to be forearmed, and he knew that what had happened to his father would never happen to him.

He was in a more cheerful mood as he turned his horse's head eastward, making for the tavern where he would find seamen who, for a gold piece or two, would be willing to do anything short of murder—and even that, if called upon.

In her flight from the house on the rue de Carondelet, Madeleine could only vaguely recall the route by which the carriage had taken her from the cheap boardinghouse, the place that had been her last residence before she was cunningly entrapped by Carrière and his sadistic mistress. But exhausted though she was from her long incarceration and spiritual and physical torment, her only real thought was of putting as much distance as she could between herself and that accursed house belonging to her captor.

Rain had begun to fall, and the air turned chilly. What she had put on at least protected her modesty, but it was hardly warm enough to withstand the rigors of a New Orleans April evening when the wind came in from the northeast, presaging a storm.

Now gasping for breath, Madeleine could run no farther. She took shelter under the stairway of a large house and there waited until the storm abated. But each clap of thunder that was announced by the sudden blinding streak of lightning made her cower and groan, and the demons that had pursued her since her father's death seemed to be all about her in the air, hovering in shadows, taunting her that her escape was only illusory and that the suave Creole who had ensnared her would find her again and punish her the more dreadfully for her audacity.

As it chanced, the front door above her opened and a liveried servant came out. He looked at the dreary atmosphere and then, as if he had seen a glimpse of her crouching below in the stairwell, came farther down the steps and peered over. "Miss," he said, "what in the world are you doing out there on a night like this?"

"W—will you—oh, please help me, please!" Madeleine blurted, moving away from her hiding place and ascending the stairs.

"This is the residence of M'sieu Claude Marbussier and his wife, miss. The master is in Natchez, but Madame Marbussier is at home—do please come in out of this rain."

"You—you're very kind, m'sieu," Madeleine faintly stammered as she moved up to the porch and faced the servant, a kind-faced, nearly bald man in his midfifties.

"Come in, come in," he said hurriedly. "I will have the maid bring you some hot tea, and I'll bring you a warm robe—you're nearly soaked to the skin, poor young lady!"

Madeleine gratefully entered the house, while the majordomo—for such he was—gestured to her to sit upon an upholstered chair in the corner while he hurried to the kitchen to ask one of the maids to prepare some tea and heat some biscuits. Then he went in search of his mistress, who was about to retire for the night. Madame Clothilde Marbussier was only a few years older than the majordomo, and she was known throughout New Orleans, as was her husband, for her support of charities. Out of her own dowry and inheritance, she had insisted that a large tithe be paid to the Ursuline Convent to help wayward girls as well as poor children in need of proper schooling that their parents could not afford.

After the majordomo had explained how he had found Madeleine hiding at the bottom of the stairwell outside the house, she put on a robe and hurried out to greet the unexpected guest. "*Ma pauvre enfant!*" she exclaimed with a benevolent smile on her wrinkled, pleasant face, "Antoine tells me that you were hiding outside my house—from what were you running away, my poor child? It's plain to see that you're a young lady of quality—"

Madeleine burst into hysterical sobs, the inevitable nervous reaction after this night of ungovernable terror and violence, and then blurted out her story. As Madame Marbussier listened, her smile vanished and she gasped in horror several times, gesturing to Antoine to come to her for orders. "*C'est incroyable!* If this is true, you have escaped with your life—and you say this man compelled you to marry him—and that he boasted of having robbed La Banque de la Nouvelle Orléans?"

"*C'est vrai, madame,*" Madeleine tearfully asserted.

"Well, you're in no condition to do anything about it now. My coachman will take you to the police station in the morning, after you've had a good nourishing breakfast and a good night's sleep, and then you shall tell your story. Perhaps this wicked scoundrel can be captured and brought to justice as he deserves! I know your name—why, of course, your father was well known in the city."

"My father—my father died—because of the disgrace of bankruptcy," Madeleine passionately avowed between sobs. "And this man brought it about by robbing La Banque de la Nouvelle Orléans, Madame Marbussier. It was because my father would not let him court me. That was his revenge."

"A monster! Come now, we must get you to a room where you shall change your clothes. Antoine, have Marie prepare a hot bath at once!"

"Very good, madame." The majordomo bowed and hurried out of the salon to execute the order.

An hour later, Madeleine had bathed and been given a light meal of broth, biscuits, a breast of chicken, and more tea. Wearing a nightshift and robe far too large for her, since they belonged to her generous benefactress, she clambered into bed and almost instantly fell asleep.

Christophe Carrière reined in his horse outside the tavern about half a mile to the north of the levee. He had halted his horse several times during the worst of the storm, seeking shelter once in the enclosed courtyard of a deserted house and, again, in one of the empty warehouse sheds of the levee itself. Now the storm had ebbed and the sky had begun to clear, and by this time his mind was cold and calculating as in the days when he had plotted his revenge against Madeleine.

There would be risks in hiring men who would have even fewer scruples than himself, and once they discovered why he had hired them and what they were digging up, there might well be real danger for him. But he had planned matters very carefully this time, and as he approached the tavern, tethering his horse to a hitching post outside, he thought again that he would seek men who had access to a flatboat or raft that could be poled upstream to the abandoned plantation that his father had once owned.

Once he had induced the men to put the silver bars aboard the raft or flatboat, he could easily kill them, as he had done with those other two, and then let the river current take him and the silver treasure down toward the wharf. Then he would pay a European-bound shipmaster to take him across the Atlantic.

He did not think that the servants would discover Amy's body until late this morning, and there was no way they could guess where he had gone. Only Joseph knew that he had left the house, but even the trustworthy majordomo had not the slightest inkling as to his ultimate destination. Let the servants ransack the house and take what treasures they would as their wages; that was totally inconsequential now.

He grinned and swaggered to the door of the tavern, pushed it open, and entered. At this early hour of the new day, it was not crowded. There were perhaps eight or ten men at most seated here, some playing cards, some dicing with their fellows, others sitting morosely over a mug of rum or mulled wine.

The fat, thickly mustached proprietor at the bar, his face lax with fatigue and drowsiness, stared dully at him as he entered and bade him a gruff, "*Bonjour, m'sieu.*"

"And to you, *mon brave.*" Carrière thrust his hand into his breeches pocket, drew out a banknote, and tossed it onto the bar. "If you have a passable wine, I'd like a bottle and a clean glass."

"I've a middlin' Chablis, though there's not much call for that fancy stuff here, m'sieu."

"It will do very nicely." He lowered his voice and leaned over the bar to engage the proprietor in a conversation that would not be overheard. "Now tell me this, *mon brave.* Do you know any of these men and, if you do, can you point out to me one who might have a flatboat or a sturdy raft he could propel upstream with a pole to do a task for me? I would pay him well and you also for the information."

"Why, m'sieu, that's very easy. You see those two at the back there, playing cards? They've a flatboat, and they wait here because sometimes a small ship that docks at the wharf has need of delivering cargo to some fancy *aristo* upriver, but the captain doesn't want to spend time sending his own roustabouts to deliver it."

"That's perfect! What are they drinking?"

"Rum."

Carrière pulled out another banknote and handed it to the man. "Bring a bottle for them, the best in the house. The change from the banknotes is yours to keep for the information you gave me."

Then, poised and unruffled as if all that had happened within the last twelve hours had never occurred, Carrière made his way to the table in the rear of the tavern. "*Bonjour, mes amis,*" he saluted the two men. "I'm buying you a bottle, and I'd like to drink to your health."

The men were bearded, stocky, in their midthirties, the one Portuguese, the other Creole. They eyed him, then shrugged in unison, and the Portuguese declared, "I'll not say no to a bottle, and I thank you for my friend here. I am Onorio Ribeiro."

"And I, Gaston Porneut," the other man spoke up.

Carrière reached over toward another empty table, drew a chair from it, and seated himself, facing both men. "My name is Charles Carnot," he glibly told them. "I'm told you have a flatboat and can haul some cargo. I'd like to engage your services."

Once more the two men eyed each other, and then the Portuguese shrugged again. "We don't much care who we haul for, *amigo;* so long as he's got the *dinheiro* to pay for it, it's all the same to Gaston and me. What's the job to be and how far is it?"

"Only about fifteen miles upriver," Carrière explained as the proprietor came forward with two bottles—one of rum and one of wine—and three clean glasses, which he set down upon the table. He had already uncorked the bottles and for a moment stood there contemplating the trio, rubbing his hands on his apron.

Carrière turned to nod at him in dismissal. "That will do nicely. *Merci bien.*" He filled the glasses of the two men with rum and his own with wine, then he went on, "My father was a smuggler, you see, off the Florida coast, and before he died he wrote to say that he had left me a legacy of treasure. I know where it is, messieurs, but I need help to get it, and then I wish to transport it on a ship back to my native country of France, which is where he was born."

The burly Portuguese roustabout squinted and leaned forward with greater interest as he studied the suave, distinguished-looking pirate's son. "Treasure, eh? How much do you think there is of it, and what's it worth?"

"I've no idea, really, m'sieu. You see, I have his letter from an old friend who brought it around to me just after my father died two weeks ago, and I've had affairs of my own to settle first. But if what I think is true, it might be rather heavy and might take several hours to dig up. Oh, yes, that reminds me—I should need some stout canvas sacks that could be used to carry the treasure."

"That's no matter. I've a stack of canvas sacks; I sometimes use them for hauling heavy cargo when a crate or sack gets broken down at the wharf. Well now, *amigo*, what will you pay us?"

Carrière hesitated a moment. To offer too large a fee might well make them suspicious. To be sure, the mention of treasure had already done that, as he could see from their suddenly avid looks at him. Nonetheless, there was no other way out; once they began to dig in that hole where the silver ingots had been buried, they would be certain to discover what the "cargo" really was. It was as well to be direct with them. They were both simpleminded rogues, in his estimation, and it should not be too difficult to trick them, any more than it had been those two fools who had come along with him the first time to bury the treasure. Pursing his lips, he finally declared, "Let us say fifty dollars to each of you now and an additional hundred for your work in loading whatever we find into sacks and taking them back to the wharf where I can find a ship for France."

"That's a fair price, Onorio," the Creole roustabout spoke up. "We're not likely to be busy until tonight, and if we start now, no reason why we can't be back in time to take another job."

"We don't want to get into any trouble with the civil guard, m'sieu," Onorio now put in. "If what we're to dig up belongs to you, that's one thing. If it's stolen and belongs to someone else, that's another matter."

"But after all, I've told you my father was a smuggler," Carrière said with fake indignation. "And as to exactly what he left buried—for you understand I haven't yet seen it, and I'm only trying to claim my property as his son and heir—I can't tell you the honest answer to that. He would procure goods that were wanted by special individuals and charge them accordingly. And since some of the things he brought back were prohibited at the port where he did his trading, it's natural that he had to have them packed a certain way."

"We know something of smuggling," Gaston said amiably, "for the pirates smuggled into Baritaria in the days when old Andy Jackson fought the battle against the British down here.

What you offer is fair. We'll drink a toast to your health now, and then Onorio and I will be ready to follow you."

The men raised their glasses and drank, and then Carrière anxiously demanded, "How long do you think it will take to get there?"

"You said fifteen miles? Well now, you'll have to pole against the current. Figure four, five hours, so we don't wear ourselves out or ground our flatboat. There are plenty of shoals and turns in the river as we leave the city, you know," Gaston again contributed.

"I'll admit there are difficulties, messieurs," Carrière said, "but I'm paying you well." He put his hand into his breeches pocket and drew out the rest of the bills he had taken just before leaving the house. "Here is the down payment I said I'd give you."

The Portuguese roustabout extended a grimy, thick-fingered hand and drew the bills toward him, sharing them with his companion.

"It's a pleasure to do business with the likes of you gentlemen," Carrière smugly said, again lifting his glass and then draining it. Now, despite the prodigious quantity of wine and brandy that he had consumed the night before, he had never felt more clearheaded, never more certain of himself nor what he must do to get free of New Orleans forever with a booty that would have tempted Sir Henry Morgan himself.

"Well, Gaston, let's drink up and go along with the gentleman." Onorio Ribeiro cleared his throat and reached for his glass. Downing his drink, he rose, and his companion followed his example, not without muttering, "Thanks for standing us the drinks, m'sieu."

"My pleasure. I'll show you the way." Carrière kept his voice calm and his demeanor equally impassive, but inwardly he was exulting over the cleverness of his scheme.

He followed the two men a few hundred yards south of the tavern to where they had left their flatboat in a narrow little cove, tied to a stanchion set deeply into the muddy bank. They took their long poles, which lay near the stanchion, gestured for Carrière to step aboard, and then Gaston untied the rope and flung it onto the flatboat as he took his station at the southern end of the large raftlike vessel while Onorio remained at the front.

"We'll do better, senhor," the latter observed over his

shoulder to Carrière, "if you take the tiller and do a bit of steering. Try to stay away from the banks, and when I shout, look out for a shoal and steer clear of it—I know this river like the back of my hand. Fifteen miles, you said?"

"That's about right, yes, m'sieu."

"Well, the rain's stopped, and that's a blessing. And what we've drunk keeps us warm inside against the nippy air," the roustabout commented. Then he began to dig his pole to force the flatboat up against the current, which, luckily, was not very strong. Both men strained, and the flatboat forged upstream, while Christophe Carrière held the tiller as instructed by the gruff Portuguese.

Early that same morning, Madame Marbussier's major-domo, Antoine, arranged for the coach to be brought out to take Madeleine to the offices of the civil guard. The kindly matron had given Madeleine a dress to wear that was far too large for the young woman, but she had no thought of her appearance as she hastily ate her breakfast, eager to go to the civil guard and tell them all that had happened.

When she had eaten a croissant and coffee, Madeleine rose and went up to Madame Marbussier at the dining-room table. She said, "Thank you for everything, madame. I will certainly let you know what happens. And I shall be indebted to you always for taking me in last night—"

"My dear child, my conscience wouldn't have let me sleep at all if I'd turned you away. How bedraggled you were—and no wonder, seeing what you'd been through. That's why I call you 'mademoiselle,' for I'm certain that the marriage can easily be annulled. It was done through coercion, and without your consent. My husband knows about such things, and he will help you when he returns to New Orleans. In the meantime, in the event you make no other arrangements, you are welcome to stay at our house for as long as you wish."

"Thank you again." Madeleine shuddered. "I never want to have the name of that man associated with mine again."

A few minutes later, she was in the carriage, and Henri the coachman, a cheerful Haitian black in his late twenties, was plying the whip over the two spirited brown geldings as he urged them toward the police station. "I'll wait for you, missy," he volunteered as he descended to help Madeleine out of the carriage.

She thanked him distractedly and hurried into the historic building. A uniformed guard directed her to the office of the civil guard, and in a few moments she had told her story.

Jules Vernier, who was in charge of the Creole contingent of the city's patrol, listened with almost spellbound interest, and then he exclaimed, "You've done us a great service, M'amselle de Courvent! I know that M'sieu Fabien Mallard, who is one of the most important factors in our city, has been doing his utmost to learn what he could about the identity of the mysterious robber who looted La Banque de la Nouvelle Orléans. I shall myself take you to M'sieu Beaubien, who is the director of that bank, as you may possibly know."

He now rose and escorted Madeleine out of his office. In the hallway, he snapped his fingers toward the back of a uniformed member of the civil guard who promptly whirled and saluted his superior. "Edmond, we have just learned from this charming mademoiselle the identity of the man who robbed La Banque de la Nouvelle Orléans. She has reason to believe that he will attempt to leave New Orléans and very likely take with him the booty that he accumulated in the robbery. I have written down on this paper, as M'amselle de Courvent spoke to me, his description. Send four armed men at once to the wharf, and make inquiries among the captains of the vessels now at anchor to determine whether he has already booked passage on any of them."

"At once, *mon capitaine!*" The guard saluted and hurried away to transmit his superior's order to the contingent of guards who would go to the great wharf of the port.

Ten minutes later, having dismissed Madame Marbussier's coachman, the French captain of the civil guard climbed out of his own calash and handed Madeleine down in front of La Banque de la Nouvelle Orléans. He took her directly to the office of Eugene Beaubien, to whom Madeleine promptly told her story.

"So that is where the silver ingots of M'sieu John Cooper Baines of Texas went!" the bank president exclaimed. "I thank heaven that you have survived this horrible experience, M'amselle de Courvent, and you have shown great courage. I know that every one of my depositors will be eternally grateful to you, as I am myself, for your courage in coming forward. And now, Captain Vernier, of what assistance can I be in helping you find this Christophe Carrière?"

"I sent some men at once to the wharf to ascertain

whether he may have booked passage, most likely to a foreign country," the captain of the civil guard responded. "There is, of course, the possibility that he may have gone upriver."

"Yes, an excellent possibility," Beaubien agreed. "Perhaps to connect with some steamboat that would take him out of the state and perhaps on to St. Louis, or some such other town." Then, frowning and rubbing his forehead with his knuckles, the bank president suddenly exclaimed, "But I've also got a feeling that when he stole all those silver bars, an extremely heavy weight that required a number of men to transport it, he may have hidden them."

"He did say to me once," Madeleine now timidly interposed, "that he had taken the money and the jewelry from the bank and gone to Europe, where he deposited the proceeds of the sale of the jewelry, as well as the money, in various banks in cities like Paris and London. But he said nothing of the silver—"

"All the more reason why I believe he must have hidden it somewhere, possibly not in the city, but beyond it in some deserted place to which he would have access," the bank president excitedly volunteered. "I wish to go at once to consult with M'sieu Mallard. He will be delighted to know that we may at last have a chance of recovering the capital that was stolen from his vault by this ingenious rogue."

"There is room in my calash, M'sieu Beaubien," the captain at once proffered, "and I shall be delighted to take you and M'amselle de Courvent to the factor's office. It is not far from the wharf."

"Thank you, Captain Vernier. Take my arm, M'amselle de Courvent. Alas, you have lost more than anyone else, and to think that that wretch drove your father to bankruptcy and that, in return, led him to lose all hope of life—it was a crime that in my estimation deserves worse than the hangman's noose!" Eugene Beaubien fiercely declared as he offered his arm to the dark-brown-haired young woman.

John Cooper Baines had chosen his sons Andrew and Charles to ride with him on a drive to New Orleans that would bring a thousand head of cattle to the market. Also accompanying them would be Epanone, the wife of the young Jicarilla brave Lortaldo. She was greatly looking forward to this reunion with her husband, who had left for New Orleans with Dr. Malmorain several weeks earlier to study as his apprentice and learn about the medicine of the white man.

The party would also include a dozen of Miguel's best *vaqueros*, as well as young Diego de Escobar. For Carlos as well as Doña Inez had agreed that it was high time that young Diego should begin his apprenticeship to a lawyer in New Orleans. He would study for the bar and, if fate so willed it, one day represent the Double H Ranch in any legal transactions.

Diego could hardly conceal his eagerness to leave, and if the truth be known, he was secretly hoping to see Francesca again, even though he well understood that any serious relationship between them was not permissible. Yet he was drawn to her, and her absence had made him miss her sorely. The thought also occurred to him that perhaps she would have made friends among some of the pretty young ladies of New Orleans and might introduce him to one who well could be his *novia*.

John Cooper's two sturdy sons had accompanied him once before on a cattle drive to New Orleans and were assigned this time to drive the supply wagon. Their father permitted them to carry along their rifles, and he told them both, "You'll also be partly responsible for adding to our supplies of fresh meat and fowl, boys."

They had left the Double H Ranch about ten days before Madeleine made her daring escape from the house on the rue de Carondelet. The weather was pleasant enough, and they caught sight of no Mexican patrols or raiding parties of hostile Indians to deter them. Andrew and Charles competed with each other, and Charles held his own, to his own great satisfaction, by shooting a young buck on the second day of the drive, and two wild rabbits and a wild *jabalí* on the fifth day. Andrew was able to bring down a deer and several rabbits as well, and a brace of mallard ducks. And both boys flushed with pride as their father praised them; the *vaqueros*, too, called them each a *gran vaquero* as they sat around the campfire at night.

They entered New Orleans early on the same morning that Madeleine appeared before the captain of the civil guard. The tall Texan directed his men to drive the cattle to a large pen at the southwestern end of the wharf, adding, "I will go to my factor's office and let him know that the cattle are there waiting for him to sell, *mis amigos*. The storm held us up a little, and I apologize that you've had to stay out in the open and make your last camp during such foul weather. But as soon as M'sieu Mallard pays me for the cattle, I will treat all of you to the best meal you've ever had, and you will have a little bonus in addition to your wages, for you have made superb time and without the loss of a single head."

At this, the *vaqueros* cheered him and began the task of driving the herd along the well-worn trail, away from the main thoroughfares, to the back end of the wharf where there were huge cattle pens. Many buyers for the local restaurants visited such pens and bid on the beef they wished to serve their patrons, but the majority of the cattle were often sent abroad or to New England, or, in some instances, to Havana, where the wealthy plantation owners paid a premium for choice meat.

John Cooper held back one of his men so that he could escort Epanone to Dr. Malmorain's house, then he, his two sons, and Diego rode on to the office of Fabien Mallard. As they tethered their horses to the hitching post outside, John Cooper started with surprise. "Why, there's M'sieu Beaubien, president of the bank I do business with, in the office with Fabien. There's also a woman in there with them and a uniformed civil guard officer. Come along, boys! I wonder what's happening."

"*Le bon Dieu* must have sent you to us at a time like this!" Fabien joyously exclaimed as he saw the tall figure of the buckskin-clad Texan approach him and came forward to shake hands with John Cooper. "Do you know what has happened? A miracle, no less! M'amselle de Courvent, may I present M'sieu John Cooper Baines, my esteemed client and the most honest and courageous man I've ever had the pleasure of meeting."

"A pleasure to know you, M'sieu Baines." Madeleine curtsied.

"An honored pleasure, M'amselle de Courvent," John Cooper said with a courtly little bow, much to the delight of his sons and of Diego as well, who admired his uncle enormously.

"M'amselle de Courvent has been the victim of the criminal who robbed M'sieu Beaubien's bank and took all my money and your silver, *mon ami*," his factor declared. "His robbing the bank bankrupted her father and drove her into poverty, which then enabled him to lure her into a most depraved, sordid captivity. Oh, I won't go into the details now. Just trust me when I say that she is a very brave young woman, and what she has endured has earned M'sieu Christophe Carrière the gallows many times over—a statement with which M'sieu Beaubien certainly concurs!"

"Indeed I do!" the bank president fumed, smacking his clenched right fist into his left palm.

"Captain Vernier has already sent a patrol to the docks to inquire as to whether this Carrière has booked passage on a vessel bound across the ocean," Fabien explained to John Cooper. "M'sieu Beaubien, however, thinks that the scoundrel may have buried the treasure somewhere outside the city and has probably gone there. Since I'm so familiar with almost every type of conveyance that goes out upon the water of our great river and the ocean and the Gulf, I may have some ideas how to find out exactly where this rogue has taken himself. I think we may learn something from the owner of the little seamen's tavern not far from the wharf. It is a place where stevedores, roustabouts, and captains often meet to wait for customers. Sometimes," he added with a knowing wink, "they also engage themselves in transporting contraband or even stolen goods. From M'amselle de Courvent's description of Carrière, I think that if he has made an appearance in that tavern to recruit any help in locating some of his treasure, the owner would certainly remember him. Let us go there and see what we can accomplish!"

John Cooper had remained silent the whole time Fabien was talking, carefully taking in everything his factor had told him. The fact that this Carrière was not only the man who had robbed the bank but also a man who had brutally victimized a young woman and her father caused the Texan to seethe inside. Indeed, death was almost too good for this slimy individual, and John Cooper couldn't wait to get his hands on him. His voice controlled but steely-sounding, he now said to the small group of people assembled in Fabien's office, "Christophe Carrière has a great debt to pay to many of us in this room. I will not rest until I personally see that debt paid!"

Seventeen

+--+

It was late morning when the two roustabouts edged their flatboat into a shallow inlet near the abandoned plantation and Christophe Carrière nimbly leaped onto the bank. All during the slow, laborious four-hour journey, his quick mind had been busy in speculating how to get Gaston and Onorio to load the bars into the sacks and put them on the raft before their inevitable cupidity might lead them into trying to kill him and take the treasure for themselves. He had observed that their only weapons were sheathed knives fixed to their belts, as well as a long-poled grappling hook. This Onorio had used to reach out to the bank, imbed into the earth, and draw the flatboat as close to the bank as was feasible. Well, he, Carrière, would think of something to outwit these two rogues.

A round, heavy wooden stanchion with a metal ring set at its top was used for mooring the flatboats and dinghies in which Carrière's father had at times transported supplies as well as tarpaulin-concealed contraband from the wharf in New Orleans. It served now for holding the flatboat against the impelling downstream river current.

Long ago Carrière's father had bought this plantation in the hopes of being accepted into New Orleans society. Now the building that overlooked the river was forlorn and forbidding, having been abandoned all these years and said to be haunted. It was an old frame house with a cupola and portico, faded to a dull gray over the years, with boards missing and shutters broken. The forest of gnarled cypress and live-oak trees seemed to be closing in on the house, making it look all the more desolate.

"Now then, *chefe*," the burly Portuguese grumbled as he reached for the shovel, "you show us where we dig; and you, Gaston, bring the sacks." His eyes narrowed with a crafty look as he turned to the pirate's son. "Guess you think there must be lots of treasure your father buried here, that right, *chefe*?"

"I don't know, m'sieu," Carrière crisply rejoined, maintaining an indifferent attitude so as not to arouse any further suspicions. "As I explained, my father told me that he had buried smuggled goods worth a good deal of money. I'm here now to recover what there is, and that's all I know."

When they approached the large, decaying house, Carrière moved to the left side of the porch, studying the ground carefully. Ah, yes, here was the hole covered by leaves and branches, almost exactly as he had left them. In another hole to the right of the porch he had buried Pascal and Jimson. Now he gestured at the ground. "You will dig here, messieurs."

"You're the boss." The Portuguese grunted as he pushed the shovel into the moist earth and began to dig energetically. Gaston moved over to his companion, staring at the house, then shook his head. "Once this must have been a fine house, m'sieu," he observed to Christophe Carrière.

"You're right, *mon ami*. It was that, indeed."

"*Deus*, what's this?" Onorio suddenly exclaimed, and the clank of his shovel against metal told Carrière that the roustabout had found the silver.

Onorio cast aside another shovelful of dirt, then squatted down and lifted up one of the bars. Sequestered as it had been in the earth all these months, it no longer gleamed, but it was unmistakably pure silver. Very slowly he turned his head to regard his employer. "I'd say your father left you a fortune here, *amigo*," he said, hefting the heavy bar in both hands, then straightening. "We're to put these in the sacks, isn't that so?"

"Precisely."

"Gaston, you fill the sacks—*por Deus*, there are many more of them—senhor, you are a very rich man now. And I do not think, and I am sure that Gaston feels as I do, that you have paid us enough to get all this treasure for you."

"I will see that you are very well paid," Carrière quickly responded. "All I ask is that you put the sacks onto the raft. I will go back downriver and take a ship away from New Orleans. Before I do, I'll share some of this with you."

"I would think you should, senhor," Onorio observed with a baleful look at the suave Creole. He stooped down and again lifted another bar, handing it to Gaston. Then he lifted a third bar. "*Deus*, these are heavy and this hole is filled with them! How did your father smuggle all this silver into New Orleans?"

"He had a fleet of ships," Carrière glibly reassured the roustabout. "A Spanish galleon engaged one of his armed ships on the ocean and was sent to the bottom, but not until my father's crew recovered what was in the hold."

Onorio frowned and scratched his forehead reflectively. "I think we should talk right now about what you will pay us, senhor." Once again, he straightened and regarded Carrière with wary, narrowed eyes.

"How would it be if I give each of you two bars for yourselves?" Carrière offered with an ingratiating smile.

"We will see, after we have dug up all that is in this deep hole," the Portuguese announced, glowering at the Creole. To Gaston he said, "Here, *amigo*, take some of those sacks and start putting the bars into them and then on the raft. This way, we can count as we take them out."

Carrière had worn a waistcoat whose long tails covered the rear pockets of his breeches; into those pockets he had put the brace of pistols, primed and loaded. He instinctively slid his hands back to his hips, to be reassured by the feel of the pistol butts under the flaps of the waistcoat. "I'm sure we can come to a friendly agreement, gentlemen," he smugly averred.

Onorio eyed him and nodded thoughtfully as he reached down to the hole and lifted out another bar and then another, which Gaston took and placed in one of the sacks. Hefting it, he said, "It's heavy, *mon vieux!*" And then, giving Carrière a wary look, Gaston lugged the sack over to the flatboat and dropped it onto the surface, then went back to aid his companion.

Almost an hour later, Onorio straightened and groaned, putting his hands behind him and rubbing his back, then urging Gaston to knead the muscles. By now, all the ingots had been taken from the hole; half of them were stacked on the ground and the other half had been put in sacks and loaded on the boat.

"I have broken my back with all this heavy work!" Onorio said. "Two bars for each of us? I have counted a good sixty, senhor! That is not playing fair with us. You do not wish us to tell the authorities how you came by all this treasure? Even if your father sank a Spanish galleon, I am not sure that what you say will suit the authorities. We are simple men, senhor.

All we wish to do is to be paid for our work and to be given an honest wage."

"And you shall be, I assure you," Carrière quickly put in. "Well now, if two each don't suit you, shall we say ten each?"

"That is a little better," Onorio grudgingly agreed. "But fifteen each would be still better. Without us, do not forget, senhor, you could not have had this flatboat or strong backs and arms to dig up the silver and load it for you and take you safely back to the wharf so that you can get aboard a ship."

"And you're right." Carrière laughed. "Well, then we've agreed on fifteen each, thirty in total, a full half-share of all that's here?"

"It will do," Onorio grumbled. "Well, now we'll finish loading the ingots into the sacks and on the boat, senhor."

"Yes, yes, you do that. Except for one more thing that has to be done first."

Gaston had moved closer to the flatboat and had been studying Carrière all this while. Suddenly, suspecting the Creole was up to something, he reached for the grappling hook and swung it up. At the same instant, Carrière thrust both hands behind him, lifted the pistols out of his breeches pockets, and fired both of them. The grappling hook dropped from Gaston's hands as he uttered a gurgling cry and fell backward onto the flatboat, his head resting on one of the heavy-laden sacks.

Meanwhile, the other pistol shot had taken Onorio just above the navel. Clutching his middle, he sank down on one knee and began to cough out jets of blood. "Treachery—you bastard—*demonio*, you have killed me—I swear, senhor—" His face went lax, and he rolled over onto his side, thrashed a moment, and was dead.

"Well, that is taken care of," Carrière muttered as he blew on the still-smoking pistols, then pocketed them. "Now four dead men will guard my father's plantation throughout eternity."

He grimaced as he stared at the two dead bodies, and then, his face hard and set, began the laborious and grisly task of burying them in the hole in which the silver had been hidden. It took another half hour before at last they were buried and the earth was covered with leaves and branches to mark this double grave that was parallel with the grave in

which he had buried the thugs he had hired to help him rob
La Banque de la Nouvelle Orléans.

There was still work to be done. A pity those two fools
couldn't have waited a little longer until all the ingots were in
the sacks and loaded on the flatboat. But there was no help
for it.

Cursing under his breath, dripping with sweat, for now
the sun was out and it was nearly noon, Carrière doggedly
lifted the silver bars and put them into the sacks, taking care
not to make each sack too heavy, then carried it, puffing and
grunting, over to the flatboat and set it down on the surface
with the others.

At last he had finished, and he straightened with a
groan. It was done, and there were about fifteen hundred
pounds on this flatboat, which weighted it down considerably.
Once he untied the rope from the stanchion, he would have
to climb aboard, take one of those long poles, and dig deep
into the muck and try to dislodge the crude vessel out into
the stream. Once there, to be sure, the current would carry
him down and back toward the wharf, and then all would be
well.

Fabien Mallard, Eugene Beaubien, John Cooper, and
the captain of the civil guard rode out to the seamen's tavern
on the northern side of the levee just away from the huge
wharf. The Texan's *vaqueros*, having driven the cattle to
the pens alongside the wharf, would take up lodgings in the
hotel their employer used in New Orleans. They, along with
Andrew, Charles, and Diego, would be waiting for John
Cooper there, with the young Indian squaw Epanone residing at Dr. Malmorain's house with her husband.

Fabien entered the tavern and went up to the proprietor
engaged him in conversation, then described Christophe
Carrière. The man nodded eagerly and began talking volubly.
Fabien's face lighted as he turned to his companions. "We
have extraordinary good luck, messieurs!" he said. "That
villain came here before dawn and engaged the services of
two men who own a flatboat, whom our friend here knows as
Gaston and Onorio. He's certain that they went with our
thief, and, of course, they must have gone upriver. Thus far,
they haven't returned."

"Then that's where he is!" John Cooper exclaimed. "We'll
get a flatboat and go after him."

Fabien nodded, then turned back to speak with the proprietor of the tavern. Once again the man nodded and excitedly burst out in a Creole dialect, all of the words of which John Cooper did not recognize. "We're in luck again," Fabien reported back to the Texan. "He owns a flatboat that is tied to a post at the very end of this little canal. Unfortunately, he can't spare any men, and he can't go himself to help us push it upriver."

"I will assign two of my best men to go with you, messieurs," the French captain declared. "But you, M'sieu Beaubien, had best return to your bank. It will be dangerous work to apprehend a thief like this. He will not be quick to surrender or to wish to return all the treasure that he has taken from your bank, now that he has it."

They left the tavern now, and John Cooper grimly drew his father's Lancaster rifle out of the saddle sheath. "We can leave our horses tethered here. They won't be of much use."

Meanwhile, true to his promise, the cooperative captain of the guard brought back two tall Creoles in their late twenties, sturdy and wiry, each armed with a musket. John Cooper made no comment, but he patted "Long Girl" affectionately, for the Lancaster was good at long range, and the musket only at short. He turned now to Eugene and said, "You'd best do as the captain says, M'sieu Beaubien, and go back to the bank. When this is over, I'll have the stolen silver to return to you."

"You are a great man, M'sieu Baines," Beaubien replied. "I will pray that all of you return safely and bring back that scoundrel. What is most important is to recover what he stole from my bank, for many of my depositors have lost their faith in me. I have been able to pay back out of my own capital some of the debts that I believe my bank incurred, or these good people would assuredly have gone as bankrupt as poor M'sieu de Courvent."

"His daughter is a most courageous young woman," Fabien declared. "Before we left my office to come to this tavern, I saw to it that she was taken to my house where Hortense and the servants will look after her."

Now they went down to the canal where the tavern keeper's flatboat was tied. The two Creole members of the civil guard took the poles and, after untying the rope that was fixed to the post, waited for John Cooper and Fabien to clamber aboard. Then they began the arduous task of pushing the heavy poles into the mud to propel the large, wide boat up against the current and onward toward the abandoned plantation.

Christophe Carrière was about to board the flatboat and cast off. His eyes glittered with anticipation as he pictured himself back in New Orleans, boarding a ship that would take him to Europe and safety. . . .

Suddenly he uttered an angry, incredulous cry. About five hundred yards away, as he looked downriver, he saw coming around a bend another flatboat with what looked to be four men on it, two of them poling energetically as they fought the quickening current. That bitch Madeleine had indeed got to the authorities, just as he had feared! Four men! But he had two pistols, ample ammunition—and his wits, as well. And four men, even if they were devils or angels, would not stop him now, not when he was so near to carrying off this cargo that would let him live like a prince in the finest European cities for the rest of his days.

He drew out his pistols and crouched on the bank near the flatboat, his eyes flickering to the piles of sacks. He ground his teeth in a savage resolve: No one now would take the silver from him, not after all that he had done, not after all that he had sacrificed.

The two Creole guards turned to call to John Cooper and Fabien Mallard, "There's the other flatboat, m'sieu—yes, and there's a man beside it, and he's armed."

Fabien crouched down and drew his own pistol, which he had brought along from his office. "The range is still too great for pistol fire, John Cooper," he whispered.

"That's why I brought along 'Long Girl,' Fabien," the Texan exclaimed. He cradled the rifle now, resting it against his shoulder, and looked through the sights and waited to draw a bead on Carrière.

Now the flatboat drew within two hundred yards of the abandoned plantation house and the wild thickets of foliage and gnarled trees that made it seem a house of ghosts and evil, indeed. Suddenly, Carrière aimed at one of the Creole guards and pulled the trigger of the pistol in his right hand. The poleman at the front of the flatboat was in the range of fire now, and he uttered a cry as he dropped his pole, his other hand pressing against his side where the bullet had grazed him without inflicting too serious a wound.

"Let's take cover!" John Cooper called, for when the wounded poleman had dropped the pole, the flatboat had swung close to the bank of the river and was directly exposed to the fire of the man on shore. John Cooper agilely leaped onto the muddy bank, and Fabien and the other guard followed suit, helping the wounded poleman get to shore and leaving him for the moment hidden in a thicket of grass.

Carrière fired the other pistol now but missed the approaching men. Swearing, he swiftly reloaded, and then, crouching, ran toward the porch of the dilapidated frame house. Climbing the stairs and taking care not to break through wood that seemed rotted and in immediate peril of collapsing under him, he crouched behind the rails of the veranda and waited.

John Cooper crawled on his belly, holding his rifle at arm's length, until he came to a tangled thicket of wild elderberry. He got to a crouching position and scanned the porch until he could make out the figure of the pirate's son. Then he leveled the rifle, his eye glued to the sights, and he squeezed the trigger. But for once, "Long Girl" failed him; there was a click and the mechanism jammed, without igniting the firing pan and speeding the ball to its destined target.

"*Mon Dieu!*" gasped Fabien, crouching beside him. He raised his pistol and triggered a shot that went wide of its mark. But Carrière, seeing that the rifle had failed, now boldly stood up and fired the pistol in his right hand. John Cooper uttered a yell as the ball buried itself in the fleshy part of his left arm. He ducked out of sight behind the thicket, just as Carrière, aiming the other pistol, tried to finish him off, but the ball went whistling harmlessly beyond both him and the factor. Meanwhile, the other Creole guard had taken his companion's pistol and began to crawl on his belly toward the porch from the west, hoping to take Carrière by surprise.

John Cooper realized that his enemy had to take time to reload his pistols. Straightening, heedless of the pain in his left arm, he ran toward the porch. Carrière frantically fumbled with the pistols, dropping one, but it was too late to reload the other, for already John Cooper had leapt onto the veranda and was on him. Now the two men were locked in a mortal duel, the sneering face of John Cooper's adversary looming before him, the eyes mad with rage and pain. Carrière panted, "Meddler, I'll kill you! I'll kill you, and I'll keep the silver—"

Carrière tried to rake his left hand, the fingers stiff like the talons of a bird of prey, across John Cooper's face, seeking out his eyes. At the same moment, he attempted to bring up his right knee into the Texan's crotch, but John Cooper twisted to one side and forced him back against the porch rail. The rotted wood gave way, and both men fell to the ground, rolling over and over.

The Creole guard came out of his hiding place, pistol in hand, but Fabien shook his head and called, "No, let them fight! Let them fight!"

Carrière had wrapped his right leg around John Cooper's wiry thighs and locked himself to the Texan. Seeing the sheath of the Spanish dagger dangle from John Cooper's neck, he tried to seize the dagger and to kill him.

But John Cooper now had both Carrière's wrists pinned tightly in his hands, despite the pain from the wound in his arm, and he rolled him over again and again, staring into the contorted, livid face of his enemy.

"I need no dagger to end your worthless life, M'sieu Christophe Carrière," John Cooper hoarsely panted. He released one of his adversary's wrists, and with his right hand he yanked from his neck the Spanish dagger in its sheath and flung it away, allowing neither man to use it. "Even my bare hands are too good for you!" John Cooper vehemently declared, grabbing his enemy's wrist again.

Now, realizing that John Cooper meant to kill him, Carrière used every trick he knew to fling his rival from him, as a wrestler might, pretending to go limp, then twisting and jerking, vainly trying to break his wrists free of John Cooper's hold. But as John Cooper felt Carrière's strength wane, he clamped both his hands around Carrière's throat, ignoring the pain in his arm.

The Creole's face convulsed, his eyes bulged, and with his fingernails he tried to dig at John Cooper's wrists to break that terrible grip. He arched and twisted, writhing, trying to kick, but nothing availed. He felt his windpipe being slowly choked off until he could scarcely breathe.

And now, putting the palm of his right hand to Carrière's chin while gripping his throat with his left hand, John Cooper forced his enemy's head back until there was a sudden crack. Beneath him, the struggling body went limp in death. It was an ironically fitting end, for son had died like father, from a broken neck.

After a long moment, John Cooper slowly rose from the inert body. Blood dripped from his left arm, but he ignored it.

"*Mon Dieu, c'etait formidable!*" the civil guardsman admiringly exclaimed as he came forward to stare down at Carrière's lifeless body.

"Your arm is bleeding badly, *mon ami*," Fabien said to John Cooper as he also came up to him. "Let me put a tourniquet around it, and then we must get you back to New Orleans to have that ball extracted. And the other Creole guard, who was wounded in the side, he, too, must go to the Ursuline hospital."

"It's not a serious wound for me, my friend," John Cooper declared as Fabien tied his handkerchief around the other man's arm to stop the bleeding. "What we have to do now is get this flatboat that Carrière so thoughtfully loaded back to the city. It's a very heavy weight, and I'm wondering if we shouldn't use both flatboats. I can see from here that our own boat luckily grounded on a little shoal."

"We could indeed use both boats," the factor agreed. "It will be easier going that way, and we'll have the current with us, so that one man should be able to handle each raft. I'll volunteer to be in charge of one of them."

"And I in charge of the other," the uninjured civil guardsman spoke up. "My friend, Robert, can help, too, at least to steer, even if he can't pole."

Fabien surveyed the scene of utter desolation around them, as he took a last look at the abandoned old frame house. "Well then, messieurs, if we can summon our strength for the task of transferring some of those sacks to the other flatboat, we'll make it handily."

Half an hour later, while John Cooper and the other wounded man rested, Fabien and the guardsman had completed the transfer of half the load of silver. Fabien then declared, "Out of decency, even though he was a scoundrel and, I'm sure, a murderer as well, I cannot let his body rot here for the birds and the scavengers that may prey upon it. Let us at least give him some kind of burial and pray for his soul. *Le bon Dieu* will judge him."

The uninjured guardsman and the factor swiftly dug a grave and covered the last remains of Christophe Carrière.

Only after they finished did they discover the recently filled-in hole containing the bodies of the two roustabouts Carrière had hired and killed. Fabien shook his head sadly, never realizing there was still another grave here of men Carrière had murdered.

Now the two guardsmen boarded one flatboat while John Cooper and his factor climbed onto the other. They pushed them off into the river, which at once began to carry the large crafts and their precious cargo back to New Orleans.

Eighteen

By evening, the ball had been removed from John Cooper's left arm, and the doctor at the Ursuline hospital assured him that there would be no ill effects except stiffness for some weeks. The wounded guardsman was also quickly treated, and Eugene Beaubien, who had been waiting with three stevedores and a carriage drawn by four horses, anticipating that John Cooper would recover the stolen silver, conveyed the ingots back to the bank. Out of his own pocket, he gave both guardsmen a substantial reward for their efforts in helping to regain the stolen property.

The following afternoon, Madeleine de Courvent, the two deputy guardsmen and their captain, together with Fabien Mallard, Eugene Beaubien, and John Cooper Baines, appeared before a judge in the courthouse. Madeleine, at Hortense Mallard's urging, petitioned the court to declare her marriage to Christophe Carrière null and void. At the same time, John Cooper and the other men gave testimony to the theft and the recovery of the stolen silver.

After the various testimonies were received, the judge began by declaring that all monies in the Carrière accounts that were placed in two New Orleans banks were to be impounded and were to be returned to La Banque de la Nouvelle Orléans so that the depositors might be paid back. Also, Carrière's house and household goods would be sold at auction to raise additional funds. "Unfortunately," the judge declared after reaching his decision, "it is impossible under our present laws to recover what this ingenious criminal hid away in foreign banks, and I fear that accordingly all of the depositors of M'sieu Beaubien's bank cannot be fully repaid."

"Your Honor," John Cooper said, stepping forward, his arm in a sling, "if you will permit me, I wish to donate twenty bars of silver on behalf of the worthy depositors of M'sieu Beaubien's bank as my gesture of compensation for what they lost to the evildoing of Christophe Carrière."

There was a murmur of astonishment in the courtroom, and then some of the spectators began to applaud. The judge cleared his throat and stared down at the tall Texan, then beamed. "M'sieu Baines, I think I may speak for the depositors in offering you my own official thanks for your Christian charity and your kindness toward your fellow man. In my boyhood, my father taught me that when one casts one's bread upon the waters, it is returned a thousandfold."

"That was my father's idea, too, Your Honor," John Cooper replied, a smile on his face.

"Very well, then," the judge continued, "there is a happy ending to this tragic case. As for you, M'amselle de Courvent, after what you have said before this court, I will grant your petition and declare your marriage null and void. It is true that it is now legally ended through the justifiable death of your scurrilous husband, but for the sake of the record, I shall instruct my clerk to expunge all record of your marriage to Christophe Carrière, and you may take back your name as if you had never married the rogue."

"I—I am grateful, M'sieu Judge," Madeleine said. Then she bowed her head and burst into tears.

Hortense, who had accompanied her to the courtroom, put her arm around Madeleine's shoulders and whispered, "You will be our guest until you've recovered your strength, ma chérie. Then Fabien and I will see to finding you something that will give you a new wish to live, perhaps a position as an assistant in a business office such as my husband's. And someday, you will meet the right man who will make you forget all the horrors you have endured, and you will be happy. I am sure of this, and I know that my husband and I will do all we can to help you begin this new life."

"You are so good to me—I have learned from what I've experienced," Madeleine tearfully exclaimed. "I know now that Christophe Carrière was right about me—that I was spoiled and pampered, that I lived only for myself—but no longer. *Le bon Dieu* has given me another chance, and with your help and that of your kind husband, Madame Mallard, I will do my utmost to be worthy of it!"

The day after the court hearing, John Cooper went to Fabien Mallard's office and received the money for his cattle, a portion of which the factor had sold to another factor in Boston and the balance to a captain bound for Havana. This money was deposited in the bank, along with the four silver ingots from the new mine. Eugene Beaubien had them weighed and assayed and gave John Cooper a requisite credit. Then the Texan signed a deed of gift to the banker for the twenty silver bars recovered from the robbery, to be divided up among the depositors, as he had promised the judge.

After Carrière's robbery of the bank the previous year, Beaubien had seen to it that the building was strengthened against any possibility of future attempts to rob it. Additional guards were also hired, and John Cooper, pleased with all these new measures to fortify the bank, decided it would be a good idea to bring the remaining silver from the new mine to New Orleans, where it would be immediately available when he needed it. Thus he confided in Beaubien and Fabien about the new mine, and told the bank president and his factor his intentions to have the silver transported to New Orleans.

When John Cooper and Fabien returned to the factor's office, John Cooper said, "Fabien, I want you to order several dozen of the finest rifles, a good supply of ball and gunpowder, and many good, sharp hunting knives—in fact, if you can secure a good number of the famous Bowie knives, I'd be grateful. I want these for the defense of the ranch and the Brazos settlement, as well as to give to my friends the Jicarilla, for their own protection."

"Tomorrow, there's a shipmaster leaving for Le Havre, and I will commission him to order the rifles and hunting knives, *mon ami*," the affable factor declared. "As to the Bowie knives, I have a source right here in the city, where Monsieur Bowie himself now has his own knives made. And now, as to your very personable young nephew, Diego de Escobar, I had a chance late yesterday afternoon to talk to M'sieu David Allary, who is one of the best-known lawyers in all New Orleans. As it happens, he can use an energetic young assistant who isn't afraid of work, and in the process, he'll teach him all the law he knows, which is considerable."

"Excellent!"

"Moreover, he's a widower with two daughters, ages twelve and eighteen, and a very devoted elderly housekeeper. He has a large house not too far from where that rogue Carrière maintained his prison for poor M'amselle de Courvent, and he has told me that he would be delighted to have your nephew live with him. In that way, too, as you can see, he can help the boy in all the social graces and also supervise his education more directly than if it were only an apprenticeship at the office."

"That would be perfect. Diego is a bright young man, very honest and determined."

"I see those traits in him already. Well now, John Cooper, *mon ami*"—the factor chuckled—"you've accomplished a great deal in a very short time. And I must thank you personally for what you've done for my lovely wife and myself in restoring our capital, to say nothing of our faith in human nature."

The two men shook hands and looked at each other with fervent admiration. Fabien tried to hide the suspicious moisture in his eyes by snorting and saying, "Before you leave, you'll do me the pleasure of dining at my house, and your *vaqueros*, too, and your two fine sons and Diego. Hortense has been longing for an opportunity to serve some of the finest cuisine New Orleans has to offer. The weather is pleasant now, and we can eat outdoors in the patio. We will have a lavish buffet and music, as well."

"That's very kind of you, and I know my men would welcome it, as would I," John Cooper said with a smile.

It was time for John Cooper Baines to return to the Double H Ranch, his business completed and young Diego de Escobar now ensconced in the home of David Allary, ready to begin his apprenticeship as a lawyer. A quick visit to Dr. Malmorain's residence to fetch Epanone also revealed that Lortaldo was making good progress in his apprenticeship to the Creole doctor, visiting the hospital daily and learning much about the white man's medicine. In just a few months, he would be ready to rejoin his wife at the Double H Ranch and from there return to the Jicarilla village in New Mexico and minister to his own people, using the medical techniques of both the Indians and the whites.

Andrew and Charles had enjoyed accompanying their father on the cattle drive, though both of them had expressed great disappointment over not having been able to see their father go after Christophe Carrière and bring him to justice. He had not wanted to tell them that he had been forced to kill the Creole adventurer with his bare hands, but when they had seen him return with Fabien Mallard and had observed that he had been wounded, nothing would do but that they must have the entire story.

"I didn't mean to tell you, boys," he said, frowning. "And if 'Long Girl' hadn't jammed, there'd have been really nothing to tell. In a way, it would have been more merciful. I only hope that both of you will never have to fight for your lives the way I did. Maybe there'll be more law and order on the Texas frontier by the time you're grown men—I surely hope so."

All the same, the boys could not help regarding their father with what amounted to hero worship, an attitude that was highly embarrassing to John Cooper. However, he knew just how to make Andrew, the older, think of other matters as, at breakfast this last day, he looked over at his tall, strapping son and drawled, "You know, Andy, we said we were going to visit Adriana over at the nuns' school before we left for home. I assume you still want to."

"Oh, gee, Pa," Andrew said, and promptly forgot his grown-up pose of calm indifference. He leaned forward, his eyes sparkling and his face flushed. "Of course I still want to see her! You know I'm crazy about her—"

"I'm not sure that's the right word to use about a fine young lady like that," John Cooper teased. Then, seeing the hurt look on Andrew's face, he chuckled and said more gently, "I didn't mean to poke fun at you, Andy boy. I know what you mean is that you love her and you wish you were grown-up enough to marry her. But don't forget, she's just turning fourteen. That's a little young, even on the frontier. Besides which, the education she'll be getting from the sisters at such a fine school will make her a much better wife when the time comes. But I'll arrange for us to visit just before we leave. Probably around noon, when the school classes are certain to break for *la comida*."

"Thanks, you're swell, Pa," Andrew blurted out, and

glared at his younger brother, who had adopted a patronizing smile by way of proving that he, too, was just as grown-up as his older brother. "You just wait, Charlie, until you find a girl you start dreaming about at night—then we'll see who laughs at who!"

"Now, boys, no bickering. Come along now, you've both had enough to eat, and we've a few chores before we leave. I'm glad we've settled Diego, and I think he likes the man he's going to work for. He'll come back a fine lawyer, one of these days."

"But won't he miss riding and hunting and going out for romps with Yankee the way we do, Pa?" Charles wanted to know.

"He's a little older than you, Charlie," John Cooper replied as he put his arm around his younger son's shoulders. "And he'll find so many new things in New Orleans that he won't have a chance to miss what we have back home."

Andrew would have greatly preferred to have gone alone with his father to pay a formal call on Adriana, but there was no help for it: Charles came along in spite of his older brother's exasperated feeling on the subject. John Cooper sensed exactly what was in Andrew's mind because, as they walked up the steps of the Ursuline Convent School, he murmured for only Andrew to hear, "I know you'd rather be alone with Adriana, but in any event, you can't do it with all the good sisters looking on. Get her to write you a nice letter and tell you what she really thinks. That's something you can hold onto when you're back on the ranch until you can see her again." This made Andrew brighten considerably.

One of the nuns answered the tall Texan's knock and smilingly admitted them to the parlor, saying that Mother Superior Cécile would be with them in a moment. Shortly thereafter, the kindly, elderly mother superior entered the parlor, and the two boys rose together with their father to greet her. "I wish you and your fine sons a pleasant day in our city, M'sieu Baines," she exclaimed. "My guess is that you have come to inquire about Francesca and the three Maldones girls."

"Yes, Mother Superior," John Cooper responded, "I bring a message for Paquita, María, and Adriana from their father, Raoul Maldones, and from Francesca's mother, Doña Inez."

In a few moments, after Mother Superior Cécile had sent for her, Francesca hurried out ahead of the three Maldones girls and came to hug John Cooper, then shake hands with Andrew and Charles. "It's wonderful to see you, John Cooper!" the precocious, lovely girl exclaimed. "Did you drive cattle here?"

"Yes, Francesca, we did. We also brought Diego along to study to be a lawyer. So he'll be in New Orleans, and I'm sure he'll come over to say hello to you, once he's settled."

"That would be wonderful!" Francesca declared. "I love this school, and I'm such good friends with Adriana and her sisters—here they come now!"

Andrew's heart began to beat faster at the sight of Adriana, who, in her sedate white blouse and black skirt and her unruly dark brown hair manageably combed back into a heart-shaped bun at the back of her head, looked even older than her almost fourteen years. Paquita's long black hair had been similarly styled, and she seemed less chubby and much more vivacious, while María, who was now seven, still irrepressibly giggled as she came to hug John Cooper and, far more shyly, to greet his sons.

"I—I hope you're getting along fine here, Adriana," Andrew said, with a gulp and a long face that all too candidly revealed his yearning to have five minutes alone with his Argentine sweetheart. But the smiling mother superior standing at the back of the parlor recalled to him the need for decorum, and John Cooper had to fight to keep from grinning as he observed what an effort Andrew made to appear politely cordial without breaking any of the rules.

"Oh, yes, Andrew, I like it here very much, and so do my sisters. And Francesca and I are such good friends!" At this, she reached out her hand to Francesca, who took it and squeezed it, and the two girls exchanged a radiant look. To be sure, Adriana had had many an occasion by now to tell Francesca how much she cared for Andrew and how brave he had been in helping save her father from prison. Nevertheless, quite aware of the mother superior's chastening presence, Adriana behaved quite as circumspectly as did young Andrew, though she could not help flashing him a quick, ardent look that made him crimson and shift from foot to foot, putting his hands behind his back and clasping his fingers tightly together.

It was John Cooper who made his older son eternally grateful by remarking at this point, "You know, Adriana, we're going back this afternoon to the Double H Ranch, and I'm going to take your best wishes and all your love, as well as that of your sisters, to your father. He's a great help to us at the ranch now, and he and Felipe Mintras will certainly be very helpful in the building of a community where everyone can live in peace. But it's a long way from here to Texas, and we probably won't be seeing you again until your summer holiday. We'd like very much to have a letter from you every now and again, particularly to Andrew."

"Oh, yes—I—I want to write—and I will, this evening as soon as I have time free after supper," Adriana blurted, then recovered herself as she saw Mother Superior Cécile smile knowingly. She immediately straightened, appearing for all the world like a dutiful schoolgirl who had never registered a single demerit for improper deportment.

"You be sure to do that, then, Adriana. You, too, Paquita, and María; I want you both to write so that your father will know how you are getting along," John Cooper concluded. "Well, Mother Superior, it was kind of you to let us see these sweet girls; now we'll be going back home."

"With my prayers that *le bon Dieu* will watch over you and yours always," she said, making the sign of the cross.

As Adriana turned to leave with the other girls, Andrew blurted out, "I'll write you, too, Adriana; I promise I will!"

"I—I'd like that very much, Señor Andrew," she replied, but the dazzling smile she flashed him just before she turned away took all the impersonality out of the formal title by which she had addressed him. He turned back to his father, his face aglow, and once again John Cooper had all he could do to keep from smiling, especially in the presence of Andrew's younger brother, who had watched the entire proceedings with considerable interest. Though Andrew was now acting like an infatuated schoolboy, he had already experienced far more than even men twice his age, in the two visits to Argentina and the cattle drives to New Orleans with his father. And he had proved his valor and dependability throughout. In his heart, John Cooper considered an eventual marriage between Adriana and young Andrew as a perfect match, and he hoped that it could take place in at the most four to five years. Adriana, too, because of what had happened to her father and her own courage in adapting herself to the political events that had forced him to flee, was far more mature than her actual age. Yes, indeed, here were two young people truly destined for each other, and theirs would be a long and steadfast union, once it was formed.

* * *

The same day John Cooper Baines left New Orleans, the bank president, Eugene Beaubien, wearing his most expansive smile, paused on the threshold of an office at the back of his bank. "M'sieu de Silva, have you had a chance, as yet, to total up the replenished assets of our bank?"

The forty-two-year-old bearded accountant deferentially rose from his desk and nodded, gesturing with his hand to a sheaf of papers before him. "*Mais oui*, M'sieu Beaubien. And may I say at this time how grateful I am that after I sold my little shop and came to you seeking employment, you trusted me enough to give me so responsible a post in your estimable bank."

"It was my pleasure, M'sieu de Silva. Your qualifications are very good. Besides, when I heard that you had a French mother, I was naturally sympathetic to you—for there is nothing like a French mother, as I know from my own happy experience as a boy. Such a one instills the sentiments of honor and duty as an obligation, *n'est-ce pas?*"

"*C'est bien vrai*, M'sieu Beaubien," the accountant agreed, and handed his employer the sheet of paper on which were noted the total assets. Then the accountant pursued, "Your bank is truly flourishing again! One day you will have the largest bank in all New Orleans; of this I am certain, M'sieu Beaubien, for you manage it so well."

"You're much too kind. Well then, I'll leave you to your work."

"M'sieu Beaubien, thank you again for your kindness to me. I am grateful for your trust and for the post, and I shall always be worthy of it."

"I am certain of that. *Au revoir*, M'sieu de Silva."

Enrique de Silva waited a few moments until he had seen the bank president return to his office and close the door. Then he opened the drawer of his desk and took out a letter that he had already written. It was addressed to Brigadier General Antonio López de Santa Anna at Veracruz, and it read as follows:

My revered General, the liberator of all Mexico, greetings!

I have the honor to inform you that the *gringo*, Señor John Cooper Baines, has brought back the bars of silver that were stolen from this bank last fall. In addition, he has deposited four more, from a source that the president of this bank has not confided to me. But you bade me let you know as to the disposition of the silver, and so I am happy to send you this news by the fastest post. In the event I learn any additional news of importance, I will communicate with you again, by courier if need be.

I wish now to avow again my total loyalty to your cause and to esteem myself as your humblest but certainly most willing and devoted servant in the cause of our great country.

He signed his name, sanded the signature, and put the letter back into the drawer. That evening, when he left the bank, he would deposit the letter at the post office in a wing of the courthouse. It was true that it would take a good month to reach the *libertador*, but by then there might be even more exciting news—and he, Enrique de Silva, was certain to be rewarded. Perhaps even a government post in the capital at Mexico City—and then a villa and then a beautiful young wife and a few lovely *criadas* to distract him from his conjugal duties . . .

Nineteen

Adriana Maldones was true to her promise, for the very next day after John Cooper and his party had left for the Double H Ranch, she wrote a letter to Andrew. Señora Josefa, who lived in the convent school in a little apartment that the sisters provided, conferred daily with her charges. One of her precepts was that Adriana must show to her any letter she had written before it could be posted, simply to make certain that the rules of propriety befitting a modest young girl were observed.

The letter that Señora Josefa read went as follows:

Esteemed Señor Andrew Baines,

I was very happy to see you and your brother and father, and María and Paquita want me to send their very best wishes to you and your brother and the señor Baines, your wonderful father. We are studying very hard, learning French under Sister Marguerite, and we are taking up sewing under Sister Althea. María is learning to do her sums, and Sister Louisette says that she is making very good progress.

When it is fair, we sometimes go out in the enclosed yard at the back of the school and do drawing or needlework. Of course, there are times I wish I could have my horse as I did back on the *pampas* and ride during the recreation period, but this is not permitted, and there is no way in which we could keep even a pony here. Maybe during our summer vacation at the ranch in Texas where you and your brother and father are, we will be allowed to ride real horses—all except María, who is much too small and would be scared. But I am sure there would be a little pony or colt that one of the *vaqueros* could lead her around on so she would think that she was actually riding the way I can.

Francesca, too, is my dear friend, and she said to be sure to include her very best wishes to everyone at the ranch. She is excited over knowing that Diego is going to study to be a lawyer, and she thinks that he will make a very good one because he is strong and brave and has a good mind.

I think this will be all for now and Señora Josefa is reading the letter to be sure that it is correct as to spelling and grammar. I know that I wish you all of the best in the world because of what you did to save *mi padre*.

When Señora Josefa finished reading the letter, she smiled and nodded approval. "It is a little too long, though it has good sentiments to it, *querida*," she told Adriana. "If you will give it to me, I will post it for you tomorrow when I go into town to shop for some dress material. Alas, the food here is so good that I am eating more than I should, and I need a wider skirt—I am ashamed to say it."

With her sweetest smile, Adriana handed the *dueña* the letter. But no sooner had Señora Josefa left to go back to her apartment than the girl took out another piece of stationery and wrote an entirely different letter:

Querido Andrew,

I wrote another letter to you, which Señora Josefa saw and will mail to you, but I am writing you this now for only you to see. I will have Francesca send it off tomorrow herself, since I am afraid if I did, Señora Josefa would find out what is going on.

I am so very fond of you, and it is very hard for me to be here so many miles away from you. In Argentina, when you came with your father to save mine from prison and the firing squad, I liked you very much. I did not think that you were a young boy, but really a man. You were so strong, and you knew how to shoot and you weren't afraid of anything the way a girl would be. I hope that we can be dear friends, and I do hope, too, that I can come very soon to the ranch and have some time to talk with you and ride horseback together.

Your loving friend,
Adriana Maldones

She blushed as she signed her name with such an ardent phrase, sealed the envelope, and then hurried to Francesca's room. She knocked at the door and, giving the letter to Doña Inez's daughter, said, "Do please mail it for me as you said you would, and don't dare tell Señora Josefa. But I couldn't let Señor Andrew think that I didn't care for him anymore, and he would never have known that from the way the first letter sounded—I couldn't say anything that really showed how I felt toward him because then Señora Josefa and Mother Superior Cécile would scold me for being forward."

"Of course I understand that," Francesca whispered. "Don't you worry. I'll mail it, and I won't tell a soul, even if they burn me at the stake for it!"

"Oh, you are such a good friend. I do hope that we shall all go together to Texas, and then we can ride horseback and have other secrets," Adriana avowed as she embraced Francesca.

*   *   *

Two days after Señora Josefa had posted Adriana's first letter to young Andrew Baines (Francesca having also posted the other, more ardent letter), a seaman off a freighter out of Havana came down with fever. There had been outbreaks of both typhoid and yellow fever in Philadelphia, as well as New York and Charleston, and in New Orleans the scourge of yellow fever (or yellow jack, as it was popularly called) had often manifested itself in the spring and summer. Some physicians bade their patients leave New Orleans and not return until the frost, and those who were wealthy and owned plantations upriver infallibly followed this sage advice.

The seaman had been observed to have a flushed face, scarlet lips and tongue, and a forehead that was burning with fever. His first mate, an affable Cuban, brought him to the Ursuline Convent Hospital and demanded to see Dr. Mendilever, who had come to the hospital from Liége, Belgium, eight years earlier and was now its foremost staff physician. He told the doctor, "This is Manuel Perez, who is not only my friend but also the best handler of cargo on the Atlantic. He has come down with the fever, and I will pay you many *pesos*, Dr. Mendilever, if you can cure him."

Dr. Michel Mendilever was in his early forties, tall and thin but possessed of tremendous stamina and endless patience. Married to a New Orleans woman, with whom he had two sons, he believed that it was his duty to treat with all his skill the sufferers of this malignant malady for which there seemed to be no medical cure and for whose cause as yet no indisputable medical evidence existed.

"I would not accept a fee, *amigo*," the doctor said to the first mate in Spanish, being fluent in that language, as well as in Latin, French, German, and some Greek, "but you may make a contribution to the convent in the name of the poor, of which there are far too many, as in every large city." He then turned to an orderly and said, "Please take this man to the empty bed in the west wing. Thus far, God be praised, we have seen no cases of yellow fever this year, so maybe this is a rare case."

"We shall be in port another week, *señor médico*," the first mate declared, "and I shall call here every day to see how Manuel does. I shall pray, too, and light a candle in the church."

"Prayer is sometimes a better remedy than many of the formulas prescribed for this fever, I'm afraid," Dr. Mendilever wearily observed. "And say a prayer also, *amigo*, that my skill may save your friend. *Vaya con Dios.*"

"You also, *señor médico*," the first mate said, respectfully inclining his head. Then he left the hospital.

But two days later, Manuel Perez's temperature had fallen below normal, and his skin had taken on a lemon-yellow tint. Also, he had begun to vomit, first a colorless fluid, then one mixed with blood. Dr. Mendilever did all that he could, but the seaman had been stricken with the fever well before he had been brought to the hospital, and it had taken too deadly a hold. He died on the third day after his admission, but by then there were a dozen new patients from various sections of New Orleans.

By now the New Orleans *Times-Picayune* had announced that at least fifty cases had been reported. Many of these were being treated by private physicians, their methods principally being bleeding and extreme dosages of calomel, though these dosages had the effect of acute mercurial poisoning, an effect that the doctors could not foresee. Also, there began to appear in the *Times-Picayune* advertisements by apothecaries offering remedies for the dreaded disease, such as Raspell's Sedative Water, Seidlitz Water, Labarraque's Chloride of Soda, "purging lemonade," and "Saturated Solution of Chloride of Lime."

But Dr. Mendilever was of the opinion, one shared by some of the French doctors who practiced in New Orleans, that calomel and bleeding were, far from being a cure, dangerous to the patient's well-being. He maintained that good nursing, the use of gentle evacuants, and acidic drinks employing cream of tartar and tamarind, orange, and lemon juices provided a far better course of treatment.

Three days after the seaman's death, sixty patients were admitted to the Ursuline Convent Hospital, and Dr. Mendilever consulted with Mother Superior Cécile to seek help.

"We need nurses and orderlies, Mother Superior," he said, facing her in her office, his face grave with concern. "I swear to you on my professional reputation that those who employ proper hygienic measures, as nurses and orderlies on my staff are taught to do, have no reason to fear yellow fever. I know that you have no one in your school who has had nursing experience in an epidemic—which I now believe this to be. But surely there must be those who could volunteer to do such simple tasks as the changing of bedpans, providing cold compresses, boiling drinking water, and other things that in themselves require little medical knowledge. I will personally supervise anyone from your school who wishes to volunteer her time—and it will be for the noblest cause of all, aiding the sick and easing the pangs of the dying."

"I will do what I can, Dr. Mendilever. Perhaps some of our girls will volunteer. But are you not afraid that girls in their early teens may be exposed to greater danger than you believe?"

He shook his head emphatically. "I do not, Mother Superior. My experience is that the young have far more stamina than the middle-aged or the old, and they can endure more hardships and perform more physical tasks without tiring. Believe me, no one who comes to me to volunteer will be exposed to unnecessary risks."

"I must think about your request, Dr. Mendilever. As I said, I will do what I can. And first I will pray for guidance."

"Yes, Mother Superior, as I shall, also. May God look down upon our endeavors and halt the spread of this epidemic. But there are things people can do, as well. For my own part, I intend to go before the mayor and the council and ask for strict hygienic remedies to be taken. The squalor and filth that befoul the city streets is an outrage, and we must somehow treat our water system to make it sanitary. These are things that one day, God willing, an enlightened civic administration will bring about. I am but a single voice."

"God has already told me what to do," the mother superior now said decisively. "There are three sisters who teach only a few classes, and they can readily act as nurses. I shall also ask the children if any of them wish to volunteer. I will be unable to tell their parents, since so many of them live far away, but I have been entrusted with the care of the children, and I will assume total responsibility—with God's help. We here at the convent school teach children that regardless of their faith, they must be endowed with a warm love for all humanity. Working with you in your hospital will allow them to show their selflessness and nobility."

The next morning, the kindly mother superior appeared in the classes and spoke of the illness that had fallen upon New Orleans. "Those of you who are older and who may have some free hours would be performing an act of blessed mercy to help Dr. Mendilever and the nurses. He assures me that there will be no danger to you from contagion, and your tasks will be very simple. For example, you can boil water, empty bedpans, and help with the meals; you can bring blankets and towels to those of our sisters who will be on duty and to the other nurses in the hospital."

Francesca de Escobar stood up from her seat and, in a clear voice, exclaimed, "Mother Superior, I want very much to help the sick, and I will do whatever I can, if you will permit it."

"God will bless you, dear Francesca," the black-robed mother superior avowed as she made the sign of the cross.

Now Adriana Maldones rose, for she was seated beside Francesca. "I, too, wish to help at the hospital, if you will permit it."

"And I, too," chimed in Paquita, not to be outdone.

"Children, children, this is wonderful of you! Very well, I will confer with your teachers and examine your schedules of classes and see what hours will be free for you. And, too, if you've never before seen people who are very ill and near death, it may sadden you because you feel you can do so little. I do not wish this experience to be a blight upon your happy natures, my dear children."

"At the ranch where I came from, Mother Superior," Francesca respectfully interposed, "we often had sickness among the *trabajadores* and their families. We have a doctor there, but still everyone helped as best as he or she could. We are not afraid of sickness, or at least, I am not."

"You are a warmhearted, good girl, and I am proud of you, Francesca. As I say, I will talk with your teachers, and for you, Adriana and Paquita, as well. But I am interrupting your French class, and I ask the pardon of Sister Marguerite." With this, the kindly woman turned to the tall, stern-faced nun and inclined her head, then went out of the room.

In the next classroom, which was for the younger girls, the mother superior told the class how some of the older girls were volunteering. She didn't want the little ones wondering what was going on without some reassurance that everything was all right.

Little María Maldones sprang from her seat and piped up, "Mother Superior, let me go; I can help, too!"

"Oh, no, my dear child, you are much too young."

"Are my sisters Adriana and Paquita going to go to the hospital, Mother Superior?" María petulantly demanded.

The mother superior turned to Sister Mélisande, who smiled and shook her head, then turned back to María and said, "Yes, it is true, they have volunteered."

"But they are being treated like grown-ups, and I should be, too, because I think I can be just as good a nurse as they are!" María insisted, and her face clouded up as if she were about to cry.

"You have spirit and heart, my darling. I'll tell you what I will do instead to give you responsibility among your classmates here. You shall be monitor of this beginning class in English grammar. You will help Sister Mélisande call the roll every morning and afternoon."

"That is very nice!" María admitted, and resumed her seat. "Thank you, Mother Superior."

"You are quite welcome, my darling. And I am sure that Adriana and Paquita will tell you what they do at the hospital. So in a way you can share it with them. The work is hard, and only because they are older than you and a little stronger, as you must surely realize, I am allowing them to go—but not for very long."

"I—I suppose that is right," María doubtfully admitted.

"Before you know it, now that you are monitor, you will be big and strong, and then you can do many more things and be the equal of your sisters. You must be patient, darling. Now, come give me a hug and tell me if you are content."

She held out her arms to the little girl, and María ran from her seat to go to her. Mother Superior Cécile gave her a loving hug, then kissed her on the cheek and murmured, "And now, dear María, go back to your seat and show the rest of the class what a grown-up monitor you can be!"

María obeyed and, just as the woman was about to leave the classroom, she impulsively called out, "I love you very much, Mother Superior!"

The very next afternoon, Francesca reported to Dr. Mendilever and informed him that Sister Cécile had given her permission to work between three and six o'clock, five afternoons a week.

Paquita and Adriana also followed Francesca to Dr. Mendilever's office, although the mother superior had stipulated that their volunteer work should take place only three afternoons a week between three and six. Finally, two other older girls, Aimée Cortigny and Gloria Sedrier, sixteen and seventeen respectively, had volunteered to work six days from three to seven, and the mother superior had granted their requests, for they stood particularly high scholastically. As it chanced, both girls were engaged to young Creoles whose families were prominent in New Orleans society, and their parents had sent them to the Ursuline School because they believed in the dedication and sound educational precepts of the nuns.

Although her thirteenth birthday was still three months away, Francesca had already displayed a ripening maturity of mind, thanks in part to the warmly loving devotion of her mother, Doña Inez, and the integrity of the father she so dearly admired, the late Don Diego. Moreover, even while she had been living on the ranch, Francesca had shown a great interest in reading on a great variety of subjects, and during his trips to New Orleans, John Cooper had purchased books and brought them back with him as gifts to the talented and perceptive girl.

Dr. Mendilever welcomed her with a handshake and told her that he greatly appreciated her offer to help. "I need not conceal from you, M'amselle Francesca," he told her, "that the epidemic seems to be worsening. This morning, for instance, fifteen new patients were admitted, and one of them has already died. I do not say this to frighten you, for as I told Mother Superior Cécile, my experience is that with proper hygiene, you will have no ill effects whatsoever. You'll have the reward, I am sure, of knowing that you're aiding those who are in desperate need of it. You're lovely, and you have a most engaging smile and personality—this, the mother superior has already told me—"

Francesca blushed and modestly lowered her eyes. "I want to do everything I can. I know there are some older nuns working here at the hospital, Dr. Mendilever, and I'm sure they get tired easily with all the work they have to do. I'm young, and I'm strong because I was born and lived on a ranch in Texas, where I was very active."

"Then you'll do famously. Thank you, my dear. God bless you."

Francesca, like the other four girls, was given a uniform to wear, and Dr. Mendilever had all of them first scrub their hands with a strong lye soap. "One thing I insist on in this hospital, young ladies," he told them, "is cleanliness. It is one of the countermeasures we can take against many diseases like this fever. Some of our unfortunate patients come from the poorest slums of the city, others from ships where hygiene does not exist, and therefore they are exposed to the fever. Now, Sister Laura will assign you your tasks for this afternoon. And if you have any questions, or there's anything you wish to report to me, please come to my office or else find me in any of the wards." He chuckled gently. "We are not hard taskmasters here, and all of us need one another. I think that is why God created the community of man, so that we would learn to be brothers and sisters and to help one another in time of need—at least, that's part of my own religious belief."

During her very first afternoon, Francesca showed a willingness to serve, going through the wards with a smile on her face, stopping at those beds where the patients were awake to ask them how they were feeling and whether they wished water to drink, or if there was anything she could do for them. Two of the nuns assigned from the convent school to act as regular nurses during the siege of fever were middle-aged women, and Francesca saw one of them entering a ward with her arms loaded with blankets. Quickly she hurried up to the sister and respectfully asked, "Please, Sister, let me carry these for you. You mustn't tire yourself."

"Thank you, child; that's sweet of you," the nun told her with a weary smile as she gratefully transferred her burden to Francesca's eager arms. "I'll admit that when one grows older, one's legs and arms tire fast. You, fortunately, don't have anything like that to worry about. Now, this blanket goes over to that bed by the far wall at the left. And the one under it is for the patient two beds to your left after that, and the third and fourth go to the last two beds along that wall."

"I will take them there, Sister." Francesca gave the nun a warm smile and hurried off to execute her errand.

At the end of her stint, she felt exhilarated, and when she reported to Dr. Mendilever to tell him that she was going back to the school, he thanked her. "I've already had comments from some of the patients that you're like a breath of fresh air, my dear. God bless you for coming. How do you feel?"

"Never better, Dr. Mendilever. I feel so sorry for them, and so many of them are afraid that they're going to die."

He gravely nodded. "Yes, but your cheerfulness may

help dispel the terrible fatalism that so many victims of the disease seem to have. In fact, I truly believe that a positive outlook can help in one's recovery."

By the end of the first week, Francesca was called in before her first morning class by the mother superior. "Dr. Mendilever has told me how very helpful you've been at the hospital, my child. I think that you are blessed and touched by the finger of God Himself," the elderly nun smilingly declared. "All of us have a calling in life. I knew when I was a little girl that I was summoned to serve Him, while others had their call later in life, perhaps after worldly disappointments through which they learned that to give unstintingly of oneself to strangers is His way toward an everlasting love. I do not say that you will become a nun, but it may well be that one day you will become a nurse. You have the aptitude for it, the courage and the strength, and even though you are not yet thirteen, you show a maturity that is surprising. Although, from what I know of your fond parents and especially the reputation of your wonderful father, it is not so surprising after all. God bless you, dear Francesca."

There were tears in Francesca's eyes as she humbly bowed her head before the mother superior, who made the sign of the cross over her, her lips moving in a silent prayer of benediction.

Each new day saw more patients being brought to the hospital, some of them in the very last stages of the pitiless yellow fever. Francesca herself saw three of the patients die even as she was bringing them cold compresses and blankets. She resolved to herself to redouble her efforts, for if she could help save only one patient, her work would not have been in vain. And in the silent, brooding atmosphere of men and women and even children lying in ward beds fighting the onslaught of the fever, she strove to be more cheerful than ever, to radiate an optimistic spirit that might help ease the pains of these who had been stricken and were fearful of death.

On the second Saturday evening of her shifts at the hospital—for she had begged the mother superior to let her spend a few more hours than had been originally authorized—she finished the task of taking up the bed linen and going out to a closet room where all dirty linen was put into a hamper and then burned. Dr. Mendilever had given this order for hygienic reasons and had urged the sisters to solicit from their parishioners gifts of linen, sheets, pillowcases—whatever bedding could be spared—for the epidemic seemed to spread, rather than decline, with each new day. And there was still the worst of the summer to come.

Francesca had watched two orderlies cover a victim with a sheet and gently and silently carry his body out of the ward, and she felt a sudden need to go outside for a moment and breathe in the evening air. There had been a brief rain about an hour before, which had cleared the humid atmosphere and brought a cooling breeze in from the Gulf. Dr. Mendilever, harassed and exhausted, working swiftly at the bedside of a patient who had just been brought in, watched her as she went down the ward and disappeared out the door. He sighed and said to himself thoughtfully, "That girl is going to make some man, some very fortunate man, a wonderful wife, and I only hope he's worthy of her."

Francesca had gone down the steps of the hospital and stood on the wooden sidewalk, closing her eyes and breathing deeply. The cool air was pleasant, and she tried to forget the groans and cries of the very ill and the dying, which had resounded in her ears almost all afternoon long. She thought of Diego and the happy times they had had playing as children on the Double H Ranch. The day before, he had left a note for her with the mother superior, telling her excitedly how much he liked the lawyer to whom he was apprenticed, what his duties were, and also how the lawyer had taken him to a little Creole restaurant, where he had had the best supper in all his life. He had wished her well and hoped that one day he might see her, perhaps even take her to lunch at that same restaurant, if she had the time to spare.

She smiled to herself, warmly remembering the arguments they had had and how she had first thought him such a boorish, brash creature who cared only for himself and thought that girls were his inferiors. Each of them had grown up now, and perhaps this would be her career, being a nurse to the sick, while he would aid those who could not afford his services, but yet who needed them far more than the wealthy. Each, then, would be doing a labor of love, and God would reward them both. Her faith was as serene as that of Doña Inez, her mother.

Suddenly there was the clatter of a horse's hooves, and a calash drew up in front of the hospital. A wiry, gray-haired man in his early fifties, extremely spry and muscular, leaped out of the calash.

The driver, a surly-featured, thickly bearded middle-aged man, called out in an angry voice, "Go on, now, take him out of here, I want no truck with yellow jack! For all I know, your friend there may have given me a dose—"

"Damn you for a lousy coward!" the older man snapped back as he reached into the calash and lifted out a man covered with a blanket, his head lolling to one side.

"Please let me help!" Francesca exclaimed as she hurried to the calash. She lifted the man's legs while his companion supported him by the waist and shoulders.

"Thankee, little missy, it's mighty kind of you! At least you're not scared like that fool driver!" Then, turning back to the scowling, bearded driver, he exclaimed, "All right, you coward, you've had your pay, and it's more than it was worth for all your bad-mouthing! Now be off with you!"

The driver of the calash muttered a profane oath, cracked his whip, and drove off almost at a gallop. The gray-haired man turned to Francesca as they began to walk slowly up the steps with their burden. "Me, I had yellow jack before, about twenty years ago, but I got over it—damn fool doctors nearly killed me along with whatever I had. Now here's this young man down with it. I heard tell at the hotel where we're staying that this hospital is the best place in town for fever!"

"Yes, sir. The sisters are very kind, and the doctors work hard. Is he—is he your son?" Francesca timidly inquired.

The gray-haired man uttered a curt laugh and, shaking his head, replied, "Bless you, little missy, you couldn't be wronger than that! No sirree, he's a foreman I have working for me on a sugarcane plantation upriver. Nice gent, came from the East. Said he was looking for a job, and damned if he didn't know how to get sugarcane production out of the lazy, no-'count niggers, that he did. Made me lots of money, and then when we came down to New Orleans on business and he took sick with yellow jack, I figgered I owed him a good chance to live. Selfish on my part because I want him back! Now, let's get him in so a doctor can take a good look at him. My friend's name's Jack McKinnon. Me, I'm Abner Heskins."

"I'm glad to meet you, Mr. Heskins. Come this way." They had reached the lobby, and Francesca said, "We can set him down here on this sofa. Then I'll get Dr. Mendilever . . .

but here he comes now. Dr. Mendilever," she called, "this patient is Mr. McKinnon, who works for Mr. Heskins here. He was taken down with the fever."

"Put him in bed five in the main ward, Francesca dear," the doctor said. "I'll attend to him directly. John"—this to one of the orderlies—"give Francesca and Mr. Heskins a hand here with a new patient, for bed five in the main ward."

The orderly helped Francesca and the older man carry the unconscious Jack McKinnon to the bed in the ward and to put him comfortably into it. After removing the patient's shoes, Francesca drew the sheets around him. She observed that he was well-dressed and rather handsome, with regular features, a deep cleft in his chin, a firm jawline, and a high-arching forehead. His eyelids began to flutter weakly, and she saw that his eyes were large and dark brown but glazed with fever. She shook her head in compassion, then hurried to get a cold compress to put on his head before Dr. Mendilever arrived.

A few moments after he had come to the patient's bed and examined McKinnon, Dr. Mendilever sighed and said, "Yes, it's the fever, all right. I'm going to give him some quinine, and Francesca, surely your shift's over by now. Aren't you tired? I marvel how you get your energy."

"I—I'd like to stay on just a little while longer, if you don't mind, Dr. Mendilever."

"With my blessing, but don't overtire yourself now, or Mother Superior Cécile will never forgive me," he warned. He administered the quinine, then went off into another ward after one of the sisters told him of a patient who was entering a critical stage of the disease.

Abner Heskins looked at the lovely young girl and said, "Well, missy, I have to thank you. You're sure looking after Jack as if you was his kin. I'd best be getting back now, and I don't mind telling you I'm a mite scared of hospitals, 'cause it reminds me of the time I had this yellow jack myself. I'll come around tomorrow afternoon and see how Jack's doing."

"I know he'd want you to. And I'm sure he'll be better. It always seems to be worse at night," Francesca explained.

After Heskins had left, Francesca replaced the compresses on Jack McKinnon's forehead, then proceeded to sit by his bed and keep an all-night vigil. She was confident that if need be, Adriana would cover for her at the convent.

She was not able to explain to herself why she felt

compelled to keep this vigil; she only knew that not only did she wish to but also that she must. Strangely enough, she did not feel the least bit exhausted as almost every half hour she rose to wring out fresh cold compresses and to take another cloth to wipe away the fever sweat from his face. His night was restful, and he seldom stirred. At times, he uttered a faint groan, and she anxiously leaned forward, but then there would be no sound and he would appear to be resting— which, of course, was the best sign of all. Meanwhile, one of the doctors on night duty looked in from time to time, surprised to see Francesca still there but reassured by the girl's presence with the patient.

As the first rays of dawn filtered in through the shutters, the young man awakened, wanly opening his eyes to see Francesca bending over him.

She caught her breath, then smiled joyously. "Do you feel a little better, Mr. McKinnon? You've been very sick, but I think the fever has broken. I'll get a doctor to look at you now. Mr. Heskins brought you in."

"I—I k-know. Th-thank you," he feebly managed.

She rose, and suddenly she felt very tired, but his smile and his recovery—for she was certain that it was this—more than compensated for her fatigue. "Well, I'll have to leave you now. But you'll be fine. And I'll come back to see you soon, I promise I will."

"What—what is your name?"

"It's Francesca de Escobar."

"How—how long were you here with me?"

"That's not important. Now you rest, and I'll go get the doctor. But I'll be sure to come back and see how you are, Mr. McKinnon. Good-bye, now."

She hurried out of the hospital, and the elderly night porter admitted her to the building of the convent school. "Please, Père Lenormand, don't tell Mother Superior Cécile I came back so late. I was at the hospital. There was a very sick patient, and I just couldn't leave him," she breathlessly explained to the frail, white-haired Frenchman.

He chuckled softly, put his finger to his lips, and nodded. "I won't tell on you, M'amselle Francesca. What you did was a wonderful thing. Now you hurry up to your dormitory and go right to sleep, and if anybody asks me, I'll say that you came in at midnight."

"You're a darling!" Impulsively, she kissed the old man

on the cheek, then hurried up the stairs, but as silently as she could go, to reach her room. No one was up and about, and it appeared she had not been missed.

The following evening after supper, Francesca received permission from the mother superior to visit the hospital—though it was not the agreed-upon hours—and went at once to the bedside of Jack McKinnon. He seemed much stronger, and he smiled as he recognized her approaching him. The elderly nun assigned to the ward greeted Francesca. "Good evening, my child. Yes, your patient is past the crisis, Dr. Mendilever has said. The fever broke this morning, and the worst is over. Now he needs rest and care, and we shall give him that."

"I prayed, too, Sister," Francesca murmured.

"That is sometimes better than any prescription a doctor may give, however wise," the nun responded as she crossed herself. Then, turning to Jack McKinnon, she said, "I shall leave you to the care of this sweet child who is concerned about you. Good night, Mr. McKinnon."

"And to you, and many thanks, Sister," he said.

Francesca had drawn up a stool and seated herself beside his bed. He put a hand to his face and grimaced. "I've developed a beard; my Lord, I must look a sight."

"No, no, not at all," she protested, her eyes fixing on his handsome face. His dark brown eyes were no longer glazed with fever, and he regarded her with a candid, friendly look that made her feel as if she had known him for a long time.

"I'll tell you a little about myself, if it won't bore you to tears, Miss Francesca."

Her name on his lips delighted her, preceded as it was by a title that implied that she was an adult. She nodded her head and said, "I'd love to know about you, Mr. McKinnon. I don't think you're a Texan or from the West, though."

"You're right. No, the fact is, I was born in the West Indies, and my father owned a sugarcane plantation—that's how I happen to know about the business and could be of value to Abner Heskins. Well now, when I was eight years old, the slaves mutinied, my father was killed, and my mother and I were lucky to escape with our lives aboard a cargo ship bound for this very city. We stayed here until I was twelve, and then she took me to New York to live with her sister, who had just lost her husband. I finished my schooling in

New York, and then my mother died when I was fifteen, so my aunt looked after me for a time."

"You've had so much tragedy in your life, Mr. McKinnon," Francesca said sadly.

"Not really, Miss Francesca. I still remember my father and mother, and it's as if they were still alive for me. And I've been very lucky—the latest proof of which is that I'm getting over this dose of yellow jack. But anyway, I inherited a little money from my parents, and I set myself up running a livery stable because I loved horses—still do, for a fact."

"You'd love our ranch in Texas, Mr. McKinnon, because my brother-in-law, John Cooper Baines, raises the most wonderful palominos."

"I'll bet they're wonderful! Maybe one day I will get a chance to visit your part of the country." He was lost in thought for a moment, then went on, "Anyway, when I was twenty-two, which was five years ago, I fell in love with a beautiful girl who came from a very distinguished family. I thought she loved me, too, but it turned out that she preferred an older man who had a great deal more money than I had and could give her much more luxury."

"That was cruel of her!" Francesca impulsively blurted out, then blushed furiously.

"Oh, it's just as well, Miss Francesca. If we had married, and if she had that nagging ambition to have wealth, she wouldn't have been a good wife and I wouldn't have been a good husband for her. There are lots of things more important than money to me. Like meeting kind people like you and Dr. Mendilever and the good sisters who've kept me alive through this sickness. That means a lot more to me, Miss Francesca."

"It—it's nice of you to say—but I did very little—"

"Dr. Mendilever told me how you come from the Ursuline School to work at the hospital and how you stayed all night with me, always changing compresses and seeing if there was anything you could do to make me more comfortable. To do that for a stranger shows a wonderfully kind and sweet nature, Miss Francesca. But anyway, as I was saying, after our romance broke up, I decided to do something active and exciting so I could forget Vivian. To be honest, I smuggled contraband in Mexico for a while. Then I came back to New Orleans to look up a cousin. In the process, I met Abner Heskins when he was in town to buy supplies. We had a few drinks together, and when he found out that I grew up on a sugarcane plantation, he hired me right off to be a foreman. And that's about it, until just now, when he brought me in."

"You've certainly led a very adventurous and exciting life, Mr. McKinnon. Do you like raising sugarcane?"

"Very much. Sugar is going to be even more important than cotton one of these days." His face clouded momentarily. "The thing I don't like is the business of slaves. It's true I grew up with them as a boy in the West Indies, but I've never really believed that any man should be a slave to anyone else. I understand the reasons why—it's cheap labor—but I still don't approve of it. Well, me, I've never used the whip yet on any of the slaves that Abner Heskins has on his plantation, and I never will. I try to encourage them, try to reward them for good work. To my way of thinking, I get much more out of them that way than by coming down hard on them all the time."

"I—I believe the way you do about slaves. There aren't any on our ranch. We all work together and share the profits and rewards."

"You and I think alike in a lot of ways, Miss Francesca, and you've been like an angel of mercy to me. A very pretty angel of mercy, too, if you don't mind my saying so."

Francesca quickly looked away. She felt her cheeks flaming and even put a hand up to feel the heat of that blush. She had never before met anyone like Jack McKinnon, and his treating her like a grown-up and taking her into his confidence had made an indelible impression on her.

He smiled at her discomfiture and reached for her hand and gently squeezed it. "You're a very sympathetic listener, Miss Francesca. I'd have been a lucky man if Vivian had had half of your honesty and thoughtfulness for other people. Now you take some advice from me, though probably I'm not the best person in the world to give it—don't you ever sell yourself cheap, Miss Francesca, and don't you ever mistake a man's good looks for what he might be hiding inside of him. When you grow up, you're going to have lots of fellows wanting to marry you, and I just hope you can pick the right one for yourself so you'll have a long and happy life. That's what I wish for you."

Her hand trembled in his, and he, seeing that she was blushing again and not wanting to embarrass her, at once released it. "Well, you've really set me to talking, and I guess that's a pretty fair sign I'm on the road to recovery, Miss Francesca. I hope I'll see you again before I get to leave the hospital. I know that Abner Heskins can't wait to have me back." He chuckled mirthlessly. "Now that I come to think of it, with the hot summer ahead of us, a sugarcane plantation isn't the most pleasant place in the world to live, but right now it's earning my cakes and ale, as you might say. And I always make it a point of wanting to do well in whatever I'm doing, especially because I'm grateful to Abner."

"I—I'm awfully glad I met you, Mr. McKinnon," Francesca said timidly. "And I'll come over tomorrow after classes, to see how you are. Now you'd better rest. And—and thank you ever so much for all the sweet things you said to me—I shan't ever forget them." Then, trusting herself no further, Francesca quickly rose from the stool, gave him a quick wave of her hand, and hurried out of the ward. Once again, her cheeks were crimson, and she knew that that night, when she was back in her dormitory with Adriana, she was going to tell her all about the handsome stranger whom, strangely enough, she felt as if she had known even longer than she had young Diego de Escobar. She wished that she were already four or five years older so that she could tell Jack McKinnon how much she liked him and wanted to hear more about his life and what his thoughts were about important things.

Twenty

Five years earlier, Timothy Callendar, his wife, Elaine, and their three children had come to the Double H Ranch to be reunited with Bess Sandarbal. For Bess had been Timothy's sister-in-law and was widowed when Indians killed her first husband and took her into captivity. Don Diego de Escobar had saved her by buying her from the Indians, and then she and his loyal *capataz*, Miguel, had fallen in love and married.

Timothy and Elaine Callendar's children—all boys—were now nine, fifteen, and sixteen respectively, named Peter,

Jasper, and Frank. Elaine was pregnant again, and this time both she and Timothy were praying for a little girl.

The Callendars had been given one hundred acres of farmland, and the *trabajadores* had built a sturdy frame house for the family. Bess and Elaine Callendar had become very close friends, and the latter's three boys were taking lessons in the classroom presided over by the redoubtable Sister Eufemia.

The Callendar boys had made friends among the *vaqueros*, and even the youngest of them rode almost as well as any man. The trio also made friends with Yankee and his two surviving cubs from Luna's litter. A male and a female, both animals were a year old and virtually full grown. John Cooper had shown the Callendar boys how he trained Yankee, and from that day forth they had spent many enjoyable hours training the two puppies so that these, like Yankee and, before him, valiant Lobo, would be docile toward friends, amenable to orders, and yet capable of attacking either on a hunt for game or against enemies who might strike the ranch without warning.

Little Dolores, now almost eight, the adopted daughter of Doña Inez and sister to Juan, her junior by two years, had named the female cub Maja because, as Dolores had declared, "She has a sweet look in her eyes, even if she is a wolf cub." John Cooper had chuckled at the name, for it meant "pretty," though to be sure, when one looked into Maja's gentle, brown eyes, it was evident that there was at times a beauty that justified the name. Meanwhile, Carlos's son, Diego, had called the male Fuerte because he was so strong, and his jaws and forelegs were as powerful as Yankee's, even though he was only a year old.

John Cooper was back at the ranch, serenely happy to be reunited with Dorotéa, their new son, and the rest of his family, knowing that the silver stolen from the New Orleans bank had been restored and that the other treasure from the secret cave he and Pastanari had recently discovered near Raton was on the way. For upon returning to Texas, John Cooper had sent out a messenger to Pastanari, telling the chief of his wish to have the silver taken from the mine and brought by Jicarilla braves to the ranch in Texas, then on to New Orleans. The week before, Dejari, the young brave who had initially brought the news that old Potiwaba was dying and had a message for John Cooper, had ridden in and told the Texan that the work had been accomplished. The religious artifacts were being sent directly to Padre Madura in Taos, and the rest of the treasure was on its way to Texas. It had been stored in sacks placed on travois, covered with blankets and securely bound with rawhide thongs. At once John Cooper had gone to Ramón Santoriaga, explained the mission that had taken him to the stronghold, and urged the former colonel in Santa Anna's own army, now in charge of defending the Double H Ranch, to head a force of twenty-five well-armed *vaqueros* and *trabajadores* to meet the convoy halfway and to bring the treasure safely back.

Now on this afternoon in May, John Cooper prepared to go hunting with the wolf-dog yearlings. The three Callendar brothers had decided not to join the other boys on the ranch, who were going to their favorite swimming hole, and they eagerly asked John Cooper if they might accompany him. He told them, "Of course, it'll be good experience for you. I also want to see how well these young cubs handle themselves in case they face something bigger and stronger than they are. Well, if you boys are coming along with me, best get your horses!"

The boys ran off toward the stable and saddled their wiry mustangs. John Cooper, meanwhile, decided to take Pingo, his favorite palomino, and the great horse whinnied and nuzzled his master's shoulder, turning his head as he saw John Cooper advance to put a saddle on him. John Cooper patted the horse's head, then dipped right thumb and forefinger into his jacket pocket to draw out a carrot, of which Pingo was particularly fond.

The two older Callendar boys had brought along their rifles, but the youngest had not yet been given one by his father, and he said to John Cooper, disappointment in his voice, "Gosh, in case we run into any game, my brothers are going to bring it down, and I'll just be sitting on my horse watching."

"Don't you worry, Peter," John Cooper said, wheeling Pingo to ride alongside the boy, "I'll tell you what I'll do. I'll give you a lesson in how to use a musket when we get back. Do you know, that's what my father first gave me, and he told me I wasn't fit to handle a rifle until I learned how to use a musket properly. Now, come on, let's see how fast you can race that mustang of yours to keep up with Pingo here!"

The boy grinned from ear to ear at this mark of favor, for

he idolized John Cooper, and the hurt of not having a rifle was swiftly forgotten as he urged his mustang on to match the magnificent stride of the palomino.

Suddenly Frank Callendar shouted and pointed off to the right. A small deer was racing out from behind a thicket of mesquite, and the boy cocked his rifle and fired, but missed.

Maja and Fuerte, who had kept pace with the four riders, uttered joyous barks, and at John Cooper's command, they loped after the fleeing deer. The tall Texan grinned. The wolf-dogs had the instinct of hunting wolves, no doubt about it; their training among humans seemed to have taken hold as well, for they knew how to obey the simple commands they had been taught, as had Yankee and Lobo before them.

The wolf-dogs had overtaken the deer, and Fuerte leaped at its throat, worrying it, while Maja sank her fangs into the deer's haunch. They bore it down to the ground, where Fuerte killed it; then, at John Cooper's shouted command, they backed away, growling, hairs bristling, tails stiffly pointed, awaiting a new order.

"Good dogs! Very good dogs!" John Cooper called as he rode up to the fallen animal. "Frank, since you fired at him, even if you didn't hit him, I'll let you have the honor of carrying his carcass back with us—it'll make a fine supper for your father and mother and brothers, as well as your Aunt Bess. I see you've brought a lariat with you. Let's see how well you can use it to tie the deer to your horse."

"Sure, Mr. Baines, sir," the boy enthusiastically replied as he leaped off his horse, detached the coiled lariat from the saddle pummel, and hurried off toward the deer. Maja and Fuerte watched him, their yellow eyes glowing, as the boy lifted the dead deer over his shoulders. It was small, not more than a year old, and he carried it with ease over to his horse, which stood docilely awaiting him. Then, draping the body of the deer behind his saddle, he bound it to the horse with the lariat and made a tight knot at the pummel.

"You did very well," John Cooper complimented him.

Frank grinned with pride as he mounted his horse and followed the tall Texan on the palomino. Maja and Fuerte loped ahead as John Cooper turned toward the northwest now, remembering that when he had ridden to the stronghold with Dejari, they had passed through a small valley formed between facing rows of hills, and there had been a herd of deer on the slopes. Maybe there they would enjoy some more good hunting.

The sky was sunny and bright, and the warm air exhilarated John Cooper. They had neared the small valley now, and suddenly John Cooper saw the two yearling cubs stiffen and then heard a low growl from each of them. At the same moment, at a distance beyond him, there was the roar of a cougar. He would never forget that sound. His memory was swiftly taken back to that time when he had found Carlos de Escobar thrown from his horse, with a cougar crouching and about to spring down on him. He had swiftly fired "Long Girl" and killed the beast before it could reach the young Spaniard, and that had been how he had first met the de Escobar family.

He reined in his palomino and called to the boys, "You'd better stay behind me now. I think there's a cougar up ahead. We call it a mountain lion. I didn't expect to find one in these parts, but that roar just now can't be anything else. So you boys stay out of it and leave it to me and young Fuerte and Maja."

"Can we—can we watch, Mr. Baines?" Peter, the youngest, asked.

John Cooper chuckled. "I guess you can. Just stay a good distance behind me. I don't want that big cat coming out here and scaring your horses—first thing they'll do is shy and throw you off." He urged Pingo on and called to Maja and Fuerte, "Go on; ¡adelante, pronto!"

The wolf cubs uttered a simultaneous bark and joyously loped forward. Once again, the cougar's roar sounded, and even Pingo tossed his head nervously. "Steady, boy, steady. I won't let it get you. Let's get up a little closer and find out exactly where it's hiding," he told the palomino.

But already the yearling cubs had found the cougar, for their angry barks and growls turned John Cooper's attention to the slope of one of the hills, where the great cat had emerged through a clump of gnarled live-oak trees. It was a relatively small cougar, no more than five feet long with a tail about a third that length, and it stood, lashing its tail, snarling at the approaching wolf cubs. John Cooper urged his palomino forward until he was within a hundred yards of the tawny cat, and then he called out to the wolf cubs, "¡Matad, matad!"

At once, Fuerte lunged up the slope at the cougar, who

bared its fangs and made a vicious swipe of its right paw at the courageous wolf-dog. But Fuerte nimbly darted to one side just as Maja, having made a circle that brought her around the right side of the cougar, sprang up and nipped it in the flank.

There was a ferocious yowl as the cougar whirled to drive away its new attacker. Pingo snorted, but John Cooper soothingly leaned over the palomino's neck and urged him on to within some thirty yards of the beast, while he swiftly reached for the Lancaster rifle and drew it out of the sheath.

As the cougar had whirled to drive away Maja, Fuerte went for the cat's throat with a savage growl and a sudden spring.

Well behind John Cooper, the three Callendar boys watched openmouthed, and the middle boy, Jasper, gasped, "Gosh, that's an awfully fierce cat—but look how brave Maja and Fuerte are!"

The cougar had swiped at Fuerte with its paw, but the wolf cub, as if anticipating this reaction, had released his hold and leaped off to the animal's left, while Maja again nipped the cat's flank with her sharp teeth. Now, maddened with rage, the cougar charged Fuerte. But John Cooper waited no longer, though he admired the wolf cub's courage. Swiftly leveling "Long Girl," he pulled the trigger, and the tawny beast stopped in its tracks, gave a convulsive shudder, and rolled over onto its side, its fangs still bared. Both wolf cubs now rushed up and began to worry the dead cougar, but John Cooper called them off with a sharp command.

"That was a wonderful shot, Mr. Baines!" Frank exclaimed. "I was scared there; I thought it was going to kill Fuerte!"

John Cooper returned his rifle to the saddle sheath and said, "Well, we'll take it back to the ranch and I'll have the *trabajadores* skin it. I'll have the skin made into a throw rug for my Dorotéa." He dismounted, and as he tied up the dead animal and secured it to his horse, all three of the boys stared at him with undisguised admiration that was little short of awe.

Shortly before noon of the next morning, Ramón Santoriaga and his twenty-five armed *vaqueros* rode through the gate of the Double H Ranch, their horses drawing a number of travois that Pastanari had sent, covered and sturdily bound. The Indians who had met Ramón halfway had gone back to their stronghold, with the exception of Dejari, who rode with Ramón's men.

John Cooper greeted him. "Welcome, Dejari! I am glad that you have come with our men so that I may send you back with a message of thanks for my blood brother, your *jefe*." John Cooper gave the young brave the tribal sign of friendship.

"It was a good idea for you to send your *trabajadores* to meet us halfway, and I admit that they covered the terrain in even faster time than we Jicarilla," Dejari declared with a wry smile. "The truth is, your horses are far better than ours, *Halcón*. And for my part, I did not want to bring the fine palomino you gave me on this mission."

"With this fortune that you have brought me, Dejari, I will see that the Jicarilla have many good horses like the one I gave you, and they will come from my own ranch. For now I wish you to take back a fresh horse for yourself from my stable and also a yearling palomino, which has been gelded, for Pastanari."

"You put me in your debt again, *Halcón*."

"No. It is only a small payment for what you and your tribe have done for me," John Cooper gently corrected. "I have also arranged to have my factor buy plenty of weapons and supplies, which I will send on to your stronghold when they arrive."

"Pastanari bade me give you this tally of what was taken from the cave, *Halcón*," Dejari now said. "He wrote it on bark, and I have kept it safely all this long journey for you." The Indian handed John Cooper a rolled sheet with the thinness of parchment, beautifully inscribed with dyes. As the tall Texan unfolded it, the brave explained, "You see this figure that is long on two sides and short at the ends"—he meant a rectangle, for which there was no Apache word— "this is the symbol for the bars of silver. In all, there were ninety-six."

"And the other figure, I take to be religious crosses and rosaries and other objects that were found?" John Cooper queried.

"That is so," the brave responded. "They were sent on to Padre Madura, as you requested, with the exception of some bracelets that you asked to have for gifts."

"Very good. Now, go to the *hacienda;* you will have *la comida* with us. I will talk to Miguel and see to the two horses you are to take for yourself and Pastanari. Then I will join you, and we shall eat together." With this, the Texan clapped Dejari on the back and strode off to the stable.

Ramón Santoriaga and some of his men were bringing the horses of the *vaqueros* and *trabajadores* to the stable, and John Cooper thanked him for his part in the transfer of the fabulous treasure of the secret cave. "I shall ask another mission of you, Ramón. I propose to take the treasure at once to the New Orleans bank."

"I will be happy to provide an armed escort for the journey to New Orleans, Señor Baines," the former Mexican soldier replied.

"We'll leave tomorrow. And when I return, I propose to circle and visit the settlement on the Brazos. Some of that money from the treasure will be used to give the settlers there more supplies, tools, and above all else, weapons with which to defend themselves against any raids by the Mexican soldiers."

"I heard from a friendly Tonkawa who stopped here for water and food while you were last in New Orleans," Ramón vouchsafed, "that Mexican patrols have been crossing the border at various points, raiding little towns, and demanding of *gringos* proper identification. They have even shot some of them for being enemies of the Republic."

"A term that Santa Anna uses to serve his own murderous ends," John Cooper angrily responded. "I can't forget how he went to the Brazos settlement and shot down old Henry Hornsteder in cold blood because that courageous man wouldn't kiss the ground and swear allegiance to Mexico. Well now, after you have finished with the horses, come into the house and join us at *la comida*. Then we'll talk more of our important mission to New Orleans."

Dejari did not wish to remain for the rest of the day and night at the *hacienda*, although John Cooper had invited him to do so; he was anxious to return to the stronghold as soon as possible. And as John Cooper bade him farewell, the tall Texan added, "Tell Pastanari also that I leave for New Orleans tomorrow. As I said, I have ordered weapons and ammunition for the Jicarilla, and if these have arrived in New Orleans when I reach there, I shall bring them back in wagons. And when I return to the *estancia*, I shall send the wagons on to the stronghold. Thus, the Jicarilla need fear no

attacks, for their enemies are mine—this is the oath I have
sworn as blood brother. ¡Vaya con Dios!"

"And with you, also, Halcón," Dejari said as he raised
his hand in farewell and rode off with the horses John Cooper
had given him.

Now John Cooper turned to Miguel Sandarbal and said,
"It's a blessing we still have those wagons with the false
bottoms in which we hid the first convoy of silver to the bank
in New Orleans. We shall use them tomorrow. If you will
have the trabajadores begin to transfer the ingots to them,
all will be ready tomorrow. I shall see to the supplies."

"Will you not let me accompany you?" Miguel asked.

John Cooper was about to say no when he caught the
wistfully appealing look in the white-haired capataz's eyes.
"Very well, then. But only if Bess permits it."

"What is this? What is this, now? Am I not capataz of
this hacienda? Since when does a mujer question what her
husband decides?" Miguel bristled.

"When he has a sweet and much younger wife with
children who want to see their father more than once a
month," John Cooper teased. Then, seeing how crestfallen
Miguel looked at his words, he chuckled and declared, "It
will be good to have you along, amigo. Just like old times!"

That night at supper, John Cooper told Andrew and
Charles that they would remain at home and look after their
stepmother and brothers and sisters, as well as make themselves useful around the ranch. "Work with Peter, Jasper,
and Frank and continue the training of Maja and Fuerte,
boys," he instructed them. "Fuerte, especially, showed great
courage against that cougar. Together, those two yearlings
can help defend us if we're ever attacked again—which I pray
we shan't be."

Raoul Maldones as well as Miguel sat at supper with
John Cooper and his wife and oldest sons. Turning to his
father-in-law, John Cooper declared, "Mi suegro, you're to be
in charge of the ranch while Miguel and I are gone. Carlos
will help you, but by now you're certainly familiar with every
part of the operation of this ranch, from the sheep to the
school, from the cattle to the produce gardens that the women
have planted and cultivated. When I return from New Orleans,
I hope to bring with me a good supply of weapons and
ammunition for Eugene Fair's Brazos settlement, as well as
for ourselves, and another good supply for the Jicarilla."

Raoul leaned back and took a sip of the strong coffee that Rosa Lorcas had just poured for him. "Carlos and I will look after things, rest assured. Ah, being here has almost made me forget the *pampas*."

It was a happy evening, and John Cooper was delighted to find that Dorotéa showed no chagrin or petulance at the thought of his leaving her again after having only just returned from New Orleans. Thus, when they lay in the huge bed that night, he made gentle love to her, and when they clung to each other afterward, he murmured, "*Mi corazón*, you've become a real frontier wife, hiding your feelings when you find out that your *esposo* is deserting you."

Dorotéa emitted a giggle, which was more in keeping with her little sister María than with this beautifully and magnificently mature young woman. "But I know you're not deserting me, *mi vida*," she whispered as she pressed herself tightly to him and with her soft, slim fingers began to stroke the back of his neck and his shoulders. "You are forgetting that on the *pampas*, even though I was brought up to be a very proper señorita by dear, fussy old Señora Josefa, I rode beside my father. Because he has no sons and I am his oldest, he took me into his confidence, and I learned how a man thinks and what a man must do to make a life for his loved ones. But I am lucky in that I also have the feelings of a woman and can lie in your arms like this." And now, whispering into his ear, she added, "I pray that you will give me another child soon, and that this time it will be a little girl who, when the time comes, will be wise enough to attract a man as wonderful as you are, my dearest love."

John Cooper could not speak with the tenderness that welled up in him, and unaccustomed tears stung his eyes as he held her tightly, kissed her, and then murmured, "And now let us sleep, my dear one, and God bless you for understanding. What you've said to me now makes me all the more eager to make this ranch of ours the safest and the happiest place in all the world for those who live within its boundaries."

John Cooper Baines, Miguel Sandarbal, and thirty of Ramón's armed *vaqueros* left for New Orleans the morning after Dejari had ridden back to the Jicarilla stronghold. The wagons were still eminently serviceable, and Miguel, remembering how they had taken the first cache of silver to New

Orleans almost two years earlier, harnessed four sturdy oxen to each wagon, which was driven by a single *vaquero* who knew how to handle such a team and make the animals move in unison. Oxen were far better for this task than horses because they could draw more weight.

The large party reached New Orleans in mid-June. The yellow fever epidemic had ended as suddenly as it had begun, but when John Cooper learned of it, he left Miguel and the *vaqueros* in charge of the wagons and went at once to the Ursuline Convent School, where the healthy, beaming Francesca and the Maldones girls assured him all was well. Mother Superior Cécile also reassured him, telling him how nobly the girls had acted during the epidemic by volunteering their services to the hospital, though to be sure she was unaware of the romantic undercurrents in her school. Francesca thought constantly of Jack McKinnon, who had returned to the sugarcane plantation upriver and had written her two letters, expressing his gratitude to her and firing the girl's romantic nature. Meanwhile, Adriana Maldones thought often of Andrew Baines, who had received her ardent letter and was himself counting the days till he saw her during the summer holiday, still a month away.

Visiting also Diego and Lortaldo—who were both well and thriving, the latter having done his own great service in Dr. Malmorain's hospital—John Cooper then hastened to La Banque de la Nouvelle Orléans. The silver ingots were transferred from the wagons into the now greatly strengthened bank vault, with Eugene Beaubien bringing in an assayer to weigh and evaluate the deposit. A sum of more than three hundred thousand dollars was registered to the Texan's account, and the banker again effusively thanked John Cooper for his generosity in donating twenty bars from the recovered cache that Carrière had stolen. "There is money enough for everyone now, Mr. Beaubien," John Cooper told him as he waived off the banker's florid praise. "And now I should like a draft on your bank for twenty thousand dollars, as I have some business to transact with Fabien Mallard."

The draft was quickly brought, and John Cooper then visited the office of his factor. "I've good news for you, *mon ami*," the genial Creole exclaimed. "The weapons and ammunition that you ordered have arrived, and I've kept them in one of the buildings I own not far from the wharf. They have been here a week waiting for you, and I'm delighted to see

you again. Praise the Lord all our loved ones are safe after
that pestilence that visited our city."

"Amen to that," John Cooper said. "Well, now I'll have
my men pack them in the wagons we used to transport the
silver, Fabien. I'll be in town just through tomorrow, and
then we'll turn our oxen around and head them for the
Brazos. But before I go, I'm going to give your lovely wife a
present, if you've no objection?"

"You're much too kind, *mon ami*."

"Not at all. I know how you and she took in Raoul
Maldones and made him comfortable, and how you did the
same for Diego, and how you also helped M'amselle de
Courvent. How is she getting along, by the way?"

"Why," Fabien responded, "Hortense has among her
friends a dear old woman, nearly blind, a widow these past
twenty years, who owns one of the most magnificent houses
in all New Orleans. Hortense talked to her about M'amselle
de Courvent, and the upshot was that Madame Levasseur
insisted that M'amselle de Courvent live with her, to act as
her companion, to read to her, et cetera. It is not really the
relationship of a domestic to a mistress, but rather a ripening
of friendship between old and young. During the day,
M'amselle de Courvent does some work for me and is an
enormous help to my clerks, keeping the books and checking
on my various accounts. So the young woman earns her own
income and has, in all, an admirable living situation."

"That is a very pleasant ending to what was a tragic
story," John Cooper commented.

Fabien gave him a roguish wink. "It may be even more
so. Madame Levasseur's only living kin is a nephew in his
early thirties, a very dignified and honest man who, for the
past several years, has been in charge of a large coffee plantation near Havana. This he inherited from his father, and I
understand that he has just sold it and wishes to return to
New Orleans to visit his old aunt. He is a bachelor, most
circumspect and honorable, and indeed it is said of him that
he was a curiosity on the island, since he took no native
women. Now, it is quite possible that he might admire a
charming mademoiselle like his aunt's companion, and there
might be a romance between them."

"Fabien, you are a sly dog, but in the very best sense of
the term." John Cooper laughed. "And I hope for her sake
that the two of them strike it off. If they do half as well as

Dorotéa and I, they'll be blissfully happy for the rest of their days."

"Just as Hortense and I are, *mon ami*. Well then, I'll see you tomorrow to say good-bye to you again."

And so, the very next afternoon, John Cooper stopped at his factor's office just before he and his men left New Orleans with the wagons now loaded with weapons and supplies. It had also been arranged that in a little less than a month's time, Fabien would see to it that Francesca, the Maldones girls, and Señora Josefa were sent on their way to the ranch for the summer holiday.

Before he left, John Cooper gave Fabien Mallard a silver bracelet, one of the artifacts that had been found in the cave near Raton. "To your lovely Hortense with my thanks and very best wishes, Fabien," John Cooper said as he shook hands with his factor.

"It's very kind of you, *mon ami*. And here, though it is dwarfed in value compared with this gift that you have given me for my wife, is a little gift for your Dorotéa from Hortense— she crocheted this herself, I'll have you know." He now showed John Cooper a table cloth, embroidered with the brand of the Double H Ranch and, at each rectangular end, the symbol of the hawk, done in colors of brown and gold and red and blue. Then he carefully folded it and put it into a leather case.

"That's beautiful!" John Cooper exclaimed. "Every time we use it at our table, Fabien, we'll think of you and Hortense. It's wonderful workmanship, and it must have taken her many months!"

"It is what we would call a labor of love, *mon ami*. She admires you as much as I do and, remembering the time you drew for us a picture of your ranch's insignia, thought it would be a fitting tribute. Good luck, and keep in touch with me frequently. I, in return, if I hear any news from Mexico that may concern you and your settler friends on the Brazos, will certainly see that one of my couriers reaches you at once!"

The day after John Cooper's arrival in New Orleans with the second cache of silver, a courier came to the little apartment of Enrique de Silva, who lived about a mile from the bank where he worked. The bank clerk had summoned the courier in order to have the man take a letter by ship to Santa Anna in Veracruz. It was a short message but one that would lead to far-reaching consequences and the most sinister machinations of which the unscrupulous brigadier general Santa Anna was capable. It read:

> Your Excellency:
>   I want to get this right off by courier, so I will make it brief. Be advised that the *gringo* John Cooper Baines has just deposited in La Banque de la Nouvelle Orléans the additional sum of more than three hundred thousand dollars in silver ingots. The bank president informs me that it was discovered in yet another mine in New Mexico. I await your instructions, and I have the honor to be, as ever, your most humble servant, awaiting the day when you truly become *el libertador* of our beloved country!
>   Enrique de Silva

"The faster the better, *mi amigo*," he said to the courier as he handed the envelope to him. The courier, a Mexican living in New Orleans, had already done many little tasks for de Silva, who had paid him from his own meager salary. This was the biggest assignment yet and was costing de Silva two weeks' wages, but this would be nothing compared to the reward he would receive from Santa Anna.

"I leave at once," the courier replied, with a little salute. "I shall see *el general* within two weeks. There is a ship leaving for Corpus Cristi tonight, and from there on to Veracruz. And when I see him, I shall tell *el general* that you are a true patriot. *¡Vaya con Dios!*"

Twenty-one

Roland Eberle had made camp this sultry June evening about four miles to the southwest of the little hamlet of Hearne in northern Texas, not far from the American settlement on the Brazos River toward which John Cooper and his men were now heading. Roland had managed to buy a little flour, some beans, and coffee from an elderly rancher who had just buried his wife the week before; greatly disconsolate, the rancher had told Roland that he planned to go to Sedalia, where his cousin, his only living relative now, operated a small trading post.

Himself a widower for the past decade, Roland could sympathize with the despondent rancher. Forty-five years old, tall and lean and soft-spoken, Roland was suffering his own misfortune and was now on a quest for his missing daughter and the man she had run off with, despite her father's warnings to her.

Beautiful, golden-haired, young Doris had been the light of her father's life after his wife, Ella, had died, the victim of a bite by a rabid dog. As a result of his feelings for his daughter, Roland was fiercely protective of her. Not a day went by that some trader, stopping for supplies at Roland's trading post on the outskirts of St. Louis, would ogle Doris with his eyes; and although he was not given to violence by nature, Roland had twice thrashed with his fists bullies bigger than himself who had dared to insult his daughter by venturing some indecent remarks in his presence concerning her desirability as a female.

Six months earlier, a young man named Roy Fenwick had come to the trading post, boasting that he had made several trading trips for one of Roland's major rivals. He was six feet tall, with curly brown hair and a soft beard that he kept neatly trimmed. Unlike most of the traders who visited Roland, he could read and write and speak rather better English than was customary on the frontier. Roy Fenwick was also a fickle womanizer, with a reputation for transient affairs throughout Missouri, Kansas, and Louisiana, Roland had learned from one of his customers. Because of this, Roland did everything he could to discourage the obvious infatuation that his lovely blond daughter had for the obsequiously flattering young trader who, only a week after meeting her for the first time, told her that he had fallen in love with her at first sight and wanted to marry her.

Roland told his daughter, "Honey, you know perfectly well there's nothing better I'd like to have you do than find the right man and settle down with him. But this Roy Fenwick is not for you. He's got a smooth, lying tongue, and I wouldn't be surprised if he hasn't told at least thirty or forty girls exactly what he's told you. Take my word for it, he's no good for you."

But Doris, feeling that at the age of twenty-two she was virtually a spinster, let herself be swayed by what she believed to be the dictates of her own heart. Thus it was that during the last week of April, when Roland had gone to a ferry on the Columbia River with a dozen pack mules to outfit a trading expedition, Fenwick seized his opportunity and persuaded Doris to go off with him as his wife. One of his cronies, who occasionally earned a grubstake by acting as a Methodist minister and holding revival meetings in a tent, though not ordained, volunteered to perform the marriage ceremony in return for fifty dollars in gold, which Fenwick promptly gave him. That evening, after he and Doris had been joined in fraudulent wedlock, he savored the reward of his cunning by possessing her. And for Doris Eberle, now supposedly Doris Fenwick, her romantic illusions were shattered by Roy Fenwick's gross insensitivity, for his only thoughts were of satisfying his own carnal desires, and not those of his supposed wife. However, believing that she was legally wed to the trader, and hoping that in time he would prove to be a loving, considerate husband, she left St. Louis with him.

Roland returned a week later. When he read the hasty note Doris had scrawled for him and put on the kitchen table, announcing her marriage and elopement with Roy Fenwick, he was beside himself with fury and grief. He immediately turned over the trading post to an affable old Frenchman who had been a Canadian *voyageur* and whose honesty was beyond question. Promising Henri Montfournier a share of the profits from any sales he made and asking him only to keep a running inventory of merchandise received and sold, Roland prepared to go after his missing daughter.

He knew only that Roy Fenwick traveled along the Columbia and had once hinted that he might make his way to Santa Fe and Taos for the profitable trading that existed there. For about five or six days, Roland stayed on at the post, anxiously asking all traders who came to it if they had seen Fenwick and his daughter. On the seventh day, a trader whose home was in Sedalia said he believed he had seen both of them and that they had taken a room in a cheap hotel on the outskirts of that town.

Roland promptly packed supplies in his saddlebags and took along several hundred dollars in gold for additional supplies and fresh horses or mules, if he should need them. Taking his best horse—a very obedient animal with great speed and endurance—he set out for Sedalia, a journey of a hundred fifty miles.

His first act was to visit the few hotels and inns in the town, only to learn that Fenwick and Doris had left the hotel where he had been told they were staying, but without leaving any news as to their destination. He thought that perhaps some other traders might have met the couple and learned their route of departure, and so, on the second day after his arrival in Sedalia, he went to the largest tavern in that bustling town.

It was noisy and there was the tinkle of an old spinet to greet his ears as he pushed open the swinging doors and entered. There were men in buckskin, bearded *voyageurs*, settlers, gamblers, and painted whores, one of whom at once accosted him and asked him to buy her a drink. Roland congenially begged off and made his way to the bar, where he asked the saloonkeeper if the latter knew anything of a Roy Fenwick and his blond wife named Doris.

As he was talking to the middle-aged, bald saloonkeeper, he was rudely jostled at his right. He turned to see a stocky, black-bearded man who was scowling and squinting at him. "You're not from these parts, stranger—I don't know what you're doin' here, but I'd advise you to buy me a drink, or I'll thrash you raw!" the bearded man loudly declared.

"Excuse me, mister, I don't know you. I'm here on business, and I think you've had enough to drink already," Roland politely answered, then turned back to the saloon-keeper.

His interlocutor gripped him by the shoulder and turned him around. "Hey, now, stranger, that ain't friendly! Nobody turns his back on Doug Blake, you git me?"

Roland considered the bully. He was not more than twenty-six, though his shabby clothes, thick beard, and flushed face made him look much older. "Look, Mr. Blake," Roland said, trying to placate him, "I wasn't being rude, and I meant you no harm. My daughter ran away with a trader, and I'm trying to find her. Now, you can understand that, can't you?"

"Hell, you say! You're a yellerbelly, friend!" the young bully said in a hoarse voice as he drew one of his pistols. "I think I'm gonna make you dance till you break down and buy me a drink, git me?"

"There's no need for that," Roland said, again trying to placate the drunken man. He glanced over at the saloonkeeper, who merely shrugged and shook his head. But before Roland could say anything else, Doug Blake pointed the pistol down at his feet and fired. The bullet grazed the toe of his right boot, and the St. Louis man realized that he was in mortal danger unless he tried to defend himself. "Now, just a minute, Mr. Blake," he said, backing away, "you've got me all wrong. Why don't you try to listen? If you were a father and had a daughter who ran away with somebody who was a no-good, you'd be concerned about her, too!"

"I said you're a yellerbelly, unless you prove it otherwise, mister! I'm gonna keep shootin' till you buy me that drink!" Blake's voice was thick as he leaned hard against the bar to keep from staggering. He fired again with his second pistol, and this time the bullet came very close to grazing Roland's hip.

"For God's sake, Mr. Blake, are you trying to kill me? Now, look out, I'm giving you fair warning—"

But Blake had replaced one of the fired pistols in his belt and had taken from his coat pocket a third pistol, which he waved in the air. Roland saw he had no choice, for the next ball might kill him. He drew his own pistol and fired once. Blake stiffened, dropped both revolvers, and in a startled, slurred tone, began, "Hell, mister—you—you killed me—" Then he sprawled dead at Roland's feet.

"You saw it," Roland said, turning to the saloonkeeper, "I had to defend myself."

"Sure you did, mister. Only trouble is, Doug Blake's got an older brother named Tom, and you better make tracks before he catches up with you. He won't take it kindly that you killed his baby brother, even though it was in self-defense. But you better wait here a few minutes till Sheriff Hall comes in and looks things over. I'll tell him that Blake already shot at you a coupla times and that you had to pull leather to save yourself. And once you're cleared, my advice to you is, skip town pronto!"

A quarter of an hour later, Sheriff Hall, a fat, dyspeptic man in his early fifties, entered the tavern and came up to Roland. One of the patrons had learned the newcomer's name and had identified him and pointed him out to the sheriff, who bellicosely demanded, "So you're the feller that did for Doug Blake, huh?"

"He had to, sheriff," the saloonkeeper interposed. "Doug was likkered up and wavin' his gun around for fair, and nuthin' would have it but he made this stranger buy him a drink—and when he wouldn't, Doug started shooting. Nearly creased his hip, I saw it. No, sir, this feller had to draw or else get shot down."

"That the way any of you others saw it here?" the sheriff called out, turning to the customers, and several spoke up in unison. "All right, then, Eberle," he said, glowering at Roland, "I guess I can't hold you in jail. But my advice to you is to beat it out of town fast. Maybe you heard already, Doug's got a brother that'll lay for you and tear your hide into tiny strips."

"I'm leaving anyway," Roland said. "I'm going to find the man who ran off with my daughter." He turned to the saloonkeeper. "Thanks, mister. I'll make tracks now. Sorry I had to put you to all this trouble."

Roland had to be content that he was at least leaving Sedalia a free man, even though he had learned nothing about Fenwick and his daughter. But thinking again about the chance remark that Roy Fenwick had once uttered in his St. Louis shop—that he planned to make a killing in Santa Fe and Taos—Roland surmised that it would be only logical for the trader to have made tracks for Texas and taken the route that would lead to New Mexico.

From his own trading experiences, Roland knew Texas was still a wild frontier with many hostile Indian tribes. The Karankawa, some of the Caddo and the Waco tribes, as well as the Kiowa and the Wichita, might prove troublesome. He could only hope that Doris and Fenwick didn't run into any hostiles themselves.

The next morning, at a small trading post outside Sedalia, Roland bought a pack mule and supplies, as well as additional ammunition and powder for his pistols. He also bought a Belgian rifle. He wished he could have gotten a Lancaster or one of the Kentucky rifles, but the settlers pushing to the southwest and the west had already bought up the few that were available. And then, saying a prayer that he would find his daughter and rescue her from the man who he was certain could only bring disaster into her life, he headed southwestward. The faster he got along their trail and caught up with them, the sooner he'd be able to talk sense into Doris. He only hoped he wouldn't have to have an out-and-out fight with Fenwick. Even if he managed to kill him—and Fenwick was a younger man with perhaps more stamina and quickness—Doris might go on hating her father for the rest of her life. That would make a martyr out of Fenwick, a role a womanizer didn't deserve.

Roy Fenwick had figured that Doris's father might try to track them down, so he and his young wife had kept almost constantly on the move. After leaving Sedalia, he had gone to Jefferson City, where he purchased the pack animals and supplies for the long journey on the Santa Fe Trail.

As for Doris, her romantic dreams of leading an adventurous life with the man she loved continued to be rudely shattered. Her husband treated her as if she were little better than his slave, and his conjugal usage of her was usually hurried and always rough. Still she tried to be a good wife, stammering, "I'm still new to what married folks do, Roy dear, so please be patient with me. I—I'll try my best to be a good wife to you."

From Jefferson City, he and Doris, with horses for them to ride as well as two spares, and six pack mules loaded with goods, headed down toward Joplin. There the couple remained for the night in a flea-bitten hotel, and in the morning Fenwick irritatedly urged Doris, "Shake your shanks, gal; there's work to be done. Make yourself useful; go down to the stables and see that the horses and mules have been watered and fed and are ready to start. We've got a long trek ahead of us, and I want to get there ahead of the other traders so I can strike it rich."

She obeyed dutifully, actually finding herself glad to be out of his presence. She found him dirty and unshaven most of the time now, which further increased her aversion to her conjugal duties. Yet she stoically and silently endured all the verbal and physical abuse because she kept telling herself that she was married and marriage was for life until death. All the same, by now she deeply regretted her impulsive act of running away from home.

From Joplin, Fenwick took his horses and mules and his unhappy young wife southwestward through Poteau and then Antlers, and a few days later crossed the Red River on into the Texas territory, past the little hamlet of Paris. Thus far, he had seen herds of buffalo and a few friendly Indians, to whom he had given some cheap trade goods like blankets, a few mirrors, and combs and beads for the warriors' squaws. He had not brought any whiskey, for, to give him his due, he was a wise trader and did not hold with giving Indians liquor. His feeling was that "a likkered-up Injun is a bad one, and he'll have your scalp before you know it."

From Paris, the trail took them to Waxahachie, some fifty miles from the Brazos and another fifty or sixty miles north of the growing American settlement there. By now, Doris was physically exhausted from the strenuous life on the trail, and Roy's irritation with her grew apace. On a June night when they made camp near the bank of the river in a glade of live-oak trees, he sourly splashed the coffee she had handed him in a tin mug into the fire and snarled, "You stupid bitch, you can't even make decent coffee!"

"Roy Fenwick, that's no way—I'm your wife!" She gasped, scandalized. "You shouldn't ever use such a word to me!"

He rose to his feet, thrusting his hands into his breeches pockets. Then he said, sneering, "If you want to know the truth, Doris honey, you're not much good to me, and I'm sorry I ever got tangled up with you."

Her mouth gaped, and she put a hand to it, shocked beyond credulity, horrified that he should so renounce her. She could remember now with a bittersweet anguish the sweet talk, the promises of a happy life together. Now there was only the dreary, dusty trail, his cursing and derision of her, and at night, suffering the fate of being little more than his sexual convenience. She was grateful for only one thing: He had not yet made her pregnant, she knew that much.

For the rest of the evening, she went about doing the chores assigned to her, for she could see by the black look on his face that he was in an ugly mood, and she hoped by dutiful silence to placate him. But when it was time to settle down in their sleeping blankets, Fenwick guffawed and tried to creep in with her. "No! Please, Roy, I—I don't feel like it. I'm tired—the day's been so hot, and I've had all this work," she pleaded.

"Why, a fine wife you are, Doris!" he growled. Scrambling out of the blankets and striding to the extinguished campfire, he picked up a willow switch from a pile of kindling wood. "I'll teach you to say no to your husband!" he snarled.

"No, Roy, for God's sake, don't beat me—how do you expect me to love you when you treat me this way? Oh, my God—oh, please, no—stop it, you're hurting me, Roy!" she sobbed as he cut viciously at her. She rolled over and over, trying to use her blankets to soften the blows, but with sadistic glee he kept whipping her until at last his arm was tired. Then, throwing away the frayed switch, he growled, "Listen, you stupid, useless bitch, until we get to Santa Fe, you'd best keep clear of me. Just you tend to the cooking and helping with the pack animals and doing whatever else has to be done so I get where I'm going and make my killing. If you don't get in my way too much, maybe I'll give you enough *dinero* to haul your useless tail back to St. Louis and your daddy. He's welcome to you, the Lord God knows!"

With this, he crawled into his sleeping blanket, turned his back to her, and fell asleep. Doris sobbed softly, and she wished that she were back home and could tell her father what a dreadful mistake she had made—and beg that he would forgive her and still love her.

Roland Eberle made no campfire this night, contenting himself with some jerky and water. He had been told in Hearne that a raiding party of Wichita had been seen in the vicinity a few days earlier, and he did not relish the odds of one man against a war party. One good thing was that he had at last located the trail of Roy Fenwick. It had been a stroke of pure luck that after he had left Sedalia, he had gone on to Jefferson City, and there the owner of a trading post had told him that he was just out of flour and jerky and ammunition because a man had bought up practically his entire stock. From his description, Roland recognized Fenwick. Also, Fenwick had bragged about heading for Santa Fe, taking the trail through Texas, then crossing the Brazos River. Roland was now following that same trail, and perhaps Fenwick and Doris were by now only a day ahead of him—and that was all the more reason he wished no quarrel with the Wichita.

But what Roland did not know was that he himself was being followed. With a tireless energy born of the desire for avenging his brother, Thomas Blake was on the trail of the man who had murdered Doug. Even though Sheriff Hall and a few of the patrons of the Sedalia tavern had declared that Roland had been forced to draw to save his own life, Blake had stubbornly refused this evidence, particularly since his feeling was that in a drunken condition, Doug should have been disarmed or, at worst, slightly wounded, rather than shot dead. Thus Thomas Blake had bought in Sedalia a superb black stallion as well as a spare horse, outfitted himself with a brace of pistols, powder and flints, in addition to a rifle and a hunting knife, and then set out.

Roland had now finished his frugal meal but was not yet ready for sleep. There was a quarter moon, obscured by slowly moving dark clouds, presaging a storm either late that night or early the next morning. Uneasy about the news of the raiding Wichita, he checked his pistols and rifle, to make sure they were primed and loaded.

Suddenly he stiffened, for he thought he had heard the sound of horses' hooves coming from the east. Gently soothing his animals, he made his horse lie down on its side, which the animal did readily, being so well trained. In this way, if it was a raiding party, he could hide behind the horse and shoot from that vantage point, thereby increasing his chances for survival.

He could only pray that Doris and Fenwick had not run into any Wichita war party or, for that matter, any other hostile Indian tribe. He did not care to think what they would do with a white woman captive; he had heard too many harrowing tales over the past few years of how white women were treated.

The sound of the horses' hooves came now more clearly to him, and as he lay down on his belly behind the horse he had ridden, quieting it with a touch of his hand and a soothing phrase, he leveled his rifle.

Then suddenly there was no sound at all. Squinting through the darkness, he could see nothing. The plain beyond lay flat and unmoving, and the stretch of waist-high grass northward seemed to move only with the gusts of warm wind that came in from the Gulf. He glanced at his rifle, cuddled it against his shoulder, and waited.

And then he heard footsteps behind him, and when he whirled, he saw a tall man with a short black beard, not much more than thirty, who had a pair of pistols trained on him.

"Damn me for a fool," Roland muttered aloud, disgusted with himself for not being more careful about his back.

"You're Roland Eberle, aren't you, mister?" the man with the pistols demanded.

"Yes, that's my name—"

"Then you're the man who killed my brother, Doug. I've tracked you down, and I'm going to make you pay for it. I'm

Thomas Blake. A man's got a right to know who killed him and why, I figure."

"For God's sake, man, it was in self-defense!" Roland said.

"Sheriff Hall and some of the fellas in the saloon also said it was self-defense; I don't buy it. But I won't kill a man until he's had a chance to make his peace with his Maker. Go ahead and say your prayers, mister! And don't think you can gun me down with that rifle—these pistols will kill you before you can even trigger a shot."

"I wasn't aiming to try that, Mr. Blake. Believe me—" Roland began.

There was a whizzing sound and then a *thuckk*, as an arrow buried itself in the trunk of a tree two feet to the right of where Thomas Blake was standing.

"Wichita!" Roland hissed. "We'll have to settle our differences later; right now, we'd better both join up to save our scalps."

"You're right," Blake muttered as he flattened himself on his belly and joined Roland behind his horse. Leveling his two pistols ahead of him, he waited for a sign of the attackers.

Now another arrow drew a scream from one of Blake's two horses, which he had tethered to the branch of a live-oak tree behind him. Blake swore under his breath and said, "Damn shame. Lucky I got me two mounts. See anything there, Eberle?"

"Not a thing," Roland whispered back. "But from what I've heard of the Wichita, they'll let us know where they are damn soon!" Just then, he thought he caught sight of something moving in the tall grass ahead of him, and he triggered a shot with his rifle. There was a yowl and the sound of a falling body, taken up at once by an angry war whoop. Blake shot off both his pistols in the direction of that yell and was rewarded by another cry of pain.

"Wonder how many there are?" he said to Roland. "If I've got time, I'll go back to my poor horse and get my rifle."

"Crawl fast and get back here; we need all the fire power we can get, Blake," Roland told him.

Blake crawled quickly back to his horses and saw that the stallion was lying dead from the arrow that had embedded itself in the mount's side. His face twisting with mingled anger and pity, Blake reached for the saddle sheath and drew out his rifle, which was already primed and loaded. Patting the other horse to reassure it, he then crawled quickly back to take his position beside Roland. The latter was soothing his own horse with calming words, trying to make certain it would stay in place and act as a protective shield.

"Wonder how many there are of them?" Blake muttered again.

"I'd say a dozen, maybe," Roland whispered back. "Know anything about the Wichita?"

"Only that right now they look to be after both our scalps."

"That's true enough. They're darker skinned than most Plains Indians you'll see, and the men and women are tattooed probably more than any other tribe you'll meet up with. When they win at warfare, they make marks on their arms and chests, and the men also pierce their ears in four places and dangle ornaments from them."

"I hope we don't get close up enough to see all that," Blake sardonically whispered.

Now there was the *whizzz* of another arrow, which had been fired almost straight up and fell from the sky, digging into the ground between the two men's bodies. Roland fired his pistol almost blindly. But the scream that followed instantly and the thrashing of a body in the underbrush some twenty-five feet in front of them told him that his random shot had hit the mark. "One less, I'm hoping," he told his pursuer who had now, by fate's irony, become his ally.

Two braves now burst out of the thickets on either side of the two men, brandishing tomahawks. Roland saw the one on his right and promptly fired the other pistol, killing the brave, who dropped the tomahawk with a cry and fell headlong to the ground. The other Indian came at Thomas Blake, a heavy stone tomahawk held on high, and Blake turned at Roland's warning cry. The brave, a young, hideously tattooed warrior, naked to the waist, made for Blake who, crouching and looking upward, pulled the trigger of one of his pistols. But it misfired, and the brave was nearly on him. Roland, having no time to reload either rifle or pistol, drew his hunting knife and thrust himself up from the ground to meet the charge. He lunged at the brave with his knife, opening a long but shallow gash along the Wichita's left arm.

Infuriated by the pain, the brave turned on Roland, trying to tomahawk him. Swiftly transferring the knife to his left hand, Roland feinted to the left, then lunged forward with the knife as the young brave swung his tomahawk, narrowly missing Roland's head. Then again he backed away, but in that second of indecision, Roland was on him and caught the brave's right wrist, wrenching the heavy handle of the tomahawk away. Instantly, the Wichita dropped his other hand to the sheathed knife in his belt, but before he could pull it out, Roland brained him.

"My God, man, that was a close thing!" Blake panted. "You saved my life."

"Get down, there may be more of them out there," Roland warned. "From all his tattoos, this fellow appears to be their war chief. That might drive them off—lots of Indians retreat once their leader is done for. Let's hope it works this time."

Just as he spoke, he heard the sound of horses' hooves receding in the distance toward the west. "My God, I think it did work!" he exulted. "Just the same, we'd best play possum for a spell until we see if they're up to any tricks."

"Suits me. I thought I was a goner that time," Blake admitted as he flattened himself on the ground behind the horse and began to reload his pistols and then his rifle. "I see what's wrong with this pistol—the flint was worn. Well, that's easily replaced. There, now. How are you fixed for ammunition?"

"Plenty. Powder and ball in the saddlebag," Roland softly declared.

Now the night was still, with not even the call of a bird. The slow-moving, thick dark clouds that had obscured the quarter moon began to move away and allow the moon's rays to light this clearing in the glade. There was no sign of the Wichita.

"I think we're free and clear," Roland said.

Thomas Blake was quiet for a long moment. Then he said solemnly, "You just saved my life. If it hadn't been for you, my scalp might be drying on one of those Indian wigwams I've heard about." He hesitated, then continued, "I had you all wrong. Whatever happened in that saloon in Sedalia, I guess maybe Doug had it coming to him. But now tell me, were you on the run from me?"

"To be honest, Blake, no," Roland replied. "I've been looking for my daughter, Doris."

"I'd say this was a hell of a place to look for a girl. Mind telling me what happened?"

"I guess you've got a right to know," Roland replied, and went on to tell Thomas Blake what had happened in St. Louis between his daughter and Roy Fenwick. "This Fenwick bragged that he was going on to Santa Fe to make a killing in trade goods," Roland continued. "And this is the route he took. I've got a gut feeling they're not far from here."

"I tell you what, Eberle, I owe you something for my life," Blake said. "Let's say I go along with you? You know the old saying, two heads are better than one."

"I'd be proud to have you along, Blake."

"Hell, call me Tom. And I'll call you Roland. Here's my hand on it."

Roland Eberle shook hands enthusiastically with the man who had sworn to kill him. Each sized up the other with a smiling glance. It was Blake who first broke off the handshake and, his face becoming red from embarrassment, growled, "We'd best get moving, then. I'm short one horse, but I'm sure glad I brought along another one."

"We should leave right now," Roland declared. "I just hope those Wichita don't find Fenwick and my daughter before we do!"

About two miles east of the settlement on the Brazos, Roy Fenwick and Doris had made their camp for the night. Doris had just finished cooking supper, and the trader upbraided her for the tastelessness of the meal. "Hell, bitch, you aren't even worth your salt. Couldn't you have found some wild onions or berries or something along the trail to brighten up this cruddy slop you fed me tonight? Call that stew? Putting some jerky in water doesn't make it a stew. And this coffee—it's enough to turn a man's stomach! And what did I tell you about looking over the cinch straps of the mules? Want those saddlebags with all the trade goods to go tumbling down on the ground and slow us down? Next time you don't check that, I'll take more than a switch to you!"

Doris merely sat in front of the fire, poking at the embers with a stick, afraid that anything she said or did would just lead to further abuse from her husband.

Fenwick persisted sadistically. "If you cross me any more, Doris gal, I might just up and sell you as a slave to some Ute or Comanche or Apache. Then you'd think you had a bed of roses being my wife, once you had to please one of those dirty redskins."

"My, God—you—you wouldn't," Doris couldn't help blurting out.

"Just don't try me to see if I would or not, bitch. Just you mind what I've been telling you, and see that I get better grub and that the saddlebags and packs don't slip off the mules, till we get to Santa Fe. I'll keep my promise then. I'll send you back to your father, and you can weep on his shoulder all you want. Me, I'll find me an Injun squaw—be better in bed than you could ever be, that's for certain!" He spat in the direction of the dying fire, inches from where Doris sat.

Mournfully, Doris rose and walked over to one of the pack mules and verified the tightness of the cinch strap. Fenwick gave her a contemptuous look, grumbling under his breath about the stupidity of women and Doris in particular. At least they were only a short distance from the Brazos River, where he had sighted in the distance the vague outline of a blockhouse and other buildings of a settlement. In the morning they would stop there for a rest and maybe sell some of his pack goods; settlers didn't have much chance to go to any trading posts and get the necessities. Besides, he'd still have trade goods enough left for the shindigs in Santa Fe and Taos.

As he lifted the coffee mug to his lips for another swallow, an arrow whizzed past his head, and he dropped the mug and let out a startled yell. "Holy Jesus Christ—Injuns! Get over here, Doris, bring my rifle! Goddamn it anyhow, if only we'd gone a little farther, we might have been inside that blockhouse I see way over across the river! Make it fast, you stupid bitch, unless you want those redskins to lift your pretty yeller hair!"

Fortunately, Fenwick's loaded rifle was close at hand, in the saddle sheath of his horse, which was at Doris's left. Pulling it out, she hurried over to him and then flung herself down flat, as another arrow went by. There were war whoops now and the thundering of Indian ponies racing around the little camp. The pack mules, off to the right and in front of the campfire, provided a partial shield from frontal attack, but the Wichita were famous for circling an enemy and then breaking in on him at the weakest spot.

Fenwick cocked the rifle, squinted along the sight, and pulled the trigger as a heavyset older brave rode by, brandishing a lance. The ball caught the Wichita in the throat, and a geyser of blood spouted from him as he toppled from his pony and lay sprawled on the ground. The pony galloped off, neighing in terror.

"Here's a pistol, Doris. Know how to shoot?" Fenwick panted as he dragged one of his pistols out of the right-hand holster. "Make every ball count—it takes time to reload. I'll do the reloading, but see if you can't hit something."

"I—my father taught me how to shoot," she began, as a Wichita brave rode past the file of docilely standing mules laden with their packs. The Indian aimed his lance straight at Fenwick. Instinctively, Doris lifted up the pistol and pulled the trigger, hardly taking aim. A startled look appeared on the face of the brave, who toppled back in his saddle, the lance dropping from his lifeless fingers, as the pony galloped past Fenwick and on into the woods behind them.

"Well, you did something right in your life for a change," he sourly commented as he drew out the pistol from his left-hand holster and snapped off a shot. It missed a warrior riding to his left and around beyond him, intending to circle and get behind him.

Now, while reloading his rifle and the pistols, two arrows whizzed by, one of them killing a pack mule, which staggered and fell onto its side, kicking feebly for a time. The other arrow imbedded itself in the trunk of a tree to Doris's left.

"I wonder how many there are—we'd best look all around us," Fenwick hoarsely advised. "Those damned redskins have a trick of getting behind a fella and letting him have it!"

Roland Eberle and Thomas Blake had ridden for more than an hour, when suddenly the trader reined in his horse and cocked his head, putting a finger to his lips to caution Blake to silence. "Sounds like gunfire, Tom!" he remarked. "Let's go see what it is. You know, I'm thinking the rest of that war party was heading in that direction."

"Let's go, then! It can't be too far off," Blake exclaimed as he spurred his horse forward.

As they approached Fenwick's camp, both men could hear the war whoops of the Wichita. Three of them were on horseback and the others were crawling on their bellies near the pack mules, using the darkness as cover as they laid siege to Doris and her alleged husband.

As Roland and Blake rode up, they saw two of the braves crawling under the pack mules, gripping knives and tomahawks

Leaping off their horses, they ran toward the mules, but another of the braves rose from behind and lunged at Roland with his tomahawk. Warned by the sound of the Indian's movement, Roland leaped to one side. But the momentum of the brave carried him toward Blake who, before he could level his pistol and kill the Wichita, received a blow on the side of his head from the stone tomahawk. With a stifled groan, he sank to his knees and then rolled over on his side. Roland drew his hunting knife and plunged it into the brave's back, killing him.

The other two warriors who crawled under the pack mules had reached the site of the campfire, and one of them flung his tomahawk at Fenwick, who had just fired his rifle at the shadowy figure of a Wichita going by on horseback. The tomahawk took the trader at the back of his head, crushing his skull. Without a sound he sprawled forward, the rifle dropping to the ground.

Roland quickly glanced at the fallen Thomas Blake and then, as the other brave rushed toward the campsite, he fired his pistol, killing him.

Then he ran to the campsite himself. Seeing it was indeed Doris, he flung himself down beside her. "Doris, thank God I found you in time!" he gasped. Seizing the dead trader's rifle and the leather pouch with ball and gunpowder, he hastily reloaded, then said, "Here, girl, take the rifle; I think there are at least three men on horseback out there, maybe more! And they won't give up! We met the raiding party about an hour to the east and drove them off onto you."

"Oh, Daddy, Daddy, I was a fool—he was horrible to me—" Doris began to sob.

"Don't stop for hysterics now, honey! Roy's dead, and that's an end to your marriage—if it really was one. Just forget it. What we've got on our minds now is living so I can get you back home safely! Look out there!" He saw a Wichita on horseback appear at the right, just beyond the mules, rising up from his saddle and flinging his lance. Roland pulled Doris to one side and rolled atop her, and the lance buried itself in the earth three inches away from his head where it stuck quivering in the ground. Rolling over like a cat, Doris's father leveled his pistol and shot the mounted Wichita down.

At the same moment, another rider appeared to Doris's left, brandishing his lance and grinning fiendishly. "Get him, honey!" Roland called, and Doris aimed her rifle and pulled the trigger just as the brave was about to throw his lance. The recoil from the gun bruised her shoulder, but the young brave screamed in pain, dropped the lance, slid off his horse, and rolled on the ground. Dying, he thrust his hand to the sheath of his hunting knife, but by now Roland had loaded his pistols and fired a bullet into the Indian's skull.

"I hope to God that's all of them!" he said hoarsely. "Wait—there's another one! Oh, my God!"

The last Wichita rider came at him from the rear and the right, having circled back into the clump of trees and then charging. He was armed with a longbow and guided his mustang with his knees as he loosed the shaft. Roland fired at the same moment, and the ball hit him in the chest, just as the arrow penetrated Roland's right side. He dropped his pistol, clapped a hand to the wound, sank down on his knees, and then rolled over onto his back with a groan, his eyes closed.

Meanwhile, the wounded rider rode off to the north, without looking back. Doris, tears running down her face, unable to believe that this nightmare had ended, got to her knees. When she turned her head, she saw Fenwick's corpse, the skull caved in and a welter of gore, and she grimaced and looked away, closing her eyes and shuddering. She hadn't wished any such death on him, God knew!

Then she turned, saw her father, and uttered a shriek: "Daddy! Oh, my God, Daddy, don't leave me here! I'm all alone! Oh, Daddy, I wish I'd never left St. Louis—I was so wrong. Oh, please, speak to me—" She crawled on her knees over to him, gently lifted his head in her hands, and stared down at him. But his eyelids did not even flutter, and she believed him to be dead. She could see the painted arrow, with its angling rows of feathers at the end of the shaft, protruding from his side.

Now the quarter moon shone down brightly. The clouds had vanished, and even a few stars twinkled in the sky. The North Star, held in awesome reverence by the savage Wichita, shone brightly in the distance.

She could see the expanses of prairie and the tall grass, and low sloping hills off to the northeast. And beyond, to the northwest, a shadowy outline, tiny and remote and yet visible, of the settlers' guardhouse. She was alone, deserted in this lonely Texas prairie, her father dead; and the man to whom she had given her love and her life was dead on the other side of her. And in the last moments of this ferocious battle for survival, Thomas Blake's horse had galloped off and Roland Eberle's faithful mount had been killed with two arrows in its side. Only the pack mules stood, humbly silent, burdened by their heavy loads of trade goods and supplies. One or two of them nickered and shifted or switched their tails.

The vast loneliness of this June night in Texas bore down upon the frightened, unhappy young woman. She got to her feet, wringing her hands, not knowing what to do. True, there was the settlement a couple of miles ahead, but she was afraid to go there. Perhaps there would be other Indians. No, she must hide.

She began to run, stumbling, sobbing, toward a little clump of live-oak trees, until she felt herself hidden on every side. Then, smoothing out a bed for herself by raking some leaves into a pile, she flung herself down and wept herself to sleep.

John Cooper Baines, Miguel Sandarbal, and the *vaqueros* driving the wagons now loaded with weapons and supplies had arrived at the settlement on the Brazos shortly after noon on the same day that Roland Eberle had been overtaken by Thomas Blake. The scout Simon Brown, who had been elected head of the settlement and was a proud family man with children of his own by his wife, Naomi, had gone out with some of his men to welcome the newcomers. Even old Minnie Hornsteder, whose grief over her murdered husband had been replaced by a burning hatred of Santa Anna and his soldiers, had seemed to regain her wonderfully congenial outlook and elected herself part of the welcoming committee, promising the newcomers an outdoor *fiesta*.

"We've brought you some rifles, Bowie knives, ball and powder and flint, to defend yourselves against any repetition of what happened before," John Cooper told Simon as they dismounted and headed into the settlement, leading their horses in the direction of the corral.

"Saints bless you all, Mr. Baines," the energetic widow chimed in, clapping him on the back as a man might. Then she bawled to Simon and three of his men, "Look lively now, and take care of those horses! Put them in the corral, and be careful unharnessing the wagons. What's in them is gonna make all of us keep our scalps and our lives a mite longer, that's for certain!"

That evening, Minnie organized the barbecue, with sweet yams roasting on the coals, beef turning on the spit, fruit punch, and berry pies, all of which the grateful settlers contributed to the feast. Minnie went around bossing everybody good-naturedly as was her wont, making sure the visitors ate their fill, piling their plates with second and third helpings. After her husband's death, she had plunged herself into being useful on the settlement in every way she could, from cooking to helping new settlers arrange for housing.

They had had a sumptuous feast, and the visitors, ravenously hungry after the arduous journey to and from New Orleans, had eaten well and had slept quite late through the next morning. But Minnie had wakened at dawn. After a quick breakfast of coffee and biscuits, some of which had been left over from the *fiesta*, she decided to take a walk outside the settlement. It was a clear day, and the weather was already warm and humid. She hoped there would be rain for the produce gardens, one of which was Naomi Brown's.

She breathed in the air as she went past the guardhouse, bidding a genial good morning to the men on sentry duty. Looking up at the sky, she addressed the cloudless blue heavens, "I'm mighty grateful, Gawd. I still miss Henry something fierce, You know that darn well. Only, You've been awful kind to a silly old woman, lettin' her put her nose in all the affairs of this here settlement so's I don't have time to think too much about how he was taken from me."

She sighed to herself, kept her eyes on the sky for a moment, and then, straightening her shoulders, went forward beyond the boundaries of the community for what she termed her morning constitutional. Usually she confined her walk to just outside the settlement, but today she had the strange feeling something was amiss not too far away. She continued walking until at last she stopped, put her hands on her hips, and slowly turned to survey the landscape. Suddenly she scowled and turned her head to one side. She thought she had heard something. There it came again, and it sounded like someone in pain. *Land 'o goshen, what could that be, now?* And there it was again—

Quickening her footsteps, she moved in the direction of the sound and then drew back with a gasp. She had come to the little clearing where Fenwick and Doris had been attacked by the Wichita war party, and she saw Roland Eberle lying very still, with the shaft of an arrow protruding from his side. The tethered mules were standing docilely nearby.

Roland's eyes were open now, and his lips moved as he saw Minnie through the mist of near-unconsciousness. She shook her head and said, "Good Lord, mister, who did that to you? Never mind—you just stay there and take it easy; I'll hurry back and get some fellers to bring you into the settlement and take care of that arrow. You've lost lots of blood—doggone it, why wasn't I born a doctor—I'm pretty good at helping when babies are born, but that's about as far as it goes, and that's a woman's work anyhow—all right, mister, I'll hurry as fast as I can for an old woman!" With a last worried look at Roland, she hurried all the way back to the settlement, puffing for breath in her unaccustomed haste, for she was large-boned and stout.

As she came into the settlement completely out of breath, she saw Simon Brown talking to Jack Converse, a new settler from Natchez who had moved into the community just two weeks before with his young Cajun wife and their six-month-old son. "Simon, you and Mr. Converse, you come right along with me! There's a feller out there who's got an Injun arrow in his side, and he looks awful weak!"

"We'll go get him for you, Minnie!" Simon declared. "You don't have to go all the way, just point out the direction."

Minnie bristled, put her hands on her hips, and stared angrily at the young scout. "Now you look here, Simon Brown," she said indignantly, "nobody's telling Minnie Hornsteder what to do. So maybe I'm puffing and huffing, but that don't mean I can't go back with you and point out where that poor man is. S'posin' you and Mr. Converse couldn't find him and spent all morning looking and maybe he died—he's lost lots of blood."

"You're a stubborn old woman, Minnie," Simon cheerfully declared. "All right, Jack, let's get our horses and go out and find him."

Grumbling under her breath, Minnie mounted her own horse and went along with the two men two miles from the settlement. She pointed to where she had found Roland Eberle, and explained, "It's a clearing there, and there's ashes from a fire."

"You just stay put, Minnie, we'll find him for certain," Simon reassured her. He and Jack dismounted and ran toward the site Minnie had indicated, and about five minutes later they rejoined Minnie, carrying Roland between them. "Now, don't you worry," Simon told the barely conscious man. "That arrow won't kill you, but you have lost plenty of blood. We'll get you comfortable and bedded down in the bunkhouse, where we put up our guests. I'll do what I can about the arrow."

"God—God b-bless you," he faintly murmured. "My—my name is Roland Eberle. Doris, my daughter—and Tom Blake—we were attacked by Wichita last night. Blake was brained with a tomahawk, and I don't know if he's dead or not—but my daughter must have run off—I hope to God she wasn't killed. Please try to find them both!"

"We'll go looking for them, as soon as we get you settled down," Simon stoutly declared. "We'll round up all the pack animals then, too."

Returning to the settlement on horseback with the wounded man propped up in front of him, Simon handed him down to Jack. Then the two men carried him together and laid him very gently down on a bed in the bunkhouse. Minnie Hornsteder, who had of course left her horse outside and followed the men into the bunkhouse, said, "I'll go fix a hot poultice. Best thing I know for wounds like that. Stop the infection, too, if there is any from that arrow. Darned redskins sometimes put poison on their arrows." Then, putting her hand over her mouth, she grumbled to herself as she left the bunkhouse, "You and your big mouth, Minnie Hornsteder. Now, why'd you have to go and say a fool thing like that, when this poor man's already suffering enough?" Meanwhile, Simon had Jack hold Roland steady, and the young scout gently averred, "Now then, I'm going to get this arrow out. Might hurt a bit, but it's gotta come out."

"Go ahead, I—I can take it," Roland weakly murmured. He closed his eyes and gritted his teeth as Simon took hold of the arrow with both hands, drew his breath, then yanked it out cleanly. "There, now! There's no barb, and that ought to do it," the scout said, while Jack took out his bandanna and at once pressed it against the bleeding wound.

A few minutes later, Minnie came back with the poultice, as well as some strips of cloth to be used as bandages, and with the two men helping her, Roland's wound was soon dressed. Then, with touching solicitude, Minnie carefully tucked under Roland's head a pillow filled with goose feathers which she had taken from her own bed. "Now, you just re-there and get some sleep, mister," she told him. "And the boys here'll go looking for that Mr. Blake you wuz talking about, and your daughter, too. We'll find them, don't you fret now. You just get some rest."

"Th-thank you—God bless you all," Roland said faintly. Weakened by his ordeal, he closed his eyes and lapsed back into sleep.

"Best thing for him," Simon avowed. "Jack, go see if you can round up two or three fellows for a search party. Have them bring their rifles, just in case there are any Wichita skulking around the settlement."

"I'll go get Ed Purvis and Frank Donner, they're crack shots," Jack told him.

A few minutes later, all four men, mounted on horseback, rode out of the settlement in search of Doris Eberle and Thomas Blake. They found the latter not far from where Roland had lain, and he was already sitting up, dazedly putting a hand to his head where the tomahawk had struck. Fortunately, it had been a glancing blow and only stunned him into unconsciousness, without shattering his skull. Two men helped him mount up behind Simon, who then rode back to the settlement, after bidding two men to continue their search for Roland's missing daughter, and telling the third man to bury Fenwick and bring in the pack animals.

Doris had wakened a few hours after dawn. The trying ordeal of seeing her false husband killed and her own father supposedly slain by a Wichita arrow had been enough to bear, but then there was also the fact that she was alone in this vast country, with hostile Indians seemingly behind every tree. She rose, smoothed down her homespun dress, and slowly walked out of the clump of live-oak trees that had sheltered her during the harrowing night, and she saw again in the distance the outline of the settlement. Her face took on a determined look. She would have to walk there, Indians or not, and get help. Her poor father—the least she could do for him was to give him a proper Christian burial, and she'd go down on her knees and pray for forgiveness for having caused him all this worry and bringing him out here to a death that should never have happened. Thinking of it, she began to cry, and her shoulders shook with sobs as she covered her face with her hands and bowed her head, berating herself for her folly in having had her head and heart turned by the smooth-talking Roy Fenwick.

She saw two men on horseback heading along the river-bank and about four hundred yards from her, and when she saw they were white men, she cried out and began to run toward them. Jack Converse reined in his horse and shouted to his companion, "There she is, safe and sound!" At once, he headed his gelding toward the blond young woman.

They drew up abreast of her, and Jack politely tipped his raccoon cap, which he was never without, even in the hottest weather. "Are you Doris Eberle, ma'am?" he politely inquired.

"Oh, yes! Thank God you've found me! My poor father's dead—"

"I've got good news for you, Miss Eberle," Jack said. "He's not dead. We took him back to the bunkhouse, and Simon Brown, who's the head of the settlement here, took out the arrow and Minnie Hornsteder put on a hot poultice. I think he'll pull through."

"Can you take me to him?"

"Why sure, ma'am, that's why we came out here, to look for you. Why don't you hop up behind me on my horse?" Jack suggested. Turning to the other man, he asked him to assist Roland's daughter, and soon Doris, her arms wound around Jack's waist, was riding into the settlement, tears of joy streaking her worry-lined face.

They took her to the bunkhouse, and she flung herself on her knees beside her father's bed. "Oh, Daddy, Daddy, thank God you're alive! I feel so guilty. I did this to you—I brought you out here looking for me!"

Roland stirred and vaguely returned to consciousness. His eyelids fluttered, and he saw Doris before him, tears running down her cheeks, clasping her hands and holding them out to him in a supplicatory gesture. "Honey—you're safe—I'm grateful," he feebly murmured.

"Oh, Daddy, can you ever forgive me? I was such a stupid little fool—you were right all along about Roy Fenwick—"

"Hush now, honey, he's gone. And there's nothing to forgive. Maybe I wasn't too good a father to you, after your mother died. I'll try to make it up to you, honey."

She kissed him on the cheek, and his tears mingled with hers. Minnie, who was staying near the bunkhouse to see how the patient was doing, took out a bandanna and loudly blew her nose. Then she turned around and addressed some of the younger men, who had come into the bunkhouse out of curiosity. "You young scalawags," she scolded them, "there's work to be done, wood to be chopped, horses to be looked after. Ain't you got nothin' better to do than to break in on a man and his l'il gal coming back from the dead? Now go on, get out of here before I take a broomstick to you! This is Minnie Hornsteder talking, and you boys know perfectly well I'll do just what I promise, like I always have all my life!"

Abashed, they sheepishly disappeared, and Minnie turned back with a benevolent look at Doris and Roland. Then she blew her nose again and, taking her own advice, quietly left the bunkhouse.

John Cooper Baines and Miguel, who had been preparing for their departure that afternoon, learned of the happy reunion between father and daughter and also the resolution of the enmity between Thomas Blake and Roland Eberle. By now, Blake, though still suffering a violent headache, was on his feet and perfectly lucid, and, like Roland and his daughter, he had made the acquaintance of the tall Texan and the white-haired *capataz*. "Are you going back to Sedalia, Mr. Blake?" John Cooper now asked as they talked outside the bunkhouse.

"I have to think it over," Blake replied. "I promised our folks I'd look after my kid brother, but now that Doug's gone, there's no real reason to stay around in Sedalia. Personally, I've been hankering for a piece of good farmland, and I know a little something about cattle. I could do worse than settle down here."

"That you could, for a fact," John Cooper agreed as he extended his hand, which Blake energetically shook. "Whatever you decide, I wish you the very best of luck."

"Thanks, Mr. Baines. It was good meeting you. You, too, Mr. Sandarbal."

"*Vaya con Dios, amigo*," Miguel wished him in return.

Shortly afterward, John Cooper and his party mounted up their horses and began the driving of the wagons out of the settlement en route to the Double H Ranch. Watching them go, Blake finally went back into the bunkhouse and saw Doris sitting on a stool beside her father's bed. They had already met, and Blake thought that perhaps the young woman wanted nothing to do with him because of his earlier intention to kill her father and avenge his brother's death. But she turned toward him and gave him a fleeting smile, and he came up to her and said quietly, "Your father's going to do just fine, I'm sure he is."

"I think so, too," Doris replied. Then, looking up at him, she said, "Daddy—Daddy told me everything—how he saved your life, and how you're friends now." She gave him a dazzling smile.

Blake stared at her. She was the loveliest young woman he had ever seen. Long a bachelor, he had not really courted any girl, for the chore of looking after his wild and unpredictable brother had occupied what spare time he had. But now, he felt as if there was nothing to hold him back any longer. What was more, it was wonderful land out here in Texas. With a wife to help him, a man could go far with a farm or a ranch.

"I won't disturb you and your father anymore now, Miss Eberle," Blake now said in a soft voice. "I'll come by later this evening to see how you both are."

"I'm just fine, Mr. Blake, thank you. I wasn't hurt at all. You're very nice. Thank you for asking about my father—and I'm glad that you're not his enemy anymore."

Blake smiled, and for the first time in all these nightmarish weeks of tracking down a man and then fighting against hostile Indians, he found he could crack a joke. "How could I stay mad at a man with as beautiful a daughter as you are, Miss Eberle?" he teased.

And then, as Doris's cheeks flamed and before she could stammer a reply, he turned and left the bunkhouse. She stared after him and for a long moment kept watching the door through which he had passed. Then, with a little sigh, she turned back to her father. First came his welfare, but soon, after he was fully recovered, maybe he and Doris could stay on at this wonderful settlement in Texas and get to know Thomas Blake better.

On the evening of this same day, in Heitor Duvaldo's *hacienda* near Lobos, the murdered *hacendado*'s two teen-age sons, Benito and Enrique, turned to Joaquín Ortega, whom they had made majordomo of the Duvaldo *estancia* as a reward for his loyalty to their father.

"Joaquín," Enrique said, "we are leaving for Buenos Aires tonight, there to take a ship bound for los Estados Unidos. Now do what you can to defend this *estancia* in our father's name, and enlist the loyal *gauchos* to hold fast against those *porteños* who, I am certain, plotted our father's death. And if they fight, you and the *gauchos* will fight back. Yes, it is true, Joaquín, they may send soldiers here— yet I do not wish you to risk your life in vain, and if the force is overwhelming, you must hide in the *pampas* with the *gauchos*."

"Señor Enrique," the majordomo avowed, "I would shed my blood to the last drop to protect this *hacienda* and all those who work here who loved your father and respect you both for your kindness to us all and your loyalty to the honorable name he left you. I have sworn an oath, and may *el Señor Dios* strike me dead if I do not perform it unto my very last breath, young señores," Joaquín went on, his voice hoarse with emotion. "And it is my prayer also that both of you will return one day to avenge the murder of my *patrón* by those devils who are worse than the jaguar."

"We pray for that also," Benito avowed, standing beside his brother, his eyes moist with emotion. "Our father gave us a command before he died, and it was to seek out the *gringo* John Cooper Baines in the land called Texas. We are still too young, the two of us, to lead the fight against the *porteños*. But this *gringo*, who married the oldest daughter of Señor Maldones and who helped him escape prison and the death that the *porteños* wished for him—he will teach us what we must do. When that day comes, Joaquín, we shall return. And now, Enrique, it's time to go. As we have learned, an American three-master will drop anchor not far from where the *gringo* came to meet our friend, the señor Maldones. It will arrive in a few days, and we must ride out now at night so that no one sees us. It will be a long ride to the coast, but we shall be there when the ship awaits us."

Both young men shook Joaquín's hand, and the majordomo could not hide his tears as he bade them Godspeed and a safe journey. They mounted their horses and, with a last look back at the home they had enjoyed for so long, now dark with its memories of a kind and generous father who had been treacherously assassinated by the greedy *porteños*, they rode toward the Argentinian coast and their rendezvous with the *Delphine*.

Twenty-two

—✦————————————————————————————————————✦—

Because of his wife's prolonged vacation, Brigadier General Santa Anna had determined upon a march with a small body of his handpicked troops through the provinces and on to the city of Chihuahua. His purpose was twofold: first, to meet there with a number of officers who would be loyal to him when the time came to announce himself as the true liberator of all Mexico; second, to determine at firsthand the feelings of the common people, whose cause he repeatedly claimed to represent. He had already won sufficient military acclaim to have captured public approval, but he was as shrewd a politician as he was a military officer to understand that his ascension to the official leadership of Mexico could not happen until he had even greater support of the common people.

He had left his estate near Veracruz the day after the courier had delivered the second letter from Eugene de Silva at La Banque de la Nouvelle Orléans, advising him that the señor Baines had deposited a second and even larger hoard of silver ingots. Decidedly, this unknown *gringo*, a stupid *americano*, had more money than perhaps the government itself—and if he, Santa Anna, could only find a way to acquire it, no one could stop his ruling all of Mexico!

They reached Chihuahua a few weeks after John Cooper, Miguel Sandarbal, and the *vaqueros* left the settlement on the Brazos for their Texas ranch. With Santa Anna had come Rodrigo Martínez, the private who had fallen asleep while on duty and had survived the ordeal of the torturous Spanish horse on Santa Anna's estate. He had accompanied the general with mixed feelings: Grateful though he was for having been spared a firing squad or perhaps even worse, he could not forget that his general had told him that he would be ordered to go on a mission to a ferocious tribe of Indians.

Santa Anna's orderly had arranged everything, engaging

the finest rooms in the very best inn. A banquet was held to honor the renowned general, and half a dozen officers, holding ranks from captain to colonel, shared Santa Anna's table. The general had made arrangements with his host to provide an attractive young *criada* for each of the men—with the prettiest of all, needless to say, for himself.

They had eaten and drunk very well, indeed, this evening, but Santa Anna had taken care not to imbibe too much *tequila*, for he wished his mind to be perfectly clear. He rose from the table and, beckoning to a lean, gloomy-looking man in his early forties, murmured, "A word in private with you, *mi coronel.*"

Colonel Esteban Moravada rose with alacrity. He followed Santa Anna into an adjoining room, closing the door behind him, and smartly saluted. "You have done me a great honor, *mi general*, and I am at your service, as always."

"I know that, Esteban—let me call you by your first name, for we are friends, and you have already done me many services. I remember last year how, when you returned from a patrol to Candela, you sent off a courier to me, saying that in Laredo you had heard by chance a *vaquero* talking in a *posada* to some companions and praising *el Halcón*. And you told me of the silver."

"I remember it well."

"That silver, Esteban, was stolen from the bank in New Orleans where that damned *gringo* had placed it for safety."

"*¡Caramba!*" the colonel swore.

"However, with the cursed luck of an *americano*, the *gringo* found the thief and returned the silver to the bank. Not only that, Esteban, but he learned of still another hidden mine, and he has now made another deposit even more substantial than the first. I would guess that his fortune would be in the neighborhood of eight-million *pesos!*"

"*¡Jesus María!*" Moravada gasped, his eyes bulging with astonishment.

"There we have it. You do not care for Texans any more than I do, *¿no es verdad?*"

"I should like to see them all exterminated," the colonel replied promptly. "Indeed, you may not have heard, *mi general*, that last summer I attacked the town of Benecia, and I put to death by firing squad some *gringos* who bore arms against our beloved country."

"*Bravo*, Esteban! No, I hadn't heard of it. But you

have done exactly what I would have done under the circumstances. Hear me out on this: The only way we shall keep these accursed *gringos* from penetrating into our country and taking our land is by driving them off and teaching them military lessons just as you have done, *mi coronel.*"

"Again, you do me too much honor. I am only a servant of my country."

"But a loyal one, and one who will go far—you forget that a general can promote a colonel to his own rank."

Esteban Moravada gasped, not believing his ears.

"I'll authorize you—though this must be kept secret from the junta in Mexico City—to do all you possibly can to harass the settlers in Texas. Texas belongs to our glorious country, and we must take vigorous steps to drive the settlers away before they can grow too strong for us to rout them."

"I fully agree with you, *mi general.*"

"Here, try this brandy. It is aged, French, and came from New Orleans. It is one of the few things the *gringos* have brought us for which we can be grateful; ¿*no es verdad?* Help yourself." Santa Anna made a generous wave of his hand.

Moravada basked in this cordial aura, for indeed he was ambitious, an ambition second only to the man who stood before him. In the year of 1823, he had been demoted from his colonelcy to the rank of captain for an alleged insult to a then-presiding general. After that, however, he had led several patrols against a group of bandits, captured the leader, and sent him to a firing squad. The villages and towns ravaged by that bandit band had sent off a letter to the junta in Mexico City to praise him, and as a consequence, he had regained his colonelcy. The previous year, Santa Anna had already asked him to provoke the brash Texans into overt revolt against the traditions and customs and laws of the Mexican government and had intimated that he would become one of the foremost officers in all Mexico. But now, tonight, the general had put the hope of his obtaining a general's star in no uncertain terms.

Moravada's hand trembled as he poured himself out a measure of brandy, and he took pains to pour an equal one for his host. He handed it to Santa Anna with an obsequious smile, then put his goblet to his lips to toast the general: "Long life, and may you indeed become the liberator of all

Mexico, who will dictate how the *gringos* are to be treated, and how our country is to be led to glory!"

"*Gracias, mi amigo. Mi compañero.* Now, bear with me a moment. It was told to me—correct me if I am wrong—that you have a contact with the fierce Yaqui Indians, who resent even our own loyal Mexican soldiers for encroaching upon their territory."

"*Es verdad, mi general,*" Colonel Moravada said, and nodded. "He is my cousin, Juan Cortizo."

"I did not know that you were a *mestizo,* Esteban," Santa Anna wonderingly replied.

The gloomy-featured colonel momentarily frowned; but then, remembering that he was in the presence of the one man who could further his own ambitions, he forced an ingratiating smile to his thin lips. "The fact is, *mi general,*" he haltingly explained, "that I am not a *mestizo.* Only my cousin is. *Mi tío* fell in love with a Yaqui girl and, I am sad to say, married her."

"But how could that be, in our church?" Santa Anna pursued, scowling uncomprehendingly.

"It seems that he found a willing priest who, for a few *pesos*—he had a very poor parish, *mi general*—agreed to perform the ceremony. And thus, Juan Cortizo was born and became my cousin. He was brought up near San Luis Obispo, but when he was fourteen, he found our Mexican civilization not rewarding and went back to live with his mother's people in Sonora."

"I understand," Santa Anna declared. "But it is a stroke of good fortune that you have such a contact, for we have great need of the Yaqui."

"My cousin and I are friends, though I do not see him too often. And it will be difficult to do so. As Your Excellency well knows, the Yaqui are suspicious of all those in uniform."

"Yes, I know. Let me think a moment." Santa Anna stroked his chin, already lost in speculation, then his eyes brightened and narrowed. "You could tell your cousin that I shall make certain that his tribesmen have guns and ammunition, as well as whatever they may need by way of food and horses—I am quick to tell you that the cost of this will be out of my own fortune, so that never can there be any connection traced between the government in Mexico City and the Yaqui. Well then, if his tribespeople agree, he may be able to lead them against the settlers."

Colonel Moravada nodded. "I am with you, *mi general*. I think such an attack can indeed be arranged."

"I know that the Yaqui are mostly in Sonora, but I have also heard they occasionally send out foraging parties as far as the northwestern boundaries of Texas. It would not be too much farther than that to attack the settlement on the Brazos that Señor Eugene Fair arranged under the treaty our government stupidly made with the Austins."

"Yes, it could be done, *mi general*," the colonel repeated. "The Yaqui are nomadic, and they do not mind traveling long distances if the hunting is good."

Santa Anna uttered a grim little laugh. "It will be very good. Now there is another matter I wish to discuss with you."

The colonel gave Santa Anna a quick salute and then inclined his head in token of great respect. "I am at your service for whatever projects you honor me by wishing me to help perform, *mi general*."

"As I've just told you, the silver treasure of that *gringo* has more than doubled. But this wealth can greatly aid the cause of Mexico. Indeed, my belief is that it rightly belongs to Mexico, and not to the *gringo*. Consider this, Esteban: The mountains in which the treasures were found are in Nuevo México, are they not?"

"*Si, es verdad, mi general*."

"Just so. Well, then, Nuevo México was a province of Mexico when it was under Spanish rule. And when we threw off the Spanish yoke, does it not follow, even in a court of law, that we acquired all the possessions that Spain formerly owned?"

"I should think so, *mi general*."

"If I were an *abogado*, Esteban, I would take this to the highest court, and I am certain that I should be found right. No matter. Now, since we cannot go to a court of law, and since unfortunately these stupid *gringos* would never recognize the claims of our government—indeed, would probably go to war rather than agree to the justice of our claim— you and I must both think of getting the silver ingots from the *americano*. Understand me—I do not care how they are acquired. And I need a reliable man to work for and with me in bringing the treasure back to Mexico. Imagine, Esteban, all that wealth divided among the *peones* who are oppressed by the *ricos* and the clergy!"

"It is a wonderful picture, *mi general!*"

"It is very possible, and it is more than a picture. And if you are the man who can help me recover the treasure for our country, remember that I said I have the power to appoint you to a rank equal to mine. Besides which, you may tell this Juan Cortizo that I will personally award him the rank of captain with full pay for what he does in harassing the American settlers . . . and helping get the silver from the señor Baines."

"I will at once make contact with my cousin, *mi general.*"

"I may be somewhat helpful to you in that regard," Santa Anna said negligently. "There is a private under my command, a certain Rodrigo Martínez, who forfeited his life by sleeping on duty. But because I was merciful, I allowed him to live to prove his worth. Yet I told him that one of his missions would be to take messages to the fierce Indians—the Yaqui, of course. You will use him to make contact with your cousin. But after his usefulness is at an end, let them kill him. I have heard that the Yaqui enjoy nothing better than a slow torture of an enemy or a captive."

"I fear that is true, *mi general.*"

"Then justice will be done to this man who could not keep his eyes open in my service. And yet by dying, think of what a glorious martyrdom he will achieve as one of the instruments by which I shall help set Mexico free and bring wealth to the poorest *peón* in the smallest hamlet in all of our glorious country, Esteban!"

"It is a plan that cannot fail, and it shows your genius, *excelencia!*" Colonel Moravada quickly responded.

Santa Anna clapped the officer on the back. "You will send Private Martínez to your cousin, then. Martínez will send Cortizo to you at an appointed meeting place. I shall see to it that there are presents for him and his people. There will be ammunition, superb horses, and for Cortizo himself, from my personal fortune, a sack of gold."

"I am certain that my cousin will come to this meeting. He has not forgotten what it was to live with a *hacendado rico* and to have all the luxuries that a Yaqui stronghold can never have. The promise of the sack of gold alone will bring him to the meeting."

"Then it is settled. Esteban, now we shall make a toast. Pour yourself more brandy, and more for me, as well. *Gracias.*" They clinked glasses. "And now, Esteban, as proof of the esteem in which I hold you, you will find awaiting you in your bed the loveliest of all the *criadas*. I tell you confidentially, Esteban, that she is so lovely that I very nearly weakened and chose her for myself. This alone should show you what regard I have for you. *¡Adelante!*"

Colonel Esteban Moravada did not awaken until early afternoon of the next day, having satiated himself with the lovely young *criada* whom Santa Anna had sent to his bedchamber. He had her bring a pot of chocolate, *tortillas*, and a small plate of *carne asada* to him, and he shared this meal with her, thereafter dismissing her and ordering her to go find Rodrigo Martínez and send him at once to the bedchamber.

A few minutes later, Martínez reported with a smart salute, an apprehensive look on his face. Moravada lay naked on the bed, his head propped up by three pillows, smoking a cigar and enjoying some *aguardiente*. His thin lips curved in a mocking smile as he said, "So you are the *soldado* under a suspended sentence of death, *no es verdad*, Martínez?"

"S-sí, *mi coronel*," the man faltered.

"Well, if you serve me faithfully and make no mistakes, I may let you keep your life. You will go on a mission for me at once. Do you know the province of Sonora?"

"Not very well, *mi coronel*."

"It is of no importance. You will learn the route. There is a *sargento* Almorinda attached to my personal aides, and you will find him elsewhere in this inn. He will tell you the best route to Sonora. Now listen carefully. You will ride to the village of Bacanora. It is perhaps a little less than two hundred miles from here. You should make this in a week, and the *sargento* will give you a fast horse, supplies, and two *pistolas* and ammunition. Now, when you reach Bacanora, there is a little *posada* known as Los Tres Cruces. You will ask the owner to send word to Juan Cortizo to meet you at the *posada*. And when you see him, you will give him this message." He handed over a small scroll sealed with wax and bound with two yellow ribbons. "Do not dare to open it, or Juan Cortizo will put you to the torture stake. Only he is to read what I have written, *¿comprendes?*"

"Sí, *mi coronel*, I will do exactly what you tell me."

"That is very wise. You may yet live a little longer and perhaps be lucky enough to have a *novia* such as I bedded last night." The colonel smirked. Seeing that the private shifted from booted foot to foot and looked more and more uncomfortable, he uttered a sardonic laugh. "You won't end up before a firing squad—that much I can promise you—if you do what you are told. I will also tell you this much of the message: Juan Cortizo is to meet me in the town of Guerrero, which is between Chihuahua and Bacanora. I shall be there within ten days and wait for him."

"Am I to return here, *mi coronel*?"

"No, you will accompany Juan Cortizo. That is all. Now go and ride as if all the devils of hell were behind you, Martínez!"

The man saluted and hurried out of the bedchamber. Colonel Moravada burst into mocking laughter. "No, *mi amigo*, you won't end up before a firing squad. It will be the torture stake of the Yaqui."

As the colonel had promised, the sergeant gave Private Martínez pistols, ball and powder, a sack of provisions, and a large canteen of water. He had pointed out to the terrified private exactly the route to be taken, for the Sierra Madre mountain range shut off most of Sonora from the east. There was, however, a considerable break between two tributary ranges, and this would provide the swiftest possible way toward Bacanora.

To his credit, Martínez wasted no time on the trail and contented himself with very little sleep, wishing to earn his life and perhaps even a promotion to corporal.

At noon of the seventh day, he reached the little town of Bacanora. The *posada* was easy to find; it was the only one in the town. The proprietor was a black-bearded, taciturn man in his early forties, and when Martínez explained his mission, the man grunted and said, "You will stay in a room upstairs, until Cortizo comes for you. And you'd best not be on a fool's errand. The Yaqui have no love for such as you."

"But I am on a mission for His Excellency, *el general* Santa Anna, and I come with this message for the señor Cortizo from his *primo hermano*," Martínez hastily stammered.

"That may be. He'll find out soon enough. I wouldn't want to be in your shoes if you're not telling the truth. Now get upstairs with you. And don't ask me when he'll come— he'll come when it suits him, *¿comprende?*"

Martínez spent the rest of the day and night and the better part of the next day before there was a knock at the door of his squalid little room. He sprang up from the bed, already sweating profusely in his terror. When he opened the door, he confronted a man nearly six feet tall, with leathery, wrinkled brown skin. The man was clad in a poncho and deerskin leggings, with tribal tattoos on both arms, and had little black eyes that seemed to pierce into Martínez's very soul. "*Soy* Cortizo. Hernandez says you have a message for me from *mi primo hermano*. Give it to me."

"*Sí*, Señor Cortizo. Here it is!" the private almost babbled as he hastily handed the half-breed the sealed scroll tied with ribbons.

Cortizo broke the seal, tore off the ribbons, and unrolled the message. From the laconic expression on his face, the unfortunate private could tell nothing. There was a long silence until finally Cortizo said, "I will go to meet my cousin at once. Come now."

Martínez could hardly speak but nodded and followed the half-breed down the narrow steps into the *posada*. It was empty except for the bearded owner who, his palms planted on the bar, stared at both men but remained silent.

"Come!" Cortizo commanded again as he pushed open the door of the *posada* and went out into the twilight. Martínez followed him, but he suddenly stopped dead in his tracks and tried to retreat. Four Yaqui, their faces hideously painted with ochre, black, and red, stood there, each man holding a hunting knife.

Cortizo quickly mounted a waiting gray pinto pony and made a gesture. The Yaqui seized Martínez and dragged him in the opposite direction.

"*Pero*, Señor Cortizo, am I not to go with you?" the private cried out, but Cortizo had already galloped off toward the rendezvous.

Then the private knew himself to be lost, and he began to babble tearful prayers, trying to hold back as the four Yaqui dragged him relentlessly toward their horses. Two of them bound his wrists behind his back and hobbled his ankles and draped him over the horse of the man who appeared to be the leader. And then all four rode off to the southwest and the camp of the Yaqui, taking the now helpless Martínez with them.

On the morning of the third day, Juan Cortizo rode into the town of Guerrero, tethered his horse at the hitching pos of the town's only inn, and went into the *posada*. His cousin Colonel Esteban Moravada was there waiting for him and uttered a joyous cry as he saw the half-breed enter. "*¡Bienvenida, mi primo hermano!* I knew you would come, but it took two days longer than I anticipated."

"That was because, Esteban, I wished to be sure that the message you sent by that stupid dog of a *soldado* was not a trap. While I am certain that Santa Anna esteems you, *mi primo hermano*, there are other generals who would have me hanged or shot or run down like a dog at lance point, *¿comprendes?*"

"Very well. But now you see it is no trap, Juan. More than that, behind this inn, there are gifts that I had some of my men bring for you. You will see that these gifts are handsome, indeed, to win your alliance."

"Are you forgetting that the Yaqui ally with no one? We are our own masters, Esteban."

"I know, but there will be great profit in this enterprise, and much killing and looting."

"Tell me what you have brought me!" the *mestizo* demanded.

"Ten of the finest horses, four crates of rifles and ammunition, and from Santa Anna himself, from his own private fortune, a sack of gold."

"I will agree that these are handsome gifts, Esteban." Cortizo chuckled humorlessly. "Let me see them."

"The horses are tethered in a stable behind the inn, and the crates of rifles are there as well. The sack of gold I have in my room—"

"I will see the horses and rifles first. Then we will talk in your room." Cortizo gestured with his thumb toward a fat, bald little man who cowered behind the bar. "Can this innkeeper be trusted?"

"He can. I have told him that if he values his worthless life, he will keep his mouth shut. Besides, I have given him a hundred *pesos*, more money than he has seen in six months. He will not betray us."

"If he does, he will die as your courier did, I'm certain."

Moravada grinned sardonically as they rose from their table and left the *posada*, the colonel leading his cousin toward the stable. The *mestizo*'s eyes widened, and he swore under his breath. "*¡Diablo!* You did not lie when you spoke of the horses."

"The best one is for you to ride, *por cierto*. And there are the crates of rifles and ammunition that I promised. Now come to my room. We will drink *tequila*, and I will tell you more about what *mi general* asks of you and your people."

In the colonel's room, the officer paced up and down and explained what General Santa Anna wanted done. As he talked, he sipped from a glass of *tequila* in his hand, while the *mestizo* sprawled on the bed, regarding his cousin with slitted eyes and a wary expression. "Well now, you've seen that we are in earnest, Juan," Moravada said. "Are you willing to do what we ask in exchange for these fine gifts?"

"*Mis compadres indios* will not need gifts to wish to kill *yanquis*, my cousin. They will do it out of the sheer joy of killing because they hate *gringos*, as I do. You know that my father, your *tío*, deserted my mother when he had a chance to marry a rich woman in Mexico City? But perhaps you do not know that my mother took her own life out of grief and shame for being abandoned by the man who had fathered me and my now-dead brother. No, I have my own score to settle with the *gringos*. And because my people know this, they will make me their war leader against the *yanquis*."

"Good, my cousin!" Colonel Moravada exclaimed. "As my message explained, you and your men will first attack an American settlement on the Brazos River. Then, afterward, there is one particular *gringo* that my general, Santa Anna, wishes you to harass. He owns a large ranch near the Frio River; also, he has a great treasure in silver that *mi general* seeks to acquire, so that he may advance the independence of Mexico and free the *peones* from their poverty and suffering. This treasure is now in a New Orleans bank, but perhaps we can think of some way of getting the *gringo* to take it out of his own free will. Knowing your cleverness, Juan, I count on you for that, when the time is ripe."

Cortizo scratched his head and then eyed his cousin with a mocking smile. "Well, I'll talk to *mis compadres*, and as you have suggested, I'll have them march to the settlement on the Brazos and attack it. Then we shall be in the general area of this *gringo*'s ranch, as you've described it to me."

"An excellent idea, Juan!"

"It won't be an all-out attack, because we have found it is much wiser to have sudden, unplanned forays that take the *yanquis* by surprise. My people know how to conceal themselves in the woods and in the thickets, until their enemies believe that they have gone and thus grow careless and lower their defenses. Then it is that we strike—and kill!"

He said the word "kill" with a savage sibilance, and his eyes gleamed cruelly as he regarded his cousin.

"¡Excelente!" Moravada exclaimed. "There will be more gifts from *mi general*, Santa Anna, if you do this. I have been authorized to tell you that he will offer you a commission as a captain in the Mexican army, with full pay at that rank, if you succeed."

Cortizo's eyes now sparkled with glee. "I, a lowly *mestizo*, to be a full captain? You joke with me, and you tempt me falsely."

"I do not. But first, you must earn the promotion."

"Do not worry." The *mestizo* scowled, deep in thought. "Time now is important. It is the very heart of summer, and I know that the *gringos* use this time to watch their crops and their cattle, and to have *fiestas*. They are soft and lazy, not like my people. So I will ride back to our stronghold; your men must accompany me with the horses and the rifles. When I show these gifts to my people, I have no doubt I will direct at least a hundred men against the settlement on the Brazos."

"How long do you think it will take you to reach there from your stronghold, Juan?" his cousin asked.

"Most of my people are now near Bacanora and the Yaqui River. I can be back there in, at most, three days, and we shall start our march. We are nomads, we move quickly, and we have good horses. Let me think, now. It is a journey of some five hundred miles, Esteban. The horses you have given me I think are faster than ours. Even so, give me seventeen days and nights, and we shall come behind the settlement on the Brazos."

"Good, good," Moravada said gleefully. "I know you will devise a stratagem worthy of a Yaqui."

"You pay me a compliment, and I will accept it, *mi primo hermano*," Cortizo replied. "When the day comes that a Yaqui cannot outthink a *gringo* or a Mexican dog, then we shall vanish from the face of the earth—but it will not happen. I go, my cousin; summon your men to bring the gifts. You shall hear from me, and your General Santa Anna, too. ¡Adiós!"

Twenty-three

Juan Cortizo appeared before his tribe soon after his meeting with his cousin. His dark-brown leathery skin brightened by the flickering glow of the torches and the huge campfire of a feast, the *mestizo* stood with arms folded across his chest and studied the mood of his mother's people. He had just shown them the crates of rifles and the magnificent horses that Santa Anna had sent as gifts to enlist the Yaqui in his war against the *gringos,* and he believed he already had them half won over.

"I have told you," Cortizo now said, "that there will be many more such gifts as these. But all of us are sworn to driving out those who would betray and kill us, and the *gringos* on the border of the Rio Grande threaten us now. Is it not wise, then, my brothers, to strike them before they grow too strong, to harass them with quick attacks in the night, and to vanish before they can find us? Not even the Comanche can rival the Yaqui in trickery in battle. There will be many scalps, many captives for the torture stake. And great booty, besides horses and women."

A murmur of approbation rose to his ears. He grinned savagely. "I am one of you," he said. "I am proud that my mother was a Yaqui. And if I could see my father here before me, the man who abandoned my mother along with my younger brother—who was killed by a Mexican *soldado* five years ago—I would take my bare hands to him, and I would rip out the veins in his throat and let his blood gush upon the fires we light now for this feast."

A chorus of growls of agreement, war whoops, and exultant cries resounded to his harangue. "I ask for volunteers," Cortizo went on. "Let a hundred of our best warriors ride with me, and we will show the *gringos* that we are enemies to be feared!"

Fierce howls of agreement rose to greet his ears, and

Cortizo smiled knowingly. He had them now in the palm of his hand, and what they did not know was that there was a sack of gold for himself, and it was carefully hidden away. And if by bad luck or the will of the eternal Giver of Breath his people would be defeated by those lucky *gringos*, then he would have the gold and no one to account to for it.

"Who rides with me, brothers?" he thundered. "Let those who will kill and plunder cross this line past the campfire and stand before me. Come, my brothers!"

Cheers, howls, and war whoops rose as those who had listened to him now hurried forward to support him.

Sardonically, he stared at all of them, his eyes turning slowly from one group to another. And then at last he said, "It is good. Get your horses, your new weapons. We ride now, before the sun rises in the eastern sky. In a little more than two weeks, we shall attack the strongest of the *gringo* settlements!"

As war chief of the Yaqui, Cortizo rode beside the tribal chief, Topaminga, with a hundred warriors, armed with lances, bows and arrows, knives, and tomahawks. The two leaders, along with eight of their best warriors, rode the new horses Santa Anna had given them. They, along with fifty other warriors, were also armed with the new rifles; the others had their old muskets and rifles. But in the main, since they were guerrilla fighters *par excellence*, they relied on close hand-to-hand fighting with knives, hatchets, and tomahawks, striking suddenly out of darkness and then retreating, causing consternation among the enemy's ranks.

"With these new rifles, Topaminga," Cortizo boasted, "your men will kill many *gringos* and *mexicanos*. And there will be more gifts from the General Santa Anna."

"We shall see, Juan, whether the gods smile on this adventure to which you have led us," the chief retorted. He was the tallest of the Yaqui, and his face was tattooed and he was naked to the waist, with his body painted in the war colors of ochre, red, and black. He carried a long lance with pennons floating near the cruelly pointed tip, pennons that he personally had wrested from a Mexican subaltern of cavalry that the Yaqui had ambushed two months earlier. "Our life is one of raiding," Topaminga continued, "but you take us many long miles beyond familiar land."

"That is because Santa Anna knows that of all Indian

tribes, the Yaqui are the fiercest fighters. There is no other tribe that can do what we can. And do not forget what rewards there will be when we succeed in driving off the settlers."

"I do not forget, Juan. See that your general keeps his promises to us. I have killed captains and majors and colonels of this fine Mexican army with my bare hands—I can kill a general as well," was the grim rejoinder.

They rode some five hundred miles in fifteen days, and though they had taken food supplies with them, they were well able to live either off the land or off others. For instance it was easy along this desolate route to raid some of the tiny Mexican hamlets near the Rio Grande, where they would find not only horses and sometimes a woman whom they fancied but also maize, dried meat, the fiery chili peppers of which they were inordinately fond, and the corn flour with which they would make their own *tortillas*. Now, on this last day of August, 1827, they had come to a dense forest about ten miles south of the settlement on the Brazos.

"We shall attack them at night," Cortizo said to Topaminga "and they will not be expecting this. These *gringos* believe the story that Indians do not attack at night because they fear that if they die in battle, their spirits will not go to the Slayer of Enemies in the sky."

"To kill our enemies at day or at night is equally pleasing to the Slayer of Enemies," Topaminga replied in his guttural voice, and his lips tightened in anticipation. "The blood of enemies poured out upon the ground is a sacrifice to Him. and that is why He smiles with favor upon us, His chosen people. Now then, Juan, tell me of this settlement. How many *gringos* are there? What weapons do they have?"

"According to what my cousin says, they have guns, no doubt as good as the ones that Santa Anna gave us, *mi jefe*,' Cortizo replied. "Pistols and knives, too. With their women and children, there are perhaps four hundred *gringos* in this community. But there is no protection for them such as the *soldados* have at a fort, which you have already seen in the provinces of Durango and Chihuahua. There, they have tall walls of sturdy wood, and it is not easy to attack except by breaking down the gate and entering."

"That is good. And we can use fire to burn their houses. It frightens the *gringos* and the *mexicanos*, and they run

bout squealing like puling babes in their terror," Topaminga
aid, and chuckled.

"My plan, *mi jefe*," Cortizo proposed, "is to take twenty
rmed braves and cross the Brazos River at a nearby fording
lace. Indeed, it is shallow at many places, for just before
vilight I rode ahead and observed those areas that can easily
e forded. Then we shall ride up along the river on the
astern side until we are directly across from the settlement.
he river side is always the least protected, and we will find
nother fording place and strike from the east, where they
re least expecting an attack. Then we will circle to the west
nd strike from that side. Once we have struck terror into
heir hearts, then you, *mi jefe*, will send another twenty
raves from the south to storm the settlement, and we can
ut the *gringos* down as we choose."

"It is a good plan," Topaminga agreed. And then, with a
ocking little smile, he added, "What is best about the plan,
y brother, is that you will lead the first attack. And if the
lan is bad, then it will be you who will pay for the deaths of
ur warriors."

"I am no coward, Topaminga, and you know that well,"
ortizo angrily countered. "Have I not fought beside you in
any a battle against the *soldados mexicanos*?"

"It is true, it is true," Topaminga blandly agreed. "I do
ot question your courage; I question only the wisdom of
tacking so many. Yet, it is true also that if we have only a
undred men and they have two times as many, surely a
aqui warrior is better than two *gringos*—I would say that
e is a better fighter than ten of them! Very well, then.
hoose those you will have accompany you, and the rest of us
ill come up from the south to see if your plan is successful."

"It will be," Cortizo boasted. "And do not forget, for
ur help, the illustrious general will make you many more
fts as a mark of his special favor. Do not think that he will
y to trick us, *mi jefe*. *Mi primo hermano* who came to enlist
y services in these attacks has told me that if all goes well,
e will be rewarded very well."

"All these are but words, Juan. It is well known that a
og can bark at a campfire to proclaim how he will kill a wolf,
ut I wish to see what he does when the wolf is upon him.
nough of this talk! Take your men and the rest of us shall go
d watch." Topaminga lowered his lance, then raised it and
de back into the woods, along with five of his council

members, older braves who had won great honor in previou
battles against the Mexicans and on whom he relied fc
advice in both military and the social matters of the tribe.

Cortizo swiftly chose a score of braves whom he knew t
be fierce fighters, all of them equipped with the rifles sent b
Santa Anna. Quickly, he explained what they were to d
Ride north on the eastern side of the river, then sweep acros
the river and ride into the settlement. Then they would circl
around and come in from the west. "If the *gringos* ar
driven into disorder by this, *mis amigos*," he told them, "ou
mighty chief Topaminga will come with another band c
warriors from the south and cut down these *gringo dogs*
There are women here, who will bring joy to you in you
lodges, as your slaves on the blanket or preparing the foo
that strengthens mighty warriors like the Yaqui. Take then
if you find them, and carry them off with you. That, too, wi
strike terror into the hearts of these *americanos!*"

The other eighty braves rode back into the woods wit
Topaminga, while Cortizo, at the head of the twenty arme
Yaqui, crossed the Brazos River at a fording place and heade
north.

Although Topaminga had seemed to agree with his wa
chief on the strategy of the attack against the settlers, he no
changed his mind and directed ten of his best bowmen t
ride across the river also and to follow Cortizo's braves
When the first twenty braves were well inside the settlemen
the bowmen would send their arrows in every direction agains
the settlers. As the chief told one of his trusted lieutenants
"Then they will certainly know that it is the Yaqui wh
attack. These *yanquis* know the Comanche and the Apach
and the Kiowa, but we are better fighters than those tribes
and this we will prove to the *yanquis*. Let fear be struc
into their hearts!"

Well ahead, not knowing this change of tactics, Cortiz
and his braves approached the eastern side of the settlemen
across the Brazos. He now instructed his twenty braves t
come in two waves of ten each, striking at the very eastern
most boundary of the settlement. Then, with a bloodcurdlin
yell, he charged forward and fired his rifle.

It was shortly after midnight, and the hazy half-moo
gave little light. Simon Brown had just gone outside hi
house for a walk, thinking over the projects that must b
completed to strengthen the settlement. When he hear

Cortizo's rifle shot, he cupped his palms to his mouth and shouted to the sentry at the guardhouse, "Ring the bell, get the men out with their guns! There's an attack from the river side!"

The lanky young sentry, Amos Denberg, promptly seized the long rope that dangled from a large brass bell standing in a frame about twelve feet high, and pulled it energetically. Men came hurrying out of their cabins and houses, armed with rifles and pistols, most with only their breeches on, barefooted, ready for trouble. Ever since Santa Anna had come into the settlement and gunned down old Henry Hornsteder, they had been prepared to repel all invaders or unwelcome visitors, as Simon himself had put it at a recent gathering in the community's meetinghouse. Now with the new arms and ammunition John Cooper had supplied them, they were more than ready.

Two small bands of Yaqui, whooping and shouting their war cries, rode in on either side of Juan Cortizo, who reined in his horse just in time to see the ten bowmen also riding in from across the river. He realized that Topaminga had altered the orders, and he scowled, for he believed that he alone should dictate the way the raid should be directed. But there was no time to countermand the chief's orders. Five of the bowmen had dismounted, leaving their horses docilely standing as they ran forward, crouching in the semidarkness, notching their arrows and waiting for targets. One of them saw an elderly woman come out the door of a little cabin some fifty feet away and sped his arrow into her right arm. With an agonized shriek, she stumbled back, slammed the door shut, and bolted it, then fainted in her terror and pain.

But by now, sixty men had hurried toward the eastern end of the settlement to meet the Yaqui attack as Simon continued to bawl out orders to them. The men crouched down, taking cover behind sheds, tethering posts, water troughs, and the sides of houses and cabins. Since they were the defenders and could watch their enemy coming at them— and since they possessed fine new rifles—their aim was more effective than the initial rifle fire of the Yaqui, whose principal thought was to terrorize and paralyze the enemy and then pick them off one by one, as they had done in the hills of Sonora and the province of Chihuahua. Three Yaqui toppled from their horses and lay dead on the ground, and two others were wounded.

Cortizo saw a young Texan, not more than eighteen, scurry toward a barn. The *mestizo* fired and killed him, but in return, a shot from Simon's rifle grazed his right shoulder, and he very nearly dropped his rifle. Wheeling his horse, he retreated, calling orders to the mounted riders and to the bowmen to continue the attack relentlessly and not to fall back.

Minnie Hornsteder seized old Henry's rifle, which she always kept loaded, and hurried out onto the porch of her house. She saw a Yaqui bowman kneeling and preparing to launch an arrow at a settler who was running with his back turned toward the bowman. "Damned redskin, shoot a helpless man in the back, would you?" she growled, then squeezed the trigger. The bowman flung up his hands, dropped the bow, and rolled over and over and lay still.

"Climb onto the roofs, men, you'll see them plain as day when they come in," Simon called to four of the settlers near a sturdy cabin. They swiftly obeyed, flattening themselves on top of the roof of the cabin, reloading their rifles. As two more bowmen came riding in, a volley of rifle fire picked them off their horses and left them lifeless on the ground.

One of the Yaqui riflemen fired at an elderly man who had come out onto the porch of his cabin, his frightened wife crouching behind him, and the Indian's shot winged him in the shoulder, making him drop his rifle and utter a cry of pain. The Yaqui warrior, knowing that it would take precious time to reload, bared his teeth and rushed forward, swinging the rifle by the barrel to use it as a war club. But the frightened woman, fearing for her husband's life, seized her husband's rifle, leveled it, and pulled the trigger. The recoil sent her sprawling backward, but the Yaqui stopped in midflight, his eyes bulging with surprise. He sank down on one knee, blood gushing from the wound in his chest, then he rolled over onto his side, dying.

The four men atop the cabin had reloaded and sent shot after shot after the now-retreating Yaqui, for Cortizo had summoned the riders and the bowmen to the south. They had inflicted losses on the settlers, true enough, but they had lost almost ten braves.

Topaminga and his braves had already ridden up from the south and watched as Cortizo and the others retreated in their direction. Now that the settlers were thoroughly roused and armed, the chief knew it would be futile to launch his part of the attack. It was not a good beginning; the infernal *gringos* had driven off some of his fiercest warriors. Juan Cortizo would answer for this, unless there were greater successes. Not all the Mexican gold there was could buy back Yaqui lives!

When Cortizo rode up to the tall, painted chief, who shook his lance in anger, he propitiatingly declared, *"Mi jefe,* I have seen weaknesses in the *gringos.* Perhaps if we had taken more men against them this first time, and not fired until we reached the inside of the settlement, we would have taken them by surprise and killed many of them!"

"You should have thought of that when you began the attack, Juan," Topaminga scolded him, his voice harsh with anger. "Where are Martingay, Dumeido, Colcarte, Bravido— warriors whom the women acclaimed around our campfire for their great deeds? Sacrificed to this attack of yours!"

"But we took lives, also. And now they fear us. We will remain here for nine suns, great Topaminga, and strike again at night, but in a different way. We shall try fire. The fire arrows—all *gringos* fear the fire as do the *mexicanos!"* Cortizo promised.

"We will see. We did not come all this long way to be driven off like women. And yet, the Yaqui who gave their blood upon this stolen soil are gone forever from our campfire, and a few paltry *gringo* lives do not make up for them; do not forget it! Back to the woods!" He turned and waved his lance, to direct the other men to the south and out of sight from the settlers.

Again the night was still, while Simon and Minnie did their best to patch up the wounded and to arrange for the burial of those whom the Yaqui had killed in this surprise assault. And it was as well for Minnie's peace of mind that she could not know that it was Santa Anna, the murderer of her own valiant old husband, who had been the one to instigate this attack by Indians from a far-distant Mexican province.

After the first attack on the settlement, Cortizo sent a Yaqui who spoke Spanish fluently to ride as a courier to Colonel Esteban Moravada, his cousin. The officer had taken up temporary headquarters at Piedras Negras, on the Mexican border in the province of Coahuila, as he had told Cortizo he would, and now the *mestizo* wanted to inform his cousin that he had commenced the harassment of the American settlers and that he needed certain additional items.

Having delivered the message, the courier returned a week later to meet Cortizo near Carrizo Springs on the Nueces River, for the *mestizo* had decided it would be better to meet his messenger in private, away from the Yaqui camp. The man brought with him a magnificent new Belgian rifle, a mother-of-pearl framed mirror, and a sack of gold coins; these were to be given to Topaminga, who, Cortizo realized, was becoming impatient at the lack of victories and the long time spent in waiting until another attack could be launched upon the Brazos settlement. Indeed, Cortizo had directed a second attack about six nights after the first one, this time taking fifteen braves with rifles and bows and arrows, with a dozen more sending fire arrows into the settlement from their positions to the south. Two of the frame buildings had been badly damaged by the fires, and three male settlers had fallen to the Yaqui rifles, while a girl of sixteen, a woman of fifty, and two children had been badly wounded by Yaqui arrows and bullets. But Simon had again rallied the settlers to drive off the attackers, and eleven Yaqui warriors lay dead by the time the survivors retreated to their hiding place in the thick woods to the south.

When Cortizo rode back to where the Yaqui had made their temporary camp five miles to the southwest of the settlement and in a thickly forested region, Topaminga angrily strode forward, lance in hand, and, shaking it in the air, exclaimed, "We have nothing yet for all these long weeks of leaving our country and coming across the Rio Grande to attack these *americanos*. When we return to our stronghold, there will be many squaws who will weep when they do not see their warrior mates. And where are the women and booty that you have promised us? This is not our land, and the *gringos* are well armed and work as would an army of *soldados*. No, you have brought us here for nothing."

"Not for nothing, great chief," Cortizo exclaimed in a wheedling tone as he dismounted and drew from the saddle sheath the gleaming new Belgian rifle. "This is a personal present from General Santa Anna for your courage and your patience, this rifle, which is the equal of any that those *gringos* have."

"Do you speak with a straight tongue, Juan?" Topaminga asked as he began examining the rifle. He turned it over and over, squinted through the sights, fingered the trigger, and then, having planted his lance in the ground beside him, took aim at a chicken hawk soaring overhead.

"I swear it by the Yaqui blood my mother gave me, Topaminga! But this is not all. Here is a mirror, a costly one that only the wealthiest *ricos* in all Mexico could own, so that you may see your noble visage in the glass—here, see for yourself!" He drew from his saddlebag the mirror, and the tall Yaqui chief examined it, scowled and made faces at it, and then grinned, thoroughly pleased as a child might be. "And this, too, is from your general?" he asked, but in a more mollified tone.

"And finally, a sack of gold pieces," Cortizo tempted his *jefe*.

"It is good. But how long must we stay in this forest?"

"We shall attack the settlement a last time, and then we shall move toward the Frio River, Topaminga, for there is the *estancia* of the *gringo* with the treasure. There we shall be certain to count coup, for all this while I have been thinking of a plan that will be better than an attack."

"What is this plan of yours, Juan?"

"I cannot tell you yet, for I must work out the way it can be done. Besides, after we have made our last attack on this settlement, I must ride to Colonel Moravada, *mi primo hermano*, and tell him what I have thought out. And if he approves of it, Topaminga, then I will make it known to you and ask for your help."

"Good," the chief grunted, again examining himself in the mirror and first grinning, then scowling. He uttered a sound that might have passed for laughter, and then he added, "I have never had a *mujer blanca*, though I have had many *mexicanas*. Perhaps this time my warriors will capture a *gringa* for me."

"We shall try, Topaminga. Tomorrow night, after we attack the settlers for the last time, I shall go to see my cousin, and you and your men will move toward the Frio River. I have given you a map of the *Hacienda del Halcón*, and you will easily find it. Keep in hiding until I meet you at the agreed-upon place."

"Very well. But let this final attack of yours be successful, for I tell you that I weary of hiding in the forest and losing the bravest of my warriors, without making those *gringos* pay for their deaths. The fire arrows did not work, and by now they are on their guard against us, since we have struck them twice."

"That is true, Topaminga, but this last attack will be in force. Fifty braves will ride with me. Half of them will take the new rifles, the others bows and arrows and lances. And we shall wait until it is nearly dawn—surely by then most of them will be asleep. This time, I am confident we will kill many *gringos!*" Cortizo promised.

And so, for the third time, Cortizo led the Yaqui against the settlement on the Brazos. He came in from the south, on foot, with one of the new rifles and a brace of pistols sheathed in holsters at his belt. And this time he cautioned his men to come silently, and not to utter their terrifying battle cry, for that would only serve to alert the settlers, as it had before.

He had not reckoned with Simon Brown's ingenuity, however. Every night since that second attack, guards had been posted along the boundaries of the settlement; as well as ten men on the roofs, with several rifles for each man and plenty of ammunition. Many of the young settlers had the new European rifles that John Cooper had given them, almost as capable of long-range marksmanship as was John Cooper's own "Long Girl." And thus, despite the stealthy entry of the Yaqui, the settlement was awakened by the sudden crackle of rifle fire and the shouts of the scouts on the roofs, "Injuns—wake up, come out with loaded guns and be ready!"

Cortizo shot down one of the guards from a nearby rooftop with his rifle. Then, drawing both pistols, he fired at another, only slightly wounding him. The pistol in his left hand misfired, and he flung it away in anger, then drew a hunting knife as a young Texan sprang from around the side of a cabin, a Bowie knife gripped in his right hand and held out like a sword to gut him. Leaping to one side, Cortizo took his other pistol and flung it in the Texan's face, making him stumble back and lift the knife up to ward off the heavy weapon. And in the same instant, the *mestizo* plunged his knife into the Texan's heart, then drew it out and wiped it on the dead man's breeches. A rifle ball bit into the ground an inch away from his foot, and he heard shouts of the Texans near him.

The bowmen killed a woman and an old man, but by now the entire settlement was aroused and the night was made hideous with the reverberations of rifle and pistol fire and the screams and shouts of the wounded and dying. Several of the Yaqui drew their knives and engaged their enemies in hand-to-hand combat, and another Texan died, but four Yaqui went down from pistol shots and knife thrusts. Cortizo saw again that there was no chance for victory and ran like a deer out of the settlement and toward the south, shouting an order to retreat. But of the warriors who had followed him, only seventeen returned, and three were left wounded, to be killed without mercy by some of the angry settlers who had seen their children and women wounded and killed by Yaqui lead and arrows.

Cortizo mounted one of the Indian horses that had been tethered outside the settlement and galloped back to Topaminga and the rest of his men, the survivors following as best they could.

"Their defenses are too good for us, Topaminga," he said, "and their weapons are far superior to ours. We have done our best to cause hardship for the *gringo* settlers, as we were bidden, but there is nothing more we can do."

Topaminga said nothing for a long time; then, finally getting control of his emotions, he said slowly and in a dark tone, "You go now to your master, and then you come back to me with this plan for the *gringo's* ranch. This is your last chance. If the plan is not good, I tell you now, I will banish you from the Yaqui tribe. And if after that you ever return to Sonora, you will die at the torture stake!"

"My plan will not fail. It is now clearly in my head, every detail of it. And when I return from my *primo hermano*, I will be able to tell you. I know that the plan will make up for all that we have lost and gain us the glory of many dead enemies, and the loot of *dinero y mujeres!*"

At once, Cortizo rode to Piedras Negras, where Colonel Moravada awaited with growing impatience. Topaminga had insisted that two of his most trusted aides, Dorjinga and Umantis, who spoke Spanish fluently, go with him so that they might hear the words of Colonel Moravada, who spoke for the general Santa Anna.

When they arrived, the colonel glanced at the two scowling Yaqui warriors who flanked his *mestizo* cousin. "Do they speak Spanish, Juan?" he guardedly asked.

"Sí, mi primo hermano," Cortizo lamely admitted.

The gloomy featured colonel understood. The Yaqui chief had begun to doubt the word of his cousin, and this could be disastrous. If Topaminga would not allow his braves to go forward with the plan to gain John Cooper Baines's treasure, then all this would have been in vain. And his own hopes for promotion to the same exalted rank as Santa Anna would exist no longer—indeed, he might even be demoted again and sent to some desolate post in an outlying province.

"Well, we will speak freely, for I have nothing to hide from your *jefe* as I bring him greetings from *su excelencia* General Santa Anna," he declared in a loud voice, addressing himself to both silent, hard-faced Yaqui warriors. "I have had word only yesterday from the general, and he sends to your chief his thanks for the courage the Yaqui have shown in attacking the *gringos*. He also says there will be more gifts. Now he asks me to ask you, Juan, in turn, what have you planned to gain the silver treasure that will restore Mexico to its true greatness?"

"My cousin, we both know, as does the general Santa Anna, that the silver is guarded in a bank in New Orleans. Thus we must get the *gringo* to offer it to us of his own free will; *¿no es verdad?*"

Colonel Moravada impatiently nodded. "Of course, of course, *hombre*, that is the problem. What solution have you?"

"Perhaps," Cortizo said with a cunning smile, "the *mujer* of this *americano* could be taken away from him. Then word would be sent to him that he would never again see her alive, unless he ransomed her with all the silver."

Colonel Moravada's gloomy face expanded in a jubilant grin, and he slapped his thigh. "A superb idea! But do you think you can bring it off? The ranch is extremely strong, and in many ways it's guarded far better than the settlement you've already attacked so well."

"I will find a way. You see that I speak Spanish as well as you, Esteban. And with a Castilian accent, when I find it useful."

"That you do. I've always said that you were a most intelligent man. And brave, because you have Yaqui blood." The colonel made this last comment because he wished to mollify the pair of taciturn, wary Yaqui who had not uttered a word but who stared at him with unwavering gaze all this while.

"Esteban, I am thinking that the ranch has many miles of grazing land. Not all of it can be guarded. It may be that the *mujer* of the *gringo* will go for a walk, or perhaps ride her horse. I will hide near the ranch and study it. And when I see her, I will have my Yaqui blood brothers near me to seize her and take her across the border. Leave all that to me."

"It is a very good plan. I shall send a courier to the general this very evening. And if you succeed, you will be made a captain in the Mexican army as I have promised, and there will be rewards of more gold and rifles and horses for your great chief, Topaminga, and his warriors."

"My chief has sent these two who are first in the council in the lodge," Cortizo declared, "and they have heard you. And so they know that I do not speak with a forked tongue when I go back." He turned to them and said, "Now do you believe?" Both of them nodded and grunted assent.

"You will hear from me, when I have done what I will do, *mi primo hermano*," Cortizo promised. Now all his swaggering self-confidence had been restored, and he had no fear of being banished from the tribe before he did what he had to do to become a captain in the Mexican army. Yes, it had been an excellent idea for Topaminga to send these two spies—for such they had been. But now even these spies could report the wisdom of his plan, which they had heard with their own ears!

Cortizo quickly rode with the *jefe*'s two aides to the meeting place that the chief had designated, not far from the Nueces River and near the little town of Benecia, where Cortizo's cousin had, the previous year, executed two Texans on the charge of bearing treasonable arms against the Republic of Mexico. The *mestizo* addressed his chief. "Let me have six of your best men, your best fighters, trackers, and scouts. My plan is this: I will go alone, dressed as a beggar who has lost his way and has traveled many long miles. I will come from the southwestern end of the ranch, and I will talk to some of the men who work there. I will learn what I can about the *mujer* of the señor Baines. Perhaps she rides alone, or with some of the *vaqueros*, or with her *esposo*. But I shall learn. Your six braves and I shall wait our chance. And if she does ride where we shall be hiding, it will be an easy matter to capture her and bring her back to the stronghold. I know very little of her, for the story that was given to me by *mi primo hermano* from the general Santa Anna taught me much about the *gringo*, *seguramente*, but nothing of the *mujer*."

Topaminga pondered a moment, then nodded. "It is a good plan. I will give you the six braves. I and two other men will go on across the Rio Grande and wait for you in the foothills of the mountains to the southeast of Acuña. We will send you a signal when we see you. In the meantime, my other braves will go back to their lodges. I will not let any more of my warriors face needless dangers—already we have lost too many men on this mission that, aside from the gifts you have brought to us, has given us little of value."

"I agree with you, *mi jefe*. And I shall not need more men than those I have asked of you to come upon the *gringa* and bring her back as prisoner of the Yaqui. For if all of your braves remained near the ranch, the *vaqueros* who would come after the *mujer* once I have captured her would give battle, and many lives would be wasted. No, it is much more sensible this way. But as I have already said, I may need some time to learn of the coming and the going of this *mujer*."

"I understand. I will wait fourteen suns for you near Acuña, no more. If you have not come by then with the woman, I go back to the stronghold. And you, Juan, you had best not return without the *mujer*. True, if the gods do not at once smile upon you and it takes longer than you think to capture her, the bringing of her to the stronghold will still tell me that you are a Yaqui, even though your father was a *mexicano*. But if you fail—do not come back. My men would demand that you be put to the torture stake, as we did with that *soldado estúpido* who was first sent to summon you."

Cortizo shuddered, and as he stared into the grim face of the tall Yaqui chief, he knew that Topaminga would not hesitate to turn him over to the fiendish rituals of torture that made the strongest man scream like a woman and beg for death long hours before it came. "I understand," he repeated in his turn. "I will bring her."

Topaminga stared at him a long moment, then mounted his horse and uttered a guttural command to his warriors. From their ranks, six horsemen drew away and trotted up to Cortizo. Topaminga turned back to call, "They will help you to do what you have promised. And if there is treachery, they will know what to do to you, even before you reach the stronghold. May the Slayer of Enemies help you return to us still a Yaqui whom we respect—or else take you to the dark world of the traitorous dead!" With this, he brandished his pennon-decorated lance and rode off toward the southwest with the rest of his warriors.

It was a warm, sunny, mid-September day on the Double H Ranch in Texas. The summer holidays had come and gone, and Francesca de Escobar and the Maldones girls were back in New Orleans, resuming their schooling at the Ursuline Convent School. But Adriana Maldones and Andrew Baines had had an opportunity to spend much time together, riding horseback and taking walks in the moonlight, holding each other's hand, and they renewed their pledge to wait for each other until they were old enough to marry. Lovely Francesca, meanwhile, happy to be reunited with her mother, Doña Inez, and the rest of her family, kept herself occupied by reading (she had brought many books with her from New Orleans for her holiday), and no one but her best friend, Adriana, knew of her growing affection for the planter Jack McKinnon, who continued to write to her from Abner Heskins's plantation on the Mississippi.

Lortaldo, the Jicarilla Indian brave studying medicine with Dr. André Malmorain in New Orleans, wrote frequently to his wife, Epanone, as well as to Carlos, telling them of his progress. Dr. Malmorain had told him that soon he would be able to return to his wife and thence to his people in New Mexico, to help them with his knowledge of white man's medicine. Young Diego de Escobar was thriving, too, in his apprenticeship to the New Orleans lawyer, and in his letters to Carlos and his stepmother, Teresa, he wrote a great deal about the daughter of his *patrón*, Dorothy Allary. Diego had invited her to visit the ranch in Texas at some future date, and as Carlos told Teresa, "I wonder if our young son has already discovered his *novia*."

Now on the same day of the meeting between Juan Cortizo and Topaminga, a rider galloped through the gate of the *Hacienda del Halcón* with a message for John Cooper Baines. The Texan had been back at his ranch for some time now since depositing the silver in the New Orleans bank and bringing back the weapons and ammunition for the settlers on the Brazos and his blood brothers the Jicarilla. All seemed peaceful and good, and he had been able to devote himself single-mindedly to the running of the ranch and being with his family.

"A good day to you, Jim!" John Cooper greeted the exhausted young horseman, whom he recognized as one of the men from the Brazos settlement. "You've ridden that gelding of yours just about into the ground. I'd best have it looked after, if you expect to ride it back. What brings you in all this haste?"

"Simon Brown told me to let you know that we've had three Indian attacks the past fortnight, Mr. Baines," Jim Trent said, panting.

"Three of them?" John Cooper echoed, and Raoul Maldones and Miguel Sandarbal, who had just come in from riding the range, dismounted and hurried up to hear the news.

"Yes, sir. We drove them off, all right—thanks to the fine weapons you gave us—and they lost a lot of fighters. We had a few killed on our side, and some kids were badly wounded and at least one was killed that I know of—little Marcy Ellison."

"That's bad news, indeed. I met Martha and Elmer Ellison on my way back from New Orleans; they're fine people, and she was such a sweet little girl. What tribe were they, Jim, do you know?"

"That's the funny thing, Mr. Baines, they weren't Kiowa nor Apache or Comanche, either. And Simon Brown doesn't think they were Tonkawa. They were painted in yellow, black, and red war paint, and I brought along a couple of their arrows, if that's any help to you. I've heard a heap about how much you know about Indians, sir."

The young scout handed the two feathered arrows to John Cooper, who examined them carefully, then scowled. "Now this is a marking I don't rightly recognize, I'll have to admit," he finally declared. "Jim Bowie would surely know, but he's off with his Rangers somewhere along the Gulf. Simon is also familiar with most of the Plains Indians in these parts, but if he says they aren't the ones you mentioned, then I'll take his word for it. I wonder . . ." He turned to Miguel. "Is it possible these Indians came across the Rio Grande?"

"May I see the arrows, *mi compadre*?" the white-haired *capataz* asked. He examined them, and then he frowned as if trying to remember. "Years ago," Miguel said at last, "when we first rode from Mexico City up to Taos, we were attacked by *los indios Toboso*. It was many years ago, but if I recall, these feathers remind me a little of the arrows the Toboso used."

"Then it's likely they did come from Mexico," John Cooper mused aloud. His face hardened. "If Mexican Indians attacked Eugene Fair's settlement in Texas Territory, it's a certainty Santa Anna was behind it. Raoul," he said, turning to his father-in-law, "you and Ramón Santoriaga had best talk this over, and I think it wise that we have additional sentries posted along the boundaries of the ranch. They can sound the alarm if they see any suspicious movement of men or horsemen off to the south along the Frio River."

"I'll go see Ramón at once, John Cooper," Raoul agreed.

John Cooper turned to the scout. "Thanks for bringing me the news, Jim. And I'm glad that you drove them off. Now why don't you go into the bunkhouse and say hello to the *vaqueros* and then come to the kitchen. Rosa will give you the best *comida* you've ever had. You'll stay the night, of course, and if that gelding of yours isn't up to snuff tomorrow, we'll get you another horse to take you back." Then, clapping Jim Trent on the back, he went to the house to tell Rosa there would be a guest for the noon meal. The news of the Indian attack on the Brazos River settlement upset him badly, and he feared that the peaceful interlude might be coming to a sudden end.

Twenty-four

After his meeting with Topaminga, Juan Cortizo and the six Yaqui braves had ridden to a small hamlet near the Nueces River and raided it. Isolated as it was and occupied by only three Mexican families, it offered almost no resistance to the seven well-armed men, who swiftly killed the two ranchers, their four sons, a grandfather and grandmother, and spared only the wives of the two ranchers and two teenage girls, daughters of the second rancher. Cortizo had purposely planned this raid to allow his six savage aides to indulge themselves in an orgy of rape and torture, knowing that it would gratify them after the privations all Topaminga's warriors had endured during the three attacks on the Brazos settlement. He himself ravished the younger girl, while forcing her sister to watch until it was her turn. And when the Yaqui had satiated themselves with the four unfortunate females, they put them to death by torture.

But there was another reason for Cortizo's murderous diversion: It was to obtain clothing for the disguise he intended to use in effecting the capture of John Cooper Baines's wife. Until now, like the other Yaqui, he had gone naked to the waist, his body smeared with tribal war paint. In the effects of the two ranchers and their sons, he found clothing such as a frontiersman might wear: a shirt, breeches, boots, a jacket made from tanned animal hide, and a *sombrero*. Moreover, he particularly chose articles of apparel that showed considerable wear, which would authenticate the explanation of his presence if he were fortunate enough to meet the *gringa*.

This done, he and his six accomplices rode northward toward the Frio River, and bidding his men hide themselves in the thick forest on the southern bank of the river, he told them that he would approach the ranch from the southwest, where he had seen sheep grazing and several elderly sheepherders. From one of them he would learn all he could about the habits of the *gringa*.

At twilight, he crossed the river on foot, then moved cautiously through the thick, waist-high grass to the westernmost boundary of the huge ranch.

Crouching low and parting the grass with his hands, he saw that there was a *vaquero* on horseback, with a rifle in his saddle sheath, moving slowly toward the east. The sentry greeted a gray-haired sheepherder in a poncho who, with his staff, was gently nudging a fractious ewe back into the flock. "So you're done for the day now, eh, Virgilio?" the *vaquero* called. "Next week, you'll have to stir your old bones a good deal more, for it'll be shearing time."

The old sheepherder testily retorted, "Don't you think I know that, *estúpido*? But I'll tell you this, the wool of my flock this year will be the best we've ever had on this *estancia*. Now go about your business and leave an old man to his work, for I'm hungry for my supper."

"I'm going, I'm going, Virgilio. One thing more—you've

been out here all day long. Have you seen anyone across the river, any men on horseback, any *indios*?"

"*Por Dios*, the questions you ask!" the old man scolded. "I've seen no one. If I had, I'd have told you when you were out this way after *la comida*. Everything here is as peaceful as my sheep. Now be off with you!"

Cortizo smiled to himself. All was well. Tomorrow would be time enough to engage the old man in conversation and learn about the *gringo*'s wife. This also was the most isolated part of the ranch, and if good luck were with him, and if the *gringa* should come this way, it would be child's play to make off with her. Satisfied with what he had learned, he crept back toward the river, crossed it, and conferred with the six waiting braves.

"Tomorrow," he told them, "at about this same time, I will talk to the old man and learn what I can about the *gringa*. Then I will know better what to do and how you are to help me. We have provisions, and we can wait. The prize is great."

"The prize is your life," one of the Yaqui growled. "Topaminga does not yet believe you can do what you promise. But he will keep *his* promise, if you fail!"

"I'll not fail. And my way is good, for there will be no Yaqui lives wasted, as there were against the *yanqui* settlement," Cortizo stoutly declared. All the same, he could not suppress an instinctive shiver of fear.

Cortizo waited all the next day until it was nearly dusk and then cautiously made his way across the river and toward the old sheepherder. The latter, his back to the *mestizo*, was urging a young lamb to rejoin its mother, so that it was easy for Cortizo to appear as if he had been walking from the west. "*Buenas tardes, abuelo*," he affably called out.

Old Virgilio, turning suddenly, stared at the stranger. "And to you also, *amigo*. Where do you come from? I have never seen you here before."

"No," Cortizo agreed, "my horse went lame about ten miles west, and I had to kill him. I came from Santa Fe."

"And you go where, señor?"

"I had heard that there might be work at the *Hacienda del Halcón, abuelo*. I see many sheep, and there must also be many *ganado*, so perhaps there will be work for a poor man like me. I was once a *vaquero*."

"Yes, there is always work here," the old sheepherder agreed. "And this is indeed the *Hacienda del Halcón*."

"I have heard of it in Santa Fe, and of the *gringo* who owns it, the señor Baines, *¿no es verdad?*"

"Assuredly," Virgilio told the *mestizo*. "Why, he is famous throughout this frontier, and it is my honor to work for him, as you see. It is true that I am an old man and not of much consequence, but I have not lost a sheep, I will tell you, señor, not in six months, and then it was a stray lamb that went so far that we could not find it until we discovered that a wolf had killed it."

"You are to be praised, *abuelo*," Cortizo said, grinning. "And this señor Baines, he has an *esposa?*"

"Oh, *sí, señor*. He is married to the señora Dorotéa, and they have a little son."

"I am happy to hear that," Cortizo glibly declared. "Well, perhaps after I have had some of the beef jerky and the maize I have brought with me for my supper, I will sleep, and then in the morning I will go ask the *capataz* for work here."

"I am sure that if you can work hard, señor, he will be happy to talk with you. There are always things to be done."

As the old man slowly turned to go on his way, Cortizo called out, "A moment more, *por favor*. Tell me something of this señora Dorotéa. Does she ride horseback, or does she stay in the *hacienda* all the time?"

"Oh, no, señor," the old man said almost indignantly. "Her father, who has come to be with her, brought her up to ride as well as any *vaquero*. The señor Baines has given her a palomino mare, and she rides it now very often, since the *niño* is almost half a year old by this time. But now, if you'll excuse me, I must go to my supper. I have a little stew, and some tortillas. I would offer to share it with you, but there is only enough left for myself, and I am very hungry, for I have been out here all day long, as you understand."

"I would not think of taking any of your supper from you, *abuelo*. And thank you for what you have told me. I will see the *capataz* tomorrow, for certain. *Gracias*."

"*De nada, amigo. ¡Buenas noches!*" The old man nodded and smiled, then went to his cottage, a few hundred feet away. Cortizo chuckled to himself. It required only a little patience, after all, and all things came to him who waited. Another day would not matter much, not with stakes as high as these.

He went back across the river that night, and he and the six Yaqui shared their evening meal together as he told them what he had learned. "It may well be that she will go out riding tomorrow, and I will be there to watch for her. Now, I wish two of you to come with me on foot and to wait. The other four, on their horses, should be near the river, but still not able to be seen by the sentries. I have seen only one sentry at this boundary, but of course there will be many more as one nears the *hacienda* itself. Everything works into our hands, and it will be as I promised."

During breakfast the next morning, a *trabajador* hurried to the *hacienda* with the news that one of John Cooper's prize breeding bulls had broken out of its stall and, since the stable door had been only partly secured, butted it open with his horns and lumbered off toward the east. John Cooper and his father-in-law rose from the table and took their leave of the rest of the family members, the tall Texan remarking, "It would be good sport to see if I can handle a lasso as well as our *vaqueros*. I only hope our bull doesn't run afoul of a mountain lion or a wild *jabalí*. Come along, Raoul, it'll be good exercise after this very satisfying breakfast Rosa has been kind enough to prepare for us."

After John Cooper and his father-in-law left the dining room, Carlos turned to his lovely wife. "Speaking of exercise, my dear one, what about our having a little bout with the foils?"

"Why, that's a charming idea, *mi esposa!*" Teresa gaily retorted. "We haven't practiced in a long while."

"Shall we play for forfeits, *querida?*" Carlos teased her, then leaned over to whisper something that made her blush.

"With such stakes as you just now whispered, you would be the winner whether you won or lost," she primly rebuked him. "That is no bet, *mi esposo*." Carlos burst out laughing, after which he leaned to her, took her in his arms, and gave her a resounding kiss.

"I shall leave you lovebirds to your own devising," Dorotéa declared as she rose from the table. "But one day, you must teach me how to use the foils. It's a most energetic sport, and I should like it very much."

"I'll be happy to teach you, Dorotéa," Teresa smilingly volunteered.

"Perhaps this afternoon, after *siesta*," John Cooper's

lovely young wife agreed. Then, bidding Carlos and Teresa a warm *hasta la vista*, she went on her way. Everyone seemed to be so eager for exercise today, and suddenly she decided that she, too, would go out and engage in her favorite activity. Thus she headed directly for the stable, where one of the *trabajadores* saddled the palomino mare that John Cooper had given her when they had returned to the ranch after rescuing her father. She had brought sugar in her palm for the horse, and it very delicately mouthed it, then licked her palm and nickered softly to indicate its pleasure.

"How beautiful it is out today! Oh, it would be a shame not to take little James with me," she said aloud. "Wait, my beauty, I'll be back with the baby, and then we'll all go for a ride—but you must be very careful, as you have been on our previous rides, for the little one is not yet six months old." The mare bowed its head as if agreeing, and Dorotéa, thoroughly happy with the warm glow of being loved and here with her father among people she found most congenial, burst out in a joyous laugh. Then, leaving the mare with the *trabajador*, she hurried back to the *hacienda*'s nursery, took little James from old Estancia's arms, and put a robe over him so that if there were a sudden chilly wind, it would not harm him.

Since horseback riding was a passion with Dorotéa, she had made provisions for continuing to ride after bearing her child. She had coaxed the assistant *capataz*, Esteban Morales, into tool-working a little leather sling that she could loop about her neck and use to carry the child behind her, safely and securely, while riding horseback, much as an Indian squaw might do. She had ridden with the baby in the sling a number of times already, and now she very carefully edged him into it, making certain that the robe was not too tight and that there was no pressure around the throat or chest. He was as secure as in a cocoon, and when the *trabajador* brought out the mare, Dorotéa made so lovely a picture in her riding jacket and trim skirt, her soft doeskin boots, with the baby in its sling behind her, that he could not help looking at her as he might the image of the Madonna.

Embarrassed and yet touched, she said gently, "Humberto, *muchas gracias* for saddling my mare. And I see you have put my rifle in its sling."

"*Sí, señora patrón,* and I just pray you never have any

need for it. I would not want anything ever to happen to you."

"You are so kind, Humberto."

"Who would not be kind, señora, to one like you?" he blurted out in obvious idolatry. He was only seventeen, gangling and tall, and at the age when he suffered the torments of the damned in wondering if any *señorita* would ever deign to look at him.

Again, Dorotéa was deeply touched. "You will turn my head with such flattery, Humberto. One day soon, I am sure that one of the sweet *criadas* here on the ranch will say to herself that Humberto Rigaldo is the finest, *más caballero trabajador* of all, and that she will pray to the *Madre Santísima* to have you fall in love with her."

"Oh, no, *señora patrón!*" he gasped, overwhelmed by such lavish praise.

"It will be as I say. Now then, if you will give me a hand as I mount into the saddle . . . *gracias* again, Humberto. And now will you call Yankee for me? As you know, the *señor patrón* insists Yankee come along with me when I go out."

"At once, *señora patrón!*" Humberto replied, and headed in the direction of the shed near the kennel buildings where Yankee slept. The wolf-dog was lying outside the shed in the warm sunlight, his head raised, his ears pricked up, surveying all the activity around him with a watchful eye. At Humberto's call, he bounded forward with alacrity, ready to do what was asked of him.

In a few moments, the young *trabajador* was back with Yankee, and the wolf-dog wagged his tail and growled softly as Dorotéa called down to him, "Yankee, *adelante*, we go for a ride, and you will go with me!"

Yankee barked happily and loped ahead of Dorotéa on her mare as, holding the reins lightly in her left hand, she spurred her mount into a lively gait.

Juan Cortizo lay on his belly in the deep grass, the two Yaqui braves not far from him. Parting the grass with both hands, he could see the old sheepherder emerging from his cottage, grumbling to himself, looking up at the sky. The *mestizo* whispered to the braves, "If that old fool is in the way when the *gringa* should come riding this way, I'll kill him quickly and hide him in the grass. If he were near the *gringa*, he might cry out and give the alarm to the sentry."

"I can see sentries on horseback," one of the Yaqui observed as he, too, peered through the tall grass, separating the thick sheaves with his stubby, strong fingers. "They ride to the east."

"That is good. Let us hope that the *viejo* spoke with a straight tongue when he said that the *mujer* of el Halcón goes riding. Wait—in the distance I see a rider, and there is something running alongside the horse—"

"Perhaps a dog," the other Yaqui said.

"That, too, may give us trouble. Well, I will take care of the dog. You have your knives and *pistolas*, do you not?" Cortizo asked.

"Yes, we are ready," the brave who had spoken before now reassured him. "At your signal, we will come out and take the horse of the *mujer*."

But Cortizo was still thinking of the old sheepherder. It would not do to have him stand gossiping with the woman, if indeed that were she coming from the east. He whispered his intentions to his two companions and then stealthily crept out of the grass and toward the unsuspecting old man. Swiftly locking his left arm around the sheepherder's throat, he plunged his knife into the old man, who slumped dead without uttering a sound. Just as swiftly, Cortizo dragged the corpse far into the grass so that it could not be seen, then wiped his knife on the old man's shirt, thrust it back into his belt, and called softly back to the two braves, "He will not bother us now. And look, I see the rider comes closer to us, yes—aiiyee, the Slayer of Enemies is good to us, it is probably the *mujer* we seek! I will speak with her and find out."

Cortizo moved toward a clump of mesquite, while his two companions remained hidden in the grass a dozen feet to the south of him. He observed that one of the mounted sentries had greeted the *gringa*, who, he could also see, rode a truly magnificent mare. After saluting her, the sentry rode on toward the east, and again Cortizo rejoiced. The Slayer of Enemies had surely answered his prayer, for now there was no one to guard the *gringa*!

Dorotéa came closer and then slowed her mare to an ambling gait. Reaching with her hands, she lifted the sling in which little James was cradled, drew it over her head, and then, letting the reins fall on the mare's neck, carefully lifted the baby out of the sling and held him in her arms. "See, *mi hijo*," she murmured to the baby, "the blue sky and the green grass and as far as you can see, only this wonderful ranch where we live. How beautiful it is, James! You will grow to be a man like your father, and you will love the land as he does, I'm certain of it." She drew a deep breath and rapturously exhaled as she looked around, for everything was at peace.

From his hiding place, Cortizo stared intently at her. He was certain that no one was in sight. Now was the time! Straightening, he moved out of the clump of mesquite.

Yankee at once bristled and uttered an angry growl, but Dorotéa, seeing that the man carried no weapons and appeared harmless—perhaps was even one of the workers on the ranch she had not met—quickly called out, "No, Yankee, *es bueno, es amigo—amigo!*" The wolf-dog, still taut with vigilance, backed away, his yellow eyes fixed on the stranger.

"Forgive me, señora, I did not mean to frighten you or your *perro*," Cortizo unctuously declared. "I have come from Santa Fe, señora, but three days ago, *mi caballo* broke its leg and I had to put it out of its misery. Since then, I have walked all this way, and I am hungry and thirsty. Indeed, not since yesterday morning have I had a morsel of food."

"*¡Que lástima!*" Dorotéa sympathetically murmured, an expression of solicitude on her lovely face. The man had spoken to her in pure Spanish with an almost Castilian accent, which disarmed her. "You are fortunate, señor, for you are now upon the ranch of *el Halcón*."

"I have heard of this ranch. You see, señora, in Santa Fe I was told of this great place. Is it not a señor Baines who owns it?" Cortizo asked in an innocent tone.

"*Pero sí, señor*," Dorotéa promptly replied with a compassionate smile. "And I am his *esposa*. If I did not have my *niño* with me, señor, I would tell you to mount up behind me and ride back to the *hacienda*. But if you will follow me, I will take you there, and I promise you that our *cocinera* will see that you are given food and drink. And if you seek work, our *capataz* will be happy to talk with you. There is always work at the *Hacienda del Halcón* for an honest *vaquero* or *trabajador*."

Cortizo respectfully inclined his head. Inwardly, he was gloating. What a stroke of good fortune—here was the *mujer* he had sought! From the corner of his eye, he saw that there was no one there except the wolf-dog, which still regarded him with baleful yellow eyes, his hair bristling. But there was no sentry to help the *mujer* now. That accursed *perro* must be disposed of swiftly.

Cortizo took a step toward Dorotéa's mare, and Yankee growled angrily, his tail stiffening, baring his fangs. "No, no, Yankee, *amigo*," Dorotéa called. Then, to the *mestizo*, "Do not be afraid. He is trained to protect me, but he answers to commands. If you wish now, we'll go back to the *hacienda*."

"Not so fast, señora," Cortizo gloatingly murmured. He put his right thumb and median finger to his lips and whistled shrilly. The two Yaqui braves sprang out of the grass and surrounded Dorotéa's mare, one of them taking the reins and the other grabbing her rifle from its sheath.

At the same moment, Yankee, with a savage growl, sprang at Cortizo. But he had already prepared himself for this and, having drawn his pistol, fired point-blank. The ball struck the wolf-dog's left shoulder just at the juncture of the leg, almost breaking it. Yet, undaunted, Yankee continued his lunge at the *mestizo*. With an oath, Cortizo reversed the pistol in his hand and with all his might struck at Yankee's head, stunning the animal and dropping him at his very feet.

Dorotéa was paralyzed with horror and disbelief, but she gained control of herself when Cortizo suddenly flung aside the pistol and came over to her mount, reaching up to seize little James from her. She held the baby close, clawing and slapping at the *mestizo*, but one of the Indians by her side grabbed her arms, allowing Cortizo to get the baby. Gripping the infant by the ankles and lifting him up in the air, he declared, "And now, señora, either you'll go with us, or I'll dash the *niño's* brains out!"

Dorotéa had no fear of the two stocky Indians, naked to the waist in their war paint of yellow, black, and red, but seeing her child in the *mestizo's* hands did terrify her. "Please, señor, I beg of you, my little child has done no harm. Do not harm him, I beg of you—I will do what you wish, only do not harm him!" she tearfully pleaded. "At least, take him back to the *hacienda*—"

Cortizo now lowered James and righted the baby, cradling him in his arms as he regarded the tearful young woman. "Do you think I am a fool, Señora Baines? You would have your sentries shoot me on sight. No, you will go with me across the Rio Grande, and I'll leave the child where it can be found."

"I—I have no choice," Dorotéa sobbed. "Just please don't hurt James."

Cortizo barked an order, and one of the Yaqui braves pulled on the reins of Dorotéa's mare and led it toward the south. But suddenly the *mestizo*, still holding the child, saw that the mounted sentry who had greeted Dorotéa earlier had come back. "Kill him!" he hissed to the other Yaqui brave, who nodded and then disappeared into the waist-high grass.

The *vaquero*, José Minaldo, had seen Dorotéa on her mare, with a painted Yaqui holding the reins of her horse and another man standing with her child in his arms. He spurred forward and cried out, "Halt, do not move. Let go of the reins of the señora's horse!" At the same time, he drew his rifle out of its saddle sheath, cocking and aiming it at the Yaqui who held the mare's reins.

But the latter's companion suddenly rose out of the bushes and flung his knife with unerring aim into the *vaquero's* throat. He dropped the rifle, clasped both hands to the knife, and then toppled from the horse and lay still.

Dorotéa uttered a cry of horror. "Oh, *Dios*, how cruel!"

"No, señora, it was not cruel," Cortizo mocked her. "He would have shot my blood brother here. And now, Señora Baines, come with us, and let Tomaso lead your horse, or I swear to you by the Slayer of Enemies I will kill your child."

"No, no, I'll do what you want," Dorotéa said excitedly. "In the name of mercy, do not harm the little one!" She stared first at James in the stranger's arms, then looked back at the fallen wolf-dog, who lay on his side, seemingly dead. Bowing her head, she prayed silently.

The Yaqui, Tomaso, chuckled as he jerked the reins and made the docile palomino follow. "Topaminga will believe you now, Juan!" he said.

"Did I not tell you as I did him that I would bring back the *mujer* of the señor Baines?" Cortizo gloatingly avowed. "Now let us go meet our four brothers across the river. But first, I will take care of the *niño*." With this, he left the helpless infant on the ground, near where the slain *vaquero* lay, saying to his companions, "This will show her husband that we have his *novia*." Dorotéa watched but said nothing. The baby was alive, that was the main thing. She would think of something to save herself.

And now the two Yaqui led Dorotéa's mare across the

river, where the four other braves awaited them on horseback. The young woman forced herself to show no fear, despite the glowering looks the Yaqui gave her. Quick-witted as she was, she began to think of how she could leave some clue for her beloved John Cooper to follow, for as they were heading to the river Cortizo had boasted to her that she was to be held for ransom, that a courier was going to be sent to the *gringo*— her husband—telling him that he would never see his wife again, unless of his own accord he brought the silver treasure to the Yaqui stronghold.

"We have let you keep your horse, señora," Cortizo said, turning to her, "but you will do well not to try to run back to the *hacienda*. My Yaqui brothers will kill the mare, and you may be hurt in the fall. It would have been too much trouble to let you ride with one of them—indeed, such a beautiful *gringa* as you would inflame him, and he would want to have his way with you. So you see that we are taking good care of you, señora."

They started their journey, all the Indians—including Cortizo—on horseback now, with two of the braves surrounding the young woman.

As they rode on to the south, Dorotéa said nothing, handling the reins of her mare, showing the utmost docility. Presently she saw that the riders on each side of her no longer bothered to glance at her quite so frequently. Retaining the reins in her right hand, she surreptitiously lowered her left to her skirt and tore off a tiny bit of needlework trim at the hem. This she let drop to the ground. A little farther on, she repeated this maneuver, though the third time she tried, the brave at her left sullenly glanced over at her. She quickly pretended to be merely adjusting her skirt.

The brave at her right now called out, "Juan, where shall we make camp for the night?"

"Do not think of resting so soon, Porgamina," the *mestizo* angrily rebuked him. "We must put distance between ourselves and the *gringo* and his men, who will surely come after us. But we will have a start of several hours over them, I'm certain, and we will come to a little creek soon and ford it, then go back and forth several times so that the tracks will be blurred and not easy to follow. Then we shall ride swiftly, and I do not think that the *gringo* and his men will go so deep into Mexico. We will cross the Rio

Grande, and Topaminga will be there to meet us, *seguramente*! Now, enough of this useless talk, and ride, my brothers!"

Yankee had at last stirred, feebly wagging his tail. His yellow eyes blurred. He tried to move his head, but there was an aching pain, and he growled.

Very warily his paws scrabbled at the ground as he tried to lift himself up to all fours. He bared his fangs at the excruciating pain in his right leg. There was matted blood in his fur where the shoulder met the leg, and as he tried a tentative step or two forward, the pain grew worse. Still, he took two or three more steps forward, and though the pain seared him, he knew he must find his master. He lifted his muzzle to the sky and uttered a ferocious yowl, one of hatred and frustration and pain. And then he began to hobble back toward the *hacienda*, heedless of the pain it cost him, ungainly and stumbling, with the throbbing ache of the ball imbedded so near the bone.

Meanwhile John Cooper had lassoed the prize bull, and two of the *vaqueros* had gentled it and were leading it back to the stable. John Cooper and his father-in-law headed back to the *hacienda* at a fast gait as the *vaqueros* riding with them shook their heads in admiration and spoke admiringly of the warm friendship between the two men.

John Cooper leaped down from his horse, exultantly laughing, feeling the physical pleasure of the warm sun and the sweet air and the landscape of this vast ranch that made him relish life. As he and Raoul walked toward the *hacienda*, he stopped in his tracks, seeing one of the sentries race from the house and come running toward him. "Señor patrón, señor patrón," the sentry panted. "I was out on duty and came across José. He's dead, señor patrón, with a knife in him! And then I found old Virgilio in the grass, dead, too! And, señor patrón, I found your little baby out there, too— he's fine, thank *Dios*, he's fine—and I brought him back to the *hacienda*. But Señora Dorotéa and her horse are missing!"

"My God, Dorotéa!" John Cooper whirled and ran to Miguel, who was working near the new schoolhouse. "Miguel, get me eight of your best *vaqueros* and have them armed and with plenty of ammunition. Dorotéa's gone, a sentry's been murdered, and old Virgilio with him!"

Miguel wasted no time. He hurried to the bunkhouse

and bawled out an order. A few moments later, eight men ran out to the stable, saddled their horses, and rode up to John Cooper, who had mounted his palomino again.

"Miguel, come with us! Oh, Lord, I wish I'd asked Dorotéa to come out with me this morning!"

"Let me come, too," Raoul urged.

"Agreed, *mi suegro*, I need you!" Frantic with his sudden agony, John Cooper galloped off, bidding the sentry ride with him and point out what the rider had seen.

Miguel and Raoul had mounted and now rode after the *vaqueros* and John Cooper. The horsemen hadn't gone very far when another distressing scene awaited them. Yankee was hobbling in their direction, the dried blood clotted in his fur, looking more dead than alive.

"Oh, my God!" John Cooper yelled, and held up his hand to halt the little troop. "There's Yankee; he was out with Dorotéa and got badly hurt." The Texan hastily dismounted, then strode toward the crippled wolf-dog who, recognizing his master, growled and whined, wagging his tail, and came limping toward him. Squatting down, John Cooper examined the matted hair and the dried blood from the blow with the pistol butt, then saw that there was a pistol ball in the wolf-dog's leg. "Whoever did this to you will wish he hadn't!" John Cooper said, fighting back the tears, praying now for Dorotéa's life. "Gently, Yankee, gently. I'll try not to hurt you—there, there." With both hands, he very carefully took Yankee's right leg, touching it here and there until he reached the pistol wound. Yankee showed his fangs but stood docilely still, understanding that his master sought to help.

"I'll take him back to the *hacienda*, John Cooper," said Raoul, who had also dismounted and stood over his son-in-law. "We'll look after him there."

"We'll need a cart," Miguel now put in. "I'll have to go back and get one. Raoul, you wait here with Yankee while *Halcón* and the other men go on their way. I'll be back with the cart as soon as I can, and then we can bring Yankee back to the ranch, to remove the ball from his leg." The *capataz* mounted his horse and turned its head toward the *hacienda*. "God be with you, *Halcón*!" he called back. "I wish I could go with you and help you find your Dorotéa." Then he raced off.

"I will wait here with Yankee," Raoul said to his son-in-law. "You go on now."

John Cooper clasped Raoul's hand for a moment, then turned to the sentry. "Take me to the place where you found your *compadre*, Paco."

"At once, *patrón*," the young *trabajador* exclaimed as he waited for John Cooper to mount his horse, then rode off with him and the other *vaqueros*.

They rode to the southwest, and again John Cooper halted his palomino and dismounted, staring down with a compassionate look on the lifeless body of the murdered sentry. "Off to the left, *patrón*," Paco explained, "I found old Virgilio."

"There isn't time for us to bury them, Paco. Ride back to the *hacienda* now and tell Miguel to bring some additional *trabajadores* to take care of these two loyal friends. The other *vaqueros* and I will continue on to look for Dorotéa. And now," John Cooper said to the men, his face grim and lined with concern, "we'll ride on. I see the footprints of three men off this way—yes, southward, to the river. And the hoofprints—it must be Dorotéa's mare—come, we'll find them! I don't know how much of a head start they've had on us, but we'll find them! *Vaqueros*, be sure your rifles are loaded and your pistols, too!"

He directed the palomino toward the shallow ford of the Frio River, and once again, he halted, staring at the ground. "Here are more prints of horses' hooves," he told the *vaqueros*. "I see at least four horses—no—there are more now—seven, and the mare's—there are only seven men who carried off Dorotéa, and we're more than a match for them! Let's ride, *mis amigos!*"

Dorotéa and her seven Yaqui captors rode at a swift pace until late at night, when they made camp at the top of a small canyon whose bottom had once been an ancient riverbed. By this time, the young woman had managed to tear off five or six small bits of trim from her skirt and to let them flutter to the ground as she rode on, and thus far her ruse had not been discovered. Now if only John Cooper and others were on the way—and if they had found the baby, and if the baby was all right . . . and Yankee, too! Dorotéa fought hard for self-control.

Cortizo himself helped her down from her horse and jocularly declared, "You are very sensible, *mujer*, not to try to escape. We wish you no harm, only the silver. Perhaps my blood brothers do not understand this so well when it is a matter of a *mujer hermosa*, but I will see to it that no harm comes to you, if you continue to be obedient as you have so far."

"I can do nothing, not against seven armed men," Dorotéa replied evenly. "But what if my husband should not give you the silver? There is much of it, and it will take many *trabajadores* to bring it in carts all this way into Mexico."

Cortizo shrugged. "Perhaps if he hesitates too long, señora," he said with a cruel little smile, "we might quicken his reply by sending a courier to him with one of your fingers, or perhaps an ear—beginning, of course, gently, with some of your hair so that he knows we have you. Do not concern yourself with this, however, for now we shall eat something. There will be no fire, since we wish to leave no traces that your husband and his *vaqueros* might find— though, by now, I am certain they have lost our trail and have gone back to the ranch in defeat."

"How far are you taking me?"

"We shall meet with our *jefe*, Topaminga, by tomorrow night, once we cross the Rio Grande," Cortizo said in an indifferent tone, "and from there, when he has seen that you are who you are, we shall ride back to the stronghold in Sonora. From there, our courier will be sent to your ranch telling your *esposo* what we wish of him and how he is to do it. But that is enough talk. Now I shall bring you something to eat, and here is my canteen with water."

Dorotéa drank thirstily and docilely followed the seven Yaqui to the little clearing, surrounded by scrub trees, that they had selected for a temporary camp. Cortizo explained, "We shall not stay here long but will ride on into the night. You are strong and young; some discomfort will not harm you. If you resist, then there will be harm—I think you know this already."

Dorotéa nodded. Their evening meal was meager, but to keep up her strength, she forced herself to eat a few handfuls of dried corn and a strip of meat that, after she had managed to swallow it, Cortizo grinningly explained was the dried flesh of the iguana. Half an hour later, Cortizo led her back to her palomino and assisted her to mount it. Then again, as before, a rider flanking her on each side, the *mestizo* at the head, and the four other braves following behind her, they headed southward toward the Rio Grande.

This time, she managed to tear bits of thread from the cuffs of her blouse and drop them after they had left the canyon and headed down toward level ground. It was desolate countryside, with no grazing for cattle or sheep, arid ground, cracked and reddish and browned in the sun, with dried-up streams and creeks. All that she saw was an occasional jackrabbit or she heard a not too far distant howling coyote and the occasional hoot of a screech owl.

At dawn, the Yaqui again made camp for an hour or two of sleep, with three of them standing guard over the young woman. They tethered her horse to a nearby tree, and Cortizo stretched himself out nearby and dozed, waking at times from his intermittent sleep to stare greedily at her. The three Yaqui conversed among themselves in their own tongue, but from time to time they looked at her and she felt a wave of scarlet diffuse her cheeks, for she comprehended that they were discussing her physical attractions. Yet her mind was not on fear for herself, only thoughts of little James: Had he been found and taken back to the *hacienda*? And her beloved John Cooper, and how he could find her in this wasteland, which would become even more difficult as they pushed on deeper into the desert and mountainous region of southwestern Mexico.

She prayed silently, and she felt fortified by that, as well as by her knowledge of John Cooper's love. She dozed a little herself, only to be wakened by Cortizo's harsh and impatient, "¡Vamanos! Mujer, get up; we ride now!" Turning to the braves, he declared, "The rest of you will sleep the next time we make camp. Late tonight, if all goes well, we shall cross the Rio Grande to meet the *jefe*."

She rode on, and fatigue began to claim her. But she prayed again, and she was certain that her husband and his men would come after her. What strengthened this faith was what she had been told by John Cooper himself of his life with the *indios norteamericanos;* he would have learned enough from that experience to be able to track riders and even men on foot. And if he did, he would be sure to see one or two of the little threads from her skirt and blouse that she had left whenever she had the chance.

Cortizo urged his companions to gallop now, putting still more distance between them and their pursuers. By now, he was supremely confident that there would be no pursuers. At noon, they stopped again for about two hours, and the Yaqui who had not slept before were granted that short repose while their companions stood guard.

Then again they mounted their horses and rode on.

At twilight, they made camp again, and the *mestizo* cheerfully announced to Dorotéa, "A few hours more, and we shall cross the Rio Grande. Once there, it will be easier on you. But after we reach the *jefe*, I shall have to bind you. He will not believe that you will not try to escape if he sees that you are not tied as a captive should be. Remember, when the courier is sent to your *esposo* to claim the silver, he will be told that we have treated you kindly and gently—and this is not our custom with *mujeres*." He leered at her and added, "Especially not with one so very beautiful!"

She tried not to show the shudder of revulsion that went through her at these words, but only listened to him, her eyes lowered, her demeanor totally submissive.

Twenty-five

It was nightfall. Juan Cortizo uttered a cry of joy as he turned his horse and called to the six Yaqui following him, "*¡Es el Rio Grande, mis amigos!* Topaminga should be waiting for us before we go much farther on! We have done well!"

They crossed the great river at a point where there was only a trickle of water, for the summer drought had made it shallow in many places in this locale. Cortizo looked back at Dorotéa, whose face showed the lines of exhaustion that the enforced swift ride had cost her. He grinned. "Soon, *mujer*, there will be no need for us to tire you by galloping. We shall meet the *jefe* of my tribe, and then you will be taken to the stronghold, where you will be an honored guest." Then, to his men he called "*¡Vamanos!*" and, kicking his booted heels against the belly of his weary horse, he urged it onward at a gallop again, the six braves following with Dorotéa in their midst. She had soothed her mare, whispering to it, crooning to it, patting its neck, and the sturdy yet gentle horse responded now, weary though it was. She saw that her captors were staring ahead, watching for their chief, and one more time she surreptitiously put her left hand to her blouse and tore off a last piece of thread, which she let flutter behind her.

They rode on some ten miles, and the full moon shone in the cloudless sky as they neared a range of small hills to the southwest of Acuña. Suddenly, Cortizo reined in his horse and held up his hand, cocking his head to listen. "It is the call of the coyote, three times! It is the signal of our *jefe!*" he joyously exclaimed.

He rode toward the direction of that sound, and a few minutes later the Yaqui chief Topaminga and his two trusted lieutenants rode out from behind a huge thicket of chinquapin.

"I have kept my promise, Topaminga!" Cortizo cried out he dismounted. "Here is the *mujer* of the *gringo.*"

"She is very young and *muy hermosa,*" the chief grunted, his beady little eyes swiftly appraising Dorotéa in the luminous moonlight. She shivered uncontrollably, for the savagery and lust in his gaze were undisguised. Now perhaps for he first time she felt fear for herself. Her prayers redoubled that somehow her beloved John Cooper would have found the bits of thread she had left along the trail and that he and his men would come to rescue her before her captors could make the long, terrible journey to desolate Sonora.

"We shall make camp for the night at the end of that range of hills," Topaminga curtly decided, gesturing with his pennoned lance. "There are caves, and no animals in them. We shall be hidden if any men try to follow us."

"All this while, Topaminga, we have heard and seen no one. There was no way the *gringo* could find our trail. I saw to that myself, for we doubled back many times. The *gringos* would not know how to read the signs we left, and they would go back whence they came. As I told you, I have done all I promised I would."

"So you say," the Yaqui *jefe* said. "And have you brought gold to pay for the help my courageous warriors have given you, Juan? Have you remembered the women who weep and strew ashes on their hair and their bodies when they learn that their mates have gone to the spirit land?"

"Do you not understand, great *jefe*, that we are holding this *gringa* for ransom? Her *esposo* has many bars of pure silver. We will make her send a letter to him that will say we shall free her when the silver is brought to our stronghold. And as soon as the letter is sent to the *yanqui*, I myself shall send a message to my *primo hermano*, Colonel Moravada, and demand that he send the general Santa Anna's soldiers to protect us, if the *gringo* should try treachery and bring his *vaqueros* to try to take his *mujer* back from us."

Topaminga stroked his chin and scowled. "Yes, it is a good plan." His eyes shifted to Dorotéa, and once again she trembled at the naked lust of that appraising glance. "But all the same, why should we not have our pleasure with her? It is the Yaqui way to use a woman taken from enemies, for this destroys the enemy and makes him less a man."

"I would agree with you, if she were a *mexicana*, or a *mestiza*, great chief," Cortizo wheedlingly countered, "but she would be spoiled if you did this to her, spoiled in the eyes of the *gringos*. And then she would not be so valuable; perhaps her *esposo* would somehow find out and then not wish to pay such a ransom."

"Perhaps you are right," Topaminga declared. "But let us go to our hiding place and prepare for the night. And this *gringa* must be tied so that she cannot run away. You, Coljardi, take her horse from her and lead it behind yours to the place where we shall hide our horses, behind the row of hills."

Cortizo grimaced, for it was plain to him that his chief had now wrested authority from him in the presence of the other braves. However, it would be dangerous to oppose the chief's will, and besides, when the sun rose again in the sky, there was time enough to be alone with Topaminga and show him clearly how he must proceed with the señora Baines, if he hoped to glean the great reward that would be turned over to the Yaqui for her safe return.

They moved toward the row of hills, and this time Dorotéa was obliged to walk beside Topaminga's horse. At his sign, one of his two aides bound her wrists in front of her with a rawhide thong, and the chief stared down at her, again appraising her with lust in his eyes.

They came to the slope where the caves were located, and two of the braves took the ten Yaqui horses and Dorotéa's palomino and led them behind the hills to a little ravine fringed by live-oak trees, where they tethered them for the night.

The brave who had bound Dorotéa's hands roughly gripped her by a shoulder and, grunting words that she could not understand, forced her to crawl into one of the caves then shoved her down on the ground and stood glowering her. He moved outside and took his station at the mouth of the cave, seating himself and folding his arms across his chest. Cortizo chose a cave beside that of Dorotéa, but the chief, glaring at him, shook his head and, with a wave of the lance, indicated that he was to take the one beyond that. When Cortizo obeyed, Topaminga himself crawled into the cave beside the one in which John Cooper's young wife lay captive. The other braves, after a quick discussion among themselves, separated into two remaining caves, with two warriors staying outside as sentries.

Dorotéa sat up and stared out at the narrow opening of the cave in which she was confined. She tried to free her wrists, but the Yaqui warrior had tied the thong far too tightly, and it already chafed her soft skin. She could not loosen it in the slightest. She dropped her hands to the ground with a weary sigh, and she suddenly felt a hard, round object. It was a heavy rock the size of a cannonball. Her heart began to beat faster, for she had the terrible presentiment that the savage-looking tall *jefe* of the Yaqui would attempt to ravish her while the others slept. She could not let this happen, and she would somehow use the rock as a weapon against him.

All the same, she was exhausted, and so she leaned her back against the wall of the cave and closed her eyes to doze. These two days and nights of strenuous riding piled upon the growing anxiety of how her captors might treat her and the terrifying thought that perhaps John Cooper might not be able to find her trail had taken their toll. She dozed only fitfully, and when she opened her eyes, she turned to stare at the opening of the cave and saw that the guard who had been sitting there as a sentry had vanished and that the mouth of the cave was open.

Thoroughly wakened now, and more apprehensive than ever, she tried to straighten herself, and her fingers gripped the rock she had found, hiding it in her lap.

She thought that surely the Yaqui must hear the loud pounding of her heart as she waited in a terrified anticipation, knowing that she must keep alert at all costs. And then suddenly, the faint light of the moon was blocked out as a man's head and shoulders lowered to the ground and began to edge into the cave toward her.

It took all her presence of mind to keep from crying out as she saw Topaminga get to his knees and face her only a few feet away. His eyes glittered with lust, and his lips worked convulsively. He muttered something she could not understand and then suddenly lunged at her, clamping one hand over her mouth as with the other he began to tear at her blouse.

Dorotéa lifted her bound hands and with all her strength brought the rock up against the side of Topaminga's head. His body jerked convulsively, and then he slumped over her. Nauseated by the scent of his unwashed, painted body, she arched and twisted herself to roll him away from her onto his back. And then suddenly she recalled that she had seen a knife at his belt when he had stared down at her from horseback. She crawled slowly and painfully toward his inert body, and her fingers began to touch him at the waist until at last she encountered the sharp hunting knife thrust through the belt of his breeches.

Gripping the bone handle of the knife in her right hand she strained at the rawhide thong and managed to turn the knife sideways so that it would rub against her bonds. Then she began to saw desperately, back and forth, exerting all her strength, panting and trembling with a nervous reaction after the near-attack by the Yaqui chief.

At last, she felt the strands of the rawhide weaken and yield. She was free!

Breathing a prayer of thanksgiving, Dorotéa crawled slowly toward the mouth of the cave, holding the knife in her right hand. Very carefully, she peeked out the opening and saw that to her left, the two guards who stood as sentries in front of the caves where the other braves slept were engaged in muttered conversation, their backs to her. She remembered now that Topaminga had said that they would tether the horses in back of the row of hills. Breathing a prayer, she crawled out of the cave, straightened, and began to run toward the end of the little row, behind which the horses were tethered and hobbled. And then suddenly her heart almost stopped beating as a hand gripped her ankle and sent her sprawling.

She now heard the sneering voice of Juan Cortizo: "You are more clever than I thought, *mujer gringa!*" he hissed. "And that is Topaminga's knife—have you killed our *jefe* then?" He stood with a drawn pistol leveled at her, jeering at her, as she slowly righted herself with her palms, sobbing in frustration and despair.

"You don't answer Juan Cortizo? I will teach you to crawl to me and to lick my boots; I will make you a *puta!*" He reached down and plunged the fingers of his left hand into her hair. "Drop that knife, or by the Slayer of Enemies, I will kill you with this pistol!"

The knife fell from her nerveless fingers, and he tugged at her hair and dragged her toward his booted feet. "Kiss them and say you will be my *puta!*" he hissed.

The pain was excruciating, and Dorotéa closed her eyes and ground her teeth to withstand it, but it was beyond her endurance as he twisted his fingers savagely.

Then suddenly there was a cry from the Yaqui sentry farthest to his left. "Look out, look out, there are horses riding upon us!"

Cortizo swore under his breath as, still holding Dorotéa tightly to him, he saw John Cooper and the *vaqueros* ride into the little valley fronting the hills. A rifle cracked, and the Yaqui who had sounded the alarm spun around, one hand groping for his forehead, where a bloody hole appeared. Then he fell like a plummet, his body rolling down the gently inclined slope.

The other braves hurried out of their caves now, kneeling down to take cover and firing their pistols and rifles at their attackers. But the eight *vaqueros* were galloping past, and each of them opened fire as they rode by the hills. Four of the braves went down with fatal wounds, and a fifth was wounded even as his pistol shot grazed the arm of the youngest *vaquero*.

John Cooper sighted "Long Girl" and fired as Topaminga, his head bleeding, stunned but conscious now, groped his way out of the cave where Dorotéa had been imprisoned, waving his pennoned lance and drawing it back to hurl it at one of the riders. He uttered a groan, dropped the lance, and sank forward on his knees as blood gushed out of his throat and darkened the dry earth as he died.

The other two Yaqui tried to run for their horses, firing as they went, but rifle shots dropped them before they had gone more than a few paces. And now only Cortizo faced Dorotéa's avenging husband and his *vaqueros*.

Like a desperate, cornered animal, his eyes shifted from *vaquero* to *vaquero*, all of whom had reloaded their rifles and were leveling them at him. The *mestizo* suddenly pressed the barrel of his pistol to Dorotéa's temple and called down to John Cooper, "If you kill me, my finger will pull the trigger and your *esposa* will die with me, *gringo*! I am a Yaqui, and I am not afraid to die."

John Cooper quickly took in the scene on the slope. In a harsh voice, he declared, "If you are a man, you will fight me hand to hand. I know something of Yaqui customs. And my men will not interfere in a fair fight. Not with knives or pistols, but with our bare hands—well, *hombre*?"

Cortizo's eyes shifted first to Dorotéa and then to the *gringo* on horseback. "How do I know that if I agree and cast away my *pistola*, your *vaqueros* will not kill me?" he hoarsely stammered.

"You have my word, and I have never lied. There will be no tricks. You deserve death a thousand times over for kidnapping my wife and perhaps very nearly harming our little son. But I will give you a chance to fight for your life, though you don't deserve it."

"And if I kill you? What then, *gringo*?" Cortizo said panting.

"Then you will go free." John Cooper turned in his saddle and called to the *vaqueros*, "You have heard what said, *mis compañeros*. If this man beats me in our duel, his life is to be spared. And then you will take my wife home safely to our son, *¿comprenden?*"

Reluctantly, all of them nodded, muttering among themselves. "There's your answer, *hombre*," John Cooper called. "You will gain nothing by using that pistol against my wife or me, for then you'll be shot down like the dog you are."

Despite his bold claim that he was not afraid to die, Cortizo decided he would prefer to take his chances in a hand-to-hand fight. He called down to John Cooper, "*Bueno* I will agree to it. With bare hands, did you not say, *perro yanqui?*" he added with a sneer.

"That is what I have said. Here, Emiliano, hold my rifle for me. And this Spanish dagger in its sheath around my neck—take it. You, Dorotéa, my sweetheart, come down here and stand beside the *vaqueros;* they will protect you," John Cooper ordered.

"Oh please, please, I'm afraid for you, *mi corazón*!" Dorotéa sobbed.

"There is no need to be. Well now, *hombre*, throw down your pistol. You see I've given my rifle and my dagger to one of the *vaqueros*. I keep my word, and now keep yours."

Cortizo stared at the grim-faced *vaqueros* who held their rifles leveled at him, then he looked at Dorotéa who, her eyes blinded with tears, had stumbled down the slope to one of them and stood beside his horse, watching in anguish. And then he looked back at John Cooper, who had dismounted from his palomino and stepped forward, looking like an Indian himself in his buckskins, sinewy and lithe, his body taut with anticipation of the duel.

For a moment Cortizo was frightened. But then was he not a fighter trained in all the crafty arts of the Yaqui, knowing how to gouge out a man's eyes, or to press his thumb pads against the place in the temples that would make a man slump in a long sleep that might even end in death? And there were other ways of crippling or killing a *gringo* like this—he would fight with his fists, as *gringos* did, the *estúpidos*! It was surely better than being shot down. True, there was the silver and Santa Anna and the gifts—but his life was first. He must live, because now he, Juan Cortizo, would be the rightful *jefe* of the Yaqui! So the gifts Santa Anna promised could not be his—but as chief of this tribe, he could terrorize all Mexico, pillage and loot, have all the women he wished!

With a contemptuous gesture, he flung the pistol from him and stepped forward. "I agree. And I have your word that if I kill you, your *vaqueros* will not shoot me down?"

"My wife will witness what I have said, and my wife knows I do not lie, *hombre*. Let's get to it!" John Cooper growled.

"I am coming," Cortizo said softly with an unctuous smile on his face as he began to walk slowly down the slope toward where John Cooper waited. Then suddenly he launched himself in a flying leap, his thumbs reaching for John Cooper's throat. There was a gasp from the *vaqueros* and a cry from Dorotéa, but the tall Texan had anticipated just such trickery and nimbly stepped to one side. The *mestizo* sprawled heavily on the ground, and there was a sound of derisive laughter from the *vaqueros*, which infuriated Cortizo.

He got to his feet, circling warily, and this time let John Cooper come toward him. But John Cooper was in no hurry, suspecting what the *mestizo* would next attempt, and he waited where he was, hunched over, his arms outstretched, ready to fight.

The *mestizo's* patience broke, as John Cooper sensed it would, and suddenly Cortizo lowered his head and lunged forward, butting the Texan in the middle and felling him to the ground. They rolled over and over, and again the *vaqueros* gasped as Cortizo was momentarily atop John Cooper, trying to dig his thumbs down into the latter's eyes. With both hands, John Cooper gripped Cortizo's wrists and forced them back, then almost effortlessly flung the *mestizo* from him and scrambled to his feet.

Once again Cortizo rushed with his head lowered, and John Cooper brought up his knee sharply, hitting the *mestizo's* jaw and sending him sprawling to the ground. Cortizo shook his head groggily like a prize fighter who has received a violent uppercut as John Cooper backed away, watching his foe with narrowed eyes, his body tense and alert.

Cortizo's left hand slowly slipped to his boot as, surreptitiously, he drew out a knife he always kept there for emergencies. Then, with the bloodcurdling war whoop of the Yaqui raiders, he sprang at John Cooper and lunged at him with the hunting knife.

"Let me shoot him, *señor patrón!*" Emiliano Colderón shouted, his voice hoarse with anger and fear for his *patrón.* "He broke his word, he deserves to die!"

"Leave him to me, Emiliano!" John Cooper called out as he moved carefully, feinting with his hands, wanting to tempt the *mestizo* into a rush that would leave the man's knife-hand vulnerable to be seized and twisted back against him.

"Now things are different, eh, *gringo?*" Cortizo snarled as he brandished the knife. "Now I'll kill you, and your men must keep your word; *¿no es verdad?* You've cost me a great deal, and you're going to pay for it!"

"Come ahead, if you think you can! Or are the Yaqui able to fight only helpless women and little babies?" John Cooper said with a sneer.

"You offspring of a diseased coyote, my blood is purer than yours ever could be! *¡Muerte, gringo!*" Cortizo shrieked, beside himself at the insult. He ran at John Cooper now, brandishing the knife like a dagger, swooping it down in a savage lunge that would have killed his enemy had the latter not twisted to one side. As it was, the sharp blade tore through the Texan's buckskin jacket and drew blood from his left arm. Again the *vaqueros* gasped with apprehension, but John Cooper, seeing that another one of them had cocked his rifle, shook his head and cried out, "No, I forbid it; I've kept my word, don't dishonor it—he's not worth it, not even worth a ball from your rifle!"

"You'll wish for death when I cut your tripes out, Yankee swine!" Cortizo said. Again he lunged, this time crouching, thrusting the blade upward toward John Cooper's belly. At that moment, the Texan reached out and deftly caught Cortizo's wrist in his left hand, twisting it so violently that with a cry of pain the *mestizo* dropped the knife. At the same moment, John Cooper's right fist crashed against Cortizo's cheekbone, sending him spinning to the ground, once again dazed and on all fours, shaking his head as he sought to recover.

The knife lay only a foot away, and John Cooper saw it, just as Cortizo was about to reach out his right hand to seize it. John Cooper's booted heel ground down on the *mestizo's* fingers, and he shrieked aloud and dragged his hand away as the Texan kicked the knife into the distance. "And now, let's finish this, *hombre!*" he said in a cold tone that made the gaping *vaqueros* shudder with its merciless intensity.

Dazed by the blows, his fingers numbed from the crushing boot, Cortizo had a moment of panic as he found himself with only his hands as weapons. All his cunning vanished now in the face of this man whose remorseless hatred seemed to dwarf him for all his savagery and cunning as a fighter. In a last frantic attempt, he seized John Cooper's ankles with both hands and upended him. The two men rolled over and over as the *mestizo* used his ebbing strength to bring his hands against John Cooper's throat or, at least, to thrust a thumb into one of the cold, narrowed eyes that fixed him with unwavering fury.

As Cortizo twisted and tried to find a way to gouge or to strangle his opponent, John Cooper swiftly seized his enemy's wrists in both hands and flung them out beyond the *mestizo's* back, pinning him on the ground, as he moved atop him, his wiry thighs pinioning Cortizo's legs. Very slowly, with all his strength, he drew the Yaqui's arms down behind his back, lifting the man up to place them there, and finally gripping both wrists in his left hand. Then, with the palm of his right hand pressed against Cortizo's chin, tightening the hold of his legs so that the *mestizo* could hardly move, he began to thrust back the contorted face of the man who had kidnapped his wife and endangered the life of his little son.

Savage agony seared Cortizo's spine, and his eyes goggled as he felt his death upon him. "No, no, wait," he gasped out. "Don't kill me—I'll tell you something you must know— please, in exchange for my life, *yanqui*, I've something to tell you—"

"Tell me, *hombre!*" John Cooper muttered for only the *mestizo* to hear.

"It was Santa Anna and *mi primo hermano*, Colonel Esteban Moravada, who bribed me to do this. I swear I meant your *esposa* no harm—I was only going to hold her for ransom, and you would bring the silver to the Yaqui stronghold—that is all. I didn't touch her, ask her; in the name of *Dios* the merciful, Señor Baines, don't kill me—no—*aiiiarrghh!*"

Hearing the *mestizo's* words, which confirmed the terrible presentiments he had had all these months, John Cooper Baines forced Cortizo's head back until he heard the snap of the man's neck and saw him stiffen and die.

He got to his knees, drawing in great gulps of breath, and slowly rose from the corpse of the *mestizo*.

Dorotéa, sobbing joyously, ran to him and clutched him in her arms as she covered his face with kisses. "Oh, *mi corazón, mi esposo, mi vida*, I was so afraid for you! Oh, thank God, thank God you found me. They didn't harm me—truly, they didn't. I would have killed myself rather than let those animals touch me. I love you so—God has been very good to us. Are you hurt, my dearest husband?"

"There now, my sweetheart, I'm fine. The baby's safe. It's all over," John Cooper murmured. His arm around her shoulders, he turned to his *vaqueros* and said, "She is truly a woman of great courage, *mis compañeros*. And of cleverness too, for if it were not for the pieces of thread from her skirt and blouse that she dropped along the way, we might not have found these devils. And now, let's bury the dead and go back home again."

"My—my mare was taken around the hill where the other horses are, my dearest John Cooper," Dorotéa told him, hugging him and kissing him repeatedly through her tears. "Home, what a lovely sound that word has!"

"Yes, my dearest one. But I want you to rest a little

while we bury the dead. You've had a terrible journey all that way from the ranch to this Godforsaken place—"

"No, no, I feel strong now. We're together again, and I want to see James! That's all that matters. Let's ride back now, right away, *mi corazón!*" she entreated.

John Cooper thought it might indeed be better to get Dorotéa away from this scene of carnage right away, so he decided to leave without burying the Yaqui dead. Retrieving "Long Girl" and the Spanish dagger, which he draped around his neck, John Cooper mounted his own horse, while the other men rounded up the Yaqui horses. They led them as they followed their *patrón* and his wife, leaving the grisly scene behind them forever as they headed back toward the Double H Ranch.

But as it happened, one of the Yaqui, the young brave named Coljardi, still lived, his rifle wound serious but not fatal. He stirred after he heard the horses gallop away and found that he could get to his feet with great effort. Stumbling as he went, he knew there was a village not far from here, where perhaps they would take him in and care for him. Then, when he was a whole man again, he would take one of the villager's horses and ride out to meet Colonel Esteban Moravada, Juan Cortizo's cousin. He had heard the *mestizo* say where he and his cousin would next meet, and the thought of himself being the one to meet the colonel of General Santa Anna gave Coljardi strength as he slowly, painfully made his way across the desolate Mexican landscape.

It was dawn as they crossed the Rio Grande back into Texas territory. John Cooper turned a moment to look back across the river, and then he said to Dorotéa, "We're not yet done with that treacherous devil of a Santa Anna and that henchman of his, Colonel Moravada. Santa Anna won't ever be content until he gets the silver, and it's up to me to see that he never does."

"I know," Dorotéa told him. "That man who tricked me and brought me here with the Yaqui told me what was to be done with the silver. You were to bring it all to him, in return for my safety, *mi corazón.*"

"It was Santa Anna who enlisted the Yaqui, Indians who hate Mexicans as much as they hate us *gringos*, my darling. He would do anything to have the silver because it would mean great power for him, to become even emperor. I think he is ready to plunge all Mexico into war for it. And because he hates *gringos* and Texans, he could buy many weapons to kill innocent men, women, and children." He rode alongside her, and he put his hand on her shoulder and smiled lovingly at her. Once again, he turned back for a last look at the Rio Grande. "Dorotéa, we must grow even stronger on the Double H Ranch. We must form a mighty fortress on this soil, built on the loyalty and the love of all of us. Only this will protect us against the powers of evil that a man like Santa Anna can invoke against God-fearing people who, like you and me, sweet Dorotéa, want to make the future secure and happy for our children. I must see how poor Yankee is doing and shall have Padre Pastronaz give a mass of thanksgiving for your return, my sweetheart. And I shall pray that God will grant my prayer and help us triumph over the evil ones who value power more than life itself."

Coming in Fall 1985 . . .
**A SAGA OF THE SOUTHWEST:
BOOK VIII**

SHADOW
OF
THE HAWK

by Leigh Franklin James

Following his encounter with the bloodthirsty Yaqui
Indians, John Cooper Baines must face new challenges. . . . His old nemesis, Santa Anna, still covets
his store of silver; though it is lodged in a New
Orleans bank, there are spies who stand ready to aid
the *generalísimo* in its capture. . . . Meanwhile, two
old friends, the Duvaldo brothers, Enrique and Benito,
leave their native Argentina for a new life in distant
Texas, only to be captured on the high seas by
raiding slavers who sell them into bondage in Cuba.
Only a priest escapes to bring word to John Cooper,
who must mount an ambitious rescue expedition to
Havana. . . . Upon his return, a bizarre invitation
awaits him: Santa Anna wishes to meet with him in
the remote Mexican village of Piedras Negras. Riding to this unprecedented confrontation under a
flag of truce—but with an armed escort—John Cooper is gambling with his future . . . and riding into a
trap.

Read **SHADOW OF THE HAWK,**
coming in Fall 1985, from Bantam

Hawk